THE MC TRAIN

A Spiritual Journey in the Footsteps of Blessed Teresa of Calcutta via the Letters of Father Sebastian Vazhakala, MC -

VOLUME TWO

iUniverse, Inc.
New York   Bloomington

THE MC TRAIN
A Spiritual Journey in the Footsteps of Blessed Teresa of Calcutta via the Letters of Father Sebastian Vazhakala, MC - VOLUME TWO

iUniverse books may be ordered through booksellers or by contacting:

iUniverse
1663 Liberty Drive
Bloomington, IN 47403
www.iuniverse.com
1-800-Authors (1-800-288-4677)

Because of the dynamic nature of the Internet, any Web addresses or links contained in this book may have changed since publication and may no longer be valid.

ISBN: 978-1-4401-8445-1 (sc)
ISBN: 978-1-4401-8446-8 (ebk)

Printed in the United States of America

iUniverse rev. date: 2/18/2010

"Injure not the poor because they are poor,
Nor crush the needy at the gate.
For the Lord will defend their cause,
And will plunder the lives of those who plunder them."

(Proverbs 22:22-23)

DEDICATED TO
THE HOLY FAMILY OF NAZARETH

PROLOGUE

Here am I, Your Train, Lord,
A title that I least deserve,
The child of many minds, confused or clear
And the work of many hands, feeble or tired,
A path that is set but still to be trodden,
A seed that is sprouting but still to be grown.
Effort so persistent, care so constant,
Much love and patience need my growing…
Even though very young, a desire so strong
To travel lands and oceans around and across,
To proclaim to the nations the unspeakable truth,
To clear the path, to manure the soil,
Fields so bare, crops so poor.
Blame me not for what I can't,
Nor misunderstand me for what I am not.
Expectations so high, hopes so full
May bring great sadness, heaviness of heart.
My task is not to do the things
That one can and must do for oneself.
My task is simply to stimulate thoughts more sublime,
Words more profound, deeds more noble.
But I want to tell to all who may meet me
That I am mere words, lifeless and dry,
Unless I become part of everyone.

ACKNOWLEDGEMENTS

These two volume letters covering a period of many years have now come into book form. Although desired by many for a long time, this project would not have taken place without the help and contribution of so many, both while they were being circulated in the form of letters and now more so in the form of books.

My gratitude goes to the Triune God, Father, Son and Holy Spirit, who inspired me to write and illumined me with thoughts and ideas beyond my ability and knowledge. Special thanks to the unfailing help of the Holy Spirit for whose glory and honour these volumes of letters are put together, along with the Holy Family of Nazareth: Jesus, Mary and Joseph. I am a mere pen in the hands of the Holy Spirit, who moved my hands to his way and to his direction.

The Holy Spirit also provided and assisted other persons, without whose unforgettable help and untiring effort these volumes would not have come to light. There are so many to be mentioned here. I am deeply indebted to the Brothers of my community and the members of our Society as a whole, who encouraged me with their gentle words, supported me with their unceasing prayers, enlightened me by their edifying examples and consoled me by their keen interest in reading the letters. I am especially indebted to Br. André Marie M.C., who is the first person who went over them before anyone.

It is difficult to thank Gianna Tommasi LMC, not only for the typing and diffusing and making them available to reach to the people, but above all by doing the tedious work of translating them into Italian and making them available to the Italian readers. She is also fully responsible for the publication of the first volume in Italian, including its cost.

With her there are several who worked side by side in season and out of season; chief among them were Msgr. Francesco D'Elia for his untiring work of correction and revision of the Italian translation, Mr. Ken Lipe for the English version, and Mr. Miquel Bassas and Félix López LMC for the Spanish translation. They went over every single letter more than once, checking for proper grammar and word usage. What incredible patience these people have! It could easily be said that they are anointed by divine patience.

I am particularly grateful for the team that worked on the Italian edition, under the leadership of Dr. Giovanni Cubeddu, the assistant director of the monthly review known as *30 Giorni*.

A good number of LMCs have also looked through the English edition of these letters, chief among them are: Mrs. Susie Aki LMC, Mrs. Ann Burridge LMC, Mrs. Laurie Dwyer LMC, Mrs Tai Pearn LMC, Juan Mayol LMC, Fr. Boniface OSB, the U.S.A. Spiritual Director, and many other Spiritual Directors and other LMCs from different parts of the world, among whom many of our M.C. Sisters take the place of prominence. Thanks to Mr. Adolfo Costa LMC from Parma, who had already tried to present all the available letters in Italian in chronological order in a book form.

While thanking all those mentioned and hundreds of others, I also hope and pray that the Holy Spirit and the Holy Family may continue to work on all those who may find the time and interest to read these letters.

I conclude these few lines with the words of St. Paul: *"I command you to preach the message, to insist upon proclaiming it, whether the time is right or not (in season and out of season); to convince, reproach, and encourage, as you teach with all patience."* (2 Tim: 4:2)

God bless you.

Fr. Sebastian Vazhakala M.C.

Contents

FOREWORD

"Let us love until we die of love."

*The General Letters – (1984-Present) of the Founder
of the Lay Missionaries of Charity:
Fr. Sebastian Vazhakala, M.C. as the
Primary Source for Formation of the Lay Missionaries of Charity*

Our whole lives are a series of choices in which we are always moving farther away from, or closer to, the will of God. Every choice is a spiritual choice. A Saint is a person who has consistently, over time, with God's grace, chosen to do His will

Mother Teresa has often said to make a firm resolution to *"will, to want, to be holy." "Holiness is a simple duty."* This duty to God must be of our will. To help us, to guide us, God has given us His commandments, and He has given us the example of His own life, and the example of the lives of the Saints, and sanctifying grace. With the Eucharist, with the Sacraments, and with our will to grow in holiness, we journey.

We have been given a most special gift of God. We have received a special call, specifically, personally, and for a purpose: we have been called to be Lay Missionaries of Charity. Not only have we been called, we have been called to a particular community of souls whom He has also called.

To each of us personally, and to our LMC community worldwide, has been given the beautiful grace of learning from the life and the teaching of Fr. Sebastian Vazhakala, M.C., Superior General of the

Missionary of Charity Brothers Contemplative, and Founder of the Lay Missionaries of Charity in 1984 in the presence of Blessed Teresa of Calcutta. We are "Mother Teresa's Grandchildren" because he was first, her spiritual son. As Blessed Teresa said of Fr.Sebastian: *"We know each other by heart."*

Some time before March of 1947, Blessed Teresa wrote a most significant and historic letter to Archbishop Perrier which refers to our very origins. Our Founder, Fr. Sebastian , writes of this letter that it can be considered the very foundation of the Movement of the Lay Missionaries of Charity (LMC). Quoting Fr Sebastian, he writes: " In the letter she expresses and explains the fundamental motive for which God wanted her to found the Congregation of the Missionaries of Charity: *"Your Grace, tell the Holy Father. . . that the Institute will be especially for the unity and happiness of family life- the life of which he has so much at heart"* Fr. Sebastian wrote that Blessed Teresa was "very happy to know that the Movement is entrusted to the care and protection of the Holy Family of Nazareth, Jesus, Mary and Joseph, who are their mirror and their model in everything. Their families are meant to resemble the Holy Family, which has been the first domestic sanctuary of the Church."

In "Life With Mother Teresa" (Servant Books) Fr Sebastian observes that in all that Mother said and wrote was the call to holiness. Running through the letters of our Founder this is the call: to union with Christ, to the life of sacrifice, service, virtue, mercy, faithfulness, forgiveness, goodness, and most especially the Cross.

The Statutes of the Lay Missionaries of Charity themselves, written by Fr Sebastian over a period of about six months with intense prayer and reflection, in response to the desire of the first four Lay Missionaries of Charity for a life more closely united to the life of the Missionaries of Charity. Fr. Sebastian found his inspiration in the heart of the Church- her Documents, foremost among them for the laity- *Christifideles Laici,* expressing and articulating the universal call to holiness. Within the Statutes of the Lay Missionaries of Charity we find these luminous passages:

"To awaken and satisfy the hunger for God is the heart of the Vocation of the L.M.C.s"

*"It is through prayer that the L.M.C.'s maintain their intimate union
with Christ and the Church and become authentic Missionaries of
Charity in their own families, toward the members of the Movement, and
the poorest of the Poor."*
*"The Lord Jesus Himself will teach us how we should pray. He is the
One key-stone of our religious life and exercises. He is the creative
Word whom we receive in the silence of our heart and the fruitful soil
of our life. We listen attentively to what He will say, and what He will
ask of us. He has promised to give His Holy Spirit who will bear our
poor little efforts before the throne of grace and into the intimacy of
the living God."* (from the Contemplative Bros. Const. 125)

"It is almighty God in person who calls you."

Holding in your hands, and reading with your heart – the General
Letters of Fr. Sebastian Vazhakala, M.C. to the Lay Missionaries of
Charity, you learn much about our Founder, but are also lead most
profoundly to an insight into the mind of Christ, and into the depths
of the love of the Sacred Heart of Jesus in union with the Immaculate
Heart of Mary, Cause of Our Joy. These two hearts, that of our Saviour,
and that of Our Lady, are the root and foundation. As Our Lady said
to St. Catherine Labouré at the Rue de Bac in Paris, regarding the
image she intended for what was to become known as "The Miraculous
Medal" - *"The two hearts say it all."*

This holy teacher, his Priest, and instrument of the Holy Spirit,
Fr. Sebastian, brought us to this place of the giving of the Miraculous
Medal when the LMCs experienced their journey to France, and as
Our Lady did, taught us to pray: "O Mary, conceived without sin, pray
for us who have recourse to thee." Given by Our Lady, a prayer of
intercession, we have the assurance of her role as Mediatrix and the
graces of Our Savior - *"one heart"*. We go with love and obedience, to
be carriers of God's love. *"Do whatever He tells you"* Our Lady said at
Cana, at the wedding feast, to the servants. They, responding, filled the
jars to the brim, setting the metaphor for love and grace overflowing,
obedience to the fullest. *"Do – whatever He tells you."*

In 1996 in Lourdes, France, the Lay Missionaries of Charity held
their second International Conference. Writing of Lourdes, Msgr.
John Moloney PP of Dublin, Ireland notes: " The definition of the
Immaculate Conception of Our Blessed Lady in 1854 was like a great

light in a dark age. It was preceded by her appearance at Rue-de-Back in Paris in 1830: *heaven's preparation* and followed by Lourdes in 1858: *heaven's approval.* Saint Bernadette said to Our Lady: *"Lady, would you have the goodness to tell me who you are, if you please."* The Lady smiled on her in silence. Three times she repeated the request. The fourth time the Lady placed her rosary on her right arm, opened her hands looking to the ground, then raising her arms she lifted her eyes towards heaven and said: ***I am the Immaculate Conception.***"

We pause in the silence of these timeless moments, and wonder in our hearts: to what **depths of holiness** are we called as Lay Missionaries of Charity in our life of contemplative prayer, and our life of service in the heart of the world. Heaven prepares, heaven provides. All the work we will ever do, all the love that flows from our hearts, has its source in Him, and with Our Lady, he has given us every grace. **"To Jesus, through Mary."**

You find, throughout all the Letters of Our Founder, Fr. Sebastian, the inspiring **zeal for souls,** the deepening in understanding through his words and teaching of ***Mother's Founding Grace,*** and the beauty of the Holy Spirit. Truly these are "A *Message of **Love** Through a Collection of Letters."* They are immersed in the Chalice, and in the Book of the Gospels.

The Letters of the Founder can be studied by various means. They can be studied chronologically, they can be studied by theme, and they can be studied in a synthesis of the graces and teachings of the MC Charism and the life, for the laity, as contemplatives in the heart of the world. By theme, the Letters are notated as follows:

❖ **MC Train**
❖ **Missionaries of Charity Charism**
❖ **The Missionaries of Charity Contemplative Brothers**
❖ **The Lay Missionaries of Charity**
❖ **Our Lady**
❖ **Pilgrimages to India**
❖ **Mother Teresa**
❖ **General Letters**
❖ **Giving Thanks**
❖ **Grateful Memories**
❖ **Lent and Easter**
❖ **Advent and Christmas**

On March 19, 1979 Fr. Sebastian Vazhakala M.C. was Co-Founder with Blessed Teresa M.C. of the Missionaries of Charity Contemplative. In 1984 he founded the Lay Missionaries of Charity. Since 1978 he has been in Rome, serving as Superior General of the M.C. Brothers Contemplative at Via S. Agapito. The M.C. Brothers Contemplative were erected into a Diocesan Religious Congregation on December 8, 1993.

Fr. Sebastian M.C. 's work has included "Casa Serena" at Via S. Agapito 8, in Rome (May 29, 1993); "Deepashram" (House of Light) in Gurgaon, Haryana, Delhi, India (July 3, 1994); "Yesu Fié" (House of Jesus) in Pankrono. Kumasi, Ghana, "Bethel" (House of God) at Bushat, Shkodra, Northern Albania (February 2006) and "Anandashram" (House of Bliss) in Gurgaon, Haryana, India (6 August 2003).

There were years of united work, united prayer, and the graces of God in the lives of Fr. Sebastian Vazhakala M.C. and Blessed Teresa of Calcutta, M.C. Yes, Mother's words succinctly expressed the reality of God's gift to us all in these two souls, our Founder and Blessed Teresa M.C.: *"We know each other by heart."*

In the early years of the Lay Missionaries of Charity, Fr. Sebastian wrote of **LMC Fundamental Values and Priority,** and from these pages among a quarter century of writing and teaching during our growth, expansion, and development, these points should be noted from the Fundamental Values:

"If I meditate on the LMC, in the light of our faith, I can find one basic value, the source value of all the others, and this value is: Total surrender to God." "Here I am, for you called me" (1 Sam) as a safe child in the arms of the Father. An act of total faith, the root of the four vows, especially the fourth vow which differentiates the Lay Missionaries of Charity from other consecrated laity."

And further, he notes:

"There is something beyond that starting from God and is waiting for an answer."

Later, in the ninth point, Father notes that:

"The fundamental value of the Lay Missionary of Charity is according to the Service. "Here I am Lord" is strictly connected with the service. It appears in the Fourth Vow: to move forward to Christ, the poorest. Everything is given for everybody. Christ

comes to share Himself: "I AM the Bread of Life, take and eat" (Jn 6:34,51) God's communion. The LMC, the messengers of Love in the world, cannot be but Communion. In a circle, I and the neighbor, in receiving and giving at the same time."

The Letters of the Founder, numbering most recently 146, from 1984 to the present, with their major themes, principal teachings, documentation of the history, and direction of the Way of Life, with their scriptural reference and inspired teaching, are a sure foundation in the Formation of a Lay Missionaries of Charity. Paired with the LMC Statutes, and read and studied, these primary source materials provide us with rich resources for growth and a sure path to holiness in a universal and accessible way for all who have been called to the life of a Lay Missionary of Charity.

They can be fruitfully studied in a format of three interrelated parts:

PART I	THE DOCUMENTS OF THE CHURCH THE STATUTES OF THE LAY MISSIONARIES OF CHARITY
PART II	THE LETTERS OF THE FOUNDER TO THE LAY MISSIONARIES OF CHARITY *FR. SEBASTIAN VAZHAKALA, M.C.* *BLESSED TERESA OF CALCUTTA, M.C.*
PART III	THE TEACHINGS OF THE LMC SPIRITUAL DIRECTORS AND THE RESOURCES OF THE LMC ARCHIVES INCLUDING IN PARTICULAR THE AUTOBIOGRAPHY OF THE FOUNDER, **Life with Mother Teresa, my thirty year friendship with The Mother of the Poor by Fr Sebastian Vazhakala M.C.**

By attentive and faithful study of the LMC Statutes and the Letters of the Founder, and enhanced by teachings to the LMCs affirmed at General Assembly, we can " give Saints to Mother Church."

"To Jesus, through Mary"
"LET US LOVE UNTIL WE DIE OF LOVE."

LAURIE DWYER, LMC

INTRODUCTION
M.C. TRAIN

A spiritual journey in the footsteps of Mother Teresa, M.C.

New Year 2008

In the dark hours of the night of Tuesday, 10th September, 1946, Mother Teresa IBVM was in a running train, heading toward the hill country of Darjeeling, in the high ranges of the mighty Himalayas.

She was going away from the crowded and noisy city of Kolkata, careless and chaotic, to go into the silence of contemplation, as she knew very well that the call to holiness is accepted and can be cultivated only in the silence of contemplation. She did not know or realize that the crowd she was trying to get away from was following her all the way.

Her eyes being closed, her mind being still, the noisy train running in the dark hours of the night, without warning there appears a big crowd of people: emaciated bodies, eaten up by worms; abandoned babies, orphaned, unloved, uncared for; disfigured faces of lepers, lost limbs and lost feet. Their feeble hands raised towards her, spoke very softly but very firmly without complaints: *"Mother Teresa, come, come, save us, bring us to Jesus."* We are being abandoned, sheep without a shepherd and guide; we are in need of a guide, a helper, a Saviour!

The crowd knew before she knew the plan God had for her. There would be a radical change in her lifestyle, her vocation and her mission. Her eyes had not yet seen, her mind had not yet grasped what God was preparing her for!

Although she was getting away from the crowd, it was following her They were with her, and she found herself in the midst of the crowd she was going away from! The hungry and the thirsty crowd saw in her the one to bring them to the Saviour. Jesus was still hiding himself. He wanted her to see him in faith.

"Thomas, you believed because you saw me, but blessed are those who have not seen and yet believe." (Jn 20: 29) Within minutes he was going to make her meet someone very special to him: his very dear Mother in the crowd: *"Mother Teresa, do you see the crowd? Take care of them. They are mine. Bring them to Jesus,"* who is their true Saviour. Neither the crowd by themselves, nor Mother Teresa by herself, nor even Our Lady can save people. Jesus alone is their Saviour. He alone is our Saviour. He alone saves all. He alone is the Lamb of God who takes away the Sin of the world. (cf. Jn 1: 29)

Our Lady was now entrusting the world of the poor to her. She also knew that Mother Teresa wouldn't be able to do it alone. She was in need of Our Lady and her beloved Son. So she said: *"Fear not, Jesus and I will be with you and with your children. Fear not, teach them to pray the Rosary, the family Rosary and all will be well."*

Who are Mother's children? She did not know yet. It was not yet revealed to her. But the crowd knew. Our Lady knew that she was chosen for her Son's beloved spouse, his partner in the new and very special mission!.

The train continued to run in the dark hours of the night, passing through many hills and dales. Her sleep was being interrupted again in a more dramatic way. The Bridegroom was now going to meet his bride. He made the crowd and his Mother meet her first, making the crowd and his Mother say to her to bring them to Jesus. That was her new vocation: to bring the souls of the poor to Jesus.

And now it was his turn to meet his little spouse face to face: *"You are my little spouse, the spouse of Jesus crucified."* This was still a voice. But now he would make her see him in the midst of the crowd covered in darkness. She would see him in the presence of his beloved Mother. Yes, *"It is in the contemplation of the crucified Christ that all vocations find their inspiration."* The Cross is the origin and the structure of all consecrated lives; and *"the more they stand at the foot of the Cross, the more immediately and profoundly they experience the truth of God who is love."* (V.C. 24)

Mother Teresa's new vocation found its origin; she took her inspiration from the Cross. From then on her songs would be joyful and sweeter, even if there were many long and sharp thorns on her path. The light was going to be dim and her path rough, but she must step it bravely.

The crowd was covered in darkness, and yet she could see the people…and *"Our Lord on the Cross, Our Lady at a distance."* Mother Teresa was in front of Our Lady, just like a little child protected by a Mother's arms. Our Lady's left hand was on Mother Teresa's left shoulder; her right hand was holding her right arm. Both of them were looking at Jesus on the Cross, who told her: *"I have asked you, the crowd has asked you. My Mother has asked you. Will you refuse to do this for me, to take care of them, to bring them to me?"*

The train had not stopped running, nor had the morning broken. There was no time to wait until morning to give him the answer. The answer had to be immediate and direct. There was no more time to doubt, to hesitate. Besides, Jesus was still hanging on the Cross; Our Lady's arms were not going to be removed. Yes, Mother Teresa was to answer quickly. Do not wait; there is no time to waste. Jesus is on the Cross. The more she delayed, the more there was suffering for Jesus… Speak Mother Teresa, speak, fear not. Yes, she did. Her heart could no longer resist; there was no more doubt. The answer came and was positive and creative. Here she followed the example of Our Lady at the Annunciation: *"Behold the handmaid of the Lord, be it done to me as you say."* (Lk 1: 38) *"I answered – you know, Jesus, I am ready to go at a moment's notice."* *"Yes, my Jesus, of my free will, I shall follow you wherever you shall go in search of souls, at any cost to myself and out of pure love of you."*

Neither Jesus nor Mary could accomplish their mission alone; they need human hearts to love the poor… human hands to serve them, as Jesus himself would serve them. *"My little one, come, be my Light."* **"I cannot go alone to their homes"**… to the lepers, to the homeless, to the crippled and handicapped, to the dying destitutes. *"You carry Me, with you into them"*… into the homes of the poor, into the street corners, into the byways of the world, gather them, feed them, satiate them, clothe them, shelter them, visit them, comfort them…yes, do these things for Me…yes, Mother Teresa do it for us. *"Your vocation is to love and suffer and save souls."* *"Nothing gives such pleasure to God as the conversion and salvation of men, for whom his every word and every revelation exist,"* says St. Gregory of Nazianzus.

With Mother Teresa, Jesus started a new railway company… the M.C. train… from Kolkata to the end of the world.

The M.C. train is running ceaselessly, quenching the infinite thirst of Jesus everywhere in the world. The M.C. train is full of poor people, unwanted people, homeless people, crippled and handicapped ones, unwed mothers, unloved and uncared-for babies, aged and forgotten ones, victims of leprosy and AIDS, those who live in despair and in the shadow of death, those who are upset, angry, bitter, or revengeful on account of their social status, colour, religion, nationality or whatever reasons. All without exception can find room in the M.C. Train.

The M.C. train is Jesus' train. He owns it. It is continually gathering and picking up people who fall on both sides of the roads of the big cities of the world. There is always room in the M.C. train for one more. There are plenty of opportunities for everyone of good will to get into the train and offer wholehearted and free service; to be members of the M.C. Family; to be LMCs, co-workers, benefactors, to offer voluntary service.

There are always more people to be fed,
Thirsty ones to be quenched,
Naked ones to be clothed,
Homeless ones to be taken in,
Sick ones to be visited,
Imprisoned ones to be befriend,
Crippled ones to be cared for,
Handicapped ones to be looked after,

Leprosy patients and AIDS victims to be cured.

Yes, Jesus, if you wish, you can touch all these and heal. You said to Mother Teresa back in 1947 that you need M.C.s, because *"there is absolutely no one for your poor people."* You want first and foremost your poor and helpless ones to be loved and cared for, served and healed. All that we ask you, Lord, is to *"Make us worthy to serve you in our fellow men and women throughout the world, who live and die in poverty and hunger, in cold and in nakedness, lacking the basic necessities of life. So we pray, Lord, give them through our hands this day and everyday their daily bread and by our understanding love, give peace and joy."*

The M.C. train must run. It must run continually without seeking rest or reward. The M.C. train must always have room to take in, to love, and to serve.

The M.C. train belongs to the Holy Family. It is the Holy Family train, as every M.C. community, without exception, is meant to be another NAZARETH. It must have the Holy Family Spirit. It must have the Spirit of warm welcome and generous hospitality. The M.C. train must be filled with the perfume of prayer…all the time trying to pray more fervently, all the time trying to smile more tenderly, all the time trying to offer more sacrifices.

Jesus is the centre of the M.C. train. Every one must remember that Jesus is the Centre, the Captain, the Owner. Therefore, we must always be ready and willing to consult him, to ask for guidance…ever more to receive him in the Bread of Life in daily mass and Holy Communion, without which the M.C. train cannot run, nor can the people in the train be fed.

Jesus' beloved spouse writes: *"One thing I request you, Your Grace, is to give us all the spiritual help we need. If we have Our Lord in the midst of us, with daily mass and Holy Communion, I fear nothing for the Sisters nor for myself. He will look after us. But without him I cannot be, I am helpless."* (Mother to Archbishop Perier S.J., 1947)

Jesus is the Epicentre. Yes, Jesus, you too have said: *"Without me, you can do nothing."* Jesus is the epicentre of our lives. He is the Vine and we are the branches. St. Paul said: *"I can do all things in him who strengthens me."* Years later Mother Teresa wrote to one of her Spiritual Directors: *"…I want only God in my life. The 'work' is really and solely His. He told me what to do. He guided every step, directs every movement I* take. *The Sisters, all that and everything is in me is His…when the world receives me, it really does not touch not even the surface of my soul. About the work, I am convinced it is all His."* (Letter to Fr. Neuner, 1961)

"Injure not the poor because they are poor,
nor crush the needy at the gate.
For the Lord will defend their cause,
And will plunder the lives of those who plunder them." (Prov 22: 22-23)

God himself will come to save the poor and he came in Jesus Christ. That is why we read: *"The Spirit of the Lord is upon me, he has anointed me to preach the good news to the poor… "*(Lk 4: 14 ff.)

The year 2007 has passed into oblivion, taking with her a good number of people, some of whom were our own family members, while some others were acquaintances and friends; there were also strangers and foreigners. They are from all walks of life, belonging to the various religions of the world or of no religion at all. All without exception of caste, colour, creed, nationality or status have died and gone. Sooner or later it will be our turn too to surrender and sacrifice even the most precious gifts, including our dear and near ones. Here there is no exception: once we are born we have to die. This is absolutely certain. What we are not certain of is **the when, the where and the how** of our final and definitive departure from this valley of pain and sorrow. There is a little piece of poem that says: "Today is my turn, tomorrow can be yours. Be ready, then; it is your call"…ready to go home to God at any hour of the day or night: *"Watch out, because you do not know the day or the hour."* (Mt 25: 13)

Unforgettable memories. The year 2007 has left with us many unforgettable memories, good and bad, sad and happy, pleasant and unpleasant. It can be helpful, enriching and beneficial to attempt to bring to our attention or to recall to mind some of the most important ones. We should try to see the meaning and significance of the work that our good God is doing for his poor people through all of us. We should also realize like Blessed Mother Teresa M.C., our foundress and our Mother, our own weakness, sinfulness and unworthiness. It is not because we are better and holier that Jesus chooses us, but as he told to our Mother: *"Precisely because you are weak, sinful and unworthy, I want to use you for my glory."*

I would like to take a moment to express my sincere gratitude to God for all of you, dearly beloved LMCs, co-workers, benefactors both spiritual and temporal, poor people and all those who have helped us in any way. Your lives have become a living exegesis of Jesus' words: *"As you did it to one of the least of my brethren, you did it to me."* (Mt 25: 40) Your concern and tender care for the needy, expressed in prayer, assistance and hospitality, has become a normal part of your life. This goes in line with the document "Vita Consecrata," which says: *"And how could it be otherwise, since the Christ encountered in contemplation is the same who lives and suffers in the poor"* (V.C. 82), in the handicapped, in the homeless, in the sick and the aged, in the lonely and the forgotten.

There is an apparent tension here between the active and the contemplative life which could be found in many saints like St. Bernard of Clairvaux, St. Catherine of Siena…Blessed Teresa of Kolkata, the servant of God Pope John Paul II, who writes: *"In Joseph, the apparent tension between the active and the contemplative life finds an ideal harmony that is only possible for those who possess the perfection of charity."* (Redemptoris Custos: 27) The perfection of charity then is its solution. Therefore one has to work on charity.

I also would like to thank all of you who have shared your joy of the season of Christmas and New Year with us and with our poor people through telephone calls, letters, cards, e-mail, etc. So many of you have shared your joy with and for the poor in various ways: some by coming and serving them in person, some in kind, while some others in cash. I commend each one of you earnestly to God, that he may reward you a hundred times more with everything you need in this world and eternal life in the world to come.

The "M.C. Train," with its various compartments, is running slowly but surely, taking us all to our final destination for which we all are created, i.e. to be with Jesus, where he is: *"Father, I want them to be with me where I am."* (Jn 17: 24)

Love and prayers.

God bless you.

Fr. Sebastian Vazhakala M.C.

Blessed Teresa of Calcutta

The train I desire, the M.C. Train,
Ever alive and fresh, alive and well.

CHAPTER ONE:
MOTHER TERESA

The Eucharist, Blessed Teresa and the poor

The Most Holy Eucharist is the lifeblood of the Church. In it the whole spiritual wealth of the Church is contained, for the Eucharist is the source and summit of the whole Christian life.

There is little wonder, then, that the Holy Father, Pope John Paul II, declared from October 2004 to October 2005 the "Year of the Eucharist" (Cf. *Mane Nobiscum Domine* n. 4). We are invited to contemplate the great mystery of the Eucharist and live as far as possible the Eucharistic life: true Christian life is Eucharistic life.

The Holy Mass and Communion are inseparable from the life of a Christian. Its fruitfulness depends on how we prepare ourselves and how we participate in the Holy Mass.

Many saints spent half a day in thanksgiving for the Mass and Holy Communion, while devoting the other half to its preparation. In the sacristies of the Missionaries of Charity all over the world, one can see a little board hanging to remind each priest that he should celebrate each Mass with devotion, freshness, contemplation and enthusiasm. The board says:

"Priest of God,
Celebrate this Mass as if it is your first Mass,
Your only Mass and your last Mass".

Of course these words apply to the celebrant as well as to the participants.

Three parts of Holy Mass. The celebration of the Mass has three distinct parts.

'Way of purification'. The first part is a very short Penitential Rite. Its main purpose is to prepare and to dispose the celebrant as well as the participants to listen to the Word of God and receive the Eucharist in a worthy manner.

The fruitfulness of the Mass depends on our inner disposition, how prepared we are to receive God's rich graces. This initial short Penitential Rite can be compared to the "way of purification" in the beginning of our spiritual life. It is the first step in our spiritual life. It depends much on one's effort, generosity, good will and above all, one's cooperation with the graces of God.

It can be and it is always a very painful process, because it necessarily involves sacrificing one's will to accept God's will

'Way of illumination'. This purification process is repeated and renewed in each celebration of the Mass. It prepares us to the next step, which is known as the "way of illumination", and as part of the Mass is known as the Liturgy of the Word.

No sower sows the seed if the field is not cleaned and properly prepared. The sower invariably knows that it will be a sheer waste of time to sow seeds in a field that is not ploughed, cleared and manured.

The same principle applies to each celebrant and participant of the Mass, especially with the Word of God being sown into our hearts at every Mass. The Liturgy of the Word is not only an essential part of the Eucharistic Sacrifice, but also an integral part of our spiritual nourishment and growth. We must be well prepared and disposed to listen to it; this means, if possible, to read the texts beforehand, to reflect, meditate and contemplate on them, not only on the part of the homilist, but by all who celebrate and participate in the Holy Mass.

The homily should awaken the seed of faith in the listener, which may be dormant in the hearts of some believers. The quality of the homily does not depend on length but how well it is prepared and how convincingly it is delivered. There is a big difference between what we copy from a stereotyped homily book and what we speak from the heart with our life experience.

The Word of God and the homily are meant not only to illumine our hearts and minds, but also to prepare us to celebrate the most important part of the Holy Mass: the Liturgy of the Eucharist and the Holy Communion.

'Way of union'. If the second part - the way of illumination or Liturgy of the Word - concludes with the Creed (on Sundays and solemnities) and the prayer of the faithful, the third part concludes, practically speaking, with Holy Communion. This part can be called the "way of union".

Just as in our spiritual life we have to pass through the way of purification and the way of illumination to arrive at the way of spousal and mystical union, so also in every celebration of the Eucharist these three ways are not only remembered but renewed and relived.

Blessed Mother Teresa of Kolakta writes. *"These desires to satiate the longings of our Lord for souls of the poor - for pure victims of His love – goes on increasing with every Mass and Holy Communion."* (MFG, p. 19) For this reason back in 1946-47, when she was writing the very first *Constitutions* for the future Congregation of the Missionaries of Charity which she was asked by Jesus, her Crucified Spouse, to found, she writes: *"The Sisters should use **every means** to learn and increase that tender love for Jesus in the Blessed Sacrament."* (R. 34; MFG, p. 31)

Blessed Teresa not only renewed daily her "call within a call" to give wholehearted free service to the poorest of the poor at every Eucharistic celebration, but she also drew her strength from its daily reception. She writes: *"One thing I request you, Your Grace, to give us all the spiritual help we need. If we have our Lord in the midst of us, with daily Mass and Holy Communion, I fear nothing for the Sisters nor* (for) *myself. He will look after us. But without Him I cannot be – I am helpless."* (MFG, 26)

She even wanted the Sisters to do the work of priests. In her original Rule book, she writes: *"As each Sister is **to do the work of a priest** – go where he cannot go and do what he cannot do, she must imbibe the Spirit of Holy Mass, which is one of total surrender and offering. For this reason, Holy Mass **must** become the daily meeting place, where God and His creature offer each other for each other and the world."* (MFG, p. 31; R. 33)

Here we see Blessed Teresa's deeper understanding of the reality of the Eucharist and her mystic union. It was this unbroken spousal union that gave her all the energy, strength, vitality and enthusiasm to go on doing what she did. The life she lived was no longer her life, but it was Jesus who lived in her and worked through her. She was able to do all things in Jesus, for Jesus and with Jesus, who strengthened her through daily reception of the Eucharist.

What did Blessed Teresa hear?

In her first letter to the Archbishop of Calcutta, Ferdinand Périer, SJ, written on 13 January 1947, she wrote: *"One day at holy Communion I heard the same voice very distinctly."* (MFG, p. 10)

What did Blessed Teresa hear from the Eucharistic Jesus?

The kind of the nuns she should have and the qualities they should possess:

- *"I want Indian nuns, victims of My love, who would be Mary and Martha, who would be so united to Me as to radiate My love on souls.*

- *I want free nuns, covered with the poverty of the Cross.*

- *I want obedient nuns, covered with the obedience of the Cross.*

- *I want full of love nuns, covered with the Charity of the Cross."*

She heard the kind of people she and her nuns should take care of:

- *"There are plenty of nuns to look after the rich and well-to-do* people, *but for My very poor people, there are absolutely none. For them I long, them I love. Wilt thou refuse?"*

The name of the Congregation Jesus wanted her to found:

- *"I want Indian Missionaries Sisters of Charity, who would be My fire of love amongst the very poor, the sick, the dying, the little street children."*

4) She heard very distinctly that she and her nuns should bring the poor to him:

- *"The poor I want you to bring to Me.*

- *The Sisters who offer their lives as victims of My love should bring these souls to Me."*

5) The Eucharistic Jesus told her that:

- *"You are, I know, the most incapable person, weak and sinful, but just because you are that, I want to use you for My glory. Wilt thou refuse?"*

6) Jesus told her the kind of habit she should bear:

- *"You will dress in simple Indian clothes or rather like My Mother dressed-simple and poor,...your sarie will become holy because it is My symbol."*

7) Jesus told her very clearly what exactly was her vocation:

- *"Your vocation is to love and suffer and save souls."*

8) He told her that she is his little spouse and she will suffer very much:

- *"You are My own little spouse, the spouse of the Crucified Jesus; you will have to suffer these torments in your heart."*

It was her Eucharistic Spouse who promised that he would never leave her provided she trusted him lovingly and blindly, obeyed him cheerfully, promptly and without any questions (cf. MFG, p. 18)

In the account of the second vision Our Lady told Blessed Teresa to take care of her poor people and carry Jesus to them. Her exact words were: *"Take care of them-they are mine-bring them to Jesus-carry Jesus to them."* (MFG, p. 19) Here our Lady apparently wanted Blessed Teresa to continue to do what she did immediately after the Annunciation. At the Annunciation she received Jesus first in her heart and then in her womb, and then with Jesus she went in haste to give him to her cousin Elizabeth and others. *"The Annunciation was our Lady's first Holy Communion day"*, Blessed Teresa said.

Just as our Lady received Jesus at the Annunciation and then went in haste to give him to others, so too all Missionaries of Charity Sisters and Brothers receive Jesus in Holy Communion and go in haste to give to the poor. Our Lady told Blessed Teresa to bring the poor to Jesus and carry Jesus to them. She also promised her unfailing help: *"Fear not, Jesus and I will be with you and your children."*

Christ in the poor. Hence we see the inseparable twofold presence of Jesus in the Bread of Life and in the distressing disguise of the poorest of the poor. Jesus told Blessed Mother Teresa: *"Carry Me with you into them, for I cannot go alone. They don't know Me-so they don't want Me-you go amongst them."* (MFG, p. 18) Jesus wants Blessed Teresa, the Sisters and the Brothers to go amongst the poor, not as social workers, politicians or even masters, but as unworthy servants asked to carry Jesus with us into the people's homes and holes.

Jesus wants us to visit the people, but he cannot go alone. Jesus is helpless to do his work amongst his people without us; we are helpless to do his work without him. *"Apart from me you can do nothing."* (Jn 15: 5) *"I can do all things in him who strengthens me."* (Phil 4: 13) There is a reciprocal helplessness and a mutual strength. In a sense Jesus depends on us to save souls and we depend totally on Jesus for our life and work, as electricity and bulb. Through the bulb the electricity becomes luminous and useful.

Our Blessed Teresa goes further and deeper with her Eucharistic Jesus. In her own words: *"Just as Jesus allows Himself to be broken, to be given to us as food, we too must break, we must share with each other, with our own people first, in our house, in our communities, for love begins at home. Every Holy Communion fills us with Jesus and we must, with our Lady, go in haste to give Him to others. For her, it was on her first Holy Communion day that Jesus came in her life, and so for all of us also. He made Himself the Bread of Life that we, too, like Mary, become full of Jesus. We too, like her, be in haste to give Him to others. We too, like her, serve others."* (Talk to the Brothers and co-workers, Los Angeles U.S.A., July 1, 1977)

According to Blessed Mother Teresa, Jesus in the Eucharist keeps us zealous, fervent and enthusiastic. Love for the Eucharist helps us to love our poor people, for she says: *"Try to be Jesus' love, Jesus' compassion, Jesus' presence to each other and the poor you serve. Humility always is the root of zeal for souls and charity. We see that in Jesus on the Cross and in the Eucharist."* (Letter, June 1990)

The Eucharistic Jesus little by little took possession of our Mother Teresa, transforming her whole being so utterly into Him so that she could become Jesus for all. People looked up and saw no longer her, but only Jesus. Like a piece of iron stuck to the magnet, she became one with her beloved Spouse, whom Jesus himself addressed as his little spouse: *"You are my own little Spouse-the Spouse of the Crucified Jesus."* (MFG, p. 11)

'To be really only his'. In Blessed Teresa there was the insatiable spousal longing, which became identical with the thirst of Jesus on the Cross for love of souls. From now on, she was going to pray, suffer and work day and night for Jesus, because her beloved Spouse was everything for her: *"Jesus, my own Jesus, I am only Thine... I love you not for what you give, but what you take, Jesus."* (MFG, p. 17) She continues in writing to the Archbishop of Calcutta: *"I long to be really only His-to burn myself completely for Him and souls. I want Him to be loved tenderly by many...I have already given my all to Him."* (MGF, p. 13-14)

The Eucharist and the poor are inseparable. This is not anything new for the Church as we can clearly see it in the Gospels. The one who said: *"This is my body"* is the same one who said: *"I was hungry and you gave me to eat..."* (cf. Mt 26: 26; 25: 35) Some of the Fathers of the Church like St.Ambrose, St. John Chrysostom, etc. were very clear and emphatic in their pronouncements. St. John Chrysostom, for example, said: *"Do you wish to honour the body of Christ? Do not ignore him when he is naked. Do not pay him homage in the temple clad in silk, only then to neglect him outside where he is cold and ill-clad. He who said: 'This is my body' is the same who said: 'You saw me hungry and you gave me no food,' and 'whatever you did to the least of my brothers you did also to me…' what good is it if the Eucharistic table is over loaded with golden chalices when your brother is dying of hunger. Start by satisfying his hunger and then with what is left you may adorn the altar as well."*

In conclusion we can say that it is a great need for each and every person to rediscover the importance and the necessity of the Eucharist in his or her life, the Eucharist which necessarily urges everyone to go in search of the poor.

The Holy Father, John Paul II, writes to the youth of the world on the occasion of the XIX World Youth Day 2004: *"Dear friends, if you learn to discover Jesus in the Eucharist, you will also know how to discover him in your brothers and sisters, particularly in the very poor…*

It is with such inner freedom and such burning charity that Jesus teaches us to find Him in others, first of all in the disfigured faces of the poor. Blessed Teresa of Calcutta loved to distribute her "visiting card" on which were written the words: 'The fruit of silence is prayer; the fruit of prayer is faith; the fruit of faith is love; the fruit of love is service; the fruit of service is peace.' This is the way to meet Christ…"

Let us go out and meet him in the poor, making our love all the more fruitful in service. Let this be our unquenchable thirst, constant effort and fervent prayer.

Love and prayers.

God bless you.

Fr. Sebastian Vazhakala M.C.

Who is Jesus to Me? 2006

From the end of May, 1983, Blessed Teresa of Kolkata went through some serious health problems. It was in Rome that she had the first of a series of heart attacks and was admitted in the "Salvator Mundi" Hospital in Monteverde, Rome. She was there for over a month.

One evening Sr. Sylvia of happy memory telephoned me and told me that our Mother (Blessed Teresa) – the Sisters still speak of her that way – wanted me to celebrate the liturgy of the Eucharist in her hospital bedroom on the following afternoon. So I went to "Salvator Mundi". As I was passing through the corridors of the hospital I saw many of the patients watching television from their hospital beds. When I walked into Mother's room she was not only watching, but contemplating another kind of very powerful television – namely, she was having adoration of the Blessed Sacrament exposed on her bed. She was lying in bed with her head lifted up and the Blessed Sacrament, exposed in a big monstrance, was right in front of her facing her; she was surrounded by a group of Sisters.

It impressed me so much that even today I not only remember it so vividly, but see it so clearly before my eyes. She had her holy Rosary and other prayers, together with the Sisters, who then asked me to give them the benediction, after which we had the Holy Mass.

What an edifying and encouraging witness of faith in the Eucharist that was! The Eucharistic Jesus gave her all the strength and energy she needed to accept whatever Jesus gave her, and to give whatever he took from her, with a big smile.

Her freedom to go around in haste to save and to serve him in the poorest of the poor was now curtailed because of the heart attack; so she decided to bring souls to Jesus by prayer, sacrifice and by Eucharistic adoration, etc. She bloomed where the Lord planted her for that period of time. She did not think of her many yesterdays filled with apostolic and missionary work, nor did she envision a wonderful tomorrow, when she would be out in the world, discharged from the hospital. No, she lived her present moment with enthusiasm. From her sick bed she equally did her missionary work, satiating Jesus' thirst for love and for souls. In a word, their thirsts were no longer two, but one. Jesus' infinite thirst became her thirst, as she knew that Jesus had chosen her to be his spouse, the spouse of the crucified Jesus.

In a spousal relationship there is the fusion, first of all, of the two wills, communion of the two hearts and of the whole being. In this spousal and mystical union they are no longer two, but become one in love, and from that spousal union souls are being born. Spouses in love long for each other, especially when they are away. Their temporary separation only strengthens their bond of love, making them love each other ever more ardently. Blessed Teresa was in love with Jesus and Jesus was in love with her.

This spousal love led Blessed Teresa to suffer more for the members of the mystical body of Christ, the Church. She saw the presence of her beloved spouse in the hungry, and the more she fed the hungry, the more hungry she became for Jesus in the hungry.

The more she satiated the thirsty ones, the thirstier she became for her beloved spouse. The more she clothed the naked, the more she took the homeless in. The more she healed the sick, the more she felt to be united to Him in love in the least, in the lost and in the last. The more she loved the poor and served them, the more her love for Jesus grew. *"Love grows through love."* (Pope Benedict XVI)

Her heart longed for him burning within her. And so she expressed it in the form of a Litany. On Sunday, 19 June 1983, from the hospital bed she expressed her insatiable thirst for her beloved, who came to her in many different forms. Her questions were two: "Who do you say I am?" (Mt 16: 15) and the second was: "Who is Jesus to me?" Here we allow her to speak to us. Her words are not mere human words, but words of eternal truth, life and light. They are the sure way of loving and serving Jesus; they are the *evangelion*, the good news to all people of good will. Here we quote the second question:

WHO IS JESUS TO ME?

Jesus is the Word made Flesh.
Jesus is the Bread of Life.
Jesus is the Victim offered for our sins on the Cross.
Jesus is the Sacrifice offered at the Holy Mass for the sins of the world and mine.
Jesus is the Word – to be spoken.
Jesus is the Truth – to be told.
Jesus is the Way – to be walked.
Jesus is the Light – to be lit.
Jesus is the Life – to be lived.
Jesus is the Love – to be loved.
Jesus is the Joy – to be shared.
Jesus is the Sacrifice – to be offered.
Jesus is the Peace – to be given.
Jesus is the Bread of Life – to be eaten.
Jesus is the Hungry – to be fed.
Jesus is the Thirsty – to be satiated.
Jesus is the Naked – to be clothed.
Jesus is the Homeless - to be taken in.
Jesus is the Sick – to be healed.
Jesus is the Lonely – to be loved.
Jesus is the Unwanted – to be wanted.
Jesus is the Leper – to wash his wounds.
Jesus is the Beggar - - to give him a smile.
Jesus is the Drunkard – to listen to him.
Jesus is the Mental – to protect him.
Jesus is the Little One – to embrace him.
Jesus is the Blind – to lead him.
Jesus is the Dumb – to speak to him.
Jesus is the Crippled – to walk with him.
Jesus is the Drug Addict – to befriend him.
Jesus is the Prostitute – to remove from danger and befriend her.
Jesus is the Prisoner – to be visited.
Jesus is the Old – to be served.

TO ME:
Jesus is my God.
Jesus is my Spouse.
Jesus is my Life.
Jesus is my only Love.
Jesus is my All in All.
Jesus is my Everything.

JESUS, I love with my whole heart, with my whole being.
I have given Him all, even my sins and He has espoused me to Himself
in tenderness and love.
Now and for life I am the Spouse of my Crucified Spouse. Amen.
God bless you.

    M. Teresa *M.C*

Love and prayers. God bless you.

Rome, 10 September 2006

Fr. Sebastian Vazhakala M.C.

September 1997
A TRIBUTE TO OUR BELOVED MOTHER

We all have witnessed something extraordinary happening around and across the world since the night of September 5, 1997, when Mother Teresa's thirsty soul abandoned her frail and worn out body to quench once and for all the infinite thirst of her Lord and Saviour whose thirst she tried to quench over the years with all the powers and fibres of her being, on the streets of Calcutta and of the world. Although it is hard for us to accept the reality of her not being with us, the fact is that she returned to the Source of Love and Grace, from where she will continue to shower many graces.

On the other hand it is absolutely necessary for us to accept the "Kairos of God", the divine hour of God's visitation, for which she was always ready. So our beloved Mother whom we all loved and who loved us all so dearly within minutes disappeared from the visible horizons of our lives to be totally united to Jesus, like a piece of iron stuck to the magnet and never to be separated.

From a distance she might have heard the words of the Master: *"Come, blessed of my Father, inherit the kingdom prepared for you from the foundation of the world"*. We can imagine that there in heaven, waiting to welcome her, was a long line of the Missionaries of Charity (M.C.) Community, with Sr. Agnes and Sr. Sylvia in the front; as well as an endless line of the poorest of the poor whom Mother Teresa fed, clothed, sheltered, visited and buried; those in thousands who have lived like animals on the street but have died like angels with dignity, loved and cared by her and the members of the M.C. Family in the homes of the dying destitute, and the many lepers and AIDS patients.

I wonder if there has ever been such a reception in heaven or a funeral of the same sort for any person of any time or place. For her, everything was so unique and unprecedented. Never before has any religious had a State and Catholic funeral at the same time.

Moving on from all these unique privileges that our Beloved Mother received both in life and at her death - not only from her beloved daughters and sons of the Family of the Missionaries of Charity, but also from the whole world - we now proceed to some of the principal teachings of our "Little Mahatma" Mother Teresa.

If Calcutta can be taken as a cesspool, especially in the 1940s, Mother Teresa can be seen as the Lotus. Immediately after the World War, India became independent from the British, but not independent from problems. There was a continual exodus of millions - especially from East Pakistan - the majority of whom found their home on the sidewalks and in the old, unused buildings of Calcutta. Many could be found lying prostrate on both sides of the roads, a phenomenon that is still present in Calcutta. Deprived of all human comforts and consolations, the poorest and the rejected cried to God for help. God saw the affliction of the poor and heard their cry. He called this woman - simple, humble, and small in stature and until that time quite unknown to the world - to be his messenger of love and tender care while she was on the way to Darjeeling on 10th September 1946.

What did she learn from September 10th experience? She learnt that the crucified Jesus of Nazareth is still hungry and thirsty for love of souls - especially among the poorest of the poor, irrespective of caste, colour, creed or nationality - and that she was being called to satisfy the hunger of Jesus and of the poor through prayer, penance and whole-hearted free service to them.

She also learnt that the needs of the person take precedence over any other consideration, such as religion, colour or nationality. Her first question was not what religion a person belonged to or what country he or she came from, but whether that person was in need of any help or what she could do to alleviate the pain.

When I began working in the home for the dying in Kalighat, Calcutta, in 1967,, there was a man close to death who was brought by the Calcutta Corporation Ambulance. Once inside, with care and love, the simple medicines and some food, he was able to regain his strength; as soon as he was a little better he would go out to the street again and then within a few days an ambulance would bring him back. This happened over 15 times within a couple of months. I used to get upset and even angry with him for this. One day when he was brought back, I told Mother Teresa, "This man has been here over 15 times; there is no sense in taking him in again. In a couple of days' time he is going to go back to the street. Mother looked at me and said: "Listen, Brother Sebastian, does this man now need your help now or not?" I said yes. "Then do whatever you can to help him. The question is not how many times he has been to us but how we can help him now. Plus, whatever we do to him we do to Jesus".

This then is the point: although the religion of the person was not her first consideration, every person she served was Jesus for her. She was always aware that whatever we do to the least of our brothers we do to Jesus. And therefore she decided to make a fourth vow of whole-hearted free service to the poorest of the poor in whom she loved and served Jesus.

Mother Teresa understood that the same Jesus whom she loved and adored in the Bread of Life is the same Jesus whom she loved and served in the distressing disguise of the poorest of the poor. From the presence of Jesus in the Blessed Sacrament, she went to the presence of Jesus in the poorest of the poor and vice versa. She used to say: "The more repugnant the poor is, the more faith is required to help him".

Mother Teresa also repeatedly said: "Our work is not social work; it is God's work we are doing. We are not social workers, we are consecrated persons who are called to do God's work".

This gives a clear answer to the question: what is going to happen now to the Missionaries of Charity? Because [ours] is the work of God and of love, it is going to continue, as long as we remain faithful to her Spirit and Charism.

Mother Teresa realized that she was not called to do extraordinary things, but rather ordinary things with extraordinary love. She always said: "It is not how much we do that matters but how much love we put in our actions".

15

She learnt that not only should she hear the words of Jesus: "Come blessed of my Father..." but that she should help all men of good will to hear it. She was called to build the bridge between the rich and the poor, for the rich can find peace and joy in giving and sharing and the poor in receiving and returning. Both the rich and the poor give and receive mutually.

Mother Teresa knew that it is in giving that we receive, in dying that we are born to eternal life. She was called to live the words of St. Paul: "It is more blessed to give than to receive" (Acts 20: 35). Through Mother Teresa God opened the eyes of many to see their own poverty and misery and that of the poor who surround them, and to understand that they must be their "their brothers' keepers".

Mother Teresa made showed the world that there are two kinds of poverty: material and spiritual, both of which have positive and negative aspects. Spiritual poverty, however, is worse than the material poverty.

In conclusion we can say that although Mother Teresa died, had a most solemn funeral and her mortal remains laid in the tomb, her immortal spirit will continue to operate until the end of time. From heaven she will go on satiating the infinite thirst of our Crucified Saviour for love of souls, as she has become more powerful than ever.

"Each sigh, each look, each act of mine shall be an act of love divine, and everything I shall do, shall be, dear Lord, for love of you. Take this my heart and keep it true: a fountain sealed to all but you. What is there that I would not do today?" This was her prayer and her life. Let this be our prayer and our life as well.

God bless you.
Fr. Sebastian Vazhakala M.C.

September 2009
Tribute to Blessed Mother Teresa

"Trials bring us to the foot of the Cross, and the Cross to the gate of heaven."
(St. John Maria Vianney)

Every year, on 5th September, the Church celebrates the feast of Blessed Teresa of Kolkata; and every feast day celebration calls for a renewal of our life in the Holy Spirit. Every time we celebrate the feast of a saint we come to know the way he or she lived and loved God and loved his/her neighbour, lived the Gospel of love in action. We are meant to have a "double portion" of the Spirit, the desire, the longing, the hunger and thirst for holiness, his or her unquenchable thirst for the salvation and sanctification of souls. It cannot be limited to a simple liturgical celebration, but calls for a deeper understanding of the zeal and fervour, of the spirit of joy and enthusiasm, the spirit of self-denial and heroic sacrifices with which the person lived and worked. We come to realize that the saints were very much like us in many ways and lived and worked in similar situations and milieu with the difference that they were really in love with God and nothing and nobody could or did separate them from the love of God. St. Paul expresses it so eloquently in his letter to the Romans: *"What will separate us from the love of Christ?...For I am convinced that neither death, nor life, nor angels, nor principalities, nor present things, nor future things, nor powers, nor height, nor depth, nor any other creature will be able to separate us from the love of God in Christ Jesus our Lord."* (Rom 8: 35-39)

Whenever we have a feast or a solemnity, we are asked to take the psalms of Sunday, first week, for our morning prayer; and the first psalm for the morning prayer is Ps 63: 2-9. Why is this psalm prayed on a feast or a solemnity? There is a reason. This psalm expresses in so many words the insatiable thirst of the human heart and soul for God and for the salvation of souls. Psalm 63 starts with an act of profound faith and strong desire: *"O God, you are my God, for you I long; for you my soul is thirsting."* Not only does the soul of a saint thirst for God, but even his body. We continue to pray: *"My body pines for you like a dry, weary and waterless land."* The thirstier we are for God, the thirstier we become. Our thirst for God is like sea water. The more we drink the sea water, the more thirsty we become.

This was true of Our Lady; this was true of our Blessed Mother Teresa. Back in 1947 Blessed Teresa writes: *"The attraction for the Blessed Sacrament at times was so great. I longed for Holy Communion. Night after night the sleep would disappear - and only to spend those hours in longing for his coming. This began in Asansol in February-and now every night for one hour or two, I have noticed it from 11.00 p.m. to 1.00 a.m. the same longing breaks into the sleep."* (from Blessed Teresa's letter to Fr. Van Exem S.J., 1947)

The experience of Our Lady, of the saints and of Blessed Teresa herself must become ours as well. This desire, this longing and thirst, is meant to be dynamic. Every time we pray this psalm, we are meant to renew our experiences of this insatiable "nostalgia", this unquenchable thirst for God.

On the other hand, God's thirst for us is even greater, stronger and infinitely more insatiable, as God is infinite. The "Catechism of the Catholic Church" rightly defines prayer as *"the encounter of God's thirst with our thirst. God thirsts that we may thirst for him."* (CCC 2560)

We see this insatiable thirst in Jesus, not only on the Cross: *"I thirst"* (Jn 19: 28), but perhaps even more in the Eucharist. The Eucharistic Jesus and the Immaculate Heart of Mary, little by little, not only draw souls to Jesus, but they make them resemble Him. Blessed Teresa writes: *"Try to be Jesus' love, Jesus' compassion, Jesus' presence to each other and the poor you serve. All this will be possible only if you keep close to Mary, the Mother of Jesus and our Mother. She will guide and protect you and keep you only all for Jesus."* (Mother's General letter, May 1990) Jesus is the way, and Mary is the one who shows the way.

Our Lady's heart and soul longed for the salvation and sanctification of souls. In all her apparitions, whether in Lourdes, Fatima or Kolkata, invariably Our Lady demanded assiduous prayer, generous sacrifices and heroic penances for the salvation and sanctification of souls.

In Kolkata our Lady told Blessed Teresa to take care of the crowd, bringing them to Jesus. Her exact words were: *"Take care of them. They are mine. Bring them to Jesus, carry Jesus to them…"* (MFG p. 19) If the insatiable thirst for souls was a normal experience of all the saints, how much more Our Lady longed to save souls. It is not a thirst that finishes with one's death. No, it only increases, as they are much more close to Jesus. St. Thérèse of Lisieux wrote. *"My heaven will consist in doing good on earth."* In other words, in saving souls. Our Lady never stops working for the salvation of souls. Saints are the closest co-workers of Jesus. The closer one is to Jesus, the more insatiable and tireless he will be to work for the salvation and sanctification of souls. This is why Blessed Teresa M.C. worked day and night, wrote endless number of letters, and made people to join in her train of Charity. The more people share the works, the more they become thirsty and try to satiate the unquenchable thirst of Jesus. There are thousands and millions of souls to be saved. Jesus' thirst is infinite; it extends to the ends of the earth, embracing all people of all faiths or no faith. Jesus continues to demand from all of us: *"Will you refuse to do this for me, to take care of them, to bring them to Me?"* (MFG p. 19)

The second psalm of morning prayer for the feast day of a saint is from the book of the prophet Daniel (3: 57-88). It is very important to know the context of this psalm and why it is chosen for the feast of Our Lady, or an apostle, or a saint. This psalm is a canticle sung by Daniel and two of his companions in the fiery furnace. They were thrown there for refusing to worship the golden image. The furious king Nebuchadnezzar ordered the furnace to be heated seven times more than usual. And he chose certain mighty men of his army to bind Shadrach (Daniel), Meshach and Abednego and cast them into the burning fiery furnace. Then these men were bound in their mantles, their tunics, their hats and their other garments, and they were cast into the burning fiery furnace. Because the king's order was strict and the furnace very hot, the flame of the fire slew those men who took up Shadrach, Messhach and Abednego, who were thrown bound into the burning fiery furnace. And they walked about in the midst of the flames while singing hymns to God and blessing the Lord: *"Bless the Lord, all the works of the Lord, praise and exalt him above all forever..."* (cf. Dan 3. 52-90)

This is the background of this second psalm for the feast day of a saint. In the first psalm (Ps 63: 2-9), we saw the insatiable thirst of the human soul for God and the infinitely more insatiable thirst of God for man's love and for souls. In this psalm we see what Jesus, Our Lady and the saints went through during their earthly sojourn. Jesus, for example, told Blessed Teresa: *"You did not die for souls...your heart was never drowned in sorrow as it was my Mother's. We both gave our all for souls..."* (MGF p. 10) Jesus continued to say to Blessed Teresa that her vocation consisted in love and suffering: *"Your vocation is to love and suffer and save souls."* (MGF p. 11)

The sword of sorrow had to pierce the heart of Mary (Lk 2: 35), which came to its climax at the foot of the Cross: *"There stood"* – *Stabat Mater, the Mother of Jesus* (cf. Jn 19: 25-27) Our Lady's heart was drowned in sorrow, pierced with a sword of sorrow.

Years later Blessed Teresa wrote many letters to some of her spiritual directors of her own fiery furnace experience: *"If you knew what I am going through. He is destroying everything in me...I want God with all the powers of my soul – and yet between us there is a terrible separation. I don't pray any longer. I utter words of community prayer...I have been on the verge of saying 'No'. It has been so very hard – that terrible longing keeps growing and I feel as if something will break in me one day – and then that darkness, that loneliness, that feeling of terrible loneliness. Heaven from every side is closed...and yet, I long for God. I long to love Him with every drop of life in me. I want to love Him with a deep personal love..."* (from her letter to Fr. L.T. Picachy)

Blessed Teresa continued for many years with her fiery furnace experience, as she wrote: *"As for me – what will I tell you? I have nothing since I have not got Him whom my heart and soul longs to possess. Aloneness is so great – from within and without. I find no one to turn to...If there is hell – this must be one. How terrible it is to be without God – no prayer – no faith – no love – the only thing that still remains is the conviction that the work is His…And yet, Father, in spite of all these I want to be faithful to Him – to spend myself for Him, to love Him not for what He gives, but for what He takes."* (from a letter to Fr. Neuner S.J., 1965)

It is easier and even exciting for us to read and speak about other people's dark night experiences and enjoy in doing it, till the dark night, i.e. the night of the senses and the night of the spirit, hits us. It is then that we have to go through their writings with an altogether different spirit and profit from it.

"According to St. John of the Cross", writes Fr. Albert Huart S.J., *"the chief signs for distinguishing the night of the Spirit from psychological depression or spiritual sluggishness are:*

Most importantly: the person is unremitting in his/her commitment to duty and to his/her mission, even if he/she encounters trials and failures in these.

Although the person experiences prayer as dark, painful and fruitless, he/she feels drawn to prayer. Blessed Teresa continues: "and yet Father, in spite of all these I want to be faithful to Him, to spend myself for Him, to love Him, etc."

Gradually, underneath the darkness that weighs in one's soul, he/she discovers a quiet and growing spring of peace.

Later, when he/she ultimately emerges from this dark trial (which may take years), he/she looks back on it as a most blessed and life-giving period of one's life."

Saints like Blessed Teresa, and every saint went through the crucible of intense pain and purification. The sufferings were twofold: on the one hand the souls literally pass through the fiery furnace, but with an ardent longing and an insatiable thirst for God. They almost come to the verge of despair, but then the overwhelming power of grace envelops them. The inner self is not destroyed, but purified and remoulded in Jesus Christ, the perfect God-man.

"Trials bring us to the foot of the Cross, and the Cross to the gate of heaven.", says St. John Maria Vianney, the patron saint of all priests. It may be good that all priests and religious be aware of and be prepared for any sort of fiery furnace experience in their life and ministry. The dryness and darkness that we experience must not become a stumbling blocks in our life or apostolate, but stepping stones to go closer and

closer to Jesus and resemble him as the saints like St. John Vianney, Blessed Teresa and others did.

God bless you.

Fr. Sebastian Vazhakala M.C.

Saints, Signs and Miracles

Jesus said: "*I solemnly assure you:*
> 'Whoever believes in me will perform the same works as I do myself, and will perform **even greater works**, because I am going to the Father. Whatever you ask in my name I will do, so that the Father may be glorified in the Son. If you ask Me for anything in my name, I will do it' (Jn 14: 12-14).

"The believers remained faithful to the teaching of the apostles, to the brotherhood, to the breaking of bread and to the prayers…the apostles worked many signs and miracles" (cf. Acts 2: 42-47).

The story of every canonised saint is very intimately interlinked with the mystery of "signs and wonders". This is true especially after the death of a person who lived his or her earthly life in close contact with God. Many saints work even harder after their death than before. St. Thérèse of the Child Jesus and of the Holy Face who, for example, was quite unknown to the world while she was within the confines of a cloistered convent, said: "*My heaven would consist in doing good on earth*". The mission and ministry that she accomplished while alive was mostly known only to Jesus, her beloved Spouse. She wanted to make sacrifices without even Jesus knowing it, although she knew too well that that was impossible.

Blessed Padre Pio on the other hand performed innumerable miracles while he was still living. His reputation for holiness, coupled with the practice of the heroic virtues, had become a legend in his own lifetime. And yet it took 30 long years for the Church officially to recognise his heroic sanctity. The miracles done during his lifetime were not sufficient to prove that he was a saint, because a real miracle is required after the death of any Servant of God, unless the Servant of God is a martyr, in which case no miracle is required for his or her beatification; but one miracle after the Beatification is required for the Canonization, even of a martyr.

Many have been asking whether, through the intercession of our beloved Mother Teresa, the Lord has already performed the required miracle for her beatification. It is possible to think that her reputation for holiness and her heroic Faith and Charity, the various awards, honorary doctorates, the unique and unprecedented state funeral that she received, are more than sufficient ground to dispense from performing other miracles. It is up to the Holy Father to make any exception for her beatification.

Before going further into Mother Teresa's beatification and the required miracle, it would seem necessary to explain in detail the meaning of a miracle, its significance and its importance in the life of the Church.

God's Revelation comes to us in words and deeds. The words explain the deeds and the miracles; God's special interventions confirm the words. From the first pages of the Bible to the last, from the beginning of Christianity up until now, the Church has believed firmly in the importance and the necessity of miracles as a confirmation of God's direct intervention in human history. As Creator and Law-giver, God has every right and power to make exceptions to the laws of nature, which He does all the time through those persons whom He chooses to be His special instruments to keep mankind from going astray. This is also because God is not only the Creator, nor does He simply want to show His power and might, but primarily because He is a loving Father who really loves His beloved children: "*All this I tell you that my joy may be yours, and that your joy may be complete*" (Jn 15:11). This is the heart and mind of our God, and he will ask some of His sons and daughters to make heroic sacrifices, endure many tortures, and even martyrdoms, as He did with Jesus, His "well-beloved Son," to save the rest of the world. Suffering accepted with love is redemptive. No pain, no gain. In our wounds others are healed; in our trials others are strengthened; in our suffering others find salvation.

"Unless the grain of wheat falls to the ground and dies, it remains just a grain of wheat. But if it dies, it produces much fruit" (Jn 12: 24). Jesus, the grain of wheat, falls no more to the earth, but He does so now in the members of His mystical body, who are especially chosen by Him to collaborate with His work of redeeming the world and whom we call saints: confessors and martyrs. They are made to recognise that Jesus is the one who does the work in and through them, for He says, *"without Me you can do nothing"*: *"I am the vine and you are the branches..."* This explains to us in clear terms why and how Mother Teresa or Padre Pio or others could do what they did or can do what they are doing. There will always be saints and martyrs as long as there is the Church. Saints and martyrs have become so much the part and parcel of the Church's life that we can no longer think of a Church without them. Saints are co-redeemers of the world.

The divine call to sanctity is a birthright, and we are duty-bound to aspire to it and make every effort to be holy, as God Himself is holy. Children very much resemble their parents in appearance, in behaviour and in every way; they learn to speak the language of their parents. There is very little wonder then that we as God's children resemble God. If we do not, then there is much room for wonder. Imagine a child of five or six who did not speak the language **of his** parents. We would all feel strange. As children of God, it is so natural for us to speak the language of God, and the language of God is mainly 'love', and the work of God is 'Charity'. How can it be otherwise!

This brings us to the main point: how and why persons like Mother Teresa of Calcutta and others could see God as the Father not only of one group or one colour or race. Our God cannot be confined to any particular colour or caste. He is Father of all, Father to all, Father in all. He is *our* 'Our Father' and we are all brothers and sisters, sons and daughters of the same Father. All have the same immortal soul, the very same physical, psychological and moral needs...share exactly in the very same life of God. No matter what colour our skin may be, under that skin the blood is always 'red'. *The cows can be of different colours but the milk is always white.* We kill our brothers and sisters in the name of religion, and for political and geographical reasons...brothers killing brothers like Cain killing his brother Abel; mothers killing their children...etc. There is an endless chain of fratricide, infanticide...or homicide. And our God as Father of all suffers! "*What am I to do with you Ephraim? For your love is like morning mist, like the dew that quickly disappears*" (Ho 6, 4).

Mother Teresa has been a protagonist of the common brotherhood of mankind for our time. **She,** through her simple but profound faith, her intimate union with God in prayer, especially through the Eucharistic union and her ardent and heroic charity, particularly to the poorest of the poor, bridged the gap between races, religions, cultures and social status. She was able to see the "hungry Christ" in everyone: in the poor she saw Jesus who was hungry for a piece of bread, and in the rich she saw Jesus, who was hungry for love. For her it was the same to go to the dying man on the street of Calcutta or to go to the president of any country, as she saw Jesus in both, respected Him, and loved and served Him according to their specific needs. This has been the work of God. The world is called to recognise it and the M.C. Family is called to perpetuate the mystery of this great "*Mother Teresa Heritage*".

By her words and example, Mother Teresa taught the world that the value of a person does not consist in what he or she has or what he or she owns or produces, but in what he or she is, in what he or she does for others...and in the way of doing it. Created in the image and likeness of God, man is called to collaborate with God in the on-going re-creation of the universe, always moving towards the *eschaton*, where the entire cosmos will be made new in Christ. Herein lies the dynamic of Christian life!

For the beatification of a Servant of God, one real miracle performed through his or her intercession is required and sufficient. Pope Benedict XIV laid down several criteria according to which the miraculous cure of a sick person is to be judged:

a. the sickness must be serious and difficult, if not impossible, to be cured by human means.

b. The healing must be instantaneous.

c. The cure must be perfect. The sick person is to be totally healed through the intercession of the servant of God.

d. No medicine of any kind is to be administered while invoking the servant of God's intervention, nor is the help of any other saints to be sought.

e. The cure must also be constant and lasting.

All these elements have to be verified by qualified doctors and testified by the beneficiary in person by oath, and other valid documents proving the occurrence of the miracle. There is also the need for true witnesses who have known the cured person before, at the time of and after the miracle.

While we eagerly wait for the Church's recognition of Mother's heroic sanctity, let us continue to pray unceasingly: *"Make us worthy, Lord to serve our fellowmen throughout the world who live and die in poverty and hunger. Give them this day their daily bread and by our understanding love give peace and joy. Amen"*.

God bless you.

Fr. Sebastian Vazhakala M.C.

Prayer to Blessed Mother Teresa: our Foundress and our dearest Mother

Blessed and beloved Teresa of Kolkata, our foundress and our Mother,
bless your own Missionaries of Charity-Contemplative family.
help us to do all the good we can.
Enable us to love and adore Jesus in the Bread of Life
as you loved and adored Him; to love and serve Jesus
in the distressing disguise of the poorest of the poor
as you loved and served Him.
Mother Teresa, our dearest Mother and beloved Foundress,
filled with invincible love, profound humility, unshakeable faith and
undaunted courage,
you went in haste like our Blessed Mother
to give wholehearted free service to the poorest of the poor.
Help us to go forth with greater zeal and fervour
to meet human needs, to bring help, and above all
to bring Jesus to the poorest of the poor
and thus to satiate the *infinite thirst* of Jesus on the Cross
for love of souls.
Assist us, we pray, to proclaim the mighty works
the Lord has accomplished in and through you,
so that the entire M.C. family may extol the greatness of the Lord,
together with the poorest of the poor of the whole world.
Help us to give wholehearted free service
to the hungry, the thirsty,
those who lack the basic necessities of life,
those who live in despair and in the shadow of death,

the broken families, the little ones,
and all those who seek God with a sincere heart.
Beloved Mother Teresa, you never refused
assistance to any one
who sought your help or implored your guidance.
Look upon your own children and beg of Jesus,
your beloved crucified Spouse, the pardon of all our sins,
particularly our sloth, tepidity, negligence, indifference, coldness,
pride and other sins committed against our vows
of Chastity, poverty, obedience and Charity.
Our beloved Foundress, you who ardently
desired and tirelessly worked to satiate
the *infinite thirst* of your Crucified Spouse,
help us to continue satiate the *infinite thirst*
of Jesus on the Cross for love of souls,
with even greater thirst and ardent zeal and with complete dedication.
Obtain from Jesus the grace we need
to remain faithful to our M.C. vocation;
to serve the Lord freely, joyfully and wholeheartedly through prayer,
penance and works of mercy,
desiring nothing except to love
Jesus in the poorest of the poor,
and make Him loved and served in them,
as He has never been loved and served in them before,
until we die of serving them in love as you have done.
Blessed be the holy and undivided Trinity. Amen.
God bless you

Fr. Sebastian Vazhakala M.C.

CHAPTER TWO:
GENERAL LETTERS

FRATERNAL CORRECTION
NOVENAS *Growing together in holiness with Jesus, Mary, and Joseph*
OBEDIENCE – 1982
OCTOBER – 1989 *Time has no pity for the human heart*
DECEMBER - 1991
JANUARY – 1993
DECEMBER - 1994
JUNE – 1995
MARCH – 1999
NOVEMBER – 1999
HOLY YEAR – 2000
JANUARY – 2002
BAPTIZE YOUR SUFFERING – 2003 *Recycle your trials*
DO WHATEVER HE TELLS YOU – 2003
WE HAVE COME TO WORSHIP HIM – 2005
JOURNEY THROUGH AUSTRALIA - 2006
YEARNING FOR GOD – 2007 *Yearning for holiness*
ST. THERESE
TRANSFIGURATION – 2008 *Let us listen to God in prayer*
OCTOBER – 2008 *Love travels faster than the wind and the light*
CHRISTMAS 2008
PENTECOST 2009 *Linger not on the way, stray not from your aim*

Fraternal Correction

Dearly beloved Brothers and Sisters,

It is said that *"to err is human, but to forgive is divine"*. This means that all of us are prone to stumble and fall…all of us can make mistakes, commit blunders, errors, and sins. By nature we are weak, sinful and unworthy. God alone is perfectly holy!

From the cradle to the grave we are in need of every kind of help: physical, psychological, moral and spiritual. This also means that there will always be the need for good friends who will tell us our mistakes and errors…who will show us the right path when we go astray.

The following reading from the book of the prophet Ezekiel is really interesting and challenging. Let us take time to read it, reflect on it, and put it into practice in humility and charity.

"Son of man, I have appointed you as watchman for the House of Israel. When you hear a word from my mouth, you shall warn them for me.

If I say to the wicked man 'You shall surely die', and you do not warn him or speak out to dissuade him from his wicked conduct so that he may live: that wicked man shall die for his sin, but I will hold you responsible for his death.

If, on the other hand, you have warned the wicked man, yet he has not turned away from his evil, nor from his wicked conduct, then he shall die for his sin, but you shall save your life.

If a virtuous man turns away from virtue and does wrong when I place a stumbling block before him, he shall die. He shall die for his sin and his virtuous deeds shall not be remembered; but I shall hold you responsible for his death if you did not warn him. When, on the other hand, you have warned a virtuous man not to sin and he has in fact not sinned, he shall surely live because of the warning, and you shall save your own life" (Ezek 3: 17-21).

There is a duty and responsibility placed on us to correct a wicked person, to call a sinner to repentance, to tell a person who is off the track, who may have a glaring weakness and who may even lose his vocation if he is a priest or religious, and if we do not warn him.

We are liable to severe punishment for the sin of omission, for not correcting the person in time and thus saving him from spiritual death.

More surprising still is what is said about the virtuous man who happens to turn away from virtue and does wrong when God places a stumbling block before him…God himself places a stumbling block before a virtuous man, and God said to Ezechiel that he would hold him responsible for the death of that virtuous man if he did not warn him.

Two things emerge from this. First, God himself places a stumbling block before a virtuous man and he is meant to turn it into a stepping stone. Each stumbling block must become a stepping stone. Secondly, the duty of each brother who loves his brother is to warn him on time; this becomes more frightening when we think of the duty of superiors and Brothers in charge of formation to correct the Brothers who are under their care. They should not be afraid to tell things or correct a Brother on time. "A stitch in time, saves nine". But the way of correcting is very important. Fraternal correction is a 'must'. If it is given with due respect and inspired by love, it is a favour for which we should be grateful, even if it hurts our pride.

We have far more faults than we know. We must become more and more grateful to those who correct us with love and respect. Blessed Pope John XXIII, when he joined the seminary asked two of his friends to tell him his faults and mistakes every day. This helped him much and he did not go about with the idea that he was all perfect. None of us is fully perfect. There is so much bad in the best of us and so much good in the worst of us. All of us are in need of help from each other. We also have to help one another. We are commanded to love one another as Jesus loved us on the Cross and as he loves us now in the Eucharist.

This love must be transmitted; by our love all will come to know who we are.

Jesus encourages fraternal correction, privately if possible, but failing that, it may be done in company or with the assistance of the Church. Remember Jesus' teaching on the subject:

"If your brother sins against you, go and tell him his fault, between you and him alone. If he listens to you, you have gained your brother.

But if he does not listen, take one or two others along with you, that every word may be confirmed by the evidence of two or three witnesses.

But if he refuses to listen to them, tell it to the church; and if he refuses to listen even to the church, let him be to you as a Gentile and a tax collector.

Truly I say to you, whatever you bind on earth shall be bound in heaven and whatever you loose on earth shall be loosed in heaven" (Mt 18: 15-18).

"And if he sins against you seven times in the day and turns to you seven times, and says, "I repent," you must forgive him" (Lk 17: 4).

In the dramatic story of King David's sin in Chapter 12 of the second Book of Samuel, there is an example of man's utter weakness, complete blindness and terrible fall. We see the divine pedagogy at work when we read how God, through the prophet Nathan, brought David to understand and accept his terrible sins. Not only this, but David became his own judge without realizing that he himself was the culprit who had committed a crime that deserved not only restitution but even death. Listen to David's reaction and his judgement: *"David grew angry with the man. 'As God lives' he said to Nathan 'the man who did this deserves to die. For doing such a thing and for having shown no pity, he shall make fourfold restitution for the lamb'"* (2 Sam 12: 5-6). Nathan said to David: *"You are the man"*. How often may we have to hear such words as these: "That man is you"; or, "You are the man", in the Jerusalem Bible translation. As a result of David's terrible, tragic and humiliating experience, we have the beautiful psalm known as "The Miserere" (Ps. 51).

Here we have an example of divine correction…how to correct a "Brother" who errs, who sins, who is inclined to go astray. God does not crush the person, but makes him understand his faults, sins and even makes him his own judge without letting him know that *He is the man* in question. God is more merciful than man. He wants the sinner to repent and accept his mercy and become a saviour. David had wanted the man to die: *"As Yahweh lives, that man who did this deserves to die"*. Yahweh, on the contrary, forgives David: *"Yahweh for his part, forgives your sin; you are not to die…"* (2Sam 12: 14). *"God is slow to anger, rich in mercy and quick to forgive"*. We are often just the opposite of what God is: *quick to anger, slow to forgive, rich in vengeance*.

Before we rush to correct a person, we should pray to the Holy Spirit to inspire and guide us to help the Brother. Make some sacrifice for him, especially if the matter is grave. *"Again I tell you, if two of you join your voices on earth to pray for anything whatever, it shall be granted you by my Father in heaven. Where two or three are gathered in my name, there I am in their midst"* (Mt 18: 19-20).

How important it is for us to pray before we do anything; that means that our help is in the name of the Lord, that all is grace, that we depend totally on God and that everything good in us comes from Him, while we are fully responsible for all that is bad and evil in us. It is also true that we are in need of help and that we cannot live in isolation, that our spiritual growth and even our human maturity are partially dependent on social and communal interactions. We must allow ourselves to be formed and shaped into a better person, prepared for heaven. We also come to realize that we have an irreplaceable role to play, that we are held responsible for our Brothers as well, that we have to be our brother's keeper.

God will ask us, as He asked Cain: *"Where is your brother?"* Our reply cannot be like that of Cain: *"I do not know. Am I my brother's keeper?* (Gn 4: 9). God wants us to be saviours of one another, the Brother to save his Brother in community; the husband to save his wife and the wife her husband. It is easier perhaps to blame and accuse, condemn and judge, to separate or divorce, or leave the religious order if he/she is a religious, than to save and heal. When we are physically sick we look for a good and experienced doctor; and according to our means we go and choose our doctor. The surgeon may have to cut open certain parts of our body or remove part of it so that the rest of the body may be healed and saved. The doctor cannot pretend to be merciful and kind by fearing to hurt the patient and so refraining from operating on him, though he is desperately in need of surgery. The doctor's intention is not to harm the patient or to kill him, but to heal and save and to make him feel better.

In our spiritual life there are various kinds of cancers: dangerous and deadly ones, some of which require long term treatment, while others are in need of surgery. We may be told to cut out useless conversation and gossip, to keep away from unhealthy friendships and unedifying behaviour. At times we may require to shorten our hours of sleep or to reduce the quantity of food we consume; at other times we may need to prolong our hours of work, to improve the quality of our prayer, etc. We may be asked to be a little more faithful to our community exercises, keeping silence and remaining more recollected throughout the day; to be more cheerful, obedient, loving and caring. Failing to recognise and accept the need of a proper cure will result in spiritual death like a cancer patient who refuses treatment.

If 45,823 priests left their priesthood between the years 1970 and 1995, it is because many of them failed to recognise and acknowledge that they were sick, weak and sinful, and that they were in need of spiritual help; instead they allowed their beautiful and noble vocation to die a natural death. The cancer gets into our system like a parasite and eats our body from within little by little, finally causing death. Similarly, there are so many spiritual cancers, which are like parasites that cause spiritual death. First of all these are attacks on our prayer life: meditation, examination of conscience, spiritual reading, etc. To begin with we shorten our prayers, then we pray at random, and finally we give up praying altogether. Our reason begins to convince us that our prayers are no longer relevant; there are so many people to be helped and many other activities that can appear to be more profitable, useful and meaningful. The end result of such reasoning is disastrous, and can cause terrible spiritual deaths. It is here that we come to realise the importance of fraternal correction, spiritual dialogue, frequent confessions and regular spiritual retreats: all of which will not only weaken our spiritual enemies but make our apostolate a hundred times more useful, fruitful and beneficial.

It is time for us to act, to wake from sleep, to be sober and alert. Our opponent the devil is prowling like a roaring lion looking for someone to devour. Resist him, remain solid in your faith (cf. 1Pt 5: 8-9a).

Let us not be a victim of our own weaknesses, nor fall into the snares of our adversary the devil who is prowling around us, nor be blown away by the raging wind of this world. Let us resist all our spiritual enemies and remain solid in our faith, which is the basis of our spiritual life; in our unfailing hope, which is its driving force; and in invincible love, which is our goal. May the most beloved Mother of the Lord, after whose example we have consecrated our lives to God, obtain for us in our daily journeying that lasting joy that Jesus alone can give. May our life be a continual witness to Jesus' love, humility and charity. For only a humble person can receive correction and grow in holiness. Only a humble person can feel grateful to God and to everyone for everything. Let us enrol ourselves in Jesus' school of humility and charity and learn each day how to become more and more humble, gentle and grateful. *"Come to me all of you who labour and are overburdened, and I will give you rest. Shoulder my yoke, and learn from Me, for I am gentle and humble in heart and you will find rest for your souls"* (Mt 11: 28-29).

God bless you.

Fr. Sebastian Vazhakala M.C.

Novenas

Growing together in holiness with Jesus, Mary and Joseph

Throughout the year we make several novenas individually, in community and as a Society. Some novenas the Church encourages all believers to make.

There are novenas to the Holy Spirit, to the Sacred Heart of Jesus, to the Divine Mercy, to Our Lady, to St. Joseph, to Sts. Peter and Paul and to the other Apostles, to the Archangels, especially to St. Michael and St. Raphael, to our Patron saints, to St. Thérèse of the Child Jesus, to blessed Teresa of Kolkata, to St. Jude, to St. Anthony and to any saint of our own choice. Some of the novenas are seasonal, like the novena in preparation for the feast of Christmas, for the feast of Pentecost, etc.

There are also quick novenas. Blessed Teresa of Kolkata was very fond of making quick novenas of ten "Memorares" to obtain favours. The tenth one was a "Memorare" in thanksgiving for the favour Our Lady was going to grant. Once we were going to see an important person in one of the offices in Rome for a big permission. She told me that we would make a quick novena to Our Lady and we would not use the elevator, but climb the steps to make a more sacrificial novena. Our Mother looked very tired and there were quite a few steps to climb, but she kept on praying the "Memorares" as she went on climbing the steps. Periodically she stopped to take her breath. For me it was a real lesson. I understood that making a novena means not only simply saying some prayers but offering more sacrifices and praying more fervently. In any case what looked almost impossible to obtain, Our

Lady obtained for us: the fruit of our Mother's simple but profound faith, expressed through prayer and sacrifice!

Our Mother also doubled the quick novena if she did not get the favour she wanted to obtain. Once at the airport in Rome, she had fifty-eight boxes to check in. The man in charge of the airline at the desk told her that it was impossible to allow her to carry all those boxes. She tried her best to make the man understand, but he wouldn't. Mother said: "Let us start a quick novena to our Lady", and she began. We all prayed with her. She was praying with her whole being. The usual ten "Memorares" were finished, and still there was no change in his decision. So she told us to start again another quick novena, and she started. When we reached the eighth one the man came from inside and told Mother: "Alright, Mother Teresa, you may check in everything for your poor people". It is not enough to say a few prayers, but we must pray the prayers with faith, which she always had. She trusted more in God and in Our Lady than in her own power, ability and intelligence.

There are also people who make nine-day novena with fasting, abstinence and intense prayer. Some of them make it not only for nine days, but even up to forty-one days to obtain the desired benefits, both spiritual and material. Sometimes the entire community goes into such form of prayer to discover the will of God, to obtain a very important favour, personal and communal. I remember when I was a boy my beloved mother used to lead us into such form of penitential novenas, especially when the family was going through some serious crisis. One time my father was dying and he said good-bye to everyone around and was taken to the hospital, practically giving up all hope of return. This was back in May 1959. We doubled our prayers, especially praying all fifteen mysteries of the Rosary on our knees every evening and abstaining from things we liked most, until we received the news that he was going to live. It became a very long novena of almost two long months and he was perfectly cured by then; he is almost ninety-one now. What prayer and sacrifices can do!

The origin of Novena, as we read in the Acts of the Apostles, can be seen how Our Lady and the apostles prayed for nine days and where they prayed. The place of the first novena was the Upper Room, the first Chapel, where Jesus celebrated the first Holy Mass with his beloved apostles, ordaining them to the priesthood, asking them to do what he did in remembrance of him: *"Do this in remembrance of Me"*. *"The apostles returned to Jerusalem from the Mount of Olives near Jerusalem…Entering the city they went to the Upper Room…Together they devoted themselves to constant prayer."*…*"There were some women in their company, and Mary the mother of Jesus, and his brothers"* (cf. Acts 1: 12-14).

A novena, strictly speaking then, consists of nine full days. *The number nine* seems to be an important factor. It seems to bring certain maturity. The Sacred Heart of Jesus told St. Margaret Mary: *"I promise in the excess of the Mercy of My Heart, that My all powerful Love will grant to all those who receive Holy Communion on the **First Friday of nine consecutive months**, the grace of final repentance, and that they will not die in My displeasure, nor without receiving the Sacraments, and that My Heart will be their safe refuge at the last hour"* (Jesus' promise to St. Margaret Mary of Paray-le-Monial). This was the twelfth and last promise made to St. Margaret Mary, who lived in France in the seventeenth century (1647-1690).

It is interesting to note that normally a child stays in its mother's womb for **nine months**. So the number nine plays an important role in every person's life, even if one does not think of it. Definitely in the case of the little one in the womb of its mother for nine months, it is practically an absolute necessity; the little one becomes mature enough to be born.

It is clear from what has been said that making a novena does not only mean saying a little more prayer to obtain a desired favour, but making more sacrifices in joy, trying to do one's duties more faithfully and more perseveringly, offering prayers more fervently, obeying more promptly and cheerfully, thanking God for the graces and blessings we daily receive through the Brothers, the Community and the Society, depending on for whom we make the novena, offering many ejaculatory prayers for our continual growth in holiness and holy perseverance. So every time we make a novena we offer nine days of prayer with great love and devotion, observing real silence and recollection as our beloved and Blessed Mother Teresa's business card pointed out. She writes: *"The fruit of silence is prayer, the fruit of prayer is faith, the fruit of faith is love, the fruit of love is service and the fruit of service is peace"*

In any prayer, whether personal or communal, we can invite Our Lady and the apostles to pray with and for us. Our Lady not only gave birth to Jesus, not only took care of him, but lived with him, prayed with him, ate and drank, walked and talked with him. In a word, she did everything with him for thirty-three years. She will not only be too happy to join us in prayer, but teaches us to pray, and prays with us. But when we make a novena to the Holy Family, invariably we could invite the Holy Family to pray with us and for us.

The novena for our Society Feast can be found in our "Spiritual Path", Of course it must be read, reflected and explained by our elder Brothers to the younger ones. It cannot be limited to a few minutes before our night prayer. It has to be and it is a serious programme for nine days; a personal and community retreat with the Holy Family.

The Tridium is a still more intense and immediate preparation. The fruitfulness of our novena depends on how earnestly, how fervently and how prayerfully we spend these nine days. Our positive and profound silence will lead us to have deep faith experience. This faith then becomes living and active in ardent love, which will be made more fruitful in service. This kind of service, which is the fruit of love, is bound to give peace to us and to all those who come in contact with us.

In conclusion we can say that the purpose of the nine days of intense prayer, sacrifices, reflection and contemplation are meant to obtain special favours and graces for each individual, for the community, and in fine for the whole Society. In all our prayers and novenas we must ask for the grace to do God's most holy will more and more perfectly. The growth in holiness and perseverance in our vocation depends much on how disposed and ready we are not only to do God's holy will but also to accept his will. As our Blessed and beloved Teresa of Kolkata used to say: *"To accept whatever He* (God) *gives and give whatever He takes, with a big smile, is holiness."* Our novenas and our prayers as a whole are meant to do that. So we pray more fervently and more assiduously for our continual growth in holiness and for our holy perseverance. If perseverance and constancy are qualities of all prayers, the novena prayer demands even more earnestness, fidelity and sacrifices.

Let us hope and pray that our preparations, both remote and proximate, for the Society Feast may help us to understand more profoundly our call to follow Jesus in the Society of the Missionaries of Charity. Love and prayers.

Happy and holy Society Feast to all.

God bless you.

Fr. Sebastian Vazhakala M.C.

Prayer to the Holy Spirit:

Come, Holy Spirit, and from heaven direct on us the rays of your light.
Come, Father of the poor; come, giver of God's gifts; come, light of our hearts.
Kindly Paraclete, in your gracious visits to our souls you bring relief and consolation.
If they weary with toil, you bring them ease; in the heat of temptation, your grace cools them;
If sorrowful, your words console them.
Light most blessed, shine on the hearts of your faithful — even into our darkest corners;
For without your aid we can do nothing good, and everything is sinful.
Wash clean our sinful souls, rain down your grace on our parched souls
And heal our injured souls. Soften our hard hearts, cherish and warm our ice-cold hearts,
And give direction to the wayward.
Give your seven holy gifts to your faithful, for our trust is in you.
Give us reward for our virtuous acts; give us a death that ensures salvation;
Give us unending bliss. Amen. Alleluia.
"Be with us, Mary, as you were with the Apostles in the Upper Room, to prepare our hearts to be the worthy dwelling place of the Holy Spirit"

Novena to the Holy Spirit:

Oh Holy Spirit, You are the Third Person of the Holy Trinity! You are the Spirit of truth, love and holiness proceeding from the Father and the Son, and equal to them in all things! We adore you and love you with all our heart, mind, soul and strength. Teach us to know and seek God in all persons we meet and live with, and to serve them in humility and charity. Fill our hearts with a holy fear and a great love for Him. Give us compunction and patience, and do not let us fall into sin.

Increase our faith, hope and charity and bring forth in us all the virtues proper to our state of life. Help us to grow in the four cardinal virtues, your seven gifts and your twelve fruits.

Make us faithful followers of Jesus, Mary and Joseph, and obedient children of the Holy Catholic and Apostolic Church and joyful givers of whole hearted free service to the poorest of the poor beginning with our own. Raise us to holiness in the state of life in which you have called us and lead us through a happy death to everlasting life.

Grant us also, O Holy Spirit, giver of all good gifs, the special favour for which we now ask (name it), if it be for your greater honour and glory and for our growth in holiness and increase in number. We ask this in the name of Jesus the Lord.

One Hail Mary and one Glory to the Father.

Oh Holy Spirit, Spouse of the Blessed Virgin Mary, have mercy on us and bless us.

OBEDIENCE TO THE WORD OF GOD

A <u>word</u> can be defined as a verbal expression of a thought, an idea, a desire or a feeling. It can be expressed in spoken or written words. It stands for the things, not merely materially representing them, as a label, but expressing their meaning; it stands for the concept of things. Hence the word expresses the specific way in which the world of things is presented in the human minds. Thus all the languages of the world are born of words with specific meanings which are true ways of communication.

Among all creatures on earth, man alone is capable of speaking and sharing because God created man in his own image and likeness (Gen.1: 26). He alone is able to understand and appreciate the work of God's hands. "Yahweh, our Lord, how great your name throughout the earth ..."(Ps. 8) He is said to be the loud speaker of the universe and the cosmic priest who is capable of offering prayers of praises and thanksgiving to His Creator. "Give thanks to Yahweh, call His name aloud, and proclaim His deeds to the peoples. Sing to Him, tell over all His marvels!" (Ps.105: 1-2). Being creation's finality and its king man makes history through the interaction of a given world that surround him and his freedom by means of his words and deeds.

Through his words man not only expresses his ideas and thought but also reveals himself and his plans. Though very interesting and extremely useful to make a detailed study on the place and importance of the human word in our day-to-day life, we limit ourselves to our topic, namely Obedience to the Word of God.

Right from the beginning the Bible, i.e. the Word of God in the words of men - presents God's "Word" as a medium not only of communication but also of creation and revelation. By the Word of God heavens were made. (Ps 33: 6; Gen 1: 3) In contrast to man God does not speak "about" things, but their very being is rooted in the free creativeness of His Word.

Man is bound to obey God's Word, through which God spells out his designs for man (Gen.2: 16).Placing the first parents in the Garden, Yahweh tells them to obey in order to be united with Him and to be happy and at peace(Gen.2: 16-17). From now on man's life, his happiness, comfort and enjoyment depends on whether he obeys God, or not. A disobedient man can never be with God: he has to be out of God's garden. (Gen.3: 22) He has no part with Him. Before the clear command of God man has no excuse and so he suffers the consequence of his own disobedience. The first sin committed by our first parents was the sin of disobedience to God 'a Word. The tree of the knowledge of good and evil in the middle of the garden (Gen. 2: 9) symbolizes our conscience in the heart of our being, as we know that conscience is the voice of God speaking in me to do good and avoid evil (GS: 16).It is that power of deciding for oneself what is good and what is evil and acting accordingly. In a word, every sin is a disobedience to one's own conscience, which is the transgression of an express command of God spoken in me.

In contrast to our disobedient parents, we meet Abraham, the hero of obedience to God's Word, in the opening verses of the 12th chapter of the book of Genesis. He was asked to "leave his country, his family, and his father's house" and every thing he knew and was familiar with for the past 75 years of his life. "Abraham went", says the Bible, "as Yahweh told him" (Gen. 12: 4). Abraham humbly obeyed God's word; he obeyed his conscience. Abraham had to go to an unknown land, leaving all the human securities, relying only on God's word, which from then on was going to be the light for his path, food for his soul, strength for his life. Having no other support, he totally relied on God. Like Abraham of old in the opening pages of the New Testament, we meet Mary of Nazareth, the humble handmaid of the Lord, betrothed to Joseph from the family of David. (Mt.1: 18 ff; Lk.1: 26-28). Both of these heroes have the obedience of faith, and their life and example have become great inspiration for all generations to come.

So often and in so many places in the Bible, Abraham is mentioned as a man of heroic faith and obedience to God's word (Gen.22: 12-13; Rm.4: 1 ff.; Gal.3: 6ff: Heb.11: 8ff). He so willingly took "his only son

Isaac whom he loved" in obedience to God's word to sacrifice him on mount Moriah. Isaac was born when Abraham was about 100 years old; he was the promised one of God, born out of the normal course of time. And yet when Yahweh asked Abraham to sacrifice his only son, whom he loved (Gen.22: 2), Abraham did so willingly: "Rising early next morning Abraham took Isaac..." (Gen.22: 37). In deep faith Abraham now has come to know and believe that the God who gave his only son is Supreme and He is his Master. Abraham is only His servant who carries out his master's command, even in the case of Isaac, his only son. Not because Abraham did not love Isaac, not because God was ignorant of Abraham's love for Isaac that He asks Abraham to make such heroic sacrifice. On the contrary, God simply commands: "Take your only son whom you love"(Gen.22: 1).Is He going to give another child to Abraham? What would happen to Yahweh's promise? Abraham did not question; he simply and humbly obeyed: "Rising early next morning....." Years later we see Mary of Nazareth, virgin and Mother, who walks with her Son, who too was carrying his own wood for sacrifice to the place of the skull, or as it was called in Hebrew, Golgotha (Jn.19: 17). If Abraham is the father of faith, Mary can be said to be the Mother of faith. Before Mary's own eyes her beloved and only Son whom she loved was brutally killed, immolated on the wood of the cross: "Near the cross of Jesus stood his mother..." (Jn.19: 25) gazing, watching her only Son to die before her eyes. Mary remembered again her words at the Annunciation, "Behold the handmaid of the Lord, be it done to me according to your Word" (Lk.1: 38). Again and again as her life unfolded, Mary had to keep reminding herself of her first spontaneous 'fiat'. Her words of a total surrender were the echo of the sinful humanity yearning for redemption. Her obedience to God's word was thus paid instalment with greater or lesser demands.

Many have followed the example of Abraham and Mary down through the ages. We meet many heroes and heroines of faith as we travel through the history of the Church. St. Maxmillian Maria Kolbe, for example, in our own day is a shining example of such heroic faith. It means that they have learnt to value the world to come more precious that they sacrificed the present for the future, the good for the better, time for eternity. How could St. Maxmillian Kolbe sing praises to God in a starvation bunker, when he was starved to death there by the Nazies? Here all the human explanations fail. Only heroic faith and obedience to God's word can finally give the answer. "What is impossible with man is possible with God".

In our own time God chose a humble woman, Mother Teresa of Calcutta, to bring the good tidings to the poor and abandoned of the world on her way to a hill station in the north of India. She, too, had to leave all; from now on God's word is her light and her guide. She found her strength in the words of Jesus: "I was hungry and you gave me to eat, I was thirsty and you gave me to drink....As long as you did to the least of my brothers you did it to me..." (Mt.25: 31 ff.) She believed these words and made them real, proving to the world without wanting to do so. In the hungry and in the homeless, in the orphans and in the abandoned she began to see the face of Jesus in the distressing disguise. Jesus makes himself available to us in the Bread of life so that we can receive Him in the Eucharist. The same Jesus makes Himself available to us in the broken bodies of the poor so that we can love Him and serve him in the distressing disguise of the poorest of the poor. "O, how rich are the depths of God - how deep his wisdom and knowledge - how impossible to penetrate His motives or understand His ways!" (Rom 11: 33 ff.)

We are God's children and God's Word is our language. "Do not take the word of truth from my mouth...." (Ps.119: 43) Hearing God's word with faith and eating His body at the Lord's table we will become God's true children. "Brethren that is what we are" (St. Paul). As Christians, as religious and priests we must learn to love God's Word, live it in our daily life. Treasuring them in our hearts, we must ponder over them like Mary (Lk 2: 19). Going in haste, we must share the Word of God with our needy brothers and sisters.

"When I found your Words, I devoured them; they became my joy and the happiness of my heart. Because I bore your name, O Lord, God of hosts."(Jer 15: 16)

God bless you.

Fr. Sebastian Vazhakala M.C.

October 1989

Dear Your Grace,

"Time has no pity for the human heart", wrote R. N. Tagore, the Indian mystic poet, and how true that is! Time and tide wait for none. So we have to catch up with time, and I must confess that I have not done that. You have all the reasons to be angry for not hearing from me for such a long time. With all the good will and effort I find hard to keep up with my correspondence. I do not, however, want to justify myself, but would rather ask you to remember me in your daily prayers and sacrifices.

Recently I have been to Calcutta to visit our Mother Teresa of Calcutta. The decision was sudden, with a quick change of plans. I was supposed to be giving a retreat in Paris and I was getting ready for that when, rather unexpectedly, I was told that Mother had another serious crisis. As you may all know, she was admitted to Woodlands' Nursing Home (Calcutta) since September 5 and was slowly getting better; and then there was an influx of visitors – V.I.P.s and others which made her very sick, tired and weak. So as the news came, without any after thought I got ready and took off for Calcutta and was there on the night of 16ᵗʰ September, 1989.

The major part of 16 September Mother felt better; as a result many visitors were allowed to the point of serious exhaustion. By the time I arrived, to my bad luck, Mother could be visited by no one. My great desire to see her and the subsequent efforts were all in vain and I had to wait patiently for a few days before I could visit with her.

The interim period turned into something very beautiful: I went down to visit my parents and family. For them it was a very pleasant surprise, especially for my father, who was very seriously ill. The good

Lord arranged everything so well that those few days were extremely enriching and abundantly fruitful. Instead of going to Bombay directly to catch my flight back to Rome, I decided to try once more to visit Mother. This time I was very indifferent, as I did not want my visit to make her feel more sick. Thanks to the warm welcome and kind hospitality of my M.C. Brothers both in Calcutta (Dumdum) and in Bombay. They have been real brothers to me from my arrival to the hour I left. After Holy Mass and breakfast with the Brothers at Dundum house I telephoned to the Sisters at the Mother House. To my great surprise I was told that Mother wanted me to celebrate Holy Mass in her room at the clinic. You can imagine how happy I was to offer the Holy Mass with her in the evening of September 29, 1989. Mother was so happy and talked to me at length, enquiring about almost everything and everybody. She told me to give her prayerful greetings to all, especially to the Lay Missionaries of Charity, which I now do through this letter. Several times we blessed each other. I felt that I was carrying all of you with me: my Brothers and each one of you personally. She was very happy to receive your regards.

Mother also told me of God's mysterious ways and how her sickness has taught and is teaching so many people to pray to God. The Muslims in Calcutta very early morning cry to Allah, saying, "Heal our Mother", the Hindus in their temples, the Christians in their homes and Churches, the children and young people in schools, colleges and universities are all praying and making sacrifices for her cure. Somehow the world all over sees in her the sign of God's presence. The invisible God has become visible in and through her, like the invisible electricity becomes visible through a bulb. It was not just the miracles of Jesus that really strengthened the faith of the Apostles and the early Church, but the Paschal mystery of the suffering, death and resurrection of the Son of Man. Seen in the light of the Paschal mystery, Mother's present suffering is the completion and confirmation of her mission, strengthening the entire M.C. Family and the faith of the people; above all her final definitive identification with the poor. Strangely enough, a few weeks before she seriously fell ill I had a dream of her being sick to death. I saw her sitting in one of Calcutta's streets, dressed like a very poor old woman. She refused to come home, saying that she preferred to die on the street. It was a dream, of course; still I see some grains of truth in it. God's ways are mysterious and often beyond our comprehension!

Many Sisters told me that they have never prayed in all their life as they pray since Mother got sick. Sisters and their community all over were praying day and night before the Blessed Sacrament exposed. This reminds us of Moses in the Old Testament praying raising both hands to God to win the battle. As long as his arms were raised up to heaven the Israelites were safe (Ex 17: 11 ff).

Another mysterious combination is what happened in Calcutta on the morning of 25ᵗʰ September, 1989, namely Mother had her ransom: Sr. Premila went home to God. She died in the convent above the Home for the dying, in Kalighat, where her last breath mingles with thousands of Calcutta dying destitutes who have gone before her, marked with the sign of love and peace! A little over a year ago, one night Mother took me to Gemelli Hospital in Rome to anoint her. She offered her life in full consciousness in the place of Mother, a timely substitute indeed! God would have been very pleased with the selfless and exemplary offering of Sr. Premila. May she rest in peace!

I also would like to take this opportunity to express my sincere thanks to each one of you for all your help, spiritual and material. Our "Night Ministry" among the hungry and the homeless at the various train stations in Rome and the Brothers' work with the street boys in Sao Paolo, Brazil, are going quite well. Thanks to you, generous volunteers, for your spirit of service, prayer and sacrifice.

My fellow brothers and sisters of the Lay Missionaries of Charity, you may be very happy to know that the LMCs are very close to our Mother's heart. The sixth candle on all the M.C. altars of adoration represents you and the seventh for the Co-workers. It is very necessary for all those who try to follow the LMC way, first of all to pray to the Holy Spirit for the proper understanding of the spirit and charism of our Movement, to read and study carefully and regularly the LMC Statutes, to seek counsel and direction from the Spiritual Directors, to form group and to remain in close contact with other groups, the M.C. communities and also with the Centre in Rome. Together let us build God's kingdom of love and peace on earth. Let us desire noting except to love until we die of love!

God bless you.

Fr. Sebastian Vazhakala M.C.

DECEMBER 1991

The year 1991 has brought many graces and blessings of God to our little family of the Missionaries of Charity Contemplative. It may not be possible and even necessary to speak of them all, but just a few of the most important ones with joy and gratitude.

One of the many moving events was the ordination ceremony of Br. André Marie M.C. by the Holy Father Pope John Paul II in St. Peter's Basilica on May 26th . Thanks to our beloved Mother Teresa, Sr. Agnes and the many Sisters, LMCs, Co-workers and friends whose presence and active participation added special colouring to the day, both in St. Peter's and in our house at the first Holy Mass. At the end of the first Holy Mass Br. André Marie M.C. thanked his own mother, who was also present, very specially for not having aborted him!

An equally moving ceremony was Br. Mathew's religious profession in June. Br. Mathew has been a Missionary of Charity Brother Active for many years. During his tertianship he felt called to a deeper life of prayer and penance. With God's help he came to answer it, which as we know is a response of love. Only this love can motivate and support the privations and trials which he will necessarily encounter for Christ and for the Gospel. His personal response to the redemptive call of Christ now binds him together in a brotherly communion in the army of Christ. His freedom is now fortified by obedience. Rejoicing in the spirit, he now advances on the road of love. A true religious no longer desires anything except to love until he dies of love. To this end we all pray.

Thanks to Fr. Arturo Vella S. J. from Malta who in the last week of the month of August led us all to a high mountain for eight days to have a deeper and a person-to-person encounter with Jesus. May the Lord reward Fr. Arturo for his kindness and generosity.

For long we have been thinking of starting a new community. Several bishops were very happy to welcome the Brothers. But then came Albania into the scene; and we have been there since September 8. It is really a birthday gift of our Blessed Mother...not so much to us as to the spiritually and otherwise starving thousands of that blessed land. It may take too much of our time to go into detail of how we got there.

Albania is a country with three million people spread out in an area of twenty-eight square kilometres, two-thirds of which are bare rocky mountains. Five of our Brothers are in a place called Bushati. Bushati is in the northern region of the country, 15 km south of Shkodra (Scuteri) on the Tirana road. Our house, which was a theatre before, is now used as a church since March of this year. It has two distinct parts: the theatre, which is the church, and the Brothers' house with their own quarters. We did a lot of cleaning and converted a big room into a beautiful chapel for the Brothers. The entire complex needs to be re-adjusted, repaired and cleaned. Right now the Brothers are busy visiting the families and blessing the houses, preparing children and adults for baptism and other sacraments. There are about five hundred families in the area, half of which are Muslims. The people are very, very poor. They have absolutely nothing and nowhere can they get anything. Even the very basic necessities of life do not exist. There are many sick people, disabled children and adults.

Nowhere can one buy medicines or even soap, with the result that many suffer from various skin diseases, especially children. Not only is water rationed, but it is very cold and hardly any one has the facility to heat it. There isn't any gas or even wood to cook with. The misery of present Albania is beyond any description. One has to be there to see and experience it. It is enough to say that right now Albania needs everything, both spiritual and material help. Christmas is essentially a time of sharing. Let us do it now. This is the hour to act.

In spite of all the poverty and misery around them, the people of Albania are still very hungry for God, perhaps in a manner that we do not see anywhere else. They walk miles and miles to come to church, to get a blessing, to get a rosary or a medal or a religious book in Albanian.

They know their catechism by heart in a song form, as they could not have any religious book. Six days a week people come to our chapel to pray, to learn catechism, religious hymns and songs, etc. They join us in adoration, Holy Mass, the Stations of the Cross and other prayers. Each time invariably they sing the rosary and other prayers, children as well as grown-ups. Their faith is very simple. Ten statues of Our Lady are in the round. Every Monday of the week ten different families get them for a week. And when they bring the statues back they all get a small statue of Our Lady of Lourdes with holy water in it.

Albania is everywhere, perhaps in a different manner and intensity. In our Night Ministry on the streets of the so called "Eternal City of Rome", we discover a different kind of poverty. There is a noticeable difference between the materially poor people of a believing kind and the spiritually and materially poor people of an affluent city like Rome. Thanks to the many generous and dedicated volunteers of our Night Ministry team of Rome, who three nights a week provide a full meal to close to two hundred persons each night. May the Lord reward their kindness and generosity.

Work with the street children of Sao Paolo (Brazil) is another way of proclaiming the good news to the poor. In his recent visit to Brazil the Holy Father spoke of the children, including many of Brazil's street children, about his love for them and his distress at seeing their plight. To the children of Brazil he said: *"I want to tell you something very serious: the Pope loves the children of Brazil with all his heart...Let the children come to the Pope. I give each of you a great big hug and my blessing...Long live the children of Brazil! Long live the children of the world!"* (Salvador, Brazil, 20.10.91)

We have about thirty children living with us who come from the streets of Sao Paolo and elsewhere. The Brothers and the Co-workers with the recovered children go to the streets of Sao Paolo once a week at night to befriend them. It is always a very moving experience, although very demanding at the same time. Many come to the house at night, have a shower, a meal in the middle of the night, spend the rest of the night, and in the morning they are free to stay or to leave. This happens on every Monday night. Sao Paolo has thousands of street children. They too are God's children and therefore our little brothers and sisters.

Jesus said: *"If you welcome a little child in my name, you welcome Me"*. There are many ways of welcoming the little ones of God's children!

There are many more things to be said, but I am afraid to overstep the limits of time and space and to wear out your patience. Just a minute more to say a word about our LMCs. The LMC national meetings held in Rome and in Carmel, Indiana (U.S.A.) were unforgettable experiences of deep communion and fellowship. Everyone felt a deeper oneness and closeness and expressed a desire to repeat them. So we look forward to the October 1992 meeting in Rome.

The LMC groups in Pecs (Hungary) and Budapest had their profession in April last. They were happy to see the LMCs from Rome and Barcelona. September saw the profession ceremony of the LMCs in the U.K., at the conclusion of their national Co-workers' meeting. Thanks to Mrs. Fay (CW national link) and Fr. Michael, their spiritual director and all the CO-workers of the U.K., who incidentally adopted our baby house in Albania. Thanks to each one of you for all your help.

The U.S.A LMC now has a national spiritual Director, Msgr. Joseph Flusk, and Dr. Ned and Mrs. Emcele Masbaum as their National Links. My sincere thanks to you for what you are doing. Also Vancouver (Canada) has a very beautiful group of LMCs since July.

Wishing you all the blessings of a happy and holy Christmas and bright New Year 1992.

God bless you.

Fr. Sebastian Vazhakala M.C.

January 1993

Dear friends,

One more Christmas, one more New Year. Many memories! So many births, so many deaths: dear ones, near ones, strangers, foreigners, blacks, whites, browns, rich, poor, young ones and old, men and women!

Abortions, mercy-killings! (Euthanasia).

New experiences: happy, sad and mixed ones; enriching and encouraging ones; impoverishing and discouraging ones; temporary and eternal ones; harmful and harmless ones; useful and useless ones!

New encounters: new friends and friendships, new acquaintances, breakdowns and reconciliations, peace meetings, reunions, round table conferences.

In the political field: manipulations, outright injustices, great and expected victories, failures, disappointments, disillusions.

In the religious field: new and young vocations, ordinations, temporary and perpetual religious professions, conversions, spiritual and mystical experiences.

New avenues of actions, new homes for the homeless and abandoned, new hospitals and clinics, churches, dioceses and Bishops, new schools, new institutions.

Endlessly endless events to enlist. Time, space and interest force us to limit ourselves to those very important ones that have imprinted in our minds some sort of indelible impressions and images! We are the persons behind the scene, and what are those unforgettable impressions?

There is much to hank God for: persons unforgettable for their outgoing generosity and great spirit of sacrifice in serving their fellow men. Our many and diverse spiritual benefactors, co-workers, volunteers, especially of the Night Apostolate, Lay Missionaries of Charity (LMC), our own Brothers and Sisters...our endless ocean of persons. In the name of our Brothers and the poorest of the poor of all kinds, I say: Thank you, and pray that the good Lord and the Blessed Mother may reward your kindness. *"As long as you did it to one of my brothers, you did it to Me"*. Even a cup of cold water given in Jesus' name is a true Epiphany and is going to be rewarded.

Before we reach our desired goals, the good Lord lets us walk through fire and flood without being hurt by or drowned in them. Reflecting on the life of our little Society, we have, with God's help, made some progress in the Albanian scene. At Bushat, Scuteri, our Brothers were able to restructure a movie theatre into a place of prayer and worship for about 500 or more people. God willing, its blessing will be done by the Apostolic Nuncio, Archbishop Ivan Dias, on Saturday 23rd January, 1993, at 10.30 a.m. Joined to it is our first house of the Brothers in Albania, which too had to be renovated and enlarged. We now have a new dispensary from where an Albanian lady doctor dispenses medicines on a regular basis. Adjacent to it is room to teach catechism to children and adults. It is also used for all sorts of meetings with the people. The church, with its entrance, gives more room for privacy and solitude to the Brothers, which is so necessary for our life of prayer and work. This place is on the Tirana-Scuteri road, 15 km South of Scuteri, known as Bushat.

In the beginning of June of the same year, we made another big move by opening a second centre at Kukel (Scuteri), which is our present noviciate. It too is going through major changes, adjustments and renovations. Like the house is being renovated, so too the life of the novices slowly but surely is being transformed into the image of their Divine Master, whose food was to do his Father's will. May I ask your prayers for us all so that we may abandon completely to God's will, who alone has absolute dominion over us.

Besides the many hours of prayer, adoration, etc, the brothers also spend much time in preparing children of various ages and stages and adults for baptism, First Communion, Confession and Confirmation...

thanks to the keen interest in wanting to understand and study the basic truths and doctrines of our faith. Side-by-side they are also being taught to pray by introducing them to actual prayer, meditation, adoration of the Blessed Sacrament, etc. Besides the spiritual and doctrinal help, the Brothers also share with the very poor some material goods of various nature, such as food stuff, clothes, building material of various nature, stationary articles, school materials for children, medical assistance, etc. Thanks again to so many of our generous benefactors (the big loads of foodstuff and other things from Parma, the two loads of floor tiles from Sassuolo (Modena), the full container of paint from Trieste, the beautiful organ for the Church from Milan, one of the church bells from Frosinone and several other things, the many rosaries and religious articles, medicines from the United Kingdom, many, many gifts from Rome…an endless list of things received individually and collectively, as well as the many small donations in cash.

In Rome, our generous volunteers of the Night Ministry continue to serve the hungry and homeless three nights a week, on Sunday, Wednesday and Friday. With you, I thank God for offering you such golden opportunity, and for you we pray that you may serve the poor with greater love and joy.

Efforts are made to realize a centre for the old-homeless people of our city of Rome and around. It takes a lot of time and energy; our limited resources are coming to an end before even finishing simply the so-called prefabricated box. Thanks to the members of St. Vincent de Paul Society of Rome whose encouragement and promised help has set its work already in motion. *"God hears the cry of the poor"*. I firmly believe and pray that the good Lord will continue to inspire many generous people and organizations to complete his work of love, which is at the same time the work of peace!

Although the feast of Christmas is just over, the spirit of Christmas stays with us. IT then calls us to have a closer look at the cave of Bethlehem where the Bread of Life was born in the "House of Bread". Bethlehem means house of bead. We shall ask a few searching questions to ourselves. Why did the creator of the universe choose a cave in which to be born? Why did the Redeemer of the world chose to be born in a crib, among animals? Why did the Saviour of mankind chose the apparent weakest and poorest parents of no great importance, who were so unable to provide a proper place for their child to be born? Why? Why?

What then does the Bethlehem crib teach us in this context? That the Creator of the universe *deliberately chose* poverty to make the poor rich in this *poverty*.

The Redeemer of the world chose *humility*, losing his previous state with the Father; that the Savour of mankind chose *obedience,* an obedience unto death on a cross to set us free and save us all. Here is the rock-bottom, the foundation; here is the authentic truth, the unchangeable essence of our faith, our life, our Christian and in particular our M.C./LMC/Co-worker vocation.

But we must know that it is not enough to be poor, but happy to be poor; it is not enough to desire to be humble, but happy to be considered nothing, useless and of no importance at all; it is not enough to suffer any way, but accept suffering with love…Let us with the shepherds, with the Magi enter the Bethlehem cave of our authentic selves and see ourselves as we are in order to become as Jesus wants us to be.

The "commercials" kill the true spirit of Christmas by their cleverly worked out way of presenting things to their clients. The politicians manipulate so often the authentic truth of Christian charity and service. And it is here and nowhere else that we M.C./ LMC/ Co-workers, believing Christians, have to play our irreplaceable role to be authentic witnesses of the Christ of the gospels. How often we have followed the mentality of our so-called computer age of the greatest confusion, racism. divisions and unrest. On the one hand there is the United Europe strengthening by erecting stronger walls around it to protect it from the flow of the poor from poorer nations. It all sounds very logical, reasonable and natural. Well, let the Lord be our judge. And let him judge us mercifully!

From October 6th to 12th, our LMCs from 16 countries met together in Rome. It was their first International meeting which, with God's grace, was a profound spiritual experience. It brought to our awareness the importance of a committed and determined life in this world of chaos, lawlessness, promiscuity and licentiousness. That is why the LMCs must stay where they are, and not try to change their residence, work or work place, because they are LMCs who have made their private **vows; nor** should they try to change others or pretend to know everything of the M.C. way of life. *"Change your hearts"*, let us change our hearts and become humble in our attitudes and actions, being docile to the action of the Holy Spirit.

Our audience with the Holy Father on October 7th with all the LMC participants of the world was one of the highlights of the whole meeting. Several of them were able to touch or talk to him, though very shortly. Our little boy, Adam, from the U.S.A., was the most fortunate of all to receive many kisses and caresses from the Holy Father. The day concluded beautifully with our concelebrated Holy Mass and the refreshments prepared by our Brothers in the Mother House and Birthplace of the LMC Movement., at Via S. Agapito, 8, in Rome.

"Working for the Lord does not pay much and the retirement programme is out of this world". Still in faith, hope and love we must all work for the Lord untiringly. In this regard so many of you deserve to be thanked and the Lord needs to be praised and glorified in your name and for what you have been. Let us continue to serve the Lord even when it hurts, even when we are misunderstood, even when we are bring ridiculed and laughed at, even when others feel jealous of us, even when we are being humiliated (see the Thursday Litany, Prayer Book, p. 25).

Words are inadequate to express my heart-felt gratitude to God and to you all for your prayers and sacrifices offered for my beloved parents and family, especially for my dearest mother. As you might have known, I was home for about a month, and tried to spend as much time as possible with my own. I never found my mother so peaceful, joyful and filled with grace. Her last words to me as I was leaving home were: "My dear son, now I can die in peace; I thank God for this gift which I thought I would never have had". She received all the necessary Sacraments with tears of joy and tremendous peace. Her face lit up as she was saying: "Now I am ready to go home to God". My eyes were full and I was choked! My dear father along with my brother accompanied me to the airport. Thanks be to God. Let us desire nothing except to love until we die of love.

God bless you.

Fr. Sebastian Vazhakala M.C.

DECEMBER 1994

Dear friends of the Holy Family, Jesus, Mary and Joseph,

Thank you so much for all your letters, cards, donations and gifts. Above all for thinking of us and of our poor people in Casa Serena during the many beautiful and wonderful feasts that have passed: the feast of Christmas, Holy Family, New Year, with the feast of Our Lady, Mother of God, the feast of the Epiphany and the baptism of Our Lord, all of which are so rich in meaning and in mystery. More than once the readings spoke of us as children of God who are co-heirs with Christ the Lord. Thanks to his goodness, love and mercy.

God calls us to be persons of prayer and charity. There is such a deep hunger and thirst in all of us which will remain unsatisfied and insatiate until we are united with God in prayer. Prayer is for us as water for the fish. A fish cannot survive outside water and will die eventually, so too one who does not pray dies spiritually. In prayer we come to know **how thirsty God is for us and how thirsty we are for him**. We are restless until we rest in him who has created us for him. Our deep hunger and thirst for God and his hunger for us meet in prayer and express it more vividly in charity. Meeting with him in prayer essentially transforms our interior life, our motives, our values and attitudes, and leads us to works of love, whether within one's own family, religious community or outside. *"We are called to be contemplatives in the heart of the world for twenty-four hours"* (Mother Teresa).

Another good news I would particularly like to share with you is that on 8 December 1993, on the solemnity of the Immaculate Conception, the Contemplative branch of the Missionaries of Charity was erected into a diocesan religious Congregation by his Eminence

Camillus Cardinal Ruini of Rome. Thanks be to God and thanks to holy Mother Church, the M.C. Family is now canonically complete with its five Branches. Already on the eve of December 13, we had the Thanksgiving Mass, during which Mother Teresa of Calcutta, our foundress, read out the decree of erection in the presence of some of Brothers and Sisters. And then, on New Year eve and the Solemnity of the Mother of God, juridically and in a solemn way this event was celebrated by His Excellency Bishop Giuseppe Mani, auxiliary bishop of Rome in the concelebrated Holy Mass, during which some of us made our vows again. It too was a very moving experience. For us it has been a miracle which the good God worked through his Immaculate daughter and Mother. We are unable to thank him who alone can do such wonders. I cordially invite you to join us to thank the Lord for this wondrous gift to the M.C. Family. Pray much that we may not spoil God's gift, as we are so weak, imperfect and unworthy of such gift. To make it more fruitful and beautiful for God's glory and for the good of others we need his spoil blessing, which, as a matter of fact, will not be wanting. God is capable of doing what humans are unable to do by our own power and ability, and he will never let us down. God hears the cry of the poor, and blessed be the Lord.

The brothers from our communities in Albania came to take part in the celebration. We have two houses about 100 Km North of Tirana, near Shkoder, since September 91. Both houses are rather close to one another, within ten Km's distance. This enables the Brothers to come together often. The noviciate house is in Kukel at the foot of a huge mountain. There is much repairing and reconstructing work to be done. It needs time, patience, much work and a lot of money. It is the Lord's work, and in his own time all will be realized. *"Surrender to the Lord and he will do everything for you."* Br. Matthew, who was supervising and doing the work, is at home in India to assist his dying mother, who went home to God on January 9, in his presence and other members of his family. May she rest in peace!

Bushat house is practically complete now, although there is always some problem which has become very much part of the Brothers' daily life. Albania teaches us a lot, especially the virtue of patience.

On February 2nd we had the first profession of three of our Brothers in Shkoder cathedral, in Albania, a very moving experience indeed. His

Excellency Archbishop Ivan Dias, the Apostolic Nuncio, was the main celebrant and homilist, who was joined by twelve priest concelebrants. The Cathedral church was packed with people, lay and religious. It was another historical event, as it was the first religious profession in the renovated Cathedral in 45 years. Nine months ago the Holy Father in person consecrated four Albanian Bishops in the same cathedral, of which our main celebrant referred in his inspiring homily. The Catholic Church in Albania is slowly taking shape. It needs visible and living witnesses to the Gospel of love...love animated by prayer, penance and works of mercy.

Casa Serena, our night shelter, is slowly getting filled, and our volunteers are doing a wonderful job in preparing and serving the dinner, and cleaning and washing. The more volunteers we have, the better it is. Many of them join the guests to pray the family Rosary at 7.30 p.m. God loves the poor and those who serve them. In the poor we meet Jesus. Remember the words: *"You did it to me"*.

I would like to conclude this letter by recalling to mind one of my recent experiences in Albania while visiting a family: two persons in all, a mother and her eleven years old daughter and the animals. The mother was lying in bed with high fever and was unable to get up. The girl did everything in the house. The house is divided in two: a small kitchen and another room. The main one is the sleeping room for the mother and the daughter, and a cow and some chickens. The kitchen is used for the calf and a few goats for the night, for fear that someone might steal the animals at night, which is not very unlikely at all. The animals for them are vital, although the cow was paid off by the Brothers. I could only stay there for a few minutes and was feeling very uneasy. Even if one is healthy, in no time one falls sick in such conditions of life and living. Poverty can reduce people to live like animals. How many people live in similar or even worse conditions than this poor family!

It was an unforgettable experience and lesson for me, especially to appreciate and thank God for what He has given me, and also my duty to share with those who have less than me. One of Brothers had taken an old stove and some wood to burn, which I had thought was absurd, but my visit forced me to change my view. We need to reflect much. *In the evening of life when we appear before God, we will be judged on love".*

"I was hungry, thirsty, naked, sick and in prison…As log as you did to one of the least of your brothers, you did it to me". My next door neighbour is Jesus who is in need of my help…a kind word, a smile, a look, a few coins for a cup of coffee…

Thank you friends, for your friendship, for your generosity, for your time, for your good will and everything else. May the good Lord help you and bless you. Let us continue to be brothers and sisters and help one another to make our love more fruitful in service.

God bless you.

Fr. Sebastian Vazhakala M.C.

ROME, 17 JUNE 1995

Dear LMCS,

For a very long time I have wanted to write and share with you all of the joys of being a Christian...and also the demands and cost of being the same. One has to want it; one has to choose it; one has to long for and embrace it with all the powers and fibers of one's being. A Christian is no less or more but one who decides to follow the Master..."Master, where do you stay? "Come and see" (Jn. 1:38-39); "Master what must I do to gain eternal life? (Lk. 18:18); "Lord, to whom shall we go, you have the words of eternal life...(Jn. 6:68). A Christian is the one who accepts Jesus as his Master; a Christian is the one who considers Jesus as his Lord; a Christian's way is Jesus' way...Indeed Jesus is his way. "I am the way, the truth and the life".

There is no ambiguity, there is no wavering; there is no fifty-fifty. A Christian is called to become another Christ. He is called to reflect the Master who is "the light of the world" as much as He is so too the Christian..."you are the light of the world" (Mt. 5:14).

A Christian has to love one another as Jesus loved, as he loves us now--no less.

"Love one another as I have loved you" (Jn. 15:12)

"Lay down your life as I have laid down my life..." (Jn. 15:13)

As each year passes by we come to the decisive moment in the spiritual life when we must make the final choice between Jesus and the world, between the heroism of love and mediocrity, between the cross and an easy existence, between holiness and merely decent religious conformity.

A Christian is a conqueror of evil and hatred. He conquers evil with good, hatred with undefeatable love, with enduring love--no matter what you do to me, I will still love you. His love is not calculated nor measured. The measure with which he must love God and his neighbor is to love them without measure.

A Christian is called to abandon altogether the search for security in this world. His security is God. He has to reach to the risk of living with both arms. He has to embrace the cross like a lover. He has to accept pain as a condition of existence. He has to count doubt and darkness at the cost of knowing. He needs a will stubborn in conflict, but ready always to accept totally every consequence of living and dying.

As Christians we begin our day with Jesus and for Jesus. Without Jesus our actions do not mean anything at all. They are like many zeroes without a number. 000.000.000... but if we add 1 (one) before all the zeroes (1.000.000.000), it makes all the difference. Let all our actions be filled with full of God, full of His love.

"Life of my life, I shall ever try to keep my body pure, knowing that your living touch is upon all my limbs.

"I shall ever try to keep all untruths out from my thoughts, knowing that you are that truth which kindles the light of reason in my mind.

"I shall try to drive all evils away from my heart and keep my love in flower, knowing that you have your seat in the inmost shrine of my heart.

"And it shall be my endeavor to reveal you in my actions, knowing it is your power that gives me strength to act." (R. N. Tagore, Indian mystic poet and Nobel Prize winner)

Today I leave (17.06.95) for India and hope to be back by July 12th. The work is going on there to build a small house for the brothers and another home for the poorest of the poor. It will take a while, as we have some problems. The place is very close to the Delhi International Airport (14 Km only). Please pray that we may be able to do something beautiful for God there also.

Two of our novices, Br. Charbel and Br. Joseph, are making their first vows on July 22nd at 5 p.m. in our Holy Family Chapel, in Via S. Agapito, 8 - Rome. They need your moral and spiritual support, which I know, you do any way.

More news of us when I come back. In the meantime let us continue to pray for each other.

Our new telephone number is 21.70.77.02 / Fax Number is 21.70.77.03

Love and prayers.

God bless you.
Fr. Sebastian Vazhakala M.C.

Feast of St. Joseph the Worker, March 1999

Dearest Brothers and Sisters,

On Monday, 1 March, 1999, the Holy See officially announced the good news of the introduction of the cause of beatification of Mother Teresa of Calcutta without waiting for five years as the usual rule prescribes. This brought great joy to the whole world. Already this news had been sent in writing to the Archbishop of Calcutta in a letter dated 12 December, 1998, which read: "I am pleased to send you the Rescript of dispensation from the requirement of waiting five years before the presentation of the written petition requesting the initiation of such cause".

Since then there have been various interpretations regarding the exact nature of this dispensation, granted by the Holy Father through the Congregation for the Causes of Saints, and so it is good to spell out what this dispensation really consists of. First of all let us see what it did not say.

-It did not mean to say that Mother Teresa is already being beatified, nor is it said that she will or will not be beatified in the year 2000.

-Nor is it said that this exception means that the Holy Father is going to make exceptions also from the normal procedures of the beatification process that is required for any servant of God.

On the other hand:

-What is being said is that the Archbishop of Calcutta "may begin the Diocesan Enquiry into the life, virtues and reputation of sanctity of Mother Teresa in accordance with the norms to be observed in

Enquiries made by Bishops in the causes of saints", without waiting for the usual five year term.

-It also recalled the need "to gather all published and unpublished writings of Mother Teresa as well as all those documents which in any way regard the cause".

Two of us, Fr. Brian and myself, have attended a four month course – November to March – on the causes of saints conducted by the Congregation for the Causes of Saints in the Vatican, taking the due exams. Thank you for your prayers, sacrifices and words of encouragement: the professors were wonderful examiners, which naturally helped in the obtaining of good results... I too prayed much for the professors!

This course helped me tremendously and opened my eyes to many avenues in my life. Not only is it going to be helpful in preparing and assisting with Mother Teresa's beatification process, but also on a personal level – as it clearly set out the parameters envisioned by the Church for holiness. "Holiness is not a luxury of the few, but the simple duty of you and me", Mother Teresa used to instruct us. She taught us this on her five fingers: "I want, I will, with God's blessing be holy", and then on the other five fingers: "You did it to Me" (Mt 25:40). Both hands joined together in prayer enable us to do God's will. The closer one is to God the closer one comes to one's fellow human beings, especially the suffering ones. The closer Mother Teresa was to God, the nearer she was to the people, to the last, the least and the lost. "How could it be otherwise, since the Christ encountered in contemplation is the same who lives and suffers in the poor?" St. Vincent De Paul, for his part, loved to say that when one is obliged to leave prayer to attend to a person in need, that prayer is not really interrupted, because "one leaves God to serve God" (cf. V.C. 82).

Many have been asking about how far have we got with the preparatory work for the beatification of Mother Teresa. The entire process is rather complex, and I dare to say can even be rather tedious and involved. Let me explain a bit more in detail.

The Petitioner advances the cause of canonisation by appointing a Postulator by means of a mandate written according to the norm of law, with the approval of the Bishop. Who are the Petitioners and who is the Postulator for Mother Teresa's cause?

The Congregation founded by Mother Teresa is the Petitioner. More concretely the Superiors General of the five Branches of the M.C. Family, that is to say the Superiors General of the various branches together appointed Fr. Brian as Postulator of the cause. Theoretically, as the Postulator of the entire M.C. Family, he is meant to be neutral as far as the various branches are concerned.

One cannot be a postulator and a witness at the same time. Perhaps this statement needs further explanation. A witness in the process of beatification of a martyr or a confessor is a person who has seen or has known the servant of God and is now called to give witness regarding the practice of the heroic virtues by the servant of God. These are mainly the theological virtues of faith, hope and charity and the cardinal virtues of prudence, justice, fortitude and temperance. These virtues must be practised by all Christians, but not all practice them to a heroic degree. The supreme way of practising them is by martyrdom. This can only be achieved through profound and continuous union with God, assiduous prayer, penance and above all the practice of charity, not just once in passing, but constantly.

I am supposed to be an *ex-officio* eye-witness to Mother Teresa's cause of beatification. The good Lord granted me the grace to be with a saint for over 30 years. So my witnessing is about "what I have heard, what I have seen with my own eyes. What I have watched and touched with my own hands" (see 1 John 1-4). This is what I am called to give testimony to, and I am to testify to nothing but the truth so that my speaking the truth about the servant of God Mother Teresa may bring greater glory to the Holy Trinity and profound peace and joy to all men of good will.

There was, besides, our closeness to each other, which she often spelled out by saying: "We know each other by heart". Very often my feeling was that of being with my own mother, and even more!

I would also like to say a word about our correspondence. I have made a collection of the letters which she wrote to me from 22 September, 1971, to 23 August, 1997, i.e. 13 days before her death. These letters are all hand-written, except the last three which are typed. For ease of understanding, I divided the letters into three sections: A, B and C.

Section A: letters written to Bishops, Cardinals and to the Holy Father regarding our Branch of the Missionaries of Charity, Contemplative, and also a few notes written to our Lay Missionaries of Charity Movement.

Section B : Mother's letters written to the community and to me.

Section C : letters written personally to me.

All three sections put together and chronologically arranged amount to a total of about 81 letters.

On one of the last occasions that Mother visited us in our house in Rome, as she was at the gate she lifted up my small crucifix, then kissed it and said: "Oh, how beautiful this crucifix is, please give me one next time I come and I will wear it". Without a moment's thought I took mine off (the Sisters call it a 'shoulder crucifix') and gave it to her. She happily took it and kissed it, thanked me and went. On her last visit to Rome she showed it to me with great joy like a little child saying: "See your crucifix, now I am wearing it". Needless to say I was very happy about it, and happier still when I came to know that she went home to God with it. During the week of her wake in St. Thomas' Church, in Middleton Row, Calcutta, when there was no one else close to her body at nightime, I was tempted so many times to remove the crucifix and pin mine on her shoulder as they were identical, but a voice prompted me from within that it was better that our beloved Mother be buried with the same shoulder crucifix that she went home to God with. So I let it go and am not sorry, as she has been a mother to me and I her unworthy son, and she dealt with me with such kindness.

As everyone is so eager to see the Servant of God Mother Teresa of Calcutta to be raised to the honours of the altar, we all need to explore more deeply her life of profound and assiduous union with God, her practice of the virtues of faith, hope and charity, coupled with her practice of the moral virtues of prudence, justice, fortitude and temperance to a heroic degree, and above all her insatiable love for Jesus in the Blessed Sacrament and her equally unquenchable love for Jesus in the poorest of the poor, the last, lost and the least. In a word, from morning to night she submitted herself joyfully to the Rule; she strove to be attentive to her prayers and recollected all day long; she practised the silence of the eyes, the heart and the tongue when she felt inclined to speak unnecessarily, or out of place and time. She accepted suffering without complaints, especially the unseasonableness of the weather, and showed herself extremely kind and gentle to all. She accepted humbly and patiently the reproaches made to her; she tried her best to accommodate herself to the tastes, desires and temperaments of others; she stood contradictions without irritation. She did all this not just once in passing, but habitually, not merely patiently but joyfully, purely for the love of God.

Her hunger and thirst for holiness was so strong that she became a very powerful magnet, so inseparably united to the Source of all holiness that all those who came in contact with her were irresistibly drawn not only to her but to the Source itself. May her Beatification draw millions of people to the Source and fountain of all holiness. To this end we all pray and ask for prayers.

Prayer for the Beatification of Mother Teresa of Calcutta
Most Holy Trinity, Father, Son and Holy Spirit.
We praise you and thank you for choosing Mother Teresa of Calcutta
to be your faithful handmaid and zealous apostle of Charity to all,
especially to the poorest of the poor.
Father, in the silence of contemplation your humble handmaid
heard the echo of Jesus' cry on the cross: *"I thirst"*.
This cry, received in the depth of her heart, spurred her to seek out
Jesus in the poor, the abandoned and the dying
on the streets of Calcutta and to all the ends of the earth.
Jesus, she understood fully your Gospel of love.
Her spiritual legacy is all contained in your words: *"you did it to Me"*.
In silence and contemplation she learned to see your face
in every suffering human being. You wish to identify yourself with every person,
especially the last, the least and the lost.
O Holy Spirit, you who have infused in her that extraordinary spiritual vision,
her attentive and self-sacrificing love of Jesus in each individual,
her absolute respect for the value of every human life and

her courage in facing so many challenges, may inspire also her spiritual sons and daughters (ask for the favour....).

Raise her, we pray, to the honours of the altar, that enlightened by the radiance of her virtues we may praise and glorify you,

Father, Son and Holy Spirit, by doing something beautiful for God. Amen.

(with Ecclesiastical Approval)

God bless you

Fr. Sebastian Vazhakala M.C.

November 1999

Dearly Beloved Brothers and Sisters,

The month of November begins with the solemnity of *All Saints*, the feast of all those who have gone through great tribulations and temptations, all those who have fought with "themselves", with the "world" and the "devil" and won the crown of victory through their sweat and blood. Jesus too had to learn obedience through suffering; He had to spend His days and nights praying with loud cries and tears while on earth, as the letter to the Hebrews says: "*He offered up prayer and entreaty, with loud cries and with tears, to the One who had the power to save Him from death and, winning a hearing by His reverence, He learnt obedience, Son though He was, through His sufferings; when He had been perfected, He became for all who obey Him the source of eternal salvation…*" (Heb 5: 7-9). If this is true of Jesus, the Son of God, how much more must the members of His mystical body struggle and suffer to become holy!

The month of November then makes us remember the Church's three levels of existence. We are familiar with multi-storied buildings and skyscrapers. To clarify the concept we take an example of a building with just three floors:

- The ground floor can be compared with the Church militant or the Church in constant battle. All of us belong to this category.

- The first floor represents the suffering Church that is the state of the souls in Purgatory.

- And the second floor refers to the triumphant Church, i.e. the Saints in heaven who have been washed in the blood of the Lamb and whose sins the Lamb of God has taken away.

The people of God are in constant battle against the powers of this world, the devil and their own selves. A world without God is an impoverished one and becomes an evil world; worse still is the world that fights against God and continually tries to make His chosen people deviate from Him. A sinful world labours to distract God's people from listening to Him and from following His path. It is diametrically opposed to the world of God. The world with no reference to God is a restless world, an angry and competitive world, a deceptive world with no peace, joy or happiness. This world is not what God created; it is man's own re-creation. The more people try to free themselves from God in order to be independent, the more they become slaves to the world of sin, until they discover that the way to power lies through the realization of helplessness, that the way to victory lies through the admission of defeat, that the way to goodness lies through the acknowledgement and confession of sin, that the way to independence lies through dependence, and the way to freedom lies through surrender. Believing people therefore, with their motivation and determination, try to go above and beyond this world of so called autonomy, self-sufficiency and independence.

Let us now go up to the first floor or the second stage, which is the "suffering Church", Purgatory. Here we are dealing with the faithful departed who are on the way to the Source and Fountain of Love. But they are not yet fully washed and purified in the blood of the Lamb. On the other hand, they are incapable of doing works to merit for themselves or for others. They have become the poorest of the poor as long as they are in this state. They go through intense pain of purification and they cannot do anything to reduce their pain for the period in which they need to be there. But we humans, i.e. the militant Church, can help them through our prayers, sacrifices and works of mercy offered for their intentions as suffrages. The Church encourages us to help the poor souls through the gaining of indulgences.

What then is an indulgence? *"An indulgence is the remission before God of the temporal punishment due for sins already forgiven as far as their guilt is concerned. This remission the faithful, with the proper dispositions and under certain determined conditions, acquire through the intervention of the Church which, as minister of the Redemption, authoritatively dispenses and applies the treasury of the satisfaction won by Christ and the Saints"* (Norms on Indulgences n° 1).

"An indulgence is partial or plenary, according as it removes either part or all of the temporal punishment due for sin" (id. n° 2). These indulgences can only be applied for the faithful departed or for oneself; they cannot be applied to other living persons.

"To acquire a plenary indulgence it is necessary to perform the work to which the indulgence is attached (Praying the Rosary, for example) and fulfil the following three conditions: sacramental confession (several days before or after the performance of the prescribed work), Eucharistic Communion, and prayers for the intentions of the Sovereign Pontiff (both on the same day). It is further required that all attachment to sin, even venial sin, be absent" (id. n° 23).

"The deaf and the dumb can also gain indulgences attached to public prayers, if they devoutly raise their mind and affections to God, while others of the faithful are reciting the prayers in the same place; for private prayers it suffices if they recite them mentally or with signs, or if they merely read them with their eyes" (id. n° 36).

There are four ways of gaining plenary indulgence each day of the year, provided one fulfils the required conditions.

    i.   Adoration of the Blessed Sacrament for at least one half an hour.

    ii.   Devout reading of the Sacred Scriptures for at least one half an hour.

    iii.   The pious exercise of the Way of the Cross (n. 63).

    iv.   The recitation of the Marian Rosary in a church, public oratory, a family group, a religious community or pious Association (n. 48).

Even if a person performed all four on the same day, he or she can acquire an indulgence only once in the course of the day.

To understand the profound significance of all this, one has to try to penetrate into the inscrutable mystery of God's merciful love and His unchanging plan for man. God doesn't want man to suffer eternally and even temporarily, especially after his death; because he loves us so much he tries to free us from the domain of suffering and pain, including the souls in purgatory, who are bound to undergo such a state unless we help them by our prayers and sacrifices.

From the first floor we now move on to the second stage or floor that is Paradise. This is the state of bliss and unending happiness, which we believe that the saints are blessed with. In this world of pain and toil we mortals are reminded of the world to come. Jesus, the only Way, the Truth and the Life came to take us to that world of unending joy and peace, *which the eye has not seen, nor the ear has heard*, and when we celebrate the feast of *All Saints* we in some way anticipate our future life. By celebrating it we experience here and now a foretaste of our future glory and joy that is to come for all those who love God with all the powers and fibres of their being and their neighbour as they love themselves.

In conclusion, it can be said that God wants us all to be holy and perfect like Him, no matter how hard and difficult it can be at times. We may even go through fire and flood before we reach our final destiny in God: "*These are the people who have been through the great trial; they have washed their robes white again in the blood of the Lamb. That is why they are standing in front of God's throne and serving Him day and night in the sanctuary; and the One who sits on the throne will spread His tent over them. They will never hunger or thirst again; sun and scorching wind will never plague them, because the Lamb who is at the heart of the throne will be their shepherd and will guide them to springs of living water; and God will wipe away all tears from their eyes*" (Rev 7: 14-17).

There are so many of you who deserve to be thanked, who have been so generous and offered such wonderful help everywhere and in every way during my recent mission journeys. Since words are inadequate to express my heartfelt gratitude, I pray that our Blessed Lord may reward you for your kindness and generosity. Please remember our poor people, our Brothers and me in your prayers as we remember you in ours.

To the LMCs, I would like to say that we have fixed the dates for our Third International Meeting in Rome from Sunday, 30 September, to 7 October, 2001. It is never too early to start preparing. Details will follow. Till then, let us keep praying.

I am leaving for India on 5 November, 1999, and will be there until the 29th. We look forward to the blessing and inauguration of Deepashram, the home for the homeless handicapped boys on 18 November (99), the fourth anniversary of our beloved Mother Teresa's visit to Deepashram, which we still cherish with great delight. All of you are cordially invited to be present in body and or in spirit. To both groups I say thank you. Love and prayers.

God blesses you.

Fr. Sebastian Vazhakala M.C.

Holy Year 2000

Dearly beloved Brothers and Sisters,

We are at the threshold of the Third Christian Millennium. Our Mother Church has been continually inviting us to renew our response to the will of God. It is hard to say how many of us are really ready to make a radical response according to the "*noia*", the mind of Christ; the perfect way of pleasing His Father for Christ was to lose His own original form of God, "*to empty Himself and to take the form of a slave and become obedient unto death, death on a cross*" (Phil. 2: 5-11). This divine "*kenosis*" (self-emptying) became an indestructible power at Jesus' resurrection, which then became the source and summit of our own future life. God has put into man a tremendous sense of hope, which even if he loses it God doesn't lose it. It is precisely because of this invincible hope of God for man that He sent His only Son, who became man and lived among us

The feast of Christmas, then, celebrates God's unshakeable hope in every human being, created in His own image and redeemed with the blood of His Son. Christmas is a feast of hope and is also a feast of love. To be real, love must be shared. Each human being is a container of God's undefeatable and invincible love. Each human being is a spark of His love wrapped in human flesh, which is destined to live for all eternity.

Though born in a manger among animals in Bethlehem (the house of Bread), Jesus did not become food for animals, but rather He preferred to become the "*Bread of Life*" for man. Each Eucharistic celebration is a new Christmas, although He does not come in the form of man but in the form of bread, as He explained to the crowd: "*I myself am the bread of life. He who eats my flesh and drinks my blood has eternal life and I will raise Him up on the last day"* (Jn 6: 35 ff.).

Christmas is a feast of humility. Mother Teresa used to say: *"It is easier for us to understand the greatness of God than to understand His humility"*. How could such a great God become so humble as to become a tiny embryo in the womb of a woman? And then to be born among animals and to die between two thieves on the cross like a criminal! There is no wonder then that *"the Cross is a stumbling block (scandal) for the Jews and folly for the Gentiles"*; and only for those who firmly believe in Him is the Cross *"the power and the wisdom of God"* (1Cor 1: 23-24).

Jesus came to teach us this sublime virtue of humility as he says: *"Learn from Me, for I am gentle and humble of heart"* (Mt 11: 30 ff.).

Christmas is a feast of poverty. Unlike us who have no choice with regard to our birth, God purposely chose a poor and simple carpenter's family for His birth; He chose the unknown village of Nazareth, which had no importance at all in the time of Jesus Christ. His first disciples even remarked, saying: *"What good can come out of Nazareth?"* (John 1: 46).

More than in choosing a poor place and simple and humble parents, it is in deciding to lose His original form, i.e. the transition from God to man and in the hiding away of His awesome divinity in human flesh, that one discovers through contemplation the unfathomable depth of the poverty and humility of the "Son of God".

We need to approach the Jubilee Year 2000 with the *"noia"* of Christ, with the virtue of hope…and also with profound and positive poverty and humility in order to encounter Jesus Christ. Opening the doors of our hearts to Christ demands real and lasting *"meta-noia"*, that is to say to accept Jesus' own values and to try to live them in our day-to-day life. We also need to approach the Jubilee Year with a great sense of gratitude. Gratitude is an integral part of the *"noia"* of Jesus.

Glancing back over the year 1999, I am overwhelmed and almost speechless as I realize that words are inadequate to express our gratitude to God for all His loving providence and tender care. It is difficult to thank God enough for our poor people whom He sends to us all the time and whose sandals we are not worthy to unfasten. Each day after Holy Communion we pray: *"Make us worthy Lord, to serve our fellowmen who live and die in poverty and hunger…*" "Make us worthy, Lord to serve…" We are not worthy to serve our poor people unless the Lord makes us worthy to serve them. In the Church only special ministers are allowed to expose the Blessed Sacrament. There too we need to pray the same prayer: Make us worthy Lord, to celebrate the Eucharist, to expose the most Blessed Sacrament. Make us worthy also Lord, to expose you in the person of the poor and to adore and serve You in them with love. In as far as I served them with love and respect I served you in them. Thank you, Lord, for the 65 men in our night shelter "*Casa Serena*" in Via S. Agapito, 8, Rome. Bless them, Lord, with peace and joy. Let this holy season of Christmas and the Jubilee Year of 2000 "make us worthy" to give whole-hearted-free service to them; and may our lives be transformed by our self-less service.

"*Make us worthy, Lord to serve*" the AIDS patients who live, suffer and die in loneliness and pain. Give them this day their daily bread of comfort and consolation, and by our understanding love give them peace and joy. "*Make us worthy, Lord to serve*" the prisoners with our prayers, sacrifices and our regular visits. Give them peace in abundance and through dialogue, prayer and sacrifice may they receive the grace of real "*meta-noia*", radical reorientation of their lives. "*Make us worthy, Lord to serve*" all the families, especially those that are broken or separated; bring them back, reunite them in love and peace and may their children experience once again the joy of being loved by their parents. "*Make us worthy, Lord, to serve*" all the lonely, the abandoned, the elderly, the homeless whom we often pass-by. Give them this day the bread of comfort and friendship, and the housing they need. "*Make us worthy to serve*" our homeless handicapped boys in *Deepashram* – "*House of light*", who are in need of every form of tender care and loving service (see the letter on Distant Adoption). "*Make us worthy, Lord to serve*" every human being who is in need of material help or spiritual comfort. "*Make us worthy, Lord to serve*" all those who for whatever reasons dislike us, hate us or harm us in any way…those who humiliate us. Let us welcome the new born Babe of Bethlehem with the same sentiments of Mary and Joseph; let us approach the Third Christian Millennium with the same "*noia*" of Christ. For a few moments each day let us sit at the feet of Mary and Joseph to listen to them all about their Son, as they are so eager to share with us the Good News, that is

Jesus, the Son of God. Let us love Jesus as Mary and Joseph loved and served Him. And this is done through our life of prayer, penance and works of mercy.

God bless you.

Fr. Sebastian Vazhakala M.C.

January 2002

Dearly beloved brothers and sisters,

First of all I would like to express my heartfelt gratitude to God for each one of you: for all that you are, and for all that you do to bring souls to Jesus and Jesus to souls, as He Himself desires so much that we all do. He wants us to offer more sacrifices, smile more tenderly, pray more fervently.

There is such hunger, desire and thirst in the Heart of Jesus for souls, especially the souls of the poor, who nobody takes care of. From the Cross He entrusted to Mother Teresa this great patrimony, this ineffable gift in which we are all called to share in and share with. Let us then take time to read, study and meditate on this beautiful document so that we too may have her fervor and zeal for souls, and we too may continue to quench the infinite Thirst of Jesus on the Cross for love of souls. Jesus from the Cross said to Mother Teresa: *" I have asked you, they* (the crowd) *have asked you, and She, My Mother has asked you, will you refuse to do this for Me, to take care of them, to bring them to Me?"* Mother answered: *"You know, Jesus, I am ready to go at a moment's notice".*

Since that day our beloved Foundress Mother Teresa prayed unceasingly and laboured untiringly for the salvation and sanctification of the poorest of the poor of the whole world without counting the cost, without seeking rest or reward, and without any prejudice based on color, caste, religion or nationality. She acquired God's own Heart, Mind and Mentality; for her, every person was a child of God. She loved everyone unconditionally, as Jesus Himself would have loved them. People felt her great and personal love for each individual human being. The State funeral given to her and the people's participation in it was a clear manifestation of how they recognized our Mother's tender love as Jesus had told her years ago: *"In your immolation, in your love for Me, they will see Me, Know Me and want Me"*. And this is what happened. Jesus' words came literally true throughout her life and even after her death. She loved each and everyone to the very end. Let us follow her example and do the same.

Some news: Br. Peter renewed his vows, anticipating by a couple of weeks, since I was going to be out on mission to U.S.A., Nicaragua, etc. In the month of July Brothers Joachim, Peter and André Marie, went for their home visits one after another. Two others who went for their home visits were Br. Paul and Br Damien. Br. Paul expressed his desire to spend his one-month in India, which he happily did. He spent time in Deepashram, Trivandrum and Potta, where he participated in the charismatic retreat and said that he profited much from it. Now we will see how fruitful and profitable it was! Br. Damien concluded an itinerary home visit, visiting several people in different places, including Calcutta, and leaving them with some remembrances. Br. Damien is now in Albania, as you all may know that we are trying to build a home for handicapped boys there. The preliminary planning and meetings have taken place. We have to pray very hard for its realization in accordance with God's will. In the month of July Br. Ivan Marie went to Bosnia for his home visit plus his first Holy Mass. He was ordained priest in Rome on 25 April, 2001.

When exams were over Br. Stephen and our candidates Br. Joachim and Br. Vincent were sent to our mission-house in Bushat, Shkodra (Albania), to replace Br. André Marie and Br. Paul. So now the Bushat Community has Br. Damien, Br. Stephen, Br. Paul and Br. Gasper as members. They are trying to build up a community of love, to give loving and dedicated service to their needy neighbours, especially taking care of their spiritual needs. Let us pray for the Bushat Community, the Brothers and the poor they are called to serve, that Jesus' hunger and thirst for souls may be satisfied, that they may never be tired of serving the Lord in joy and in peace. Incidentally it was 10 years ago, on 8 September, 1991, that we began our community in Albania. We celebrated a Thanksgiving Mass on 1st September and another one on 9

September with the whole parish. It is very necessary to thank God for all that Jesus has been to us through our Blessed Mother.

In the month of May, Bishop Salvador Lobo, the bishop's delegate for the cause of Mother Teresa's beatification and canonization, called me from Briupur (W. Bengal) inviting me to participate in the closing ceremony of the diocesan inquiry, which was to be held in St. Mary's Parish Church, in Calcutta, on 15 August, 2001 at 4.00 p.m. I decided to go, but then everything became so difficult that I practically cancelled my trip, when out of the blue Mrs. Daniela Mandolesi offered me a round trip ticket to Delhi and back. Thanks to Dr. Massimo and Daniela Mandolesi. This offer enabled me to be in Deepashram for some days, to meet the Brothers and have a day of prayer with Brothers Alphonse, Benedict and Tony Mary José, who renewed their vows on the following day, 5 August, exactly a year after their first profession.

Deepashram was fortunate also to have so many volunteers, especially a very dedicated group of young people from Parma (13 of them) under the leadership of Gianluca Costa. Real thanks to the whole group, the dentist Paolo, the doctors, the priest Don Umberto and all the others. Special thanks are due to Dr. Paolo and all those who helped to set up the dental clinic. Our 63 homeless handicapped boys, many of our poor people and our Brothers will be profiting from this enterprise. Everything is God's gift; all praise, honour and glory to Him. There were still other volunteers like Sandra from Italy, and Dr. Gloria who since 1 February, 2001 have been with my niece Mini who became totally handicapped after 1 July, 1997, when she fell from five meters. I thank God for Dr. Gloria, for her tender care, loving service and kind attention, and for Mini's good will and generous cooperation. Words are inadequate to express my heart-felt thanks to Dr. Gloria for helping Mini to be practically self-sufficient, so that in her wheel chair she can for the most part take care of herself and her personal needs. Let us hope and pray that her difficult condition may continue to improve and that she may feel ever better in body and soul.

Br. Subash, our new superior in Deepashram, is also continuing his third year theology in Vidayajyoti, Delhi. It is hard for him to do justice both to his studies and to the duties of house-superior. Let us remember him in our prayers and daily sacrifices. In Deepashram we have Fr. Dariusz from Poland who took care of our novices for two years, and Fr. Deendayal from the Indian Missionary Society, whose gentle presence, example and assistance is invaluable. Fr. Deendayal also gave the annual retreat to some of the Brothers. Years ago Fr. Deendayal and I were students of theology together in Pune, and he was my faithful companion on visits to the slums almost every evening. I thank God for both of these priests for what they are and what they do for us and for our poor people.

Br. Peter and Br. André Marie, who were in Deepashram, India, for a few months are now back in Rome; Br. Benedict, Br. Tony Mary José, Br. Ramon resumed their studies at the Angelicum, in Rome. They are now replaced by two of our newly professed Brothers: Br. Basil and Br. Jan Timo. Actually, these two and Br. Barnabas made their first vows on 5 September, 2001 i.e. on the fourth Anniversary of our beloved Mother Teresa's going home to God. The ceremony took place in a Salesian Parish Church, in an area on Via Prenestina known as Borgo Don Bosco. Over 600 poor people from the various MC Sisters' houses were present, while some others were brought from the various parts of Rome where the Sisters go visiting. Some of our men of Casa Serena were also present. It was a moving experience. Thanks to Archbishop Giuseppe Mani, the main celebrant. After Holy Mass all our poor people enjoyed a delicious meal.

I also made a quick visit to our Brothers in Albania where three of our Junior Brothers, Br. Stephen, Br. Paul and Br. Gaspar, renewed their vows on 30 August, 2001 for a year. It was very simple. Thanks to the regional Superior, Sr. Nada M.C., who came with Sr. Vittoria M.C.(Shkodra superior) and Sr. Andrea M.C., the organist, who made the celebration more colourful and solemn. We had to sort out the *"Furgone"* documents and insurance, all with a lot of sacrifices, without food, without rest... Br. Paul even walked over three kilometers in the heat of the day. Thanks again to our very generous volunteers Dr. Salvatore and Dr. Paolo who worked so hard without counting the cost and without seeking rest or reward. Our return journey was even more eventful, chaotic and demanding. I felt like the Israelite just before crossing the Red Sea. Before them were the raging waters of the Red Sea and behind them was Pharaoh's army. The Lord hears the cry of the poor. Jesus saw our affliction and heard our cry and brought us to the *promised land* of Italy.

When the first profession ceremony on the first anniversary of Mother's departure from this world to God was over, Brothers Jean Marie and Br. Leo began their eight-day retreat on the evening of Thursday 6 September until 14 September. They had a lot of time to themselves, as I had to carry on with all my other engagements and appointments.

On 15 September, the feast of Our Lady of Sorrows, our community in Rome experienced deep spiritual joy and profound gratitude to God when our beloved Br. Leo solemnly made his vows for *Life* of Chastity, Poverty, Obedience and Wholehearted Free Service to the poorest of the poor in the presence of his Brothers and in the hands of the Father General. It was very significant that we had the profession in the parish Church of Our Lady of Sorrows on Her Feast day. It was a grace and we thank Br. Leo M.C. and thank God for him and continue to pray for his growth in holiness through humility and charity, and for his holy perseverance.

Thanks to God's grace, his Excellency bishop Anil Couto ordained Br. Mathew M.C., a priest on 16 October, 2001 in the Sacred Heart Cathedral in New Delhi, and on 17 October offered his first thanksgiving Mass for Deepashram Community and for our Society as a whole. Br. Mathew is now back in Deepashram, together with Br. Thomas Mathew.

So there is much to thank God for all that the good Lord is doing for us through our poor people, volunteers, benefactors and friends. Let us continue to help one another to grow in holiness through our good example, prayers, sacrifices and hard work so that we remain God's sign of hope, love, joy and peace. To this end we pray.

We also have about 10 students of Theology and Philosophy this year. It is a bit hard for the students to be fully engaged in their studies, and at the same time to remain faithful to our way of life and then to share in the work of the house and that of the apostolate. But this is a healthy tension, which will enable them to prepare themselves for their future life and ministry. Those who sow in tears will reap rejoicing. We have to shed much more tears now as we are still in the sowing stage while we patiently wait for a good and joyful harvest.

I hope that you all have prepared a hidden warm crib in your hearts to welcome the Baby Jesus. Let us take all opportunities God is offering us each day to become a little more prayerful, a little more humble, a little more obedient, a little more charitable and thus be able to put our little straws…in our crib.

"*Offer more sacrifices, smile more tenderly and pray more fervently and all the difficulties will disappear*". This was Jesus' own request to Mother Teresa. Let us do the same now more than ever and beyond doubt all difficulties and problems can be overcome one by one. Let us remain in touch.

Wishing you all a very blessed and Holy Christmas and a peace-filled New Year 2002. Love and prayers.

Fr. Sebastian Vazhakala M.C.

BAPTIZE YOUR SUFFERING AND
RECYCLE YOUR TRIALS
2003

Suffering is as old as the first human being. In fact in the opening pages of the Bible we see that man invited suffering into his life through his disobedience to God's command (cf. Gen.3, 1-19, see verses 14-19). Whereas before their fall Adam and Eve, our first parents, enjoyed a very different kind of life, which for us is now possible only in the life to come.

> On Christmas eve the younger sister of one of our LMCs was driving home to take the documents she had forgotten to carry with her. But Jesus wanted Maria Vittoria to celebrate Christmas with him in heaven instead of celebrating it with her family members on earth. For her it was great and wonderful, comforting and rewarding. What was it like for those whom she left behind, especially on the eve of Christmas? A real trial for the family to endure. If the rest of the family were not sealed with the gift and mystery of faith, there would have been an even greater catastrophe in that family.

An experience like this kind has two aspects: the human and the divine. In some cases and with some people, the human side prevails over the divine; at times it even totally ignores the divine aspect. Here one does not suffer any less. No, the suffering becomes more intense and acute. This was not the case of Maria Vittoria's family. They suffered much and are still suffering from it. But because they are graced with profound faith, they were able to overcome their pain and transform it into channels of grace. In the words of our beloved Mother Teresa of Kolkata:

"Trials and temptations are but the kiss of Jesus – a sign that you have come so close to him that he can kiss you. Don't be afraid – the little Society has to imitate only its Master – to be able to redeem the world he accepted Bethlehem, Nazareth, Calvary. You remember how frightened the Apostles were-and Jesus told them: 'O You (men) of little faith. Why are you afraid?" (Mother's letter to Fr. Sebastian M.C., 17.01.79).

In another letter to Fr. Sebastian M.C. Mother writes: *"My mother had not seen me for 46 years - months before she died, she kept calling and longing to see me - her youngest child. Albania being what it is-no Indian is allowed to go. I could go so near – and yet not to her – so she died with my name in her mouth. This is why I know what you feel – Our Lady will be your strength – I am asking her to take care of your family..."* (Mother Teresa to Fr. Sebastian M.C., 14.08.79). She baptized her pain and channeled her sorrow for the repose of the soul of her beloved mother and also for her own personal sanctification and growth in holiness.

Mother Teresa continues to speak about trials, its meaning and how to use them. She writes: *"...I know what you feel – this really* (is) *the full meaning of the poverty of Jesus. He being rich became poor. The richness of the company of his Father he gave up by becoming man like us in all things except sin. You too are experiencing that* **'giving up'** *for love of him. Do not be afraid. - All will be well – the seed has to die – if it has to produce fruit...This aloness is the beginning of great love. You are not alone – Jesus and you. Tabernacle is the most beautiful sign for you to look at when you feel lonely. Don't be afraid – he is there – in spite of the darkness and failure. It was like that for Jesus in the garden –* **'Could you not watch one hour?'** *he felt so lonely that night. Don't be afraid – put your hand in our Lady's hand and walk with her..."* (Mother Teresa's letter to Fr. Sebastian M.C., 12.10.79).

Christians, baptize your daily sufferings, humiliations, mistreatments and even calumnies. Christians, recycle your trials and direct your hardships to the waters of grace for you and for many. Let many souls drink from the waters of your pain and sorrow. You bottle your pain and distribute freely to those who are in need. Suffering is a vocation. Jesus told Mother Teresa: *"Your vocation is to love and to suffer and to save souls"*, *"You will suffer much, you suffer now"*, *"In your immolation, in your love for me, they will see Me, know Me, want Me. Offer more sacrifices..."* (MFG 11).

Jesus invites all to take up their cross and follow him (Mt 16, 24 ff.). This can means *"to accept whatever Jesus gives us and to give whatever Jesus takes from us with a big smile"* (Mother Teresa).

We are all martyrs of some kind and some time. It can be our weaknesses, sins, failures and shortcomings. It can be the terrible darkness in our spiritual life or aridity in our life of prayer. It can be the deep feeling of our own unworthiness to accept the things we cannot change in us and not having the courage to change the things we can. Even our beloved Mother Teresa constantly felt unworthy, weak and sinful. It was almost like an *antiphon* that she kept repeating. St. Therese of Lisieux wrote at the end of her autobiography that, if God could have found a feebler soul than hers - although it might have been impossible according to her - God would have bestowed on her the same graces if it had abandoned itself with supreme confidence to his infinite mercy.

Recently two of our closest friends, Dr. Salvatore and Dr. Paolo, went to visit Auschwitz in Poland. On their return they urged me to go and see that terrible monument of modern Calvary, which speaks to every human being, without exception, of the meaning of human life on earth. We are created not to wound and kill, but to heal and to save. Will there be any justification, human or divine for such inhuman cruelties and brutal atrocities? I wonder!

The Second World War was a global disaster. There are not any adequate explanations of the how and why of it except that the evil one tried to triumph over good; he wanted to capture the power of love to turn it into the power of hatred and destruction. But even if the whole world stands together with Lucifer and his minions and fight against God, God cannot be conquered or defeated. God cannot be captured and crushed. He dwells within the castle of love without limits and boundaries. There is nothing in him and all around him but love. His entire kingdom is one of love. His subjects in heaven, his army of angels and saints fight with the strongest and invincible weapons of love. All his soldiers are messengers of love and peace. *Shalom, shanti, peace!*

God is sure to conquer the world with love at the end. Mankind will bounce back and surrender to the power of love. All else is transitory and will vanish like grass in the field. Even from such disastrous monstrosity saints and martyrs like St. Maximillian Maria Kolbe. St. Edith Stein and many other known and unknown saints and martyrs of love, peace and justice were born. Yes, God is able from these stones to raise up children to Abraham (cf. Lk 3, 8). Love never comes to an end. It is eternal. It is the source and origin of all good. Even when a man dies love never dies. The charity he practiced outlives him and is going to be judged on love. Everything else is subordinated to love and everything else surrenders to the power of love.

But love never surrenders to anything or to anyone except to God who is nothing but love. It was clearly shown on 13 September 1997 when all the world came to the 'filthy' city of Kolkata to pay homage to a little lifeless body, which lay in state with no words, no gestures or power. It was the lifeless body of a woman who had become the embodiment of invincible love. She became a symbol of love. Lotus grows in muddy water. If Kolkata was a cesspool of human misery, Mother Teresa was the lotus of love and beauty in the cesspool of misery as well as mystery.

With Teresa of Kolkata God turned the city of poverty and misery into a city of rich love and joy. Thus the symbol of hatred, selfishness and darkness became the symbol of love, service and light. The scientists cannot prove this in their laboratories nor can the philosophers with their critique of pure reason explain adequately such mysteries of selfless love in action.

Our God never gets tired of loving us. He never gives us up or excludes us from the circle of his love. Beyond doubt he will purify and make us go through severe trials, which is almost an intrinsic necessity. St. Pio of Pietrelcina was forbidden to celebrate Holy Mass in public for two years and to hear confessions for about four years, especially of women. His superiors were touching the core of his priestly ministry. Among the seven sacraments, daily celebration of the Eucharist and the administration of the sacrament of reconciliation are the two main sacraments a priest is ordained generally to exercise. To forbid him from administering them was the most difficult sacrifice he was asked to make, and not so many will willingly accept such orders without reacting and trying to defend and get back their birthrights as priests. Instead St. Pio of Pietrelcina accepted the orders of his superiors promptly and without questions. Truth may be attacked, delayed, suppressed, mocked at, but time will tell where truth is and, if we believe, in the end truth will prevail.

The meek and humble of heart do not labor so much to defend against offenses nor claim one's rights. They know that God will defend them, because God is the defender of truth and justice, on which the virtue of humility is based. In the words of Mother Teresa, our beloved foundress: *"Don't worry about so and so's letter. Gifts like this I have been receiving many. Just smile and say thank you…"* (Mother Teresa to Fr. Sebastian M.C., June 1978).

The Holy Father pope John Paul II gave his Lenten message for the year 2003. Its theme is based on a quotation from the Acts of the Apostles (Ch. 20, 35), where St. Paul presents a famous teaching of Jesus which has not come down to us in the gospels: *"There is more happiness in giving than in receiving".*

It begins its message by saying, *"Lent is a season of intense prayer, fasting and concern for those in need. It offers an opportunity to prepare for Easter by serious discernment about their lives with particular attention to the Word of God, which enlightens the daily journey of all who believe".*

We need to build a culture of solidarity on the common brotherhood of men based on the common fatherhood of God. In other words we are all children of the one and the same heavenly Father, irrespective of color, creed or nationality. Created in his own image and likeness (cf. Gen 1, 26) we all have the same common desires, aspirations and needs. Our basic physical, psychological and moral needs are the same, no matter whether one is black or white, brown or red, or one is tall or short, rich or poor. The cows are of different colors but milk is always white.

Our differences are more accidental and many times we try to build our culture on accidentals overlooking and ignoring the essentials that are meant to bind us all more closely. Charity is the reason why anything should be done or left undone, changed or left unchanged. It is the natural principle and the end to which all things should be directed. Whatever is done out of love and for love will never be forgotten nor go unrewarded. Let this Lent be one of more giving than receiving, one of more forgiving and forgetting than hurting and offending.

We all can try to be a little more humble and a little less proud; a little more kind and little less arrogant; a little more hospitable, warm and caring and a little less hostile, indifferent and cold. In us there is always more room for Charity, hard work and toil. We all can be holier than we really are. Even if we do not have money and material things to share, let us at least share our joy, our smile, and our eagerness to befriend.

In this season of Lent let us be a little less critical, judgmental, angry, lazy or gluttonous and a little more understanding, appreciating, tolerant, patient, gentle, hard working, temperate and sharing. Let us control our minds from vain thoughts and useless and utopian plans, our tongues from speaking guile, lies and bad words and blasphemies, let us keep our hearts pure, humble and holy. Let there be peace, joy and harmony and let it begin with me.

In conclusion we can say, together with St. Peter Chrysologus, that *"there are three things by which faith stands firm, devotion remains constant, and virtue endures. They are prayer, penance and works of mercy. Prayer knocks at the door, penance obtains and works of mercy receive... These three are one and they give light to each other.*

Penance is the soul of prayer, works of mercy are the life-blood of penance. Let no one try to separate them... If you pray, fast; if you fast, show mercy; if you want your petition to be heard, hear the petition of others. If you do not close your ear to others, you open God's ear to yourself.

When you fast, see the fasting of others. If you want God to know that you are hungry, know that another is hungry. If you hope for mercy, show mercy. If you look for kindness, show kindness. If you want to receive, give. If you ask for yourself what you deny to others, your asking is a mockery...

Let prayer, penance and works of mercy be one single plea to God on our behalf, one speech in our defense, a threefold united prayer in our favour" (cf. St. Peter Chrysologus' Sermon 43. Office of Readings for Tuesday, Lent, week 3).

I Wish you a very holy and joyous Lent which prepares us all to the great and happy feast of Easter.

Love and prayers.

God bless you.

Fr. Sebastian Vazhakala M.C.

"Do whatever He tells you" (Jn 2:5)

Dear Brothers and Sisters,

We are on the eve of two of the big celebrations of praise and thanksgiving. One is the jubilee celebration of twenty-five years of Pope John Paul II's great and eventful pontificate and the other is the beatification of the great Venerable Teresa of Kolkata, Virgin and foundress of the Family of the Missionaries of Charity. The celebration of a Pope's twenty-five years of his pontificate is a rare occurrence, as most Popes went home to God before they were anywhere near to it. Glancing through the list of the 264 Popes starting from St. Peter, the apostle, to our present Pope there are only three of them who lived up to this kind of celebration. The first such Pope is Blessed Pius IX, whose pontificate lasted from 1846 to 1878, followed by his successor Pope Leo XIII of happy memory from 3rd March 1878 to 20th July 1903. The next one after him to complete 25 years on the Chair of St. Peter is our present Pope, who was elected on 16 October 1978. It is then very right and fitting and is our duty everywhere and everyway to give thanks to the most Holy Trinity, Father, Son and Holy Spirit for the gift of the Holy Father to the Church and to the world of our time.

It was on the very first day of the jubilee year of his long, painful and demanding pontificate that our beloved Holy Father published his apostolic exhortation: *"Rosarium Virginis Mariae"* explaining to the Christian faithful the meaning, significance and the importance of praying the most Holy Rosary, and exhorting them all to pray it daily. He did not only ask all the believers in Jesus to join in thanking God through praying the Rosary, but he also wants all the faithful to *"contemplate the face of Christ with Mary"* as *"she is the contemplative memory of the Church"* (Pope John Paul II) and she will help us to *"do whatever Jesus tells us"* (cf. Jn 2: 5), as she did in her life.

Pope John Paul II went further and deeper into the mysteries of the life and work of God's own Son on earth as he added five more mysteries from the public life of Jesus to the already existing fifteen mysteries of the Rosary. So we now have twenty mysteries with the five luminous mysteries added.

In the past year through faithfully and contemplatively praying the Rosary, the Christian faithful all over the world have been thanking God for the fidelity of our present Pope, for his wonderful example, for his profound teaching and preaching, for his endurance in the many and unceasing trials of life, his availability and approachability, for his personal zeal, for the many apostolic and missionary journeys which gave so many people of good will a chance to see, to hear and even to touch the Pope in person, as he is the Vicar of Christ, the one who is called to represent and make visible Jesus Christ on earth again, as John the apostle and evangelist writes about Jesus in his first letter: *"That which was in the beginning, which we have **heard**, which we have **seen** with our eyes, which we have **looked** upon and **touched** with our hands...we testify and proclaim to you"*...(cf. 1 Jn 1: 1-4). This is what our beloved Pope John Paul II has been doing ever since his election to the See of Peter on 16 October 1978 to this day. And so the reason for this great jubilee celebration.

If Pope Pius XI called St. Thérèse of Lisieux the *star* of his pontificate, who not only beatified her in 1923, but also canonized her within two years (1925) and then made her patroness of the Missions together with St. Francis Xavier, Pope John Paul II has another great *star* in his pontificate, whom we all know and love: Venerable Mother Teresa of Kolkata. Unlike St. Thérèse of Lisieux, who did not live during Pope Pius XI's pontificate, the Venerable Teresa of Kolkata, Virgin and foundress of the Family of the Missionaries of Charity, worked very closely with Pope John Paul II, as we all know. Mother Teresa loved the Holy Father and the Church as she loved Jesus, her Spouse and Lord, so passionately! She writes: *"I long to be only His – to burn myself completely for Him and for souls – I want Him to be loved tenderly by many..."*. She really had a very special veneration for the Holy Father: *"...If he (the Holy Father) only knew how much his children the M.C.s love him and how each one of us are ready to give our all to stand by him - everything of mine is his and for him"* (from Mother Teresa's letter to Charlotte). For Mother Teresa to love Jesus was equal to loving the Church, as the Church is the mystical body of Christ, whose head is Jesus! And the Pope represented Christ and gave visibility to Him. To love him then meant to love the Church. Like St. Thérèse of Lisieux, Mother Teresa of Kolkata too wanted to remain in the heart of the Mother Church to be only love. *"In the heart of the Church my Mother, I will be Love"* (St. Thérèse of Lisieux).

There is another reason for Mother Teresa's great love for the Pope, namely that with her profound and unshakeable faith and trust she saw Jesus in the person of the Pope, gave him love, respect and obedience as she would give to Jesus. For her all these elements were one and the same. *"Once you fall in love with Jesus"*, she used to say, *"everything else follows and becomes easy in a way"*. Her love was neither conditional nor limited to a certain circle of people, nor was it simply general. Her love was without barriers of caste, colour, religion or nationality; her love was without boundaries of status, rich or poor, young or old. Her love was Christ's love. She loved everyone individually and personally with Jesus' love. Not only did she want to recognize the presence of Jesus in everyone and to love Him in everyone, especially in the poorest of the poor, as if He had never been loved before, but she wanted all people of good will to do the same.

The really poor person is not the one who is deprived of just the material things; the really poor person is the one who is devoid of true love and generous Charity. Who really then is the poor man? The really poor man is the one in whom there is no love, no Charity. The really poor man is the one who is totally selfish, utterly self-centred with no thought of his neighbours, never responding to the needs of others. The really poor man lives just for himself, and so lives with himself, buried himself in his own miserable world. Can there be a poorer person in this world than the one who has never learnt to love, give or share? There are so many *poor-rich* people and there are so many more *rich-poor* people in today's world. This is well explained in the parable of Lazarus and the rich man in the gospel of Luke (cf. 16:19-31). It is not said that the rich man was condemned to hell for the evils he committed, the lies he told, the blasphemies and bad words he uttered, but for not doing what he should have done. The rich man was suffering from terrible torments for all eternity, for the sins of omission. *"I was hungry and you gave me no food, I was thirsty and you gave me no drink…"*, all is negative. *"Lord, when did we see you hungry, thirsty, naked, homeless, sick or imprisoned…As long as you did not do this to the least of my brothers, you did not do it to me…. These will go to eternal damnation while the just to eternal life"* (cf. Mt 25: 31-46).

Coming back to the two personalities mentioned in the beginning, let us try to see how divine Providence chose these two great prophets, mystics and charismatics of our time and how He prepared them, and through them unfolded His plan of salvation and redemption of the world of our time. Mother Teresa of Kolkata and Pope John Paul II are ordinary people to whom God bestowed extraordinary gifts and talents, above all the gift of invincible love, ardent Charity and unshakeable faith. In order to understand these two outstanding personalities of our time it is good to see their country of origin, their family background, their early upbringing, their religious formation, trials in their families and many other things that pertain to their lives and **future missions;** these really have many significant similarities.

Their countries of origin at one time or another were under communist rule. In fact Albania had the worst form of communism. By law they were forbidden even to mention the name of God.

Their Christian names	Karol Vojtyla	Agnes Bojakhiu
Pet names	Lolek (Karolet)	Ganxhe
Dates of birth	18 May 1920	26 August 1910
Countries of birth	Poland	Youguslavia, Macedonia from Albanian parents
Fathers' names	Karol	Nichola
Mothers' names	Emilia Kaczorowska	Rosa Markit

Both lost one of their parents at the age of nine:
Karol lost his mother when he was about nine years old on 13 April 1929.
Agnes lost her father when she old was nine years old in 1919.

Both suffered terribly from the loss of their dearest parent. The boy lacked a beloved mother and so he turned to Our Lady for help and guidance, love and affection; and Agnes lost her father and so she turned to the Sacred Heart and Our Lady. Both were very gifted, born leaders and organizers, good singers, much involved in parish activities...strong family discipline and religious formation under the father for Karol and under the mother for Agnes. Both were serious with their studies, extremely energetic, enthusiastic, and intelligent. Both were trained to practice kindness and Charity, not only by words, but above all by their good examples. In some mysterious way for both, Jesus became the centre of their lives, and they were unconditionally open to his call.

For both, 1946 was the year of many graces. It was on 1 November of that year that Pope John Paul II was ordained priest for the diocese of Crakow, Poland. And it was on 10 September of the same year that Mother Teresa of Kolkata had her second call, which she called *a call within a call.* Strangely enough, it was about this period that communism triumphed in Albania and the Church doors were shut; priests and religious were captured, imprisoned and killed by the dictator, Enver Hozha. He confiscated all Catholic institutions and churches, turning them into sports-stadiums, ammunition depots and other such places. That is why our good and merciful God called Mother Teresa Bojaxhiu, one of their own flesh and blood, to defend and diffuse the very God the dictator tried to make people deny and destroy. God, being Almighty, cannot be captured, imprisoned or defeated by man or by any power or ideology. No man can know more than God what is better for man. With all the powers and fibres of her being Mother Teresa preached without preaching, not so much by words, but by actions, by loving service to the poorest of the poor of the whole world. When the dictator Enver Hozha closed a small window to God, through Mother Teresa God opened hundreds of doors to himself throughout the world.

In fact, on 1 November 1996 there were big jubilee celebrations in St. Peter's Basilica for the Holy Father's 50th anniversary of his priestly ordination, and on 10 September of the same year there was the celebration of the 50th anniversary of Mother Teresa's inspiration in the Mother House of the Missionaries of Charity Sisters in Kolkata.

It was a great grace for me to participate in both these celebrations in person.

Both the Holy Father and Mother Teresa are so devoted to Our Lady, especially to Our Lady of Fatima, i.e. the Immaculate Heart of Mary. For both the Rosary has been one of the strongest weapons to attack the evil of atheistic regimes that destroyed peace and unity in the world. In fact, the Missionary Sisters of Charity of Kolkata was founded on 7 October 1950, the feast of Our Lady of the Holy Rosary.

Again the Holy Father and Mother Teresa were instrumental in the breakdown of the communist regimes in Eastern Europe in the late eighties, as Our Lady of Fatima had predicted back in 1917 to the three children. This came about through the continual praying of the Holy Rosary and through the consecration of the entire human race, especially Russia, to the Immaculate Heart of Mary by Pope Pius XII back in 1942. This consecration has been renewed several times in later years.

Our Lady of the Immaculate Heart also told Mother Teresa back in 1947: *"Fear not, teach them* (the people) *to say the Rosary, the family Rosary – and all will be well. Fear not – Jesus and I will be with you and with your children"* (from Mother Teresa's letter to Archbishop Perier S.J. of Kolkata, 3.12.1947).

I could go on with many more striking similarities between the two prophets of our time whom God used and is still using to show the world that He still loves it as He loved it once in Jesus Christ (cf. Jn 3: 16). In other words, God will never stop loving the world as long as there are human beings living on this planet, even if there is only one person.

Let us hope and pray that the jubilee celebration of our beloved Pope John Paul II and the beatification of our dearest Mother Teresa of Kolkata may bring all people of good will all the more closer to God, to the Church and very especially to the world of the poor.

God bless you.

Fr. Sebastian Vazhakala M.C.

"We have come to worship him!"

Cologne, August 2005

A look back at World Youth Day 2005:
Retreat and renewal, grace and glory, alive in Cologne

The XX World Youth Day (WYD) 2005 was one more of the milestones of a great event in the history of mankind. During those August days in the beautiful land of Germany there were different kinds of encounters: there was the encounter with God in prayer, listening and adoring Him like the Magi, and there was the encounter with God in one another, irrespective of colour, culture, language or nationality. It looked like a mosaic of great artwork. An ocean of one million young people from 193 countries of the world, many cardinals, 800 bishops and ten thousand priests met in Cologne, Germany, a city of extraordinary beauty and charm. It is in this city of history, tradition and antiquity which Divine providence chose through the Magisterium of the Church to hold such an important event of faith and history.

Blessings from two Popes

The XX World Youth Day was held in Cologne from 15 to 21 August, 2005, as announced by the late Pope John Paul II three years ago in Toronto, Canada. Unlike other World Youth gatherings, the WYD in Cologne was special. There were two popes: the servant of God Pope John Paul II in heaven and our beloved Pope Benedict XVI on earth. The assistance from heaven was very evident, especially with regard to the weather. According to the reports received, there could have been heavy showers, as the sky was grey. But it did not stop the hundreds of thousands of pilgrims from going to Marienfeld (Mary's field) and camping there for the wonderful vigil, and then spending the night in the open, as did the shepherds near Bethlehem at the time of Jesus' birth. I prayed much to Pope John Paul II to help us from heaven, as the young people were so dear to his heart until the last day of his life on earth. To the young people who gathered under the window of Pope John Paul II in St. Peter Square, where they chanted John Paul's name for two days, he said: *"I have been looking for you, and now you have come to me. I thank you for this."* While these last words of the late Pope John Paul II to the young people continue to resound in our ears, we can count on his spiritual presence and assistance from on high. I still feel that he did really help us from heaven on Saturday 20 and Sunday 21 August, 2005. The weather became pleasant and free from showers, except a rain of heavenly graces on the thousands who gathered around the altar together with our Holy Father Benedict XVI. It was a real experience of God's inescapable presence and nearness, tender care and concern. Blessed be the name of the Lord, now and for ever!.

'Spiritual Centres' of prayer

In his Angelus message on Sunday, 28 August, 2005 Pope Benedict XVI said that the adoration of Jesus in the Blessed Sacrament *"is not a luxury but a priority"*. This was proven true during the WYD in Cologne. I strongly felt among the many programs in Cologne for the young people the strongest of all was the "Spiritual Centres". "The Spiritual Centre" was a group of sixteen inner-city churches in Cologne, and two churches in Bonn and Düsseldorf. The churches were open to pilgrims from August 16 to 20, 2005. These Centres became the spiritual powerhouses of intense prayer, where there was adoration of the Blessed Sacrament for twenty-four hours a day. They became centres of reconciliation, through the sacrament of confession, and an oasis of peace, meeting, sharing and nourishing. There was an incredible sense of peace, joy, fellowship and brotherhood. The confessions went on day and night. Not only did young people come for confessions, but many older people, religious and priests. All of them made their way to Jesus, following the *"star of God's irrevocable grace and invincible love."* Opening their hearts, they offered the gold of their freedom to Jesus, as they found him in that *little manger* in the form of Bread in a monstrance. So many have poured out their hearts' desires, pain and problems to him like frankincense.

Bethlehem for us today is Jesus in the Eucharist. We are called to be the Magi, not only from the Orient, but from all corners of the world. We must come to worship him in the Bread of Life in the house of Bread. Jesus does not need our gold nor silver, but our hearts in place of gold, our free will in place of frankincense, and our body and soul in place of the myrrh.

Confession and Eucharist

Very close to the Dom in Cologne, the Missionaries of Charity were given the Church of St. Aposteln (the Church of the Holy Apostles) in the Neumakt area of Cologne. The church became an important spiritual centre for hundreds of young people, who continuously came to visit, to pray, to adore the Lord together with the five branches of the M.C. family, who were keeping vigil before the Blessed Sacrament exposed day and night. Various groups of people continually flooded into the church. As there were two main entrances into the church, there were two welcoming teams of Brothers and Sisters, who then gave them not only directions but also information about the Missionaries of Charity, distributing rosaries and medals, leaflets, pictures and novenas of Blessed Teresa and other religious articles of interest. Many wanted to talk, some wanted to pray, many went to confession.

Besides the exposition of the Blessed Sacrament, there was also a very wonderful, inspiring and inviting exhibition on our Blessed and beloved Mother Teresa's vocation, vision and mission, her life and activity, and the various M.C. Branches she founded. Many were touched by the famous poem she composed on her sea voyage to India in December, 1928. Everything spoke very eloquently of Jesus' love for everyone, and especially his love for *"the poorest of the poor,"* as he had told to Mother Teresa back in 1946: *"There are plenty of nuns to look after the rich and the well-to-do people, but for My very poor there are absolutely none. For them I long-them I love-Wilt thou refuse?"* (MFG p. 18)

From the exhibition hall people were led to the adoration chapel where, like the Magi, they could adore the Lord in the Bread of life, together with the M.C. Family, and could be reconciled in the sacrament of confession if that was wanted and found necessary. Many did come for confessions, even in the middle of the night. Thanks be to God.

The Liturgy of the Hours, and especially the daily celebration of the Holy Mass, were quite solemn. It was the most important hour of the day, and it was well-participated. The parish priest, Fr. Christopher, was a real example of liturgical order and discipline. He wanted all the priests to celebrate the Holy Mass with decorum and respect, love and devotion. He is also a real singer! His singing was not only excellent, but it was also very celestial and mystical. He loves his Church, fulfils his duty and demands and instills liturgical discipline and devotion. The celebration of the Eucharist, and all the prayers for that matter, must be the expression of our deep faith, ardent love, fervour and zeal. We must celebrate all our prayers, especially the Eucharist, with gratitude and enthusiasm. The older we are, the more enthusiastic we must all become. Our life of prayer must not be sterile and static, but it must be fervent and dynamic.

Taking a new road

The WYD gathering was a retreat and a renewal. The prayer of the "Our Father" as we prayed or sang, touched everyone and went deeply into the bottom of reality. There were people from all over the world. They spoke different languages, belonged to different countries, possessed different cultures, and were of various colours. Going beyond all these accidentals, which were true and important, the WYD went deeper and tried to build the relationship of their common brotherhood on the one and only fatherhood of God. The saying *"In essential things we must have unity, in doubtful things freedom, and in all things charity"* was followed. There was a deeper sharing. The prayer of the "Our Father" really made sense. The cows can be of different colours, but milk is always white. In everyone, irrespective of colour, nationality, culture or language, there is an immortal soul created in the image and likeness of God (Gen 1: 26). That image of God in us is hungry and thirsty for the living God; that image of God is thirsty for solidarity and sharing. In Cologne the twofold hunger and thirst of the human heart for God and for one another was enkindled and quenched...quenched and enkindled anew. Once again God's infinite and insatiable thirst for man, and our thirst for him, met in enduring love, and became our fervent prayer. The end result was healing, peace, joy, solidarity, sharing, conviction and determination. Like the Magi, who after meeting the Child Jesus did not go back on the same road but on a different one, so too the participants of the WYD cannot continue to travel on the same road, but they have to take another way, no matter how difficult and demanding that road can at times be!

Bro. Roger: sign of unity

During the XX WYD something very shocking and extremely painful took place, namely the tragic and brutal assassination of Br. Roger Schutz of Taizé, France on Tuesday, 16 August, 2005. Humanly speaking, the event was very difficult to accept and to reconcile. He was 90 years old and was praying the Vespers with his Brothers in the community, along with about 2,500 people, when suddenly a 36-year-old woman stabbed him three times, taking away his life.

The event of his assassination in the middle of the XX World Youth Day can be considered very symbolic and significant. Br. Roger not only knew the aspirations of the young people, their strength and their vitality, but he also knew how they needed to be guided to the authentic truth and lasting values of life. For he writes: *"The young people come to fix their gaze not on what divides them but on what unites them, not to reinforce their pessimism but to perceive signs of hope."* The youth need guidance in their turning points of life. It was Br. Roger who, at the age of 25, came from Switzerland to Taizé (France) and began the centre for refugees of World War II, which with time became a big centre for young people. As a matter of fact, it was Br. Roger who introduced in 1978 *'the pilgrimage of trust on earth'* for young people. For many years, he used to gather them in the various cities of Europe, including Rome, shortly after Christmas. I still remember giving hospitality to over 50 or more young people in our house in Rome back in the early 1980s. There were thousands of them. He used to take them to the Holy Father John Paul II for audiences.

Br. Roger of Taizé is no more with us in body. But his invincible love and untiring dedication, his devotion to duty, his faithfulness to prayer, his effort to bring unity in the Church through prayer and dialogue will continue to produce fruit. Though he was 90 years old, Br. Roger still loved the young people until the day he was killed. He always tried to lead them from unreal to the real, from pessimism to optimism, from darkness to light, from division to unity, from man to

God and vice-versa. Many might have seen him seated on a wheelchair at John Paul II's funeral Mass when the present Pope Benedict XVI, then Cardinal Joseph Ratzinger, gave him Holy Communion.

He lived for unity, prayed very hard, and worked harder to bring unity into the Church. He was a very inspiring and edifying example for all people of good will, including the Popes and the Magisterium of the Catholic Church. In his general audience on Wednesday, 17 August, 2005 the Holy Father Pope Benedict XVI said: "…This news is an especially heavy blow because only just yesterday I received a very touching and friendly letter from Br. Roger. In it he wrote that in the depths of his heart he was intending to tell me that *'We are in communion with you and with those who have gathered in Cologne.'* He then wrote that because of his health he would unfortunately be unable to come in person to Cologne, but would be present in Spirit, with **his** brethren. He also said that he wanted to come to Rome to meet me and tell me that *'Our community of Taizé wants to journey on in communion with the Holy Father.'* And he then wrote in his own hand: *'Holy Father, I assure you of my sentiments of deep communion. Bro. Roger of Taizé'.*" (Osservatore Romano, weekly edition NE 34, 24 August, 2005). May his martyrdom of blood, which is God's gift to him and a blessing to the world, especially to the world of the youth, bring greater unity among the various denominational Churches. May the one who loved and tirelessly guided the youth on earth continue to love and guide them from heaven.

Five Branches come together

In Cologne for the first time the five Branches of the M.C. Family met together in prayer, in adoration, in praise and thanksgiving to God, remaining faithful to the teachings of our blessed and beloved Mother Teresa, breaking bread and sharing all things in common. Each day of that unforgettable week we regularly went to the church. We shared our food gladly and generously.

The whole M.C. Family was united heart and soul, sharing the poverty and the inconveniences of the place and the difficulties caused by the common living.

The M.C. Family thus laid its foundation stone of unity in Cologne and sowed the seed of a new and important venture, which has to be nurtured, protected, weeded and watered. By their presence and prayers the M.C. Family showed the young people of the world the basic and unending values of life on earth. Never before in all these years has the M.C. Family had such a wonderful and joyful sharing as we had in Cologne. This experience of the oneness of the M.C. Family is not a luxury of a few M.C. Brothers and Sisters, nor is it limited to the city of Cologne, but a simple duty of every M.C. member of all Branches and of all times and places. This unity and brotherhood cannot be achieved or arrived at without providing a common forum of life and action. Here is the need for ardent prayer and contemplation, constant sharing and frequent dialogue. The famous saying: "The family that prays together stays together" can be applied to the M.C. Family as well.

God bless you.

Fr. Sebastian Vazhakala M.C.

A Journey through Australia

The island continent of Australia is the sixth largest country in the world. It is 2,968.000 square miles in area, stretching from the Indian Ocean in the West to the Pacific in the East. Forty per cent of its land mass lies in tropics. The vast country with varied climates is divided into six states corresponding to the six original British colonies: New South Wales, Victoria, Queensland, Northern Territory, South Australia, Western Australia and Tasmania (separate island).

Although more than double the size of India, Australia has a population of only thirty million people, consisting of various colours, customs, languages and cultures. The booklet published on the occasion of "Census night – 8 August 2006" writes: *"Australia is a multi-cultured society. In 2001 approximately one in five people were born overseas or spoke a language other than English at home."* (How to complete your census form p. 8).

Besides, when Australia was colonized, it was already occupied by a race of dark-skinned people of extremely primitive life and culture. They are known as the Australian aborigines. They are a very special and unique race equal to no other great divisions of mankind. At the time of the occupation of British in 1778, it is said that there were about 300,000 aborigines. In 1954 they totalled only to 70,680, having suffered a steady decline. Today the majority of them live in Northern Territory, Western Australia and Queensland.

The Sisters of the Missionaries of Charity of Blessed Teresa have 14 houses in the various parts of the island continent of Australia and two in New Zealand. The first community of Sisters began in Bourke on 16 September 1969. The work with and for the native Australians, whose precious and immortal souls are enshrined in and with black-skinned bodies, seems useless and fruitless, but still it is God's work and so he will reward them and those who tirelessly work for them. These people, like anyone of us, are in need of continued evangelization, which becomes then the culture of love. This can only take place on the basis of an intimate encounter with God. In God and with God I can love even the most repugnant persons and difficult characters. Blessed Teresa used to say that the more repugnant the person is the more faith is required to see the face of Jesus and serve him with tender love. Our Lady Help of Christians Region of the Missionaries of Charity dedicate their lives in service to the poorest of the poor in their 16 houses, scattered in the various parts of the geologically oldest and smallest continent of the planet. There is no proportion between what they are and what they do. In the words of our Blessed Teresa they too, like anyone of us, are *"weak, sinful and unworthy"*. But Jesus said: *"Precisely because you are weak, sinful and unworthy, I want to use you for my glory."* This is what Jesus is doing with the Missionaries of Charity. The more we have contact with Jesus in prayer, in adoration and in receiving him in the Bread of Life with humility, love and devotion, the more he can use us to bring souls to him and carry him to souls, especially the souls of the poor, who may be living like savage beasts. In fact the world is becoming more and more like savage beasts, and it is the duty of religious and priests to give authentic witness to the holy presence of God, to prove by life and action that there is God who loves us all. There is a felt need to return to the authentic truth and evangelical radicality for all religious, priests and committed Christians everywhere.

A few words of Archbishop Barry Hickey of Perth, Australia, are worth quoting: *"What I am trying to say is that the crisis of the present time will not be met by aligning ourselves too closely to the values of contemporary society, but by lives of radical love, poverty, trust and generosity. This is what Jesus said then and is saying to us now. Our personal lives are to contrast sharply with the ways of the world, as we try to enter the kingdom of love, justice and compassion by living biblical standard...*

"Asceticism may well be our proper response to the affluence with which we are surrounded. Even our commitment to the poor lacks credibility if we are not poor with them, as we must offer what we have - not gold and silver-which is the responsibility of the Society - but the life-giving

Word. A conversion of lifestyle is maybe part of the answer to the present crisis." (From an address given by Archbishop Barry Hickey at the 2005 Annual Conference of the Australian Confraternity of Catholic Clergy [ACCC])

It is absolutely vital for us to have a balanced life of prayer and apostolate, which is the concrete way of living the twofold commandments of the love of God and the love of one's neighbour. It is only when we are united with God that we are able to see God in our neighbour. Serving the poor is neither a hobby nor a way to pass our time or to overcome our boredom; no, serving the needy is an internal necessity. It is like the wings of the bird. It is not enough to have two wings for a bird to fly, but both wings must balance.

The first and greatest commandment is to love God with all one's heart, mind, souls and strength. This commandment enters into our being, our system through prayer and sacrifice, and comes out through our eyes, ears, mouth, hands and hearts in charity. In other words my uninterrupted contact with God in prayer enables me to see the existence of my needy neighbour and forces me to give wholehearted service to him. Without this contact with God I remain handicapped and will not be able to see the image of God in others, nor will I have the strength and the power to serve them with love. A piece of iron is totally different when it is in contact with the magnet. In the same way we will be totally different if we are united to God in prayer, otherwise our life will become sterile and useless.

Sr. Joseph Maria M.C., the regional Superior of the Missionaries of Charity for our Lady Help of Christians Region, invited me to give two seminars to the Sisters and a retreat to the Lay Missionaries of Charity and co-workers in three different cities of Australia: Darwin, Melbourne and Sydney. So I began my long and tedious journey via London on 1st August 2006. I reached Sydney on the morning of 3rd August 2006, where Sr. Maria Lucy M.C. and few of the Sisters were patiently waiting for me. There was a delay inside the airport as one piece of my luggage did not arrive.

Arriving home, some of the Sisters took me to visit the tomb of the Australian-born saint, Blessed Mary Mackillop (1842-1909), the foundress of the Institute of the Sisters of St. Joseph of the Sacred Heart. Her effort to adapt the new community to a colonial environment encountered a decade of lay and clerical misunderstanding and opposition, climaxing in the disbanding of the Sisterhood and her excommunication in 1871 by the Bishop of Adelaide. A compassionate Jew gave the homeless nuns a house free of rent until their restoration in 1872. In 1874 she traveled to Rome, met the Blessed Pope Pius IX, submitted her rule and got permission to work throughout the Australian colonies without restrictions.

Blessed Mary Mackillop went home to God on August 8, 1909, after a long illness patiently borne. Her congregation, which numbered one thousand at the time of her death, had 2,106 sisters serving in the 22 dioceses in Australia, four in New Zealand, and one in Ireland by 1964! *"The souls of the just are in the hands of God; no torment will ever touch them...Like gold in the fire God tried them and like a sacrificial offering he accepted them... They will govern nations and rule over people, the Lord will reign over them for ever."* (cf. Wis 3: 1-9)

From Sydney in the same evening, I traveled to Darwin to be with one group of our Sisters and to give them a seminar on our beloved and Blessed Mother Teresa's Spirit and charism. It was a real experience for me, thanks to Sr. Joseph Maria and the twenty-two other Sisters who had gathered together. Every day the Sisters devoted themselves to the life and teachings of our Mother, sharing all things in common, to the breaking of Bread and the prayers.

While in Darwin I was able to meet my good old novice mate after 38 years, Mr. Brian Laporte, and his brother, Mr. Colin, who were the first M.C. Brothers with whom Blessed Teresa began the first group of Brothers in Kolkata on 25 March, 1963. I did my novitiate with Brian (Br. Michael Joseph) from 1967 to 1968. Needless to say, we were happy to meet each other after such a long time to renew many wonderful memories of our good old days, around their family dinner table with varieties of delicious food.

Melbourne was the next city, where the Lay Missionaries of Charity and co-workers, supported and encouraged by the inspiring and edifying presence and example of the Sisters, had our retreat from Thursday 10 to Sunday 13 August 2006. The group prayed very fervently, offered many sacrifices, including the Friday whole night vigil before the Blessed Sacrament exposed. The place chosen for the retreat was exceptionally attractive and was very conducive to satisfy our hunger and thirst for God and to create more hunger. "Love grows through love"; hunger and thirst for God grows through hunger and thirst. If I am hungry and thirsty for God, how much more hungry and thirsty my God, who made me in his own image and likeness, must be! (cf. Gen 1: 26) *"Can a woman forget her nursing child…even if she forgets I will not forget you. See, I have inscribed you on the palm of my hands."* (cf. Is 49: 15-16)

In Melbourne two of the LMCs made their vows; several others began their two year formation. The couple who were supposed to make their vows with them were not able to participate in the retreat because their children were sick, and so they were asked to wait until the first Saturday of October 2006, when they with due preparation can make their vows. We need exemplary couples like these in our Movement.

It was very noticeable that the lay people too are eager to become holy by doing God's will and through Charity. They are very eager to know the way to holiness, which is simple but demanding. No one, including religious and priests, is going to become holy without really wanting it and without making strenuous efforts. Our Blessed Teresa's words come to mind: *"I will, I want, with God's blessing, be holy."* To realize this ardent desire, the way Jesus has shown us is to feed him in the hungry one, to satiate his thirst in the thirsty one, to clothe him in the naked one, to shelter him in the homeless one, to visit him in the sick and in the imprisoned one. (cf. Mt 25: 31-46) It is all summarized in five words: *"You did it to me"* (Mt 25: 40). So let us never hesitate to do good to others, whether they deserve it or not. God will never forget.

In Melbourne I was able to visit the room where Br. Andrew, who was the Co-founder and General Servant of the Brothers of the Missionaries of Charity of Kolkata, slept in the Lord at the M.C. Sisters' house on 4 October 2000. I also was privileged to visit his tomb twice during my stay. Many memories of our good old days came to my mind again as we had spent over 11 years together in the early days of our M.C. Brothers' life and existence. On 2 June 1968 we made vows together, he his final vows and five of us Brothers our first vows. We have offered holy Masses and prayers for the repose of his soul. R.I.P.

The third and final place of our meeting was in Sydney, a city where rich and poor, old and young, natives and strangers live together in peace and fellowship.

"From 1788, thousands of wretched, half-starved, imprisoned and punished convicts were sent here to be forgotten. Instead, they and the settlers who followed, struggled, survived and then thrived, spurred by the warmth, beauty and natural abundance they found around them. The more people came to live in Sydney from other parts of the world, the better it became." (From 2000 Things to See and Do in Sydney p. 3)

It is this city which has been chosen to hold the 23rd World Youth Day in 2008. It is here that the M.C. Sisters have their Our Lady Help of Christians regional house. It is here 32 M.C. Sisters had their five day Seminar on Mother's Spirit, spirituality and charism from 16 to 21 August 2006. It is here that over seventy poor people come every day to have some nourishment for the body as well as for their soul. *"Our hearts are restless until they rest in God."* (St. Augustine)

The Sisters try to provide food both for the body and the soul. They teach catechism in public schools wherever the Sisters have their houses in the various parts of this huge country. They do family visiting, teach them to pray, pray the Rosary with the people when possible, and pray for them when the latter is impossible. They do not judge or proselytize the poor, but are kind and understanding. "They preach Jesus by words and by their example, by the catching force, by the sympathetic influence of what they do and the evident fullness of the love their hearts bear to Jesus" (cf. 'Radiating Christ' prayer)

The words of Archbishop Barry Hickey of Perth are again worth reflecting on: *"The crisis of the present time will not be met by aligning ourselves too closely to the values of contemporary society, but by lives of radical love, poverty, trust and generosity."* I too felt very much the same during my short stay in Australia that the Australian Catholic Church needs saints who, without compromising, humbly and courageously venture to live the radical life of the Gospel love, poverty and simplicity. If Jesus back in 1946-47 asked Blessed Teresa of Kolkata to find free nuns covered with the poverty of the Cross, obedience of the Cross, full-of-love nuns covered with the Charity of the Cross, how much more Jesus would want from today's Church the same standard of the Cross from all of us religious, priests and committed people of the

Catholic Church?. Let there be authentic evangelical simplicity and let it begin with me, with our community!

Happy and holy feast of our beloved and Blessed Mother Teresa M.C. Love and prayers.

God bless you

Fr. Sebastian Vazhakala M.C.

Yearning for God, Yearning for Holiness
January 2007

On a Friday morning in a small Chapel in Sao Paolo, Brazil, I was in adoration before the Blessed Sacrament exposed. The word "holy" began to flash my mind for a long time and I did not know why it was happening and what to do with it, although the Lord had put into me the desire to become holy ever since I can remember through my beloved mother who too wanted to be holy. I also know that I have still miles to go; it is like someone who wants to reach the top of Mount Everest and is still at its bottom. However, I could not ignore the reality and so I took the word "holy" and began to see what those letters could stand for.

H - Humility. The word **"holy"** has four letters. The first letter is **"H"**. I began to reflect on this letter and what it could stand for. I realized that if I have to be holy I must start with **humility.** I went through the lives of the saints I knew, but I could not find that any of the saints I knew were proud. Precisely what made them saints was that they firmly believed and were convinced that without God they could not become holy, could not do the work of God, and could not live a life of holiness.

What is humility? The word "humus" in Latin means ground, earth. Here St. Thomas Aquinas' explanation on humility is important. He says humility is to believe that whatever is good in me comes from God. This includes even the place of birth, as I have not chosen it, but the good God gave me the place of birth. I did not choose my parents, but they are God's gift to me. I should therefore thank God for them and pray for them more fervently and assiduously, especially if I did not have a good relationship with my parents. Little by little I come to realize that everything and everyone is a gift of God and I must become more and more grateful to Him.

Besides, the many gifts and talents that one may have, the education one has received, all are to be recognized as God's gifts and are to be used and shared with others. Humility does not mean that we should deny the truth, but make clear the holiness of God through our gifts.

Blessed Mother Teresa used to say that it is easy to understand the greatness of God, but it is more difficult to understand the humility of God. How could a God, who is so inscrutable, become man, born of a woman, born under the law of nature and accept all the vicissitudes of this earthly life and existence? He even went so far as to tell us to learn humility from him, as he is meek and humble of heart. (cf. Mt. 11: 30)

St. Thomas of Aquinas says that humility is built on two pillars: truth and justice. The truth, he says, is that whatever is good in us comes from God; and justice means to give, therefore, all honour and glory to God. This means to give to Caesar what belongs to Caesar and give to God what is God's. In other words all glory and honour belong to God. Blessed Teresa of Kolkata is an example for us here. She received so many awards and honorary doctorates, which amount to seven hundred. But nothing made her feel that they were due to her cleverness or intelligence or capacity or power. She was very aware that it was He and not she; it was His and not hers. So, all honour and glory went directly to God, including the prestigious Nobel Prize for peace on 10 December 1979. Besides, she accepted all awards and honours in the name of the poor for the glory of God and the salvation of souls. Humility is very vital in the life of anyone who aspires to holiness, which, of course, is not a luxury of the few anymore but the simple duty of each one of us. "*Be holy, for the Lord, your God, is holy.*" (Lv 19: 2)

St. Augustine is a master in explaining the virtue of humility. Consider the testimony of the following text: "*…there is no coming* to unity without humility; there is no love without the openness of humble patience. Where humility reigns, there is love." For St. Augustine humility is not just one virtue among others; it is the basic virtue. In this way humility is the fertile soil for Charity.

St. Augustine writes: *"I would wish that you place yourself with all your love under Christ, and that you pave no other way in order to reach and to attain the truth that has already been paved by him who, as God, knows the weakness of our steps. This way is, in the first place, humility; in the second place, humility; in the third place humility... As often as you ask me about the Christian religion's norms of conduct, I choose to give no other answer than: humility."* (Letter 118, 3, 22)

It is very clear that pride is the great enemy, great adversary, of humility. All the positive qualities of humility are mirrored negatively in pride. St. Augustine writes again: *"To the extent that we are freed from the malignant swelling, which is called pride, we are filled with love."*

St. Augustine even dares to assert that *"God's hatred for pride is so strong that he would rather see humility in evil deeds than pride in good deeds."* (Sermon on Psalm 93, 15)

In religious life, love and humility are decisive, and without them the religious life is worthless. St. Augustine declared that it is better to possess a fortune outside the religious community than to go through life as a proud religious! Speaking of the celibate state of life, he says: *"It is much better to be married and humble than celibate and proud."* (On Holy Virginity, 51, 52)

When I joined the seminary, for sixty continual days we had to meditate on the necessity and importance of the virtue of humility.. At the end of two long months of meditation on humility, I then knew how to be humble...and I became proud of my humility. We can never be humble enough to think or say: "I am really a humble person". The humbler we are, the holier we become, and without it none of us will ever become holy.

O – Obedience. The next letter in the word "**holy**" is "**O**". This letter stands for **obedience**. Like for the word humility, here too I went through the lives of many of the canonized saints I knew, and I couldn't find one disobedient saint being canonized. I have come to know St.Pio of Pietrelcina, one of the saints of our times. He was forbidden to celebrate the holy Mass in public for the people for two years, and he was not allowed to hear confessions, especially of women, for four years. And what did St. Pio of Pietralcina do? He did not open his mouth against the Superiors, but simply obeyed his Superiors. He knew that his Superiors could make a mistake in commanding, but he could not make a mistake in obeying, even though Jesus granted him the gift of his five sacred wounds, which were a privilege and a burden for him. The devil tried to use them against doing God's will and thus they were going to become stumbling blocks; but instead he became all the more humble and obedient and saw in his Superiors the designs of God...like Jesus who saw the will of his Father in Pilate, when Pilate condemned him to death.

In the autobiography of St. Margaret Mary, we see Jesus telling her to obey her Superiors when her Superior did not easily accept what Jesus had been telling St. Margaret. He told her: *"Listen, my child, satan is furiously trying to destroy you, but as long as you obey your Superior he is powerless over you."*

Imagine, if our Lady refused to listen to the Angel Gabriel, what would have happened to the Incarnation? But she, without knowing what could happen to her, said in sheer faith: *"Behold the handmaid of the Lord, be it done to me as you say."* (Lk 1: 38) See, St. Joseph, how disturbed he was and how he wanted to divorce Mary in secret when he found out that she was with child. He could have exposed Mary to public shame, and Our Lady could have been stoned to death. But Joseph, a just and upright man, unwilling to put her to shame, finally accepted the will of God revealed to him through a dream. (cf. Mt 1: 19) In both cases, it was the Angel who came to Joseph and also to Mary. The Gospel says: *"Joseph awoke from sleep and did as the Angel of the Lord had told him. He took Mary as his wife."* (Mt 1: 24)

Jesus' own words and example are very clear as well. For he says: *"My food is to do the will of my Father who sent me."* (Jn 4: 34) *"In the days when he was in the flesh, Jesus offered prayers and supplications with loud cries and tears to the one who was able to save him from death, and he was heard because of his reverence. Son though he was, he learnt obedience from what he suffered; and when he was made perfect, he became the source of eternal salvation for all who obey him in and through his obedience."* (Heb 5: 7-9) Without obedience to God's will and his plan no one is going to be saved. Holiness demands the obedience of Jesus: prompt, cheerful, without any questions. Jesus told Blessed Mother Teresa: *"Fear not,…only obey, obey Me very cheerfully and promptly and without any questions – just only obey. I shall never leave you – if you obey."* (MFG, 18)

What then is obedience? *"Obedience is the wholehearted free submission of our will to God's will and plan through a serious of intermediaries, persons, events, institutions, human authorities, written rules, customs and practices. To obey is to say 'yes' to the sacred order of existence established by God in this world."* (MCC Brothers' Constitutions, R. 76)

Based on this motive there can be two ways of obeying our legitimate Superiors:

Servile obedience which is based on fear.

Docile obedience which is based on love and respect for the persons we obey, the obedience of Jesus. *"I want obedient nuns, covered with the obedience of the Cross"*, Jesus said to Blessed Teresa. (MFG, 10)

L – Love. The third letter of the word **"holy"** is **"L"**. This letter has two lines: the vertical and the horizontal. Reflecting on this letter I realized that this letter with its two lines stands for the twofold commandments of the **Love** of God and the love of one's neighbour. We are commanded to love God undeservedly and unconditionally and our neighbour as we love ourselves.

"Listen Israel…you MUST love Yahweh your God with all your heart, with all your soul, with all your strength…" (Dt 6: 4-5). Jesus joins it with the equally important commandment of loving one's neighbour as one loves oneself, which is a verse from the book of Leviticus that says: *"You shall love your neighbour as yourself."* (Lv 19: 18b) This twofold love is not only central to human beings but also natural for them.

What makes us different from other creatures is our capacity to love and to be loved. There is no substitute for this twofold love. And this capacity is common to all human beings, may they be healthy or sick, rich or poor, Christians or non Christians, white, black or brown. Irrespective of colour, culture, religion or nationality; even those who still lead a very primitive life or very highly cultured, the essential element in all is this twofold love. A person is measured by his or her capacity to love and to be loved. The highest form of culture and the greatest degree of civilization are the culture of love and the civilization of love.

Our life on earth from the time of our conception and birth to our rebirth into heaven and our life thereafter depends upon this one reality: this twofold love of God and neighbour. They are like two sides of the same coin, inseparable from one another. No bird can fly with one wing alone, no matter how strong its one wing is. Every bird has to have two wings strong and balancing to fly. The wing of the commandment of the love of God with all one's heart, mind, soul and strength and the equally important commandment of loving one's neighbour as one loves oneself should balance harmoniously in our everyday life, no matter how busy we may be.

Blessed Teresa prayed various hours of the day, participated in the celebration of the Eucharist and received holy Communion daily, and then with Jesus went in haste to serve the Lord in the distressing disguise of the poorest of the poor, the sick and the dying. *"The saints – consider the example of Blessed Teresa of Kolkata"*, writes the Holy Father Pope Benedict XVI in his first encyclical "Deus Caritas Est" *"constantly renewed their capacity for love of neighbour from their encounter with the Eucharistic Lord, and conversely this encounter acquired its realism and depth in their service to others. Love of God and love of neighbour are thus inseparable, they form one single commandment, but both from the love of God who loved us first. Love grows through love. Love is "divine, because it comes from God and unites us to God; through this unifying process it makes us a **"we"**, which transcends our divisions and makes us one, until in the end God is all in all. (1 Cor 15: 18)"* (Pope Benedict XVI, Deus Caritas Est, 18)

Love never gets old; love is eternal. Love never gives up loving; love is never tired of loving, humanly speaking, even the unlovable, the ones I don't like and even do not know. Love reaches out to all, embraces all, trusts all, and forgives all. Love does not brood over past injuries, but remembers the past with gratitude and with purified memories.

Love is a school where we learn to love through love. Love travels across the oceans, climbs mountains, without lamentation, without prejudices, barriers and boundaries. Love does not wait. In the school of love we learn to transcend superficial emotions; love breaks man-made walls of separation like the Berlin wall and removes the division, uniting one another. In the school of love one learns to transcend from affective love to effective love; from human love to Jesus' love.

This happens in and through prayer, sacrifice and works of mercy. Love enters into our being through prayer and comes out of us as Charity.

Love necessarily leads us to suffering. The twofold love with its vertical and horizontal lines makes the cross. God's love for me and my love for him is the vertical beam, and my love for my neighbour is the horizontal beam. If no cross, there is no love, and vice versa. It is impossible to love God and love one's neighbour without suffering, some pain, some sacrifice of time, personal interest, likes and dislikes, superficial feelings and emotions.

Love necessarily leads to suffering. Suffering then is the natural, necessary and spontaneous expression of love. Take the example of a good mother. How much she has to suffer from conception to birth and until the child becomes more or less independent; but the mother does not count the cost nor goes on telling everybody of her inconveniences and hardships of bringing a child into the world, educating him to stand on his feet. We all have wonderful experiences of our mother's love and tender care. If we genuinely love a person, then we do not calculate the difficulties and hardships in mathematical terms.

"God loved the world so much that he gave his only begotten Son, so that whoever believes in him may not perish, but may have eternal life." (Jn 3: 16) Jesus in turn loved us to the very end. (Cf. Jn 13: 1) *"Greater love than this no man has that a man lay down his life for his friends."* (Jn 15: 13) This is love without limits and without counting the cost. This is what the saints did. They became God's love for the poor, the sick, the lepers, the dying. The invisible God becomes visible today through works of love and Charity. *"Where Charity and love prevail, there God is ever found."* (St. Augustine)

Y – Yearning. Now we come to the fourth and last letter in the word "holy". Here I could not easily find the proper word that would fit to complete the word "holy" and make sense in the context. After I prayed hard and begged the Holy Spirit to illumine me to find the right word, I was shown the word Yearning.

This word can be equivalent to the word "Thirst" or "Longing" or "Desire". It matters very little here which word we use to express the same reality, as long as one has the real yearning for God, thirst for holiness. *"Blessed are those who hunger and thirst for holiness..."* (Mt 5: 6)

The word "yearning" can be used to express two essential elements on the path of holiness:

Prayer as yearning of the human heart for God.

Yearning for holiness.

Prayer as yearning. There is more than one psalm that expresses this reality of the human heart for God. Psalm 42 is an example of how the psalmist expressed his deep desire for God in prayer. *"Like the deer that yearns for running streams, So my soul is yearning for you, my God."* (v. 1)

Psalm 63 is another example. Who can really quench the insatiable thirst for God? Not only our soul but our whole being pines for God: *"O God, you are my God, for you I long, for you my soul is thirsting; My body pines for you, like a dry, weary land without water."* (v. 1)

Psalm 63 is the first psalm for Morning Prayer on every solemnity and feast. Every saint during his life on earth longed for God with all his heart, mind, soul and strength, even when his soul went through thick darkness, experienced terrible loneliness and rejection. Blessed Teresa writes: *"I have been on the verge of saying "No". It has been so very hard – that terrible longing keeps growing and I feel as if something will break in me one day – and then that darkness, that loneliness, that feeling of terrible aloneness. Heaven from every side is closed…gone is the love for anything and anybody – and yet – I long for God. I long to love him with every drop of life in me… My mind and heart is habitually with God."* (Blessed Teresa's letter to Cardinal Picachy S.J., 20 October 1960)

The saints live always with God; they walk with him, travel with him, work with him and for him; they speak with him. Their mind and heart are habitually with God. Isaiah writes: *"My soul yearns for you in the night, yes, my spirit within me keeps vigil for you."* (26: 9) In the night and as morning breaks the saints watch for his coming.

According to St. Augustine, the yearning of the human heart for God, the insatiable *nostalgia* is the heart of all true prayer. Without deep yearning, there is no true prayer, regardless of the many hours in the chapel and the length of formal prayers. *"Longing is always at prayer, even though the tongue is silent. If your yearning is constant, then you are always praying. When does our prayer sleep? Only when our desire cools."* (St, Augustine, Sermon 80: 7)

Even though prayer of the heart is the most important, this does not make verbal prayer superfluous. *"In faith, hope and love we are always praying with uninterrupted longing. But at particular hours and times we entreat God also with words so that, through these*

120

verbal signs of the reality we may impel ourselves to greater effort, help ourselves become aware of how much progress we have made in this desire, and rouse ourselves to grow in it with greater vitality... Therefore at certain times, we call our spirit back to prayer from the other cares and activities, which in some way cloud our yearning.". (St. Augustine, Letter 130: 9, 18) There should be real harmony of word and heart in every form of prayer.

This **yearning** of the human heart, which St. Augustine calls "desiderium naturale" – "natural desire", is common to all saints and must be a common denominator for everyone who aspires to greater holiness. How can I be perfect or merciful or holy as our heavenly Father is perfect, merciful and holy if I do not yearn for it like the saints did? God's friends become the saints' friends and they love and take care of all those God loves and wants to take care of. They know that their inner dynamism, the driving force, does not come from them, but from the Lord, whom they want to proclaim by their words and example. Without this deep yearning no one can become a saint. In the words of Blessed Teresa of Kolkata: *"I want, I will, with God's help, be holy."*

Yearning for holiness. Without this strong desire and deep yearning one cannot become holy. Even though all are called to be perfect as our heavenly Father is perfect, no one is going to become automatically holy or perfect. This inner longing for holiness is at the same time the strong desire to resemble God in his holiness. God wants us to witness his holiness in our life and work.

The real yearning is found in the heart of God who yearns for each individual soul created in his own image and likeness. He creates in each person a corresponding thirst or yearning for him. To express it graphically, let us take the example of the magnet and a piece of iron. The magnet has the power to attract the piece of iron and the iron has the capacity to be attracted by the magnet. God is the powerful magnet who draws us to him; and we are like pieces of iron drawn to him. Our capacity to be drawn to God is our thirst, our yearning or longing for God. This capacity to be attracted is not something passive but dynamic. As God is thirsty, he is in love with every human being; he creates the same thirst in each one of us for him and for souls, as long as we are in contact with Jesus. Jesus wants to suffer in us for souls, as he can no longer suffer alone without us. *"I am longing with painful longing to be all for God"*, writes Blessed Teresa, *"to be holy in such a way that Jesus can live his life to the full in me...I want to love him as he has never been loved...I did not know that love could make one suffer so much."*

Conclusion – The word "holy" can be explained and understood much more deeply. The more we understand the sublime beauty of the reality of this holiness, which is a participation in the holiness of God, the more we can appreciate and try to live it No wonder Jesus speaks of the parable of the pearl the merchant bought: *"The kingdom of heaven is like a merchant's search for fine pearls. When he found one really valuable pearl, he went back and put up for a sale all that he had and bought it."* (Mt 13: 45-46)

Among God's creations, human beings alone can become better and holier. Even the Angels remain what they are. As long as we live in the world, we can grow in holiness and can resemble our Creator more closely and perfectly. *"Be holy, for I, the Lord your God, am holy."* (Lv 19: 2)

God bless you.
Fr. Sebastian Vazhakala M.C.

SAINT THERESE

Today as we know is the feast day of St. Jerome – a friend and a lover of the Bible…who said: "One who is ignorant of the Bible is ignorant of God and of Christ". Today he invites us all to reread the Word of God, to treasure them in our heart, ponder over them as did our Blessed Mother, and then live the Word of God. We pray earnestly to St. Jerome to help us to love the Bible.

I as pardon of St. Jerome for leaving him behind this day as we are forced to, since we have decided to celebrate the feast of another saint who too in her own way knew God's Word, loved and lived it with great simplicity, clarity and originality. While St. Jerome with his incredible knowledge and intelligence translated the Bible into Latin, St. Theresa of the Child Jesus translated God's Word into life and made it easily readable. Her way was that of simplicity and total abandonment of God's merciful love…..in total surrender, in childlike trust. She cried out in Spirit of God from the closed walls of the Lisieux Convent that the secret to our life is *"Love"*, that she wished to much to be love. *"In the heart of the Church, my Mother, I will be love"*. She no longer desired anything except to love until she died of love. But she died, and disappeared from the visible horizons of this world of tears, pain and sorrow, but her love did not die, nor her Spirit of total trust. Her way of doing ordinary things with extraordinary love did not end with her earthly departure for heaven.

Thousands and thousands have been inflamed by her Spirit of simplicity, humility and charity, and took the same "elevator" to heaven – her short but sure way; her happy but difficult way; her secure but painful way….yes the way of love is the way of suffering////but that is

123

the best way to peace and joy.....Today she tells us all to have the same evangelical Spirit of the Gospel that we heard, namely *"unless you become like little children....."*(Mt. 18:1-4) – let us approach God as she did, let us accept the cross like a lover. Her way was short, hard, difficult and demanding – but she persevered////nothing and nobody could separate her from the love of her Lord....On the other hand suffering increased her fidelity, strengthened her convictions and she saw it as a means to save souls; and this is exactly what she did. Is not the reason why we celebrate her feast today – it not the reason why we find her in every Church – to remind the world that God is **"Love"**, and His love never dies....that whoever is in contact with that undefeatable love of God will live for all eternity with God!

Love is dynamic; love is creative, love never gives up....love is our interior force. It is like an engine. And God is love.

Today we see how this incredible love has become a living reality in Mother Teresa of Calcutta. The secret to her life is the same. Through her God makes the world realize that there is God; and He is a God of love; He loves us all, and especially He love the poor......He is the friend of the friends of the poor. He loves especially those who love the poor.

God opened through Mother Teresa the eyes of many and showed not only the existence and the reality of the poor but that they too are God's children.

This is an unfinished homily; it is up to each of the readers to complete it. St. Therese took three resolutions at the age of eleven while she was preparing herself for her first Holy Communion: 1. *"I will recite a 'Memorare' everyday"*, 2. *"I will humiliate myself"*, 3. *"I will never allow myself to be discouraged"*.

Transfiguration of Our Lord, 2008

Let us listen to God in prayer and listen to God in one another

Dear beloved Sisters and Brothers,

May the grace of our Lord Jesus Christ, the love of God the Father and the fellowship of the Holy Spirit be with each and every one of you.

While the M.C. Sisters all over the world are intensely preparing for the Society Feast, we, the Missionaries of Charity Contemplative, are preparing for our Second General Chapter. The last General Chapter was in June two thousand and two. Since then, with God's help and blessing, our Society has grown in many ways. The growth has been slow but steady. It is characteristic of any sort of growth to experience pain, uncertainties and even confusion. Time and patience are indispensable factors for growth and maturity.

There is an olive tree in our garden in Rome, planted in the month of April 1979, about a month after my coming to live there. Toward the end of April 1979, one of the men from the slums, as he was moving into an apartment, gave me a small olive tree to be transplanted in our garden. The neighbours who saw me carrying the tree on my shoulders began to laugh at me for two reasons: first, because it was not the season of planting trees, and secondly because the olive tree did not have proper roots.

While planting the tree in our garden I prayed the quick "Memorare novena", and then water was given each day, together with many "Memorares". As days passed by all the leaves of the tree dried up. Mr. Enzo from the nearby tennis court felt pity and so gave me a cypress tree with all the proper roots to plant in place of the olive tree. I planted the cypress tree a few meters away from the olive tree. Although the olive tree by now had practically dried up, I continued to pray the "Memorare" while watering it. Within a few weeks' time the olive tree began to sprout with new leaves...Mr. Enzo, who gave me the cypress tree, brought several people to show the miracle of the olive tree. After that the tennis people began to ask for prayers.

There is one thing more about the olive tree. I continued with my prayer and asked the Lord to give me at least one olive on the tree that year. By now the tree was full of leaves. One day Mr. Gaetano Marano, our friend and co-worker, was looking around and saw just one olive on the tree. This olive tree then has much to teach us...First of all the power of prayer – even when everything around us is dry and hopeless, we must still continue to pray more fervently. Prayer alone is not enough; the olive tree needed sufficient water as well; so "Ora et Labora" become inseparable.

God is our Father. He grants even our childish desires. In this case he granted me one olive I asked for. For me the olive tree is very symbolic.

There is something more to this olive tree. The growth of the olive tree is very slow, but very steady. The olive tree lives very long. Our Society grows very slowly, but steadily. We must trust Jesus more lovingly, trust him more blindly, pray more fervently and work more untiringly. Then all will be well.

As some of you have asked me certain particulars about our General Chapter, I thought of sharing with you a few of its aspects. This can help you to be with us in Spirit and accompany us with your prayers. We too will be very close to you in Spirit, especially in our perpetual hours of adoration and intercessory prayers. Those who live in Rome and around are most welcome to join us in adoration, as we may require some volunteers for the many hours. We will have the exposition of the Blessed Sacrament from 25th August to 5th September 2008 and then again from the evening of September 9th (08) till the end of our General Chapter (27th September 2008).

Our General Chapter is a time to listen to God in prayer and listen to God in each other.

The place of the G. Chapter: Rome, Via S. Agapito 8.

The date of the G. Chapter: Saturday 23 August to Saturday 27 September, 2008 (approximate)

1) **Seminar:** 23rd to 27th August, 2008

2) **Retreat:** 27th August to 5th September, 2008

   Mother's feast (5th September)

3) **Pilgrimage:** 6th September, 2008

4) **Day of Atonement:** 7th September, 2008

5) **Ordination to diaconate:** 8th September, at 4.00 p.m. in the Parish Church of St. Leo I.

   The candidates to diaconate are: Br. Alphonse M.C., Br. Benedict M.C., **Br.** Tony M.C., Br. Jan Timo M.C. and Br. Ramon M.C.

6) **Thanksgiving Day:** 9th September, 2008

7) **General Chapter:** 10th to 27th September, 2008

8) **Elections:** Friday 19th September, 2008:

9) **The patrons of the General Chapter:** Although all the Angels and Saints of God are ever ready to help us, we still have some special patrons for our General Chapter:

   -   The Holy Spirit

   -   The Holy Family: Jesus, Mary and Joseph

   -   Blessed Mother Teresa M.C.

10) The Theme of the G. Chapter: "Instaurare omnia in Christo"

   -   "To restore and renew our aim, Spirit and Charism, our specific vocation and mission in and with the Church for the poorest of the poor.

   -   Jesus in the Eucharist and in the poor."

As Missionaries of Charity we are called to satiate Jesus' thirst for souls not only on the Cross but also in the Eucharist. Like a magnet that draws a piece of iron, so Jesus, the divine Magnet, draws us, who are like little pieces of iron, to Him. As long as we are in contact with Jesus we will have Jesus' love, Jesus' compassion, Jesus' humility and above all Jesus' thirst for souls. The thirst we experience in the depth of our being for God and for souls is no longer our thirst but Jesus' own infinite thirst. This thirst is enkindled and strengthened by Jesus' body, the Eucharist. Jesus quenched his Father's thirst for sinful humanity by becoming obedient unto death, death on a cross. He now thirsts for souls in and through the Eucharist, and He thirsts to come to us. Jesus had felt compassion for the hungry crowd during his earthly life. He now feels compassion for the poor, especially for those who live in the darkness of poverty and misery. Today Jesus not only multiplies the loaves and the fish, but he changes ordinary bread into his body and simple wine into his blood. The Eucharistic Jesus lives in us and lives with us in our communities, walks with us to the homes of the poor, thirsts in us for the souls of the poor, suffers with us for the redemption of the world, especially for the world of the poor. How he wishes to enter the many unhappy hearts, how he wishes to console many sorrowful souls! His thirst remains unquenched until we welcome him in the hungry, thirsty, naked, homeless, sick and the imprisoned. *"Carry Me with you into them"*, he told Blessed Mother Teresa M.C. *"Bring them to Jesus, carry Jesus to them"*, Our Lady also told Mother.

Blessed Teresa M.C. gave great importance to daily Mass and Holy Communion. For her and for the Missionaries of Charity, the Holy Eucharist was and is an absolute need. Back in 1947 Blessed Teresa wrote to the Archbishop of Kolkata: *"One thing I request you, your Grace, to give us all the spiritual help we need. If we have Our Lord in the midst of us, with daily Mass and Holy Communion, I fear nothing for the Sisters nor for myself. He will look after us. But without him I cannot be. I am helpless"*.

Intercessory Prayer.

There is a very important and interesting passage in the book of Exodus where the Israelites had to engage in battle against their enemy (Ex 17: 8-16). We are in need of some brothers and sisters, especially during the General Chapter, to intercede unceasingly with the Lord, like Moses: *"As long as his arms raised, Israel had the advantage, when he let his arms fall, the advantage went to Amalek* (the enemy). *But Moses' arms grew heavy, so they took stone and put it under him and on this he sat, with Aron and Hur supporting his arms on each side. Thus the arms remained unwavering till sunset, and Joshua defeated Amalek"*.

How important for us to have intercessory prayer, together with sacrifices and penance to defeat our enemies, to win the battle and to grow in holiness and perseverance in our vocation. Assiduous prayer and generous sacrifices are necessary means for our growth in holiness and for holy perseverance.

Our Lady's intercession.

In the Gospel of John we can see Our Lady telling Jesus: *"They have no wine"* (cf. 2: 1-11). When we fall short of the wine of enthusiasm in community life, when we find it hard to smile more tenderly, when our prayer becomes dry and empty, when making sacrifices becomes a big sacrifice, when we suffer from lack of appreciation, understanding and thoughtfulness from the part of others, when we struggle with our own weaknesses, imperfections and sins, when we feel that we are no longer understood by our Superiors or others, etc., let us turn to Our Lady, who will introduce us to Jesus and will intercede for us with him. She will remind us to do whatever Jesus is going to tell us, like the servants at the wedding feast in Cana. If the servants had refused Our Lady and Jesus, what would have happened to the miracle of the fresh and best wine? The servants had all the reasons to laugh at Jesus and Mary; instead they literally and blindly obeyed. We, too, will keep the best wine of our freshness and enthusiasm till the end of our earthly life if we remain close to Our Lady.

In the name of the Capitulars and in the name of our poor people I would like to express my sincere thanks to each and every one of you who are offering fervent prayers and making generous sacrifices for the success and fruitfulness of our General Chapter.

May the Eucharistic Jesus and the Blessed Virgin Mary help us to make our General Chapter a real experience of God, enabling us to live our M.C. vocation to the full. We also ask Blessed Teresa M.C., our Mother and our Foundress, to bless us all from heaven and make our Society something beautiful for God.

Love and prayers.

God bless you.

Fr. Sebastian Vazhakala M.C.

October 2008

Love travels faster than the wind and the light

Dearly beloved brothers and sisters,

The Gospel of the thirtieth Sunday in Ordinary Time, year A, is taken from the Gospel of Matthew, Chapter 22: 34-40. The question of one of the teachers of the Law to Jesus was: *"Teacher, which is the most important commandment in the Law?"* The teacher of the Law knew very well also the answer; but he asked this question to test Jesus. Here Jesus without hesitation gives the answer, which is the most basic to our life on earth as well as in heaven. Our life in heaven is going to depend on how we live this twofold commandment of loving God with all our heart, mind, soul and strength and loving our neighbour as we love ourselves.

Unlike the teacher of the Law I asked a different kind of question to the participants of the Holy Eucharist on 30th Sunday, namely, which of the two commandments is easier to practice: love of God or love one's neighbour? The majority, including a child of seven years old, said that it is easier to practice the love of God than to love one's neighbour as one loves oneself. It sounds true, as we know that we love ourselves in spite of what we are, in spite of all our defects, imperfections, sins, failures and shortcomings and the worst part is that many a time we don't even realize them. But to love another person with all his/her defects, sins, failures and shortcomings, to love him/her without judging him/her is apparently more difficult and only very few people seem to do it. They of course enter the category of saints and heroes. One of the most world renowned persons we all know is Blessed Teresa of Kolkata. We could even say that she loved others more than she loved herself.

The next question was: "Can we love God without loving our neighbour?" There was a long silence and then came the answer: no. We cannot really love God without loving our neighbour. St. John, the apostle and evangelist, writes: «*If you say 'I love God' while you hate your brother or sister, you are a liar. How can you love God, whom you cannot see, if you do not love your brother, whom you see?*» (1Jn 4: 20)

The third question was: "Is it possible to love your neighbour if you do not love God?" Again there was silence. Then many said: no. It is not possible to love our neighbour without loving God.

These simple questions make us understand the most important and basic truth of life. This twofold love in reality is inseparable. They are like the two sides of the same coin. We could easily say that in reality there is only one kind of love and that is God's love, which is like the electricity that flows into the bulb and makes the bulb shine. In the same way the flow of God's love into a soul makes the person love one's neighbour. It is impossible for a person who loves God with all one's heart, mind, soul and strength not to love his neighbour. He no longer loves with human love but God's love, which can go beyond the external appearances of a person or his many defects and weakness. God's love is eternal, infinite, undefeatable; God's love purifies and transforms a person who is chosen to love like God. He experiences the incredible force of love. In fact in the beginning of Jesus' locutions to Blessed Teresa of Kolkata M.C., he told her that the M.C.s should be very united to him so as to radiate **his** love on souls. (cf. MGF pg. 10)

When electricity goes into a bulb, the bulb shines and gives light to all around. The bulb does not produce electricity nor does it shine for itself but for others. When electricity goes into a fan, the fan moves and releases fresh air. The fan does not produce fresh air for its own sake but for others who are around, nor does the bulb or fan or any other instrument take pride and boast of each other. When the love of God enters into our being, we will be like the bulb, like the fan, like any other electronic instruments.

How much the world of today is depending on electricity! In other words, the world as a whole cannot function any more, nor can it survive without electrical energy. It is much more with love. The world cannot even exist without the twofold love of God and love of one's neighbour. Love is the essence of our life; no love, no heaven; no love, no God; no love, no life!

When electricity fails, people feel a panic. When love fails in us, forgiveness does not work, mutual dialogue becomes difficult in religious communities, in families, among the various religions of the world, and in our world as a whole. Without love the world moves from light to darkness, from the real to the unreal; the culture of death begins to prevail; violence and terrorism will start to dominate. Man without love is worse than an animal, and his presence creates darkness in and around and makes the atmosphere heavy and tense; a world that does not recognise the presence of God and the power of his love and his tender care is a world that is being destroyed little by little. A world without love is a world without life. A loveless life is a lifeless life.

Love makes one fly; it makes people alive and enthusiastic. Love is dynamic. Love is the only and strongest weapon that can conquer the whole world. Love is a God-made weapon to conquer even our enemies and who eventually become our friends. Love does not destroy or kill, but protects, forgives and saves. Love suffers to love especially the difficult ones. Man-made weapons never save, but kill and destroy. Going back to the primitive man, when he used bows and arrows, or to our day when we use the most modern and sophisticated weapons and suicidal bombs, we see that the purpose is not to save but to retaliate, to take revenge or to covet what belongs to others. As long as we conquer evil with evil, nothing is achieved; instead when we conquer evil with good there is victory, there is joy and peace.

Love travels faster than the wind and the light; it can reach the remotest corners of the world; it can permeate even the most savage human being, transforming the person into the reflection of God. Every time there is real love, which may hurt us, there is a real return to the original image of God. (see Gen 1: 26)

All created beings come to an end and disappear when they die. But love never dies, even when the person dies: instead love becomes more alive, more powerful, more effective. Every time a person dies, there is a transition from the affective love to an effective love, from purely human love to God's love. The saints who loved God with all the powers of their soul and loved their neighbour more than they loved themselves become powerful intercessors in heaven for those who invoke their name, implore their assistance.

It would be appropriate to quote here the following passage from the first encyclical letter of pope Benedict XVI:

«...in God and with God, I love even the person whom I do not like or even know. This can only take place on the basis of an intimate encounter with God, an encounter which has become a communion of will, even affecting my feelings. Then I learn to look on this other person not simply with my eyes and my feelings, but from the perspective of Jesus Christ. His friend is my friend. Going beyond exterior appearances, I perceive in others an interior desire for a sign of love, of concern... Seeing with the eyes of Christ, I can give to others much more than their outward necessities; I can give them the look of love which they crave. Here we see the necessary interplay between love of God and love of neighbour which the First Letter of John speaks of with such insistence. If I have no contact whatsoever with God in my life, then I cannot see in the other anything more than the other, and I am incapable of seeing in him the image of God... Only my readiness to encounter my neighbour and to show him love makes me sensitive to God as well. Only if I serve my neighbour can my eyes be opened to what God does for me and how much he loves me. The saints—consider the example of Blessed Teresa of Calcutta—constantly renewed their capacity for love of neighbour from their encounter with the Eucharistic Lord, and conversely this encounter acquired its real- ism and depth in their service to others. Love of God and love of neighbour are thus inseparable, they form a single commandment. But both live from the love of God who has loved us first. No longer is it a question, then, of a "commandment" imposed from without and calling for the impossible, but rather of a freely-bestowed experience of love from within, a love which by its very nature must then be shared with others. Love grows through love. Love is "divine" because it comes from God and unites us to God; through this unifying process it makes us a "we" which transcends our divisions and makes us one, until in the end God is "all in all" (1 Cor 15:28)». (Deus carita est: 18)

Now I would like to say a few words about our General Chapter. Our General Chapter was a prayer event. It lasted over five weeks with all the various programmes. We have much to thank God for and much more to thank God for each one of you, who offered up fervent prayers and made generous sacrifices for the success and fruitfulness of our General Chapter. From Sunday 24th August 2008 we have started perpetual adoration. Mr. Thomas Paul and his team of two men, Mr. Anthony and Ginu from India, were the main adorers and intercessors during our long weeks of seminar, retreat and General Chapter. A few more days after our G. Chapter they continued with their adoration. One of them has many spiritual gifts and used his gifts in full until he went back. We also had two others: Mr. Chako and Sahodharan Anyan. Anyan is making a forty day retreat with us in total silence, fasting and adoration. He spends 14 hours of adoration a day, including six hours at night. He will return to India on 7th December 2008. Mr. Chako has already gone back.

Over the years we were and we are very fortunate to have many co-workers and benefactors, but this time we were more fortunate to have such wonderful spiritual benefactors day and night praying and interceding with arms outstretched, like Moses in the book of Exodus (cf. Ex 17: 8-13). We still are very much in need of spiritual co-workers.

Our day of election was on Friday 19th September 08. Our heartfelt thanks go to your prayers, which really helped us to have a very peaceful election. The Episcopal Vicar for Religious of the diocese of Rome, Msgr. Natalino Zagotto, came to celebrate Holy Mass with us, after which he presided over the election of the Father General.

His words both during the celebration of the Holy Eucharist and before and after the election of the Father General were very appropriate and inspiring. After his departure the Capitulars continued with the election of the four General Councillors, under the presidency of the newly elected Father General. Here too the election was very smooth and the following Brothers were elected to assist, counsel and help the Father General according to the Constitutions of the Missionaries of Charity Contemplative:

Br. Stephen M.C. from Ghana was elected as the first Councillor and Vicar; Br. Jan-Timo M.C. from Germany, Br. André Marie M.C. from Canada, Br. Luke M.C. from Canada

These four Councillors represent the four continents of Africa, Europe, South and Central America and the North America. The Father General represents the continent of Asia and the rest of the world. It will take a while to prepare all the acts and outcome of the

General Chapter. Hence we request every one's fervent and continued prayers.

The LMC General Assembly (G. A.) and Jubilee. The Jubilee of the Lay Missionaries of Charity (LMC) is very close. It has two main parts. The first part is their General Assembly. From now on we use the words "General Assembly" in place of General Chapter for the Movement (G.A.), which will commence from 14th to 21st April 2009; while the Jubilee programme will start from the evening of 21st to the evening of 25th April 2009. We have booked for three hundred persons for food and lodging, as well as one hundred more for day time events, including their meals. For the General Assembly we hope to have about one hundred to one hundred and twenty persons. Much has been done by way of preparation, including most of the registrations.

The prayer for the success and fruitfulness of the Jubilee is prayed in all the groups. During the General Assembly we are going to have perpetual adoration at Teresa Gerini, where we hold the Assembly. We hope to have enough volunteers to adore for the occasion. In our place, at S. Agapito, we will in any way continue with our perpetual adoration.

The Brothers' Society Feast of the Holy Family is celebrated every year on the last Thursday of the month of October. We anticipate our Society feast of the Holy Family, although the actual liturgical feast is after Christmas. We do this to have a real preparation for the feast, which we may not be able to do during Christmas time, the same reason why the LMCs celebrate the feast of the Holy Family on the Sunday before the feast of Christ the King.

Our heartfelt thanks to Sr. Nirmala M.C. who was so kind to send to the Capitulars two letters, one in the beginning of our General Chapter and one almost at the end. They renewed our ties with the source of the M.C. Charism and the M.C. Bethlehem. Once again thanks to one and all for all the help and support. Love and prayers.

God bless you.
Fr. Sebastian Vazhakala M.C.

Christmas 2008

Dear beloved Brothers and Sisters,

Once again we are on the eve of the great feast of Christmas, the feast that makes many people happy even in the business world. A look at the streets of the cities will speak to us without words that someone important is coming.

There are two main aspects in this sort of preparation and celebration: the material and spiritual. Each must have its proper place. Apparently the time of Christmas for many people is a time to make more money. The beautiful and incredibly mystery-bound feast is so much commercialized; so much so that many people are busy with material profit, enjoyment and satisfaction. The reality of the Incarnation, the coming of the Saviour among us, the birth of the Prince of Peace is not much contemplated. The Church's duty then is to help the people not to go to extremes, but to keep the balance; not to throw out the baby with the bath water. Many of our Christian feasts have come to that stage. We celebrate the feasts superficially and materially without having the real essence and substance of the feast.

It is our duty to maintain the pristine purity and spirit of these feasts. There is a need to return to the early spirit, to their origins…go to Bethlehem's spirit of faith, contemplation, humility, simplicity, and poverty. Is it possible for us to experience the immense love of God, which is the heart and centre of any authentic celebration?

Now I am now going to share with you, my Brothers and Sisters, a few reflections, which many of you may already know. They are the reflections made on the occasion of the «Peace Award» which the Mayor of Rome, Mr. Gianni Alemanno, is going to give me on Thursday 18

December 2008. You and I know very well that I do not deserve it, nor am I worthy for such an award. It is the Lord. There is no doubt in my mind, and so let Him be praised and glorified, and our poor people be helped and served better. I know very well that all of you have a share in this as well. For me it is also a sign from the Lord that our life and work are his and are pleasing and acceptable to him.

Now let us dwell on some of the reflections, along with some information. Working with and for the poorest of the poor for more than forty years I have come to understand many things and have discovered the various aspects of life:

- It is better to light a candle than to curse the darkness.

- It is not important where we are born, but is very important how we live our lives now and what we do.

- Man is more important for what he is than for what he has or possesses.

- We can be of different colours, different cultures, nationalities or religions, but in essential matters we are all the same.

- Let there be peace and joy and let it begin with me.

- The works of love are works of peace.

- Our work with the poorest of the poor is not merely social work, but God's work.

- We are not called to do extraordinary things, but ordinary things with extraordinary love.

- What you do I cannot do, what I do perhaps you may not be able to do, but together we can do something good and beautiful for God.

- The family that prays together stays together.

- It is not important how much we do, but with how much love and humility we do what we do.

- We learn to live today and not yesterday or tomorrow. Whatever I am able to do today I must do it now and I should not postpone it until tomorrow.

- When we see a needy person (a person in need), let us not ask what others are doing or not doing, but what we can do; and let us do it straight away, if we can.

- Love never sets; love does not put limits or boundaries.

- Destructive weapons make enemies more enemies, creating disaster and disorder, while the weapon of invincible love conquers enemies, transforming them into friends. Love never destroys, except that it destroys our egoism and pride.

- Once upon a time Rome was considered to be the "the world Capital". We could still say that Rome is "the world Capital", because Rome is the world capital of the Church, fraternal love and service. Rome has a very particular vocation: she must know that she is the servant of Charity in humility and meekness, in generosity and benevolence. Oh, Rome, recognize your dignity, your special love and tender care for the little ones, for the oppressed, for the sick, the homeless, the unwanted, the uncared and the unloved.

- Oh, Rome, become what you are…It is the work of everybody, for the Romans and those who come to live in Rome, even for a short while. No one should feel a stranger here. We must bloom where we are planted; if we live in Rome, we must bloom in Rome. The foreigners who live in Rome should not think of only profiting, but contribute and share for the good of all. Nor should we live in Rome just to ask and receive, but we must be more willing to give than to receive. "It is more blessed to give than to receive", says the Acts of the Apostles. (Acts 20: 35)

- Let us not come to Rome to be served, but to serve with love. The offices in Rome are offices of service and courtesy. The Mayor's office in Campidoglio is a centre of fraternal service because we are all brothers and sisters, children of the same heavenly Father.

- The city of Rome, where I live, is a city to be built on love every day; the people of Rome are my people as well. I am equally responsible for whatever happens. I feel like the Good Samaritan in the gospel of Luke (10: 30-37). The Good Samaritan did not judge the priest or the Levite, who passed the same way before him and who did not respond to the person in need. Instead he just got off his donkey and did what was needed. He did not waste his precious time to judge and criticize but sacrificed his time to help and save. If we waste our time in judging and blaming everyone else, we will not have any time left to love, serve and save. Through the parable of the Good Samaritan Jesus teaches the great and fundamental lesson of loving, serving and saving people more than judging and criticizing them. St. John's gospel emphasizes this fact, namely *"God did not send his Son into the world to be its judge, but to be its Saviour."* (Jn 3: 17). This is our vocation as well.

- I am more than convinced that I am not worthy to receive the "Peace award", which the Mayor of Rome is giving me on Thursday 18th December 2008. When the Mayor, honourable Gianni Alemanno, in person told me that decided to give me the "Peace award", I how is it possible, as I great to merit this award. I have never sought any recognition for our humble works of love, but only tried to bring a little bit of comfort to a sick person, a warm meal to a hungry person, to offer a bed to a homeless person, especially during the visit AIDS patients in the various hospitals, the prisoners of

- Rebibbia in Rome, the many persons who are old and lonely, etc.

- I am convinced that a man's dignity does not depend on his status in life, nor on social conditions, or on his riches and wealth, nor does it depend on his country of origin. A person can be poor, but poverty does not destroy his dignity, nor even reduce his dignity. Human dignity is much more profound. Oh, man, recognize your dignity, for you are created by Almighty God in his own image and likeness (cf. Gen 1: 26).

WHAT WE FIND AND HOW WE WORK WHERE WE LIVE.

We live at Via S. Agapito, 8 in Rome, in the old "Borghetto Prenestino", at Largo Preneste, which is about four KM east of the main train station, Termini. We came to this place on Thursday 8th March 1979, when many people were still living in little huts. It is here we have slowly begun our life and apostolate. Here we have now:

THE BROTHERS' HOUSE: the Brothers of the Missionaries of Charity Contemplative were born here. Hence we have our Mother House and Generalate since Monday 19th March 1979.

THE HOLY FAMILY CHAPEL. **We have recently found** out from the city offices (Catasto) that our chapel belongs to the Holy See. As we have notified to the A.P.S.A., in the Vatican, they gave the chapel for our free use. It is in this chapel we hold our perpetual adoration of the Blessed Sacrament.

CASA SERENA: This is our night shelter for about 80 homeless older men above 50 years of age, who are being served with breakfast and an evening meal. All the basic needs, including medical care, are met. We depend entirely on divine providence, and all our services are to be offered not only freely, but also wholeheartedly and joyfully.

THE INTERNATIONAL CENTRE OF THE LAY MISSIONARIES OF CHARITY - (LMC): the Movement of the Lay Missionaries of Charity began here on Monday in Holy Week, 16th April 1984, with four married people--two women and two men--in the presence of Blessed Teresa of Kolkata and Fr. Sebastian Vazhakala, its founder. With God's help and blessing the Movement has spread into more than 50 countries of the world. From 14 to 25th April 2009 we shall have the silver Jubilee and General Assembly, retreats and Jubilee celebrations in Rome. About 400 participants from 53 countries of the world are expected to participate in the event. We have already had three previous International meetings--two in Rome and one in Lourdes. We want to extend a warm welcome to all our LMCs of the world for the Jubilee in April 2009. Let us pray much for the success and fruitfulness of our Jubilee celebrations that they may become profound spiritual experiences.

WHAT REMAINS TO BE DONE.

Casa Serena is practically full all the time, especially during the winter period, and every day there are several requests and enquiries for a bed and a meal. We are preparing a new project for an additional place. We need two things: the required permission to build, and the funds to do so. Both look now, humanly speaking, impossible. So we have to pray much and work harder.

MY GRATITUDE TO ALL.

I would like to express my sincere gratitude to every person, to the Mayor of Rome for choosing me, the least among all and the most unworthy person upon whom to confer the "Peace award". I have accepted it for the glory of God and the good of the poorest of the poor, of those who suffer in body, mind and soul, those who feel rejected, and above all those who do not have peace of mind and joy of heart. But then, there is another side of the reality, that my life, without the help and support of my Brothers, the Lay Missionaries of Charity, the numberless co-workers, volunteers, benefactors, our M.C. Sisters and our poor people themselves, would be impossible. For me these recognitions, awards, etc. are signs that our life and our work are God's, not ours. It is he who has called us to be his light; it is he who wants us to be the channels of his peace: *"Lord make me a channel of your peace".*

THE POOR WILL ALWAYS BE WITH US.

Jesus said to Blessed Teresa back in 1947: *"I have absolutely no one for my very poor..."* (cf. MFG pg. 18) Many people in various places are trying to eradicate poverty and misery, but as long as there is terrorism, there is war and other destructive weapons around, the poverty and misery will only increase. The only weapon that can eradicate poverty and misery from the face of the earth is invincible love. Love alone can conquer even our enemies and make them our friends. *"Only in heaven we will see how much we owe to the poor for helping us to love God better because of them."* (Blessed Teresa M.C.)

I AM NOT WORTHY TO SERVE THE POOR.

Personally, I feel unworthy to serve the poor. For this we pray each day: *"Make us worthy Lord, to serve our fellowmen throughout the world, who live and die in poverty and hunger. Give them this day their daily bread and by our understanding love, give peace and joy".*

Our gratitude to each one of you is our assiduous prayer and our effort to remain faithful to our vocation. I would like to request your prayers for us that we may in no way spoil God's work; your cooperation and sharing in love and peace are our strength and our joy.

Before I close these reflections and facts I would like to extend to each individual reader a very happy and holy Christmas and peace-filled New Year 2009.

God bless you.
Fr. Sebastian Vazhakala M.C.

Pentecost 2009

**"Linger not on the way, stray not from your aim,
always strive, always move, always advance." (St. Augustine)**

Dearly beloved Brothers, Sisters and all,

May the grace and peace of this holy season of Easter and the feast of Pentecost be with you. We are all eagerly and prayerfully waiting in the upper room with Our Lady, like the Apostles, to receive the promised Holy Spirit on Pentecost Sunday, which falls this year on 31st May (09). The more we pray to the Holy Spirit the better it is. He is the sanctifier. It is worth becoming slaves of the Holy Spirit so that all our thoughts, words and works may always be holy.

Thank you for your prayers. The retreat in Haiti went quite well. Thanks be to God. There were 22 Sisters plus the Regional Sr. Jacinta M.C.; the community Sisters joined the Holy Mass and the afternoon conference. They were happy and grateful as usual.

Haiti is a very beautiful country. It is very tropical, with plenty of rain. All the tropical fruits can be found in abundance, especially mangoes and bananas, all through the year.

The M.C. Sisters have 9 houses in Haiti alone. They have been there since 1979, if I am not mistaken. They are doing beautiful work with the poorest of the poor, even risking their lives. One of the Superiors, Sr. Abha M.C, in one of the communities was shot by the thieves; thanks be to God, she didn't die. She has been there since the very beginning.

The poverty of the poor is beyond any description. There is moral degradation beyond one's imagination. It is an accumulation of human misery reduced to the lowest level. How can human beings come to live in this manner, I wonder? Abortion is not legalized, thanks be to God. It is so common to see teenage girls ranging from 14 years old with babies in their arms. I anointed a woman of about 28 who died on the same day, leaving her seven children behind, the oldest of which is about 14. They have no father(s) with them either, as they are step brothers and sisters. This kind of case is very common in Haiti, and our Sisters try their best to do all that they can to help them. Not even in Kolkata (India) have I seen such suffering, poverty and misery. M.C. Sisters are really doing a great work!

Our M.C. Brothers too have two communities in Port-au-Prince; one is their noviciate, the other one is a home for men and women suffering from TB, AIDS, etc.

I was also very happy to meet one of my old friends and brother, Michael from U.S.A., who runs several homes for boys in Haiti. It had been 31 years since we had seen each other. What a joyful and wonderful meeting it was! We recalled our life together and apostolate among the poor in Los Angeles with much joy and gratitude.

Another terrible evil that afflicts the Haitian people is their devil worship through black magic, witchcraft, etc. It is a very common, accepted custom, which continually corrupts the moral lives of the people, from birth to death. This satanic cult is a cause of much suffering in the sacred and Eucharistic heart of Jesus. We have to offer much prayer and make many sacrifices, and above all many hours of Eucharistic adoration.

Haiti is often hit by natural calamities such as storms, cyclones, hurricane, etc. The Lord wants to save his people in many different ways, but it is very hard for him, as He does not force anybody but respects the gift of freedom to choose, determine and decide.

The island is divided into two countries: Dominican Republic and Haiti. The M.C. Sisters are in both countries, but they only have three houses in the Dominican Republic, while there are 9 in Haiti, although the latter is much smaller in size and population.

What I generally feel is that the poverty of India is more material, at least in comparison with this kind of poverty of the poor, which is both, material and spiritual. There is much work to be done everywhere: "Ora et Labora" with much "poenitentia" is needed. We are in need of more and more prayer, penance and works of mercy to overcome the works of the evil one. The road to heaven is rough and narrow and few there are who would like to travel on it willingly.

Thank you, Brothers and Sisters, for all that you are and all that you do for the Lord. The things we do can be very small and insignificant, but they become great and infinite because of the love we put in our doing. In the words of Blessed Teresa M.C. whose teaching makes it clear:

"To the good God nothing is little because he is so great and we are so small – that is why He stoops down and takes the trouble to make those little things for us – to give us the chance to prove our love for Him. Because He makes them, they are very great. He cannot make anything small; they are infinite. Yes, my dear children, be faithful in little practices of love, of little sacrifices, of the little interior mortifications, of little fidelities to Rule, which will build in you the life of holiness – make you Christ-like." (Blessed Teresa's instructions to M.C.s, Nov. 1960)

It is God's work we do. It can be compared to a fan or a bulb. In order that the fan may move to give cool breeze, it requires electricity. It is electricity that moves the fan. It is electricity that shines through a bulb. If electricity is not there, the fan is useless and the bulb as well. We are like the fan, like the bulb. The invisible grace of God works in and through us like the invisible electricity. The invisible God breathes into us his very breath of love and grace and so that we are alive and are able to do his work with love. The little host we receive in Holy Communion is the secret to our strength to do God's work, for we know that without Holy Mass and Holy Communion we cannot do his work. For

"If we have our Lord in the midst of us, with daily Mass and holy Communion I fear nothing for the Sisters, nor for myself. He will look after us. But without him I cannot be, I am helpless." (Blessed Teresa, Corpus Domini 1947) Another time she writes:

"… The work we will have to do will be impossible without his continual grace from the tabernacle. He will have to do everything. We have only to follow." (ibid., Jan. 1948)

The purchase of the land in Rome is still facing difficulties. We have overcome so may obstacles already, one after another, each of which demands time, patience and money. Right now the problem we are facing is the cost of the buildings. We have to pay a certain percentage of the exact price of the buildings. We are trying to find an architect to do the work for us. Please do pray much.

Our perpetual adoration is a great source of strength, though it can be quite difficult and demanding at times. Precisely because it is difficult and very demanding, it also becomes a source of grace not only for our communities and for our Society, but for the LMCs, for the M.C. Family, for the whole Church and the world. *"Let our adoration never stop."* (Pope John Paul II)

St. Peter Julian Eymard, the apostle of the Eucharistic adoration, writes: *"Go to your adoration as one who would go to heaven, to the divine banquet. Tell yourself: 'In four hours, in two hours, in one hour, our Lord will give us an abundance of grace and love. He has invited me, he is waiting for me; he is longing for me.'* "

My trip to Haiti was via Miami,-Florida, where on my way to Haiti and the way back I met with our M.C. Sisters and the group of the LMCs, who really went out of their way to make me feel very comfortable. They put me in a food room where there were all kinds of truck loads of food stuff and soft drinks. Both times I slept in that room. They knew that I was on my way to and way back from Haiti and I needed to recuperate. How can I thank enough our M.C. Sisters of our Lady of Alta Gracia region enough for their warm welcome and generous hospitality? Special thanks to Sr. Jacinta M.C., the Regional Superior, Sr. Anthony Mary Claret M.C. who took so much care of me, the Superiors of Delmas, Jacmel, Miami and others. I was also very happy to travel back from Port-au-Prince to Miami with two of our old friends: Sr. Mahima M.C. and Sr. Carmen M.C., who periodically help us with some good vocations.

It was so wonderful to meet with our M.C. Sisters, LMCs and co-workers in Miami and talk to them and have Holy Mass with and for them. Once again it renewed and brought to memory many of the LMCs and others with whom we had retreat in Miami in 2001 and then recently in Rome for the LMC Jubilee celebrations.

I was able to explain at our meeting in Miami the meaning of the word "Miami" in Italian and Spanish. Jesus asked St. Peter three times: "Simon, son of John, do you love me more than these?"... and in Italian: "Simone di Giovanni MI AMI tu più di costoro?". "Mi ami?" – Do you love me? St. Peter answered: "Lord, you know that I love you." (Jn 21: 15) I also knew that the M.C. Sisters, the LMCs and co-workers of Miami really love Jesus and love Jesus in all those whom they meet and with whom they live, and my meeting with them in Miami confirmed that they really do.

Before I conclude this letter let me wish each and every one of you Brothers and Sisters a very happy and holy feast of Pentecost. As he, the Holy Spirit, transformed the hearts and lives of the apostles, so He may also do the same with each one of us, giving all the necessary gifts to grow in holiness and persevere in our beautiful vocation.

Please remember me in your prayer for my next mission to Kigali, Rwanda from 13th to 24th June 2009. Love and prayers.

God bless you.

Fr. Sebastian Vazhakala M.C.

CHAPTER THREE:
GIVING THANKS

ANNUAL THANKSGIVING
AMAZING GRACE – 1996

Great Thanksgiving Day New Year 2007

For all the gifts, blessings and benefits; for all the opportunities we have had to love, serve and save souls.

For protecting us from dangers, from great falls, from the loss of faith, hope and Charity.

For guiding us, leading us and guarding us.

For taking care of us, looking after us.

For our Lay Missionaries of Charity.

For sending us many helpers, volunteers, benefactors, the poorest of the poor.

For giving us the opportunity to make more sacrifices, to pray more fervently, to smile and accept and love people whom we may not have liked, to accept and serve people in whom we met Jesus and loved him and served.

For the Word of God and the Bread of Life, for the Holy Mass, for all the prayers, hours of adoration, the rosary, the Stations of the Cross, all our spiritual exercises.

For our Brothers, for our Society, for the Brothers who have helped us to grow in holiness, for the good example we gave and received.

For the suffering and pain we are able to endure and were able to use as a means for the salvation and sanctification of souls.

For all the inspirations to do good.

For so many of God's graces and blessings...*Please go on listing them......*

Great Reparation Day

For all the gifts and blessings that were wasted or not used properly, fully and solely for God's glory.

For being selfish instead of selfless; for being self-centered instead of Christ-centered.

For not seeking help and guidance.

For not being grateful enough to God for all the benefits, for neglecting the poor, for not thinking about the salvation of the poor.

For not guiding them, for not helping them to love Jesus, Mary and Joseph, the saints and the Church; for not preparing them for the worthy reception of the sacraments.

For wasting time, energy and talents.

For being moody, sad and refusing to co-operate with my brothers.

For not contemplating and not seeing and recognizing the presence of Jesus in each other, not adoring Jesus in each other, not adoring Jesus, not only in the Eucharist, but in loving and adoring him in my Brothers and in the persons of the poor.

For attracting people to ourselves and not to God, and for not glorifying God enough.

For all grace and blessings not accepted or simply wasted.

For so many failures, shortcomings, negligence...for not helping the Brothers to grow in holiness and to persevere in their vocation.

For discouraging instead of encouraging by words and actions, especially by bad example.

For not learning from the good example, but following more the bad one.

For not observing and practicing the vows of poverty, chastity, obedience and wholehearted free service to the poorest of the poor.

For missing community functions or being late. For not making up missed prayers, etc., etc.

For not praying for and making sacrifices for vocations, nor for the perseverance of those who accept a vocation.

Happy New Year.

God bless you.

Father Sebastian Vazhakala, M.C.

Amazing Grace

April, 1996

Dear Brothers and Sisters,

Thanks so much to each one of you for your prayerful, seasonal greetings and wishes with your generous gift of love so kindly sent. All of them meant much to us and made us feel that we all belong to the same family of God. We are very fortunate to be the children of God the Father and so brothers and sisters in Jesus Christ, the beloved Son of the eternal Father. Thanks be to His great love and grace.

Mrs. Ann Blaikie spoke of building a little hermitage - a postinia - in via S. Agapito, 8 overlooking Rome so that one can periodically withdraw into solitude. Somehow we all feel the need of a deeper solitude and aloneness with God more than ever in this noisy world of ours with such hectic activities. Let us try to build a little hermitage if not outside at least deep within our hearts. But if we can have both so much the better.

It was so good to know that you all did have a very beautiful Christmas. With you I thank God and for you I pray. I pray that you may continue to recognise His coming in the least little things of daily life, in the persons you live with, in the persons of the poor, in the meditative reading of the Word of God, in the reception of the sacraments and in... so that the Christmas may not be limited to one day a year but to all through the year. Every time one is able to see the coming of Christ in some form, it is Christmas for him!

Christmas is essentially a time of sharing. Visiting one our friends during Christmas made aware of it even more deeply. Sergio a 49 years old man. He told me that for him Christmas is yet to come. Ten years ago Sergio met with an accident which made him partially blind, crippled and disfigured. To most of us Christmas means sending cards and letters., greeting friends and people. The general mood is one of sharing and celebration. Our telephones are more busy, too. Poor Sergio had none of these. So he is right; he did not have a Christmas as most of us have had. It made me think and be thankful at the same time; for I am so fortunate to have so many friends, not to speak of my own good Brothers. We are able to pray together, to celebrate the Eucharist together, to greet one another etc...etc... It made me think of another truth, namely that how many Sergios there are who are deprived of Christmas joy and celebration. What can and should 'I' do?.

Many of you have asked me about how we were and how Christmas was for us. Well, we are a community of six Brothers coming from different countries: Br. Piet (Holland), Br. John Marie (Sweden), Br. Martin of the Cross (Austria), Br. Brian (Canada), Br. Francesco (Italy) and Br. Sebastian (India). Two of us are already priests, two are taking courses in theology and the other two are in formation. As we are Missionaries of the Word we devote ourselves to <u>prayer</u> and <u>Ministry of the Word</u>; thus to quench the infinite thirst of Jesus on the Cross for love of souls (Mother Teresa) through the profession of the evangelical counsels and through the additional vow of whole-hearted and free service to the poorest of the poor. Besides our intense life of prayer and living of the Word of God in a life marked by the poverty, humility, joy and freedom of the Gospel, the Brothers go out to the spiritually poorest of the poor to proclaim the Word of God by our presence, the spiritual works of mercy and by our priestly ministry when opportunity offers. Ours is a contemplative, apostolic and missionary vocation.

On Christmas eve the Brothers went to one of the prisons in Rome where we go regularly for Sunday celebration of the Eucharist, Adoration of the Blessed Sacrament, confession, counselling etc...This time the good novices of the Sisters of the Missionaries of Charity put up a Christmas show followed by the celebration of the Eucharist. The people's eyes were filled as they were separated from their homes and homelands. For many Christmas meant more sorrow than joy. All of us tried our best to make everybody happy, a little happier by sharing all we had - joy and peace, giving of gifts and carol singing. At the end all looked happier and went in peace and joy, praising God.

The Brothers also visit the sick and lonely people, especially the abandoned sick ones. Even if it not possible for us to do much for them and with them, it is vitally important to listen to them when possible and pray for them if they are found not yet ready. Since the sick lying on the bed are Christ for us, the meeting is sacramental and salvific as we are sent by the Lord to him or them to be their brother. Giovanna, for example, was a 90 years old woman, left alone in one of the hospitals in Rome to die a lonely death. Until five years ago Giovanna went to Church almost everyday. And then she was confined to bed. All her people practically abandoned her. It was a Thursday afternoon when I first came in contact with Giovanna. Over an hour I listened to her bitter complaints and curses, which was so necessary as she was in such desperate condition. Though she refused to pray, at the end she gently responded to the blessing that I gave on my leaving. On my way back I thought of the people in the home for the dying in Calcutta. There the poor starve to death for want of material food, here on the contrary they starve to death for want of spiritual nourishment. Giovanna had almost come to that stage; she had lost the taste for spiritual food. But then the grace of God comes to compliment where the humans fail.

The Brothers decided to pray very intensively for Giovanna. So we did especially during our night adoration and Friday (every Friday we have adoration all day long). On Saturday afternoon I visited her again taking the Blessed Sacrament along with me. She began her story all over again. Sitting near her bed, I began to pray silently for a while. After some time I began to pray the Hail Mary very slowly and, to my surprise, I found her praying with me. She went on praying for a while, saying all the prayers she could possibly remember, at the end of which she made her confession, received communion and was very happy. She also took my rosary. Giovanna was now ready and set for her long journey. On the following Wednesday, Giovanna left this valley of tears for her eternal home. Two weeks later in the same bed another lady - Maria Rosa - died in the presence of the Brothers. That bed seems to be meant for the abandoned sick people to die their peaceful deaths! Let us bless the Lord for His loving kindness.

Each one of us has a considerably lengthy story to tell provided there are people to listen to us with interest. Giovanna, Maria Rosa, Sergio and many others have their painful stories. At the end it always seems to me to be the story of the amazing Grace and we could all easily sing:

"Amazing grace, how sweet the sound
that saved a wretch like me...
Through many dangers, toils and snares
I have already come.
It's grace that brought me thus far
and grace will lead me home".

This is true of individuals, married couples, religious communities, families and groups. It is always the same story of the *amazing grace* which is so actively and miraculously at work in each one of us.

Very often the people who come to visit us for the first time like to see our TV room. With great joy I take them to our Chapel. For us the tabernacle takes the place of the TV. How little time is spent before Jesus in the Blessed Sacrament even by us religious, when we compare the amount of time an average person of today spends before a TV? *"Jesus wais for us in this Sacrament of love. Let us be generous with our time in going to meet Him in adoration and in contemplation that is full of faith and ready to make reparation for the great faults and crimes of the world. May our adoration never cease"* (John Paul II).

Once again I very sincerely would like to thank you and thank God for you for all your help, support and encouragement and wish you many of God's choicest blessings. Let us remember each other and all in our prayer, so that Jesus may become more and more visible to the world through us, that He may be loved and accepted by all. Prayer is our strength. Imagine a fish trying to live outside the water. As soon as it is out of the water, it is insecure and will not live long, no matter how long it has been in the water. If water is a means for the survival of the fish, for us it is prayer. Remaining faithful to our life of prayer and work of love, let us continue to spread the fragrance of His love and peace among all men of good will and especially among the poorest of the poor, sick and abandoned.

Love and prayers.

Fr. Sebastian Vazhakala M.C.

St. Peter's Basilica Rome 2007

02.06.2007

25th Jubilee Planning Committee Rome 2007

Blessing of the Contemplative Brothers' convent by Cardinal Ugo Poletti 1984

Blessed Teresa M.C. and Fr. Sebastian M.C. in Kolkata 1990

Inauguration of Casa Serena with Blessed Teresa M.C. and
Archbishop Giuseppe Mani 1993

Blessing of Deepashram by Archbishop Vincent Concessao 1995

Blessed Teresa M.C. and Archbishop Vincent Concessao at Deepashram inauguration 1995

Fr. Sebastian M.C.'s family in St. Peter's Basilica in Rome for the Jubilee Mass of the Holy Father 1996

25th Jubilee Planning Committee in Chapel at Casa Serena Rome 2007

At the tomb of Blessed Teresa M.C. in Kolkata

Inauguration of Bethel with Fr. Sebastian and the Mayor of Bushat in the presence of Archbishop Angelo Massafra of Shkodra, Albania 2006

Blessing of Casa Serena by Cardinal Camillo Ruini

Brother Andrew, M.C.

Cardinal Angleo Comastri with our poor people and some friends.

Fr. Sebastian M.C. adoration of the Holy Eucharist in Casa Serena Chapel.

25th Jubilee Celebration Cultural Night in Rome 2009

Fr. Sebasian M.C. at Casa Serena beginnings

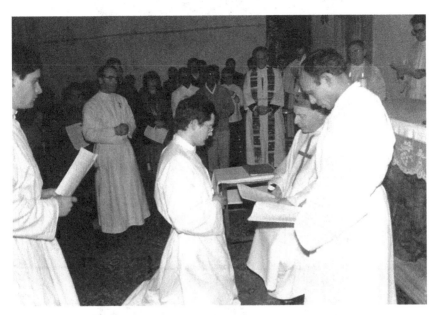

First profession of Brother Andre Marie, M.C.

Fr. Sebastian M.C. with his brothers and sisters

Fr. Sebastian M.C. with his mother and father

Fr. Sebastian M.C. with MC Sisters in Lima, Peru 2008

LMC 25th Jubilee Celebration Rome 2009

Give whatever He takes and take whatever He gives……with a smile.

...more smiles.

Blessed Teresa M.C. and Fr. Sebastian M.C. in the
Chapel of the Holy Family in Via S Agapito

The funeral carriage with body of Blessed Teresa M.C. 1997

Via Dolorosa in the Holy Land Pilgrimage 1999

CHAPTER FOUR: GRATEFUL MEMORIES

Remembering the past with gratitude

Solemnity of the Most Holy Trinity 2008

This letter is an attempt to remember the past with gratitude to the triune God, Father, Son and Holy Spirit and with purified memories. It is also an attempt to thank God for the numberless people whom two of us, Br. Damien M.C. and Fr. Sebastian M.C., in the very first group of M.C. men, have met, walked with, or walked by, worked for and worked with over 40 years. We want to express our sincere thanks to God in the first place for choosing us, though unworthy, weak and sinful, to work with Blessed Mother Teresa M.C. for the cause of the poorest of the poor. With her and in her footsteps we have fed the hungry crowd, gave water to the thirsty ones, clothed the naked ones, sheltered the homeless, consoled the sick, and visited the prisoners. We feel duty bound not only to remember the past with gratitude to God, but also to invite all people of good will, especially all the members of our M.C. Family, to join us in expressing our gratitude through prayer, especially the celebration of the most holy Eucharist, which in itself is a great act of thanksgiving.

This letter, then, is going to be very personal, and therefore I apologize if some readers find it tedious or boring. Although two of us are involved in this spiritual saga, I focus mainly on my story, leaving the space and the opportunity to Br. Damien M.C. to speak for himself, as he is of age and experience.

On Monday 2nd June, 2008 Br. Damien M.C. and I complete forty years of our first religious profession in the Society of the Missionary Brothers of Charity. We are the only surviving men from the first group of six Brothers who took vows on Pentecost Sunday, 2nd June, 1968. One of the six was Br. Andrew M.C., the co-founder of the active M.C. Brothers, who eventually became an itinerant preacher, and finally died of cancer in our M.C. Sisters' home in Melbourne, Australia, on Friday 4th October, 2002.

It was on the feast of the Sacred Heart, 2nd June, 1967, that twelve of us Brothers, together with Br. Andrew, began our historic noviciate at 7 Mansatala Row, Kidderpore, Kolkata. Br. Andrew was himself a novice, Superior of the house, Superior General of the new-born Society, its Co-founder and Novice Master. I still remember, after the Holy Mass, kneeling in a semicircle around the little altar at 7 Mansatala Row, Kidderpore, on the first Friday morning and the feast of the Sacred Heart that year, to be blessed by Br. Andrew, which then marked the beginning of the very first group of twelve novices and the men's noviciate.

One afternoon, in the month of April, 1968 I picked up a dying man from the street and brought him to Nirmal Hriday, Kalighat. Blessed Teresa M.C. was there. After doing the necessary nursing, including his bath, change of clothes, medicine, food, etc., Blessed Teresa and I started talking casually. She asked me how the Brothers were, and then said: "You know, Br. Sebastian, that six of the Brothers are going to make their first vows on Pentecost Sunday 2nd June (1968)." I told her that I did not know anything about it. She pursued and said: "Br. Sebastian, why don't you ask Br. Andrew the possibility of including you in the group of those six Brothers?" She told me to pray about it and then try to talk with Br. Andrew, which I then did one afternoon.

Br. Andrew said that the Archbishop of Kolkata, Rt. Rev. Albert D'Souza, had already granted permission for the six Brothers to make their vows after one year of noviciate. He said that he had never thought of including me at that time, but that he would speak with the Archbishop about it. After about two weeks Br. Andrew told me that the Archbishop had happily granted the indult to make my profession with the other six after one year of noviciate. My heart was filled with gratitude to God for his enduring love, to Blessed Teresa M.C. for her tender care and thoughtfulness, and to Br. Andrew for taking the trouble to get the necessary permission.

Although there were seven of us, including Br. Andrew, to make our vows, and although all of us made all the preparations for it, including the eight-day retreat under the wise guidance of Fr. Mathew Schillings S.J., in the early hours of the morning of Pentecost Sunday 2nd June, 1968, there were suddenly only six of us. The one and only first Brother, who had persevered until that day, decided the night of the profession not to make it. This was Br. Joseph Michael, who was one of the first group of the Pious Union since 25th March, 1963 to 2nd June, 1968. Strangely enough, he had been my inspiration and example. God's ways are mysterious: *"Who knows the mind of the Lord, who has been his counsellor…"* (cf. Rom 11: 33 ff.)

We six Brothers took our vows on Pentecost Sunday 2nd June, 1968: Br. Andrew M.C. (R.I.P.) took his final vows in the hands of Msgr. Eric Barber, the Vicar General for the Archdiocese of Kolkata. The other five of us, Br. Aloysius M.C., Br. Damien M.C., Br. George M.C., Br. Benedict M.C. and Br. Sebastian M.C., took vows for three years in the hands of Br. Andrew M.C. Among the six, just two of us, Br. Damien M.C. and Fr. Sebastian M.C., remain. The rest have left the Society for one reason or another. Br. Damien M.C. and Fr. Sebastian M.C. complete forty years of their first profession on Monday 2nd June 2008; the latter still has the card signed by Br. Andrew M.C. for the occasion where one can easily see the exact date of their first profession.

That day was historical for the M.C. men's world as the very first group of men added the two letters M.C. to their names, which can mean Martyrs of Charity, Ministers of Charity, Masters of Charity or Missionaries of Charity. Whatever the first word, "Charity" is the central and vital part of our graduation. It means much more now than what it meant for me then.

We have much to thank God for. Our life has been the story of the amazing grace. The Lord has led us through fire and flood. The water has not drowned us so far, nor has the fire burnt us to death yet. (cf. Is. 43: 2-3) We would then like to invite all of you to thank God with us, while asking you to remember us in your prayers, particularly on that day. We would like to have a thanksgiving celebration this year, as we are not sure that we will live to celebrate the golden jubilee of our first religious profession. We would have liked to celebrate it at our Mother's tomb in Kolkata, as she was present for that first and historic profession day. Six years later, on Pentecost Sunday, 2nd June Br. Damien M.C. and I made our final vows. Blessed Teresa M.C. was not in Kolkata at that time. She sent a card with Sr. Agnes M.C. signed by her: *"Let the Holy Spirit guide you."*

As human beings we live in time and history. We are being inserted into the history, as we all have our past as an integral part of our life, good or bad, painful or pleasant, sad or happy. As we know well, today was the tomorrow of yesterday, today is going to be the yesterday of tomorrow, and tomorrow becomes today. Each day has its own possibilities to do good and to try to live the present more enthusiastically.

I would like to go as far back as to March, 1966, when I heard Blessed Teresa speak to the staff and students of St. Albert College, Ranchi, Jarkand, India. Her words became words of confrontation, clarity, confirmation and decision for me. They were simple words, but profound and true because they were words from the gospel translated into life of loving service. Those words remained impressed into me because they were transparent and penetrating, sharper than a two-edged sword. (cf. Heb 4: 12)

What did Blessed Teresa say that evening to the staff and students of St. Albert's College, Ranchi? Here I can only quote some of her words from memory. She spoke of her life and her work. She emphasized the importance of serving not only poor, but the poorest of the poor, who are Jesus under disguise. She spoke of our duty to recognize the existence of the poor, to protect and defend their rights, as they have their unalienable right to live their lives with dignity, like any one of us has the right. She spoke of the value and importance of each person for whom Jesus shed his precious blood. Jesus made no distinctions when he spoke of the last judgment. He is not going to judge people according to caste, colour, religion or country. He simply said: *"I was hungry, you gave me to eat, I was thirsty, you gave me to drink, I was naked, you clothed me, I was a stranger, and you welcomed me, sick and in prison and you visited me. As long as you did to one of the least of my brethren you did it to me."* Yes, whatever we do to the least of our brethren, we do it to Jesus. (cf. Mt 25: 31-46) Jesus makes himself the Bread of Life for us to eat and to be nourished and strengthened in spirit; he makes himself present in the hungry and the naked, in the lepers and the sick ones to be loved and served. Blessed Teresa said that Jesus made our life on earth simple and great. He gives us the chance to do simple things with great love. To give a cup of cold water is a very simple thing; but, when we do it with love, that little giving becomes an act of love divine. (cf. Mt 10: 42) She gave the example of St. Thérèse of Lisieux, who was canonized not for doing great things, but doing little things with great love. She said: *"I will do ordinary things with extraordinary love."* She spoke of a little group of men who were in existence in Kolkata, India, who would be doing the same kind of work as the Sisters were doing.

Blessed Teresa continued to speak about the new branch of men: the Brothers' group began on 25th March, 1963 in Kolkata with five young men, three of whom were blood brothers. But now, just this last month (19th February, 1966), Br. Andrew, whom some of you knew as Fr. Ian Travers Ball S.J., has joined the little group of Brothers and changed his name to Br. Andrew. He is fully in charge now. There are just about ten or so young men. They are still a Pious Union, as there are only ten, and we need at least twelve to become a diocesan religious Congregation. We are praying much to our Lady and St. Joseph for more vocations. They will come and in time we will become a Congregation; you also pray for the Brothers and for our poor people.

Blessed Teresa's presence and her words, her serene face and penetrating look, her joy, her assurance and her conviction, touched many of the listeners and elicited, at least in some of us, a real desire to live the gospel of love in action. Her life for me was a living exegesis of Jesus' words: *"As you did to one of the least of my brothers, you did it to me."* (Mt 25: 40) I could no longer be indifferent, nor could I go on studying in a comfortable setting when Jesus was hungry, thirsty, naked, homeless, sick and imprisoned in the poorest of the poor. I felt that it was Jesus who sent her to talk to us, and to me in particular ,as I had been in search of a more radical and religious vocation. In Blessed Teresa M.C. that evening I felt I had at last found my vocation.

That night for me was too long. I could not wait to speak to my spiritual director, Fr. Leo Donelly S.J. of happy memory, who advised me as I met him the following morning after Holy Mass, to complete my philosophical studies. It was a big sacrifice for me to wait; but then the words of the Scriptures came to illumine me and I heard the whispering sound: *"Truly, obedience is better than sacrifice, submissiveness is better than rams"*. (1 Sam 15: 22) Today, looking back, I see the wisdom of his direction. If I had not obeyed him without question then, today I could have been very sorry. My human nature, my feelings and emotions were stirred and I wanted to fly on my wings to Kolkata; instead I accepted his advice, reflected continuously the words of Blessed Teresa, and waited for the day and the hour, while fully involving myself with my studies.

And then came the day. Saturday 26th November, 1966, I got permission from my Superiors – rector, spiritual director and all concerned – to go to the Brothers in Kolkata and stay with them for a few days on my way home to Kerala for vacation. Br. Andrew knew of my desire as Fr. Leo Donelly SJ was in touch with him. So I travelled the whole night by train from Ranchi and reached Kolkata early morning on Sunday 27th November, 1966.

Br. Andrew and the community were in prayer. They had just started the Holy Mass. The Brothers were also celebrating Br. Andrew's feast day on that day, as he was going to be away in Delhi on the following day. But during breakfast Blessed Teresa M.C. called and told that the idea of the Brothers moving to Delhi was no longer possible, as the place they were supposed to get had been cancelled.

It was my first meeting with Br. Andrew and the tiny little group of Brothers, who were still a Pious Union in the archdiocese of Kolkata. They had then no house of their own, no real canonical status, and no financial resources. They totally depended on Blessed Teresa M.C. and the M.C. Sisters for everything.

I met Blessed Teresa for the first time on Wednesday 30th November, 1966 in the Mother House parlour. That meeting with her was positive and challenging. She explained to me about the life and the work of the Missionaries of Charity, particularly about the Brothers. I told her that I was very interested in doing social work. She straight away told me that the work with and for the poor was not social work but God's work. For me it did not make much difference then, but now I fully understand her words. I also told her that I would like to join the Brothers and also to continue with my studies for priesthood. She was very pleased with my proposals and plan. She, as well as Br. Andrew, told me that there would be no difference in the status between the priests and the simple Brothers, except when the priest Brothers administer the sacraments.

My days with the Brothers were few, but extremely intense and interesting. I still remember the day. Br. Andrew sent me to Howrah railway station, along with Br. James, to work in the apostolate among the railway station boys, who used to run away from homes or were sent by the parents to beg, to steal, or do some odd jobs. They were often beaten up by the police. The brothers used to gather them in groups to render whatever kind of help they could give.

I went home for my one month holiday and then returned to St. Albert's College to continue with my studies, which I liked very much. However, I also felt drawn by the experience of simplicity and poverty… the direct contact with the many and varied victims of poverty, pain and diseases. So I spoke at length with my spiritual director, who was very wise and far-sighted. He told me that I should complete my studies and then go to the Brothers. With his help, however, I got a very special permission to go to Kolkata during Holy Week that year. In the meantime, Br. Andrew had come to St. Albert's to meet with me and Fr. Leo Donelly S.J., whom he knew very well. That visit helped me to get permission to go to Kolkata for Holy Week, which that year was early. I reached Kolkata on Wednesday in Holy Week, 22 March, 1967, and became a formal member of the Brothers on the following day, which was Holy Thursday that year.

The other coincidence was the visit of the Archbishop, his Excellency Rt. Rev. Albert D'Souza, in the evening of the same day of my arrival, who brought the good news that the Pious Union of the Missionary Brothers of Charity of Kolkata had become a diocesan religious Congregation. On Easter Sunday, 26th March, 1967, the same Archbishop of Kolkata, with some of the members of the diocesan curia, arrived at 7 Mansatala Row, Kolkata. Blessed Teresa M.C. and some of the senior Sisters with great joy appeared with their ambulance. It was like a new Pentecost for the little group before the liturgical feast of Pentecost. It was about 4.00 p.m. in the afternoon when we all gathered in the little Chapel to thank God. The Archbishop read the decree of erection and praised God and thanked him. We all sang the *Te Deum*. "You are God: we praise you, you are the Lord: we acclaim you…" Mother was overjoyed. There were no professed M.C. Brothers yet, not even novices, no proper constitutions. Br. Andrew, who was now in-charge of the new group, was asked to make a year of noviciate before he made his final vows in the new-born Society as he was under exclaustration.

All of us sat around the table. All were overjoyed, Blessed Teresa M.C. and the Sisters filled us with their prayerful greetings: *"Now you too are like us,"* Blessed Teresa said. *"You, too are a religious congregation. You are Diocesan; we are Pontifical. You are under the Bishop; we are under the Pope. One day you, too, will be like us, Pontifical, if you remain faithful and persevere in your vocation. Nothing and nobody should separate you from the love of Christ. We were like you when we became a Congregation on 7th October, 1950. We were thirteen. You too are thirteen… Br. Andrew and you twelve Brothers. Now you have to begin the noviciate soon. Let us pray much and also pray for Mother. All right."*

The Catholic Herald of Kolkata proclaimed the following week about the baptism of the new Congregation. Its title was: "God's Gift to Calcutta's Poor" by Br. Andrew.

Today I am still an M.C. because of the mercy of God, but my M.C. life must continue to bloom in the fertile soil of love. In me and around me there should not be anything but love. My M.C. life and ministry must be nothing but the fruit of my intimate and uninterrupted union with the source and fountain of this enduring love: the holy and most undivided trinity – Father, Son and Holy Spirit.

My M.C. life bloomed and continues to blossom in the soil and in the midst of a unique group of people, whom I consider very specially loved by God. They are the poorest of the poor, the weakest of the weak, the less than the least of all. I, too, am one like them and one of them, who is called to minister, to serve and guide them to God. To this end I pray and humbly ask the prayers of all.

God bless and reward all of you, my Brothers and Sisters.

Fr. Sebastian Vazhakala M.C.

The card signed by Br. Andrew M.C. for the first profession
A Meditation

By Cardinal Newman

GOD has created me to do Him some definite service; He has committed some work to me which He has not committed to another. I have my mission—I may never know it in this life, but I shall be told it in the next.

I am a link in a chain, a bond of connection between persons. He has not created me for naught. I shall do good, I shall do His work I shall be an angel of peace, a preacher of truth' in my own place while not intending it—if . do but keep His Commandments.

Therefore, I will trust Him. Whatever, wherever I am. I can never be thrown away. If I am in sickness, my sickness may serve Him; in perplexity, my perplexity may serve Him; if I am in so-row, my sorrow may serve Him. He does nothing in vain. He knows what He is about. He may take away my friends, He may throw me among strangers, He may make me feel desolate, make my spirits sink, hide my future from me—still He knows what He is about.

Wishing Sebastian all God's blessing on your Vow Day

Andrew M.c

2/6/65

Jubilee of Brother Piet M.C. 2004

On 4th April, 2004 Br. Piet Van Wanrooy completed 25 years of his first religious profession in the Family of the Missionaries of Charity. Since this year 4 April fell on Palm Sunday, we postponed the Jubilee celebration to Tuesday 13 April at our Holy family Church, Bushat, Shkodra (Abania). The following is the homily given by Fr. Sebastian M.C. during the Jubilee Mass, celebrated by Br. Piet, together with several other priest concelebrants, many women religious and the church full of lay people.

With you Br Piet, we thank God and for you we pray

We have come together on this chosen day to thank God for the last 25 years of your life as a religious Brother of the Missionaries of Charity of the Blessed Teresa of Kolkata. All these years your life has been the story of the "amazing grace", and you continue to sing all your life here on earth and in the world to come, "Amazing Grace how sweet the sound, that saved a wretch like me, I once was lost, but now I am found, was blind but now I see. It was grace that taught my heart to fear, and grace my fears relieved.... Through many dangers, toils and snares I have already come. It was grace that brought me safe thus far, and grace will lead me home." Yes, Br Piet, your life on earth then is the story of the amazing grace and you will continue to sing forever the eternal mercies of the Lord.

Mr. Petrus Johannes Engelbertus Maria Van Wanrooy was born in a little village called Kaatsheuvel in the south of Holland on Sunday the 2nd May, 1937. He was the third among seven children, two of whom went home to God in their infancy. For this reason Brother Piet was baptized on the very same day he was born.

Mr. Petrus's infancy and his early childhood were spent in the midst of shooting, bombing and killing; there was terrible fear and suspicion everywhere. The ages of two to eight were the war years, for World War II had broken out on 1st September, 1939 and ended only on the 6th August, 1945 with the bombing of Hiroshima and Nagasaki in Japan. Although the war ended, peace, security and prosperity were not immediately restored; the disastrous consequences continued. Practically the whole of Br Piet's childhood-adolescent years were terrible. Six million Jews were killed; many families lost their bread-winners. To grow up with such tragic a situation for an adolescent boy was very unhealthy. Fortunately, Br Piet's parents were devout and God- fearing Catholics who knew how to bring up their children and educate them in the Catholic faith. Not only did they teach their children by words, but above all by their good example in Charity, in practicing their faith. Their sweet home was the secure refuge for many Jews during the war. They often risked their lives in welcoming certain Jewish guests, as well as German, Scottish and Canadian soldiers. They went through many inconveniences. For Br Piet his home was a school of Charity, fraternal love, service and hospitality, which in later years he was able to express more convincingly, faithfully and more fully in the society of the Missionaries of Charity. How important to have good families, exemplary parents, edifying surroundings. They can be very poor materially, but can be very rich spiritually (i.e. practicing the virtues). Br Piet was very fortunate, then, to have such wonderful parents, brothers and sisters. He was 15 years old when his father died. His father's last words to him were: "Go first to Adoration, then you may go to watch football".

The family that prays together stays together. This too was true of Br Piet's family. They prayed together, every day at home as a family. Br Piet tells you and me today to remain faithful to our life of prayer, and to not give God the last place in our family, but the first place. We begin our day with God. How sad to often hear statements like "if I have time I will pray, I will go to Church, etc...."

After many years of working in a factory, Br. Piet began his military service, which lasted for 21 months. During this period several beautiful and good girls came around Mr. Petrus Van Wanrooy, some of whom were Protestants, but his mother did not want her beloved Catholic child to be married to a Protestant girl. It was not the question of Protestant or Catholic, but God had other plans for Mr. Petrus Van Wanrooy which he did not know then, but which God gradually unfolded to him. For Jesus had already looked at Br Piet with love and so kept his heart, mind and soul for himself and not for any other creature of this world. Years later, Br Piet could say: "Jesus, you alone are worthy of my love, you alone deserve my heart as you have looked at me with love and kept me for yourself". Today, after so many years of dangers, toils and snares Br Piet can continue to sing the song of the amazing grace.

Finishing his term of military service, Mr. Petrus van Wanrooy began to work in a shoe shop; and he did several other kinds of jobs. Then he went to a nursing school to get a diploma in nursing so that he could nurse the sick, the old, the widows, etc. During this period Mr. Piet came to Kolkata in May, 1974, and was a guest in our house for three weeks. I still remember so well his smiling face. He smiled all the time, even when he was sweating continually in the summer heat of Kolkata in the Brothers novitiate house at 7 Mansatala Row, Kidderpure. We couldn't talk with him much, as he could speak hardly any English. The time he was in Kolkata, he mostly went to work in the home for the homeless destitute people in Kalighat and in the leprosy centre in Titagarh.

After returning home, Br Piet completed his studies in nursing, obtained a diploma, and then shortly after decided to become a Missionary of Charity Brother. Accordingly Br Piet arrived in Los Angelus on 7th December, 1976 to be part of the Missionaries of Charity. The first thing he needed to learn was the English language, which he was able to acquire in six months' time. Br Piet began his novitiate on the 2nd June, 1977 in Los Angelus, where I was superior and novice Master. After a year of novitiate Br Andrew M.C., the then General Servant of the Missionary Brothers of Charity of Calcutta, asked Br Piet to go to Tokyo, Japan, where he made his first vows on 4th April, 1979 as a Missionary Brother of Charity. Today's Jubilee celebration is based on his very first profession he made in Tokyo.

Br. Piet, although extremely interested in helping the poor, firmly believed that he couldn't do it without a very deep and solid prayer life. He felt that he was called to lead a life of prayer, penance and works of mercy. Like a bird which cannot fly if both of its wings do not balance, so also the religious. God has given us the two commandments of the love of God and the love of our neighbour. We are asked to love God with all our heart, mind, soul and strength, and our neighbour as we love ourselves. With these two wings, like the bird we fly to God. In order to fly, the wings must balance. So Br Piet, realizing the importance of these two-fold inseparable commandments of love, decided to come to the newly founded Branch of the Missionaries of Charity-Contemplative of Via S Agapito, Rome. Accordingly, with due permission from his legitimate superiors, Br Piet arrived in Rome on 24th April, 1980. Since then Br Piet has served the little Contemplative branch in various places, capacities and times. He has been the Society's Vicar General, novice Master, house Superior and then since 2nd February, 1989, also an ordained priest.

Today we are here to express our gratitude to God for all that God has accomplished through you, Br Piet, for the last 25 years of your religious life. With Mary, you too can sing the Magnificat and say: "the Almighty has done great things for me, holy is his name". Imagine the number of poor people you have served in Los Angelus, in Tokyo, in Sao Paulo (Brazil), in Rome, in Albania, in India and wherever else Divine Providence has sent you through your superiors. You were always open and obedient, ready to accept and follow the will of your superiors rather than your own will, as you see in the superiors the will of God. You have put many young Brothers into shame with your hard work, your fervour and zeal, your readiness to go anywhere you are sent, even when the mission and the ministry seem difficult. Your concern for the orphans and your love for the poor has been exemplary. And your ministry and means of procuring black clothes for the widows in Albania has been unique.

Today, with St Paul, you may say: *"Brothers, I do not think of myself as having reached the finish line. I give no thought to what lies behind me, but push on to what is ahead, my entire attention is on the finishing line as I run toward the prize to which God calls me. Life on high in Christ Jesus."* (Phil: 3: 13-14).

187

Like Mary Magdalene of the Gospel of today, Br Piet, you too saw many a time the empty tomb. The empty tomb, however, did not make you feel discouraged, but like Mary Magdalene who stayed back, looking again and again into the empty tomb, wetting the earth with her tears, Br Piet continues to do the same. Only those who are humble enough and are filled with undefeatable love will be able to meet the Lord like Mary Magdalene did. Nothing is impossible with God. He can produce children of Abraham from the stones, says St. John the Baptist. What God needs is our faithfulness, our persevering fidelity. If Mary Magdalene left the tomb like the apostles did, she too would not have seen and talked to the Risen Lord. Br Piet, you are the one who stayed at the empty tomb and the Lord is going to reward you for your perseverance, your faithfulness and generosity.

In conclusion, Br Piet, we would ask you to remember the past with gratitude, to live the present with enthusiasm, and then look forward to the future with confidence. In the words of St Pio of Pietrelcina: *"to leave the past to the mercy of God, the present to His love, and the future to his providence"*.

Br Piet, God loves you...for what you are and for what you do for him, in him and with him, and for what he can do with you, in you and through you. Jesus tells you: "My little one, come, come, continue to be My light, My love, My peace and My joy. My beloved one, continue to love and adore Me in the Bread of Life so that you can go on loving and serving Me in the poor, in the sick and all in need. Bring them all to Me, carry Me to them". While our Blessed Mother tells you: *"Teach them to pray the Rosary, the family Rosary and all will be well. Do not be afraid. Jesus and I will be with you and with all those who come to me through you"*. We entrust you, then, to the care and protection of the Holy Family: Jesus, Mary and Joseph, who will be your secure shelter and refuge in times of need. And you may continue to love and serve the Lord until you die of love. To this end we pray. Amen. Alleluia!

God bless you.

Fr. Sebastian Vazhakala M.C.

Final Vows of M.C. Brothers Peter and Gaspar

Let us give thanks to the Lord, Let us sing forever the eternal Mercies of the Lord

Kumasi, Ghana, 21 May, 2005

Your Excellency, Most Rev. Gabriel Justice Anokye,
the V.G. very Rev. Stephen,
all the priests concelebrants,
Rev. Sisters
my dear friends in Jesus Christ,

This has been a very joyful morning. The good Lord made this celebration a very solemn one, a joyful one, a spiritually rich one.

You and I have joined with two of our beloved Brothers: Br. Peter M.C. and Br. Gaspar M.C. for their courageous step into the world of faith, like our forefathers of faith, Abraham, Isach, Joseph, Moses; like our Lady who said to the angel Gabriel: *"Let it be done to me as you say."* The response of our Brothers is an expression of their loving trust, their blind obedience in the Lord. So, our dearly beloved Brothers: with you we thank God, for you we pray. We pray that you may not only persevere in your holy vocation but may grow in it, that you may remember the past, whatever kind of past you had, with gratitude, thanking God for everyone: your worthy parents, brothers and sisters in the first place, then your good friends, including priests and religious, who have helped you in the various stages and ages of your journey of faith. You have much to thank God for: all those who have helped to form you,

189

especially Br. Subash M.C. and the community, Br. Stephen M.C., Fr. Peter Viafe, our beloved M.C. Sisters of Kumasi and also Accra. Thank God for them and pray much for them, especially today.

While remembering the past with gratitude, live the present with enthusiasm. I pray that you never lose the spirit of fervor and joyful enthusiasm. Your bodies may get old, even can feel tired and sick, but your soul and spirit may always retain its youthfulness. It may not follow the demands of the body, but your body may help the soul go above and beyond all earthly desires and ambitions. Let your ambition in this life be how to love Jesus in prayer and especially in the poorest of the poor as he has never been loved before; to desire nothing except to love until you die of love.

Blessed Teresa, our beloved Mother and foundress, so often told us to pray together, as we know that the family that prays together stays together. Br. Peter and Br. Gaspar, your journey of faith has been the story of the amazing grace:

"It was grace that taught my heart to fear, and grace my fear relieved.

How gracious did the grace appear,

The hour I first believed.

Through many dangers, toils and snares

I have already come. This grace that brought me so far,

And grace will lead me home."

So we remember the past with gratitude, live the present with enthusiasm, and look forward to the future with confidence. This means to trust all the more in God's unceasing help. It was grace that brought me thus far, and grace will lead me home, provided I do what I can and cooperate with God's grace. Courage Brothers. Br. Peter and Br. Gaspar.

"Do not stumble.

Though your path is dark as night,

there is star to guide the humble.

Trust in God and do the right."

Br. Peter M.C.

The third child among seven children, Br. Peter Dadzie M.C. was born at Akim Tafo, in the Eastern Region of Ghana on 30 March,

1953. His beloved father was first a soldier and then the director of the board of agriculture, while his mother is a housewife.

Three years later Br. Peter was baptized in Sacred Heart Church, Accra. At the age of eight Br. Peter had his first Holy Communion in St. Peter's Cathedral Church, Kumasi, and four years after he received the sacrament of Confirmation in the same cathedral Church, Kumasi.

Although he had his primary school in Kumasi, Br. Peter did the rest of his schooling at Tafo Akim in the Eastern Region. Br. Peter then pursued his studies in minor seminary and his studies in philosophy at the Regional Seminary Cape Coast, and then on his own he left the seminary and went to Nigeria to teach history, geography and first lessons in Sacred Scriptures in St. Paul's Minor Seminary for six years. In the meantime his father became very ill and so he returned to Kumasi to be at the bedside of his beloved father to prepare him for his final journey from this world of tears and sorrows to the world of joy and eternal peace. After the death of his beloved father he continued with his studies and taught in a primary school for 12 years.

Although he liked teaching children, he felt called to a deeper and full commitment. Through our beloved M.C. Sisters of Kumasi, Br. Peter came to know the existence of the Missionaries of Charity Contemplative Brothers in Rome. So in September, 1996, Br. Peter joined our community in Rome and began his religious formation. He had his novitiate mainly in Albania, and then on 19 March, 1999, on the solemnity of St. Joseph, Br. Peter made his first vows, together with Br. Gaspar, in Sacred Heart Cathedral, New Delhi, India.

Br. Peter had his juniorate mostly in Rome, during which he completed his studies in theology at the Angelicum University, Rome. On 18 September, 2003, Br. Peter came with Br. Stephen M.C. and Br. Gaspar M.C. to start his preparation for his final **vows,** which, with God's grace, he did this morning.

Let us continue to support Br. Peter Dadzie with our prayers so that he can grow in holiness and persevere in his vocation. I also would like to thank his beloved mother and his brothers and sisters, all his close relations and friends for their prayers and support and request them and all of you to continue to support him with your prayers.

Br. Gaspar M.C.

Br. Gaspar Barla M.C. was born in a little village in the state of Orissa, India on 28th December, 1966. His father is a veterinary doctor and his mother a primary school teacher. He is the first among six children.

At the age of nine, Br. Gaspar received the first Holy Communion, and then a year later on the solemnity of St. Joseph, on 19 March,1977, the sacrament of Confirmation, which not only strengthened his faith but convinced him to live and work for Jesus. Br. Gaspar is a college graduate in commerce, in banking law and practice, first in the state of Orissa, India and then in Kolkata, the city that has become the symbol of loving service. He has volunteered with several youth associations to work for the uplift of the people. But all his social activities and helping others did not give him enough joy and satisfaction. He felt the need of going further and deeper into his search for meaning in life. His aunt, his father's beloved sister, had already joined the Missionary Sisters of Charity, and currently works with the poor in South America. She inspired Br. Gaspar to join the Missionaries of Charity, leaving his sweet home, beloved parents, brothers and sisters on January 5, 1993. Br. Gaspar did his novitiate in Delhi and the second year in Albania. He took his first vows in Sacred Heart Cathedral in New Delhi, the capital city of the Indian nation, together with Br. Peter and Thomas Mathew.

After his first profession, Br. Gaspar served in several places, including our home for the homeless, handicapped and orphaned boys known as Deepashram, Gurgaon, India and then in Albania.

Br. Gaspar finished his philosophical studies in the Angelicum University, Rome.

On 18 September, 2003, Br. Gaspar, together with Br. Stephen and Br. Peter, came to Kumasi, Ghana to prepare himself to make his final and definitive commitment, which he did this morning, along with Br. Peter. Let us wish both a very happy and holy new life and pray that they may persevere in their holy vocation. We pray that many may follow their good example.

You and I are all called to become holy through humility and charity. Holiness is not the luxury of the few, but the simple duty of all. All of you are not called to be religious and priests, bishops, cardinals or popes, but all of you, all of us are called to become saints. All of us can do ordinary things with extraordinary love, simple things with great love. Jesus told Blessed Mother Teresa of Kolkata back in 1946 to offer more sacrifices, smile more tenderly, pray more fervently and everything will go well. Blessed Teresa did exactly as Jesus told her, and she became a great saint, a hero of charity, a lover and mother of the poor. Let us try, make every effort to do the same.

I also would like to thank once again his Lordship Rt. Rev. Gabriel Justice, our Vicar General Msgr. Stephen, all the priests concelebrants, our Sisters, and all of you. Please continue to support us with your prayers. Consider us as your Brothers, as we consider you as our Brothers and Sisters. We are children of the same heavenly Father. The cows can be of different colors, but milk is always white. Let us continue to light a candle rather than curse the darkness.

Love and prayers.

God bless you.
Fr. Sebastian Vazhakala M.C.

Jubilee of Brother Subash M.C. June 2006

On Friday 2nd June, 2006, Br. Subash will complete 25 years of his first religious profession in the family of the Missionaries of Charity. Since Br. Subash may be in Albania on that day, as he is the Superior of the house in Albania, and two of the councillors and I will be elsewhere, we have anticipated the jubilee celebration to this day.

With you, Br. Subash, we thank God, and for you we pray that you may continue to grow in holiness and persevere in your holy vocation.

We have come together on this chosen day to thank God for the last 25 years of your life as a religious Brother of the Missionaries of Charity of Blessed Teresa of Kolkata. All these years your life has been the story of the "amazing grace", and you continue to sing all your life here on earth and the world to come: *"Amazing grace, how sweet the sound that saved a wretch like me, I once was lost, but now I am found, was blind but now I see. It was grace that taught my heart to fear and grace my fears relieved… Through many trials and snares I have already come. It was grace that brought me thus far, and grace will lead me home."* Yes, Br. Subash M.C., your life on earth, then, is the story of the amazing grace, and you will continue to sing forever the eternal mercies of the Lord.

Br. Varghese Chittillapilly was born in a small city called Trichur, in the state of Kerala, in the extreme South West of India on 23rd January, 1956. He was the fourth child among 10 children, three of whom have gone home to God. Thanks be to God, both his parents are still alive, although presently his mother is not doing too well. Two of his sisters are consecrated religious, one of whom is Sr. Nestina M.C., belonging to the M.C. Community of Bologna, who is present here today.

Jesus called Br. Subash at an early age to be with him and to proclaim the good news to the poor, as he called Peter, James and John and the other apostles. As the apostles left their parents, their nets and their boats, Br. Subash too left his beloved parents, brothers and sisters to love the Lord more ardently and to follow him more closely. He heard Jesus say: "I'm hungry and thirsty, I am naked and homeless, I am sick and imprisoned. You can satisfy my hunger and satiate my thirst in the poorest of the poor of Kolkata and of the world. You can clothe me and welcome me. You can visit me in the sick and in the prisoners, as I have absolutely no one for my very poor people. And so Br. Subash left his beloved home, his place, and his friends to answer the call of God, to join the Missionaries of Charity in the paradoxical city of Kolkata in the year 1978. After his aspirancy and postulancy, Br. Subash began his noviciate on 2nd June, 1979, and made his first vows after two years, exactly on 2nd June, 1981, in the Mother House and Generalate of the Missionaries of Charity Brothers of Kolkata.

For Br. Subash, his home was a school of prayer, fraternal love, service and hospitality, which in later years he was able to express more convincingly, faithfully and more fully in and through the Missionaries of Charity. How important to have good families, exemplary parents, edifying surroundings. The greatness of our family life does not depend only on material wealth and prosperity, but more so on spiritual richness, peace, love, and joy. The Holy Family, for example, was quite poor materially, but was spiritually the richest family to ever live on earth, because Jesus was the centre of the Holy Family, which made not only a word of difference, but a world of difference.

The family that prays together, stays together. This was true of Br. Subash's family. Let us not give God the last place in our families, but the first place. We begin our day with God, continue with his inspiration, and end the day with deep gratitude.

Br. Subash, though extremely interested in helping the poor, believed that he couldn't do it without a very deep and solid prayer life. He felt that he was called to lead a life of prayer, penance and works of mercy. Like a bird which cannot fly if both of its wings do not balance, so also the consecrated religious person. God has given us the two commandments of love of God and the love of our neighbor. We are asked to love God with all our heart, mind, soul and strength, and our neighbour as we love ourselves. With these two wings, we, like the birds, fly to God. In order to fly the wings must balance. So Br. Subash, realizing the importance of these twofold inseparable commandments of love, decided to join the contemplative branch of the Missionaries of Charity of V. S. Agapito, Rome. Accordingly, Br. Subash joined us on 11 February, 1991. When our branch became a diocesan religious Institute, Br. Subash made his final vows on 31st of December, 1993, in Rome, with the first group of Brothers. And since then he has served the Society in various places and in various capacities. He was ordained a priest on 27 December, 2003 in Rome.

Presently he is the Vicar General of the Missionaries of Charity Contemplative and the Superior of the house in Albania.

Today we are here to express our gratitude to God for all that he has accomplished in and through Br. Subash for the past 25 years of his religious life. With Mary, he too can sing the "Magnificat" and say: *"The Almighty has done great things for me, holy is his name.* Imagine the number of poor people he has served in various places he has been sent, such as in India, in Mexico, in Rome, in Ghana (Africa), in Albania and wherever the Divine Providence has sent him through his Superiors.

Today with St. Paul, Br. Subash, you may say: *"Brothers, I do not think of myself having reached the finish line. I give no thought to what is behind me, but push on to what is ahead; my entire attention is on the finish line, as I run towards the prize to which God calls me. Life on high in Christ Jesus."* (Phil 3: 13-14)

Like Mary Magdalene, you might have seen the empty tomb. But the empty tomb did not make you feel discouraged. Like Mary Magdalene, who stayed at the empty tomb, looking again and again, hoping against all hope, wetting the earth with her tears, Br. Subash, you too continue to do the same. It is not success and human achievements we have come to thank God for today, but for your uncompromising fidelity, undaunted courage, invincible love, and above all your unquestionable perseverance, even when everything around may be dark and we see nothing but the "empty tomb". If Mary Magdalene had left the tomb like the apostles did on that first day of the week, she too would not have met the risen Lord, nor would she have talked to him. May the

Lord reward Br. Subash, then, for his persevering fidelity to God's call for the past 25 years.

In conclusion Br. Subash, we would ask you to remember your past with gratitude, to live the present with ever greater enthusiasm...which is absolutely vital...and look forward to the future with confidence. In the words of St. Pio of Pietrelcina, "to leave the past to the mercy of God, the present to his love and the future to his providence".

Br. Subash, God loves you for what you are and what you do for him, in him and with him, and for what he can do with you, in you and through you. Jesus tells once again today: *My little one come, come, continue to be My light, My love, My joy, My peace. My beloved one, continue to love and adore Me in the Bread of Life so that you can go on loving and serving Me in my very poor and all in need of My gentle love, My joy, My tender care. Bring them all to Me, carry Me with you into them, as I long to enter the unhappy home of their hearts."* While our blessed Mother Mary tells you: *"Teach them to pray the Rosary, the family Rosary and all will be well. Do not be afraid. Jesus and I will be with you and all those you live with, and with all those who know, love and serve Me through you."*

We entrust you to the care and protection of the Holy Family: Jesus, Mary and Joseph, who will be your secure shelter and refuge in times of trials, hardships and discouragements. May you continue to love and serve the Lord until you die of love. To this end we all pray. Amen. Alleluia!

God bless you.
Father Sebastian Vazhakala, MC

Ordinations of Brother Stephen M.C. to Priesthood And Brother Peter M.C. to Diaconate January 2006

"If we have our Lord in the midst of us, with daily Mass and Holy Communion, I fear nothing for the Sisters, brothers, or for myself. He will look after us. But without him I cannot be, I am helpless."
(Blessed Teresa)

Dearly beloved Brothers and Sisters,

The ordination to deaconate of Br. Peter M.C. and the ordination to priesthood of Br. Stephen M.C. took place in the parish church of St. Martin-Kumawu Ash in the diocese of Konongo-Mampong, Ghana on 17 December 2005.

The celebration began exactly at 9:30 a.m. and was over at 12:20 p.m. There were 29 priest concelebrants and the ordaining bishop, His Excellency Rt. Rev. Joseph Osei-Bonsu, the bishop of the diocese. The ceremony was held in the open. There was another candidate for deaconate from Nigeria for the diocese of Konongo-Mampong. The Holy Mass, the homily, the various prayers and most of the rite of ordination were held in the local language known as Twi. There were some dances, mainly while collections were taken; two sets of bands and trumpeters besides the big choir… all were dressed in their respective uniforms. The bishop was very warm, personal and loving. After the communion prayer he took the trouble to introduce to the crowd the two M.C. Sisters from Kumasi, who came for the ordination, a few other people, and me. I was able to thank the bishop, the parents and the family members of Br. Stephen and Br. Peter. It was very humbling and moving to see the bishop kneeling before the newly ordained priest and asking for his blessing before the entire assembly. The bishop told me that it is the Ghanean custom to give the blessings to the ordaining bishop, his Superior General, and his parents, which he did. After these he was asked to bless the entire crowd of people. Only at the end, as the main celebrant of the mass, did the bishop impart his final blessing on all.

Br. Peter M.C. served at the altar as deacon for the first time and did very well, without much confusion.

After the Holy Mass we had some packed lunch, prepared by the parish priest, Fr. Peter and the parishioners. It looked like Jesus feeding the five thousands in the Gospel on the mountain slope. (cf. Jn 6:1-15) This was also a very vast slope of a mountain, enough place for all to gather. The main problem the inhabitants of the place face is the lack of water. We really have to pray so that the very simple people of that area may have their water problem solved.

We give thanks to the presence of the group of four Italian volunteers: Teresa, Claudia, Francesca and Salvatore. They spent their days with Br. Stephen until the first of January 2006.

In the late afternoon of the same day we traveled to the home parish of Br. Stephen M.C. and Br. Leo M.C. It was a two hours' drive from the place of the ordination. About 500 m. away from his church, we were stopped by the crowd of his hometown people, so we all had to get off. Br. Stephen and his pastor got into a pick up with some of the members of his family. They stood erect at the back of the open truck. The trumpeters and the drummers used all their strength and energy, and the crowd in the meantime danced before the pick up in great jubilation. The video cameras focused on getting all the details, so that they can see it again and relive such a joyful event. The whole procession lasted for two hours, circling the small town of Anyianasu, while some of the ladies threw a lot of perfumed powder in the air and on the heads, including on the head of the newly ordained priest. The procession finally was led to the church, where they had the concluding ceremony. People thanked God again and again for the gifts of the priests, who through the words of consecration can give Jesus to the hungry people. God needed a woman to come down from heaven and live among us. What God did through Our Lady then, Jesus does through validly ordained priests through the Eucharist today. It is the same God who became flesh and dwelt among us, who becomes the Bread of life for the same purpose, namely for the salvation and the sanctification of souls.

If, through the "fiat" of Mary, God became man and dwelt among us, through the words of consecration of the priests, Jesus becomes the Bread of Life. If the former is Incarnation, the latter is "Impanation". The Incarnation was only once and for all. The "Impanation" is an ongoing event; it will be continued till the end of time, as Jesus himself told: *"Do this in memory of me."* (Lk 22: 19)

In view of the event of the Incarnation, the eternal Father did not allow our Blessed Virgin Mary to be touched by any sort of sin: original or actual. Not only was she free from original and actual sin, but each day living with Jesus, her Son, she grew in holiness. Our holiness depends on the measure and manner of our identification to and conformity with the Divine Will. Jesus possessed this perfect conformity to the Father's will, even at the cost of losing his life... dying shamefully on the cross between two thieves, becoming totally powerless – kenosis. In him there was nothing more left to empty; total annihilation!

Perfect conformity to the Divine Will brought Our Lady to go through untold pain and suffering as well. Suffering began as soon as she accepted the Divine Will to be the Mother of God. St. Joseph decided to divorce her. Her suffering did not become any less with the presence of Jesus, although her joy increased. We go through two kinds of experiences when we try to do God's will: one is a painful death to our own will, likes and dislikes, to our superficial emotions, self attachments, affective love etc., and the other is the experience of deep joy because of our effort to live our lives in accordance with the will of God.

The priest is meant to relive Jesus' life on earth again. Jesus never lived without Our Lady during his earthly life; he wanted his Mother to stand at the foot of the Cross, not only to see him suffer and die in excruciating pain, but share in it very personally. She too suffered and died with him in spirit. The sword of sorrow did pierce her heart and she was drowned in sorrow. Jesus and Our Lady gave their everything to save souls. The priest's life cannot be any different from the life of Jesus and Mary. We too must become humble and obedient like Jesus and Mary and grow in holiness each day by doing God's will, no matter what it may cost us!

Br. Stephen's first mass started at 10:00 a.m., on Sunday 18 December 2005 and finished exactly at 2:20 p.m. The mass was celebrated in their local language, Twi. Although I do not speak their language, I could understand and join in the expressions of their faith, hope, charity, joy and gratitude. They expressed those virtues in prolonged and repeated prayers, gestures, through music and sound of trumpets, sounding and rhythmic beating of drums, and above all through joyful dance.

The homily was given by a very young priest, Fr. Clement, who comes from the same parish. The people listened attentively and showed signs of agreement as the homily was delivered very convincingly. Father gave the impression that he lives what he preaches. After the profession of faith, the trumpets once again sounded and resounded together with the beatings of drums. Once again people began to jump and dance from one corner of the church to the other, and they went in procession with music and dance. The whole church was in feast. This was the time of Sunday collection. After the general collection, in which every single human being in that church participated, the next collection was made according to the day of one's birth. They began with Friday, since Br. Stephen was born on Thursday and he had to be the last. In this also the priest has to participate, so I joined the dance of the group of Wednesday, as I am Wednesday born. When Br. Stephen's turn came, which was the last one, once again the whole crowd followed, joining the first of all Thursday born, including the priest concelebrants.

There was then the offertory procession, for which people brought food, drink and various sanitary items. The priest received the gifts with due respect, blessed the people who brought them to the altar, and the gifts.

The Eucharistic celebration for them is life; it is a feast, a banquet, a joyful sharing of life in common. People forget all their problems and worries and think of celebrating the great day of the Lord. Not only because it was the first holy Mass, but it was Sunday, the day of the Lord, the day of the resurrection of Jesus, and so it is a day of great victory. People, even after four hours of singing, dancing, speaking and praying in the heat of the day, did not seem tired. On the contrary, they get more energy as they give and share. There is the inexhaustible spirit of God working in them, the infinite fountain of love and strength. The more one draws with joy from the fountain of life-giving waters of love, the more is there to draw, because God is infinite and he is the inexhaustible well-spring of love and life.

Those two days of Saturday and Sunday just before the great feasts of Christmas 2005 were inscribed in the hearts of so many and will be recalled to memory again and again in order to relive their first experiences. The eternal Father unceasingly allows the tenderness of his fatherly care to be shared with the hungry and thirsty ones, wanting to manifest the glory of the Cross of his Son, Jesus Christ, and the splendour of the Holy Spirit to shine through the priest.

Because he loved us, God became man through the unconditional "fiat" of Mary. Because he loves us now, Jesus becomes the Bread of life through the words of the priest, so that Jesus through the priest can satisfy the hunger of the human heart and satiate the thirst of the human soul.

And then with Jesus we must go about doing good, as he cannot do his work alone without us. We cannot do his work without him either. Jesus wants to visit everyone in need. Back in 1946-47 he told blessed Teresa of Kolkata: *"My little one, come, come; carry Me into the holes of the poor, come, be My light. I cannot go alone, they don't know Me, so they don't want Me. You come, go amongst them, carry Me with you into them. How I long to enter their holes, their dark unhappy homes. Come be their victim. In your immolation, in your love for Me, they will see Me, know Me, want Me. Offer more sacrifices, smile more tenderly, pray more fervently and all the difficulties will disappear."* (MGF 18)

The priest of the Missionaries of Charity Contemplative then has a clear and definite vocation. He is ordained for the community of the Missionaries of Charity and for the poorest of the poor. In accordance with the Constitutions of the Missionaries of Charity Contemplative he exercises his priestly ministry under guidance and direction of his superiors. *"Father, I abandon myself into your hands...Let your Will be done in me and in all your creatures. I wish no more than this…"* (Blessed C. De Foucault)

The M.C. priesthood must bloom in the soil and in the midst of a unique group of people, who are very specially loved by God. They are the poorest of the poor, the weakest of the weak, the less than the least of all; we are one like and one of them who are ordained to minister, to serve and guide them to God.

I would like to conclude this letter with the following words:

"To live in the midst of the world,
Without wishing its pleasures;
To be a member of each family,
Yet belonging to none;
To announce the good news to the poor,
To heal the broken hearted,
To share all their sufferings;
To penetrate all secrets;
To go from men to God
And offer Him their prayers;
To return from God to men
To bring pardon and hope;
To have a heart of fire for charity
And a heart of bronze for Chastity;
To teach and to pardon,
Console and bless always.
What a glorious life! And it is yours,
O priest of Jesus Christ!"

God bless you.

Fr. Sebastian Vazhakala M.C.

Ordination of Brother Peter M.C. to Priesthood

Feast of St. James, Apostle 2007

Dearly beloved Brothers and Sisters,

As part of the golden jubilee of his priesthood, the Servant of God Pope John Paul II published an account of his priesthood called "the Gift and Mystery". How true it is to say that priesthood is and will always be an ineffable gift and an unfathomable mystery!

On Saturday 14 July 2007, in Kumasi, Ghana, West Africa, one of our beloved Brothers, Br. Peter Dadzie M.C., together with 14 other men, was ordained priest by His Grace, Rt. Rev. Peter A. Sarpong, the Archbishop of Kumasi.

Among the 15 "ordinandi", 8 of them belong to the archdiocese of Kumasi, 6 to the Congregation of the Holy Spirit Fathers and Br. Peter M.C. to the Missionaries of Charity Contemplative.

The solemn Eucharist was concelebrated together with the Archbishop of Kumasi, his auxiliary bishop Rt. Rev. Gabriel Justice Yaw Anokye, the Vicar General Msgr. Stephen, the Superior General of the Missionaries of Charity Contemplative Fr. Sebastian Vazhakala M.C., the assistant General of the Holy Spirit Fathers and their Provincial, and over a hundred priest concelebrants from the archdiocese of Kumasi and around. The solemn Eucharistic celebration lasted for exactly five and half hours.

Word of God and presentation of candidates.

After the Gospel there was the calling of the names of the candidates to be ordained and the subsequent presentation of them by the respective parents of each one. There was perfect order and harmony from the start to the finish of the entire function.

Homily. Finishing the presentation, the Archbishop asked some of us to give a one minute long message to the "ordinandi", before he would give his homily. I too was asked to speak for one minute, which I did in front of such an immense crowd of people. The following was the message that I gave:

"Today, dearly beloved Brothers, you became the priests of God because of his mercy. Remember that your priesthood is a great gift and a mystery. And your priesthood must bloom in the fertile soil of love. In you and around you there should be nothing but love. And your priestly life and ministry must be nothing but the fruit of your personal, intimate and unbroken union with God in prayer, especially in the Holy sacrifice of the Mass. Let the celebration of the Holy Mass be your life and let your life be a prolonged Mass. Thanks to each and everyone of you and God bless you all."

His Excellency Rt. Rev. Peter A. Sarpong, the main celebrant and homilist, then took up some of the points spoken by the various kinds of people. He spoke very strongly about the importance of having a very healthy community life. The vows make sense only when there is real love, sacrifice, caring and sharing among themselves.

We all know very well that the community is the first place where we make God's kingdom incarnate. In community we learn to give and share instead of demanding, to trust others instead of compelling their trust, to serve others instead of being served. Here one has to put aside all ambition for power, popularity and wealth. And only to the extent that we are ready to die together that others may live, will our community bear fruit for the coming of the kingdom. We have to be very grateful to God for the variety of gifts and also thankful for the differences of personality. When each one puts his own potential and insights at the service of our brothers and the poor, our unity will grow stronger and richer. Let us not take vengeance, not even in thought. We must try our best to avoid every tendency towards depression, moodiness and sadness. It is death to our souls.

The quality of our communities does not depend on age or numbers. The only thing that counts and will bring us a blessing is that we should always be seeking each other in the Spirit of Jesus. From him alone comes salvation.

We also have to learn more and more to have great respect for the seniors in the community. Let us not distress them by our talk or behaviour. Instead, let us be gentle towards their weaknesses and incapacities, as we are building on what they have begun.

Everything in our life can have love as its motive, its end. The four vows by which we bind ourselves are precisely our own way of embodying our love for God and man. The more, therefore, we grow in love, the more clearly we will understand what the vows demand; and the more seriously we live our vows, the more we will grow in love.

Our faith and love must be constantly renewed; our weaknesses and faults constantly corrected.

When the homilist started speaking about obedience, he said: "Here I want to dramatize the notion of obedience". He then called to the front a young military Chaplain and made him stand in front of the "ordinandi", their family members and the entire assembly and said that the priest was asked to go to Congo on the following day by his Superiors. There was no question of whether he was ready or not or whether he liked the place or not; he just has to go. For us, who are religious and priests, our obedience must be prompt, joyful and without any questions, as we are meant to obey Jesus, who is our King and Lord. Our obedience must be Christ-like. He was obedient unto death, death on a Cross. (cf. Phil 2: 6-11)

Invitation to pray. After the homily the celebrant did the final scrutiny. Finishing the questions and answers, the Bishop invited everyone present to pray for the candidates; the choir began the litany of all saints during which all the "ordinandi" prostrated themselves on the floor. The entire assembly on their knees, invoked the assistance of the heavenly court.

The profession of faith and the promise of obedience. Each candidate, holding a big crucifix in hand, made the profession of faith and the promise of obedience. It was very impressive and moving. There was no rush. Every part of the liturgy was well prepared and celebrated.

The candidates then came forward one by one and in the hands of the bishop promised obedience and respect to him and to his successors.

Br. Peter M.C., as religious, promised obedience and respect not only to the Archbishop and his successors, but also to his Superior General and his successors. To do that Br. Peter had to hold both our hands and answer to the Bishop's questions: "Do you promise obedience to me and to my successors, to your Superior and his successors?" to which Br. Peter's answer was: "I do". The bishop then said: "May the Lord, who began his good work in you, bring it to its completion".

The laying on of hands. All the fifteen candidates knelt down and the Archbishop and his auxiliary, followed by me, the provincial of the Holy Spirit Fathers and the priest concelebrants laid hands in silence on every single "ordinandi". What an incredible moment that was for all the candidates who were kneeling on the ground, in the open air, under the sky, in the heat of the day! The solemn moment of the descent of the Holy Spirit upon each one of them. My prayer in silence for each one as I placed my hands on the head was: *"Spirit of the living God, fall afresh on him, melt him, mould him, fill him and use him"*. The candidates were there for hours in the open air, bathed in the sun's scorching heat, but their eyes were fixed more on Jesus the Son, their mirror and their model, rather than the sun that bathed them in sweat. Nobody showed any sign of restlessness, but all were absorbed in the divine interventions and sacramental encounters that were transforming those ordinary "sinners" into saviours of men. It was as if Jesus was telling them as he told St. Peter at the miraculous catch of fish (cf Lk 5: 1-11), who then, falling at Jesus' feet told him: *"Go away from me, Lord! I am a sinful man"*: *"Do not be afraid; from now on you will be catching people"* (Lk 5: 10).

The vestition was very simple. The parish priest of each candidate was asked to help to put on the priests' stole and chausable. Br. Peter M.C. was blessed to have three of us Brothers plus his parish priest to put his priestly vestments on.

The anointing was very solemn and moving. Each newly ordained priest approached the celebrant, and knelt down with hands wide open to be anointed with Chrism. The archbishop was very lavish. He literally poured the consecrated oil into both hands of the priest and the priest got up with both hands tightly closed; extending them he returned to his place, holding the hands raised until all were anointed. They then went to wash their hands and got ready for the kiss of peace.

Taking of collections and offertory procession. There was then the collection, and every single person participated in it, followed by the offertory procession in which they brought to the altar all sorts of food stuff, fruits and other items for everyday use, including soap and toilet paper.

Br. Peter M.C. was chosen from the newly ordained to be one of the main concelebrants, which, thanks be to God, he did quite well.

Liturgical dances. There were also many liturgical dances at various important moments of the celebration, after the doxology, for example, to show profound reverence and adoration, and after communion to express "one's joy". These dances were performed by a special group of well-trained people in the African way.

Blessings by the newly ordained. Before imparting the final blessing by the celebrant, some of the newly ordained priests were chosen to give blessings to the Bishops and some of the important people. Br. Peter M.C. gave blessings to the Bishops, who knelt before him. Another newly ordained gave blessings to two of us Superiors, who represented the two religious Congregations; another one to all the parents of the newly ordained priests, etc. All in all the entire function was very moving and well participated in.

Community in Kumasi. A word about our Kumasi community. Right now our community in Kumasi, Ghana, consists of five finally professed Brothers: Br. Matthew M.C. (House Superior), Br. Peter M.C. (Assistant), Br. Gaspar M.C. (Accountant), Br. Tony M.C. (In-charge of candidates), Br. Leo M.C. (In-charge of "Jesu Fié", the home for homeless men).

The city of Kumasi is about 300 Km North of Accra, the capital city of Ghana. It takes about six hours by bus to drive from Accra to Kumasi.

Our house is about 8 km north of the centre of the city of Kumasi, a place called Pankrono. It is here we began our little community on Wednesday 1st October 2003.

The Brothers started a little home for the homeless older men. Right now we only have two of them. We hope to get more men, as we can accommodate up to 8 persons. We are looking for a bigger place.

The Brothers also try to practice the spiritual and corporal works of mercy in and around the area. With the help of some generous benefactors from Rome, the Brothers were able to dig two tube wells for drinking water in the slum area not too far from our house. So many people still come to our place to take water, as some of them do not have the basic necessities of life.

The harvest is plenty, the labourers are few. Let us pray to the Lord of the harvest to send more generous and enterprising labourers into his vineyard (cf. Mt 9: 36-37).

Jesus said to Blessed Teresa of Kolkata back in 1946: *"There are plenty of nuns to look after the rich and well to do people, but for my very poor, there are absolutely none. For them I long, them I love. Wilt thou refuse?"* (M.F.G. pg. 18).

Conclusion. We M.C.s are called to live and work in the midst of the world with a unique group of people who are the poorest of the poor, the weakest of the weak, the less than the least of all. Every M.C. realizes as he lives and works with them that he is one like and one of them. He is called to announce the good news to the poor, to heal the broken-hearted, to share all their sufferings; to go from men to God and offer him their prayers; to return from God to men to bring freedom and hope; to have a heart of fire for charity and a heart of bronze for Chastity; to teach and to pardon, console and bless always, everywhere and everyone. What a wonderful life! It is yours, oh MCs of Jesus Christ!

Love and prayers.

God bless you.

Fr. Sebastian Vazhakala M.C.

Final Vows of Brother Ramon M.C.
2007

"...The treasures of the Church"

Dearly beloved Brothers and Sisters,

Glory to God in the highest and peace to his people on earth of good will and humility.

Hearty congratulations, happy and holy new life to Br. Ramon M.C., to Br. Francois Marie M.C., Br. Victor M.C. and Br. Michael M.C.. Br. Ramon M.C. made his life long commitment to Jesus through the profession of the evangelical counsels and the fourth vow of wholehearted free service to the poorest of the poor. On our heavenly Mother's earthly birthday, 8th September 2007, in the Basilica of St. Anthony of Padua, in Rome, at 4.00 p.m., Br. Ramon M.C. said to the Lord, like and with our Lady: "Fiat voluntas tua" – "Let your will be done". The Basilica was packed quite full. The main celebrant was Rt. Rev. Msgr. Agostino Marchetto, Secretary General of the Pontifical Council for Immigrant aliens and Pilgrims of the world. After the words of welcome by Br. André Marie M.C., the celebrant began to sing by himself the "Kyrie", which surprised everybody, especially the choir. The entire celebration lasted for two long hours. The singing was angelic. The responsorial psalm sung by Mini touched every one's heart.

The homily was simple and rather short, delivered in both languages of Italian and English. The celebrant started with our Mother's meetings with his Eminence Cardinal Camillo Ruini, which His Eminence recalled lately for the 10th anniversary of the death of Blessed Teresa of Kolkata. "Every time Blessed Teresa went to the Cardinal she invariably told that she came to offer him a gift, and he was expecting the gift... but her hands were always empty...while her heart was full of love and gratitude. He came to realize that her gift was the good works of mercy she and the Missionaries of Charity Family do for to the poorest of the poor, *"who are really the treasures of the Church."* (St. Lawrence)

"Br. Ramon is that kind of gift being offered and consecrated this evening to God to be with him and to be sent out to proclaim the Good News to the poor," said the homilist. Like and with Our Lady, Br. Ramon M.C. now says: "Behold the handmaid of the Lord, be it done to me as you say". He then goes in haste with Jesus as she did in her time to her cousin Elizabeth. Today we have to go with Jesus and Mary to meet the needs of the poor, to bring help, but above all to bring Jesus, wherever they may be found.

He spoke about the difficulties of communal living. He quoted St. Berchmans, who used to say: *"Vita comunis est maxima penitentia mea – The community life is my greatest penance"*. We must also know that we do not have a ready-made community, but one that is to be made and remade, corrected and perfected. We also know very well that our community is not composed of those who are already saints, but those who are trying to be saints. We grow holy together, drawing upon one another's virtues to combat our own weaknesses. We should therefore be extremely patient with each others' faults and failures.

We must pray daily to the Holy Spirit to unite us all in love, praising and thanking God for each other. Praying together as a community is our strength and protection. **The community that prays together stays together**.

Since the celebration of the final vows of Br. Ramon M.C. was part of Blessed Teresa's 10th death anniversary program, which we began in Rome from Sunday 26th August to Monday 10th September 2007, so many of our poor people, many M.C. Sisters, M.C. Fathers, LMCs, co-workers, volunteers and others were present for the profession. Br. Ramon's sister Josi Lusterio came all the way from the Philippines, while two of her friends from Canada, Vicky and Violyn, joined her in Rome. Their stay in Rome was limited to a week in all. Bushat community had its representation in the person of Br. Luke M.C....a big sacrifice for the community over there. Both Br. Luke M.C. and Br. Ramon M.C. will return, God willing, to Albania on 15th September 2007.

Our celebration this time was more spiritual in nature. The night of 8th September 2007 was spent in adoration, thanking God, as well as in vigil for our Brothers Francois Marie, Br. Victor and Br. Michael, who were going to make their temporary profession on the following day, i.e. on Sunday 9th September 2007.

His Excellency Msgr. Oscar Rizzato from the Vatican presided over the Eucharistic celebration, which was held in our Holy Family Church, in V. S. Agapito 8, Rome, at 5.00 p.m. Our Church was full. It was a combined celebration of the first professions, of thanksgiving for Casa Serena men before we close it for cleaning and repairing works, and also to choose those who are really the poor and homeless, and of the official conclusion of the 10th anniversary of Blessed Teresa's entrance into heaven. Of course the main emphasis was given to the religious profession of our beloved Brothers. The Archbishop spoke about the "wisdom of the heart - la sapienza del cuore". It was the Sunday psalm response sung by Mini. The choir again was very angelic. At Holy Communion Br. Piet M.C. on both days sang the "Panis Angelicus". It lifted up the spirit of the Archbishop, Msgr. O. Rizzato to the third heaven. He thanked Br. Piet M.C again and again for singing "Panis Angelicus" so well.

Although most of the M.C. Sisters went for the closing Mass of Mother's 10th death anniversary celebrations in the Basilica of St. John Lateran, still a good number of them came for the Brothers' profession as well..

The three Brothers took their Masters' degree in Charity from the Missionaries of Charity University of Blessed Teresa of Kolkata. From now on till the last day of their life on earth they will add M.C. to their names, provided they persevere in this great gift of their M.C. vocation. They have to do their practical training for five years, which we call Juniorate, before they are fully inserted into our Society. Let us support them by our fervent prayers, words and good example, and by our generous sacrifices. The M.C. can mean:

- **Martyrs of Charity**

- **Masters of Charity**

- **Ministers of Charity**

- **Missionaries of Charity.**

What is common to all is Charity, without which we can be mere social workers: But Jesus wants the Missionaries of Charity to be his fire of love amongst the very poor, the sick, the homeless, the handicapped, the children on the street, etc. (cf. M.F.G. p. 17)

Thanks to each and every one of the Brothers, LMCs, co-workers and others, who have not only offered up their prayers and sacrifices for the Brothers, but also sent telegrams, cards and letters, besides the many telephone calls. Heart felt thanks to Adolfo LMC who, all the way from Parma, travelled to Rome to participate in the Brothers' professions. For us it was very encouraging and edifying. Let us remain faithful to our vocation. This call of Jesus to "love and suffer and save souls" is an ineffable gift of God for which we all must remain eternally faithful and grateful to him. Our fidelity to our life of prayer, penance and works of mercy will not only help us to grow in holiness, but also to persevere in our vocation.

On Wednesday 5th September 2007, on the 10th death anniversary of Blessed Teresa M.C., the M.C. family together with our poor people, Lay M.C.s, co-workers, benefactors and others—about 1,500 persons in all—went to St. Peter's Square to participate in the general audience. At the end of the general audience the Holy Father Pope Benedict XVI delivered the following message to the Missionaries of Charity family:

> *"Greetings to the members of the Missionaries of Charity, who have come here with their co-workers, on the 10th death anniversary of Blessed Teresa of Calcutta. The life and the witness of this authentic disciple of Christ, dear friends, whose feast is liturgically being celebrated today, is an invitation to you and to the whole Church to serve God always faithfully in the poorest and the needy. Continue to follow her example and be instruments of God's mercy everywhere."* (Message of the Holy Father, Benedict XVI, 5th September 2007)

After the audience Fr. Brian M.C.F. (postulator), Sr. Fatima M.C., responsible for the Contemplative Branch of the Missionaries of Charity (Sisters), Sr. Patrick M.C., the regional Superior for South Italy, and Fr. Sebastian M.C. were able to meet with the Holy Father and talk with him personally. Sr. Maria Pia M.C., the regional Superior of Rome and North Italy, made a big sacrifice since only four of us could have the special tickets. Fr. Brian presented the Pope copies of the book "Mother Teresa: come, Be My Light" in German and in English.

I, on the other hand, took the entire M.C. Family with me and presented it to the Holy Father asking him to bless all our Family members, our Brothers, Sisters, our poor people: the blind, the lame, the crippled, the maimed, lepers, the AID patients, widows, orphaned and handicapped, our LMCs, co-workers, benefactors, all people of good will, and those who have no desire for God. I stood there in the presence of the Vicar of Christ on earth, and received his blessing for each and every person. I felt very small, humbled and unworthy to stand for all of you, speak to the one who represents Jesus on earth and request his blessings and prayers. When I said: "Holy Father, please remember us all in your prayers", he said: "Pray for me as well." I said to him that we remember him several times a day and pray for his intentions. He was extremely happy to hear it. He again blessed me and I kissed his ring. During the entire time we were holding each other's hands, as you may see in some of the photos taken for the occasion.

I would like to conclude this letter with the following prayer to the Holy Family, which may help us to make our Communities and families "Another Nazareth" (cf. Blessed Teresa M.C.):

"Jesus, Mary and Joseph on my mind,
That I may always think of you.
Jesus, Mary and Joseph in my eyes,
That I may always look for you.
Jesus, Mary and Joseph in my hearing,
That I may carefully listen to you.
Jesus, Mary and Joseph on my lips,
That I may always talk to you.
Jesus, Mary and Joseph in my heart,
That I may always love you.
Jesus, Mary and Joseph in my walking,
That I may always walk toward you.."

God bless you.
Fr. Sebastian Vazhakala M.C.

Tribute to Brother Martin M.C. 1996
June, 1996

We write to tell you of the joyful and sorrowful, but most of all glorious news that our dearly beloved Brother Martin Amponsah M.C. has gone home to the Father. He died after a short but acute phase of a long-standing illness on the night of 27 / 28 May in his room at our Church in Bushati (Shkoder, Albania). He was 39 years old.

Brother Martin, from Ghana in West Africa, had lived and worked for some time with the Active M.C. Brothers in Ghana, and only later decided to come and join us in Rome. He had also been employed as a school teacher and a car body mechanic.

He came to us on 14 February, 1992, and on 20 June, the Vigil of Corpus Christi, he began the Noviciate in Rome. On 11 July of the same year he traveled to Albania as a pioneer member of the novitiate, which was being transferred there, and he remained there in the village of Kukel until making his first vows, along with two other novices in Shkodra Cathedral, on 2 February, 1994, the first such ceremony which had taken place there since the closure of the churches in 1967.

He then moved to Bushati, where our church is on the busy main road to the North of Albania, and he put himself wholeheartedly at the service of the poorest from the surrounding villages, many of whom were lacking the basic necessities of life...helping them as far as possible at our own gate and conducting many missions by van to outlying areas to distribute food and clothes. He also made special efforts in the local area to help those who had no land and no employment... generally people who had come down from the mountains and who are not over-popular with the local residents. He took a lot of criticism from some quarters in his strife over this matter, as it was quite clear that his service to the poorest of the poor had to be without partiality.

In preparation for the visits he made to the poor people, Brother Martin generally preferred to work alone; and he did an immense amount of work: lifting, packing and organizing single-handedly. He was the procurator and treasurer to the community and provided for all the Brothers' needs with great dedication and selflessness. He often worked late into the night to organize everything efficiently in the way he thought best.

He had a very powerful spirit of spontaneous and profound joy, at the same time taking his vocation as a missionary of God's charity to the poorest of the poor very seriously. His contribution to our liturgical life gave evidence of a man who truly and evidently loved the Lord his God with all his mind, soul, heart and strength. Some of his contributions to the intercessions at Morning and Evening Prayer were a fruitful source of inspiration and reflection for all of us.

During the two and half years he spent in Bushati he returned to Rome at least once for medical reasons, and he also went to Ghana in the summer of 1994 to be with his family after his mother's death. For a period of a few months he also acted as a superior in Bushati, a task he fulfilled with much energy and enthusiasm, initiating many constructive projects around the house.

For a few months before his death his state of health, which had often appeared to be a little erratic, became more marked in its swings between his usual strength and a state of abnormal weakness, though he did not wish to see a doctor. However, in the last few days he seemed to be quite well: he was happy and showed no indication of any serious difficulty or ailment. He had been making arrangements for various routine activities in the future, when the Lord quite unexpectedly took him to Himself on the night of Monday, 27 May. May he rest in peace and joyfully take his place in the resurrection of the just on the last day.

The funeral Mass and burial of Brother Martin were most beautiful occasions. The Mass was celebrated by Bishop Zef Simoni from Shkodra and eleven concelebrants. Missionary of Charity Sisters came from all over Albania, some of them traveling for over eight hours to come to wish their brother farewell.

After the Mass his body was taken to our Novitiate in Kukel in a long motorized procession, including a bus full of local people, and there he was laid out again for people to pay their last respects. Then we buried our Brother in our own ground in Kukel, our first professed member to die, and an inspiration for the perseverance of those who, with God's grace, may come in the future.

We can see that Brother Martin's life was a reflection and a practical application of the Gospel of St. Matthew (25: 31-40), which was also the Gospel text chosen for his funeral Mass, namely *"... The King (Jesus) said: 'Come, blessed of my Father! Inherit the Kingdom prepared for you from the creation of the world. For I was hungry and you gave me food, I was thirsty and you gave me drink. I was a stranger and you welcomed me, naked and you clothed me. I was ill and you comforted me, in prison and you came to visit me.' The just will ask Him: 'When did we see you hungry and feed you or see you thirsty and give you drink? When did we welcome you away from home or clothe you in your nakedness? When did we visit you when you were ill or in prison?' The King will answer them: 'I assure you, as often as you did it for one of my least brothers, you did it to Me.' ...and the just thus go to eternal life!"*

Hence when we die and go home to God, Jesus is not going to ask us of our place of origin, or how much money we have accumulated in the bank...No, we will be asked what we did with our life. *"In the evening of our life, when we appear before God we will be judged on love"* (St. John of the Cross). Brother Martin's life speaks loudly and eloquently to us all to give with joy, even when it hurts...to give without counting the cost!

Now that he is with God, it is sure that he is praying for us all. We thank you and thank God for you for all your spiritual and material help.

God bless you.

Fr. Sebastian Vazhakala M.C.

Tribute to Sister Sylvia M.C. and Sister Kateri M.C.
July 1996

"Come blessed of my Father, inherit the kingdom prepared for you from the foundation of the world" (Mt 25: 34).

Dearly beloved Sr. Nirmala M.C.,

How are you? It is hard, difficult and painful, heart-rending even to think that someone who was so dear to us is no more visible to the human eyes and no more to be with us to enjoy her company. But still there is joy that is born of pain and sorrow... every death is a rebirth, every separation is a reunion, and especially our bodily separation is a return to the Father's house. For Srs. Sylvia and Kateri it was their "home visit", so it will be for all of us one day or another when that hour strikes.

And yet we did not want it to happen to them so quickly and so tragically. Yes, Sr. Sylvia and Sr. Kateri should not have died. Without faith we could not have accepted it. Thanks be to God for the gift of faith which alone comes to our rescue. Sr. Sylvia and Sr. Kateri are not dead, nor finished their mission. Their life has not ended, but changed into the fullness of happiness and peace, changed into the fullness of God's love...love without measure, love without admixture, love without pain and sorrow, love without human limitations, a pure, unadulterated love! That love consists in giving, sharing and creating. Love purifies, sanctifies and makes one glitter, shine like God.

With you we suffer; for you we pray that the eyes of our faith may give us the strength to surrender to God, to be ready for all, to accept all without reserve. "Lord do with us what you will; whatever you may do we thank you. Let only your will be done in us and in all your creatures" is our humble prayer.

Since my personal acquaintance with Sr. Kateri is much more limited than with Sr. Sylvia I stay on with the latter, leaving space for the former to someone else who may have known her better and longer.

Sr. Sylvia's life has been a light to all. She was humble but courageous, human and holy...a rare combination of holiness, humility and humanity. Her sacrifices and self-denials were not easily visible to the human eyes, but to the eyes of God. He saw it all: He accepted everything.

"She died in her habit", worthy of the habit she was wearing, because she had the habit of dying to herself. She was decreasing all the time, while Jesus was increasing, He grew and matured in her, bearing fruit in abundance and abiding at the same time. He smiled through her consecrated lips, her pure eyes. He loved, he shined through her. She was like a transparent bulb, a spotless glass that let the light of Christ shine through her. So when we saw her, we saw no longer her but Jesus...

Like a sapling, she grew up in arid ground as well as in moistened soil. Even-minded in pleasure and in pain, courageous in her steps, reflective and thoughtful, understanding beyond human calculations, accepting beyond conditions, drawing all not to herself but to God.

Sr. Sylvia has not died; she is alive and active in another form, in a stronger form. Now she acts as a realized person in the Fatherhood of God.

Joy is the infallible sign of the presence of God. She was found always joyful, a joy that was pure and holy. Joy to be real has to be tried, purified, filtered and perfected. Her joy was the grace of God shown forth through her big and capturing smiles.

Problems she had like everybody else; but they were secondary in front of others' pain and sorrow. Her problems she saw through a microscope, while others' through a telescope...and in Jesus she found the solutions for all. Unlike many she had an outstanding virtue which made her free and noble. Name it if you can, practice it as she did: she was magnanimous i.e., she was never jealous. Jealousy kills and destroys a person; jealousy is like a parasite, it does not give room for others to emerge, grow and mature. In her case this was one of her great gifts of God and the secret to her leadership. A jealous person is afraid and angry at others' gifts and progress, a jealous person wants himself/herself to be the centre of attraction, gradually cuts and breaks away from everyone else. Jealousy chokes love and becomes more and more fearful. In her presence others could feel at home, comfortable, at peace and at ease.

She lived the word Holy, as she was holy without ostentation, obedient without rigidity. If holiness is built on humility we can easily say that she was genuinely humble, obedient and yet free.

Love: she was filled with the love of God. She lived in God and for Him alone. The letter L has two lines: the vertical and the horizontal. She lived both dimensions to the full: love of God and love of one's neighbor.

Yearning for God, for the living God and God's yearning for us. Like a magnet and iron...If God is the magnet, we are little pieces of iron. She was the little piece of iron stuck to the magnet that is God, never again to be separated from Him. To Him be glory for ever and ever. Amen.

God bless you.
Fr. Sebastian Vazhakala M.C.

Tribute to Elizabeth
June 1998

ELIZABETH (born on 07,10.1913-died on 22.06.1998)
"The souls of the just are in the hand of God and no torment shall touch them." (Wis: 3:1)

Dearly beloved brothers and sisters,

So many of you have made me reflect so much these days on the words of St. Paul: *"Rejoice with those who rejoice, and weep with those who weep."* And that is what you have done with me through your many telephone calls, telegrams, fax messages, cards and letters. Your prayers and sacrifices made our sorrow lighter and the soul of my mother Elizabeth enter Heaven faster. May the good Lord continue to reward you for your great kindness and sublime generosity. *"We are one in the spirit, we are one in the Lord. By your love they will know we are Christians, by your love! In the evening of life, when we appear before God, we will be judged on love."*

My mother showed exceptional strength and vitality, and above all joy in the last days of her earthly life. On the morning of Wednesday 17th June she went to Church on her own, made her confession and received Communion at Holy Mass. Although it is only a fifty metres' walk from where my parents lived, it is a very steep climb; and she had not been that way to Church on her own at least for four or five years. She always took the round about way or went by jeep. That morning was special.

Coming back from the church she decided to go on another adventure, namely to go and visit my older brother's family, which is about two kilometres' distance. My father, Devasia, wanted her to postpone her trip to another day or wait for the bus, or go by jeep. But she decided to walk, and it took her over three hours to reach the house, where she stayed until the morning of the 21st, sharing all things in common in joy and in peace.

On the morning of Sunday 21st she returned home by bus, renewed in spirit and radiating joy. She prepared lunch and supper. All noticed in her something extraordinary, showing greater joy and tranquility. Strangely enough, she asked one of our cousins to tie a hand bell above her bed before going to bed for the last time. At about 11.15 p.m. (Indian time) she woke up and started rubbing her chest. By this time my father woke up and put the light on, realizing that my mother wasn't feeling too well. He got the usual tablets to give to her. She made the sign for him to grind the tablet and put it her mouth. By this time, though she could understand, she was unable to speak. So she was taken to St. Joseph's Hospital (Josegiri), next door to the Bishop's House, run by the Adoration nuns, where she received the sacrament of the anointing of the sick. In the presence of my father, my brothers, Emmanuel and Zachariah and his wife, she breathed her last on Monday, 22nd June at 9.30 a.m. The Angels welcomed her into Abraham's bosom. My brother Joseph, my sisters Terese and Leelamma, and I, as we live many miles away, were unable to witness to that unique moment of her final and definitive departure from the world of darkness and death to the world of perpetual light and unending life of peace and joy, even though we were informed straight away of her falling ill. She went home to God as she lived, without giving trouble to anybody. We had the funeral on the afternoon of Thursday, 25th June. It was a moving experience for all. It indeed was a unique week! I could feel the support of your prayers and sacrifices so strongly.

Every mother is not only a mother but also a teacher. What I have learned from my mother could be of some help to others. The following are some of the things I still remember:

> She was a wonderful mother who loved and took care not only of our bodily needs but more so of our spiritual growth and maturation.

She taught us the first lessons of life: how to pray, how to practice mortification, how to make sacrifices.

She taught us to be devoted and dedicated to duties of everyday life and to be hard working.

She showed us how to observe the commandments of God and to practise the precepts of the Church.

She taught us to be sincere and honest and to keep our word. Think twice before you say something, but once said you should keep it, she used to say.

Never flatter anybody to get something out of a person.

Never refuse to help a needy person, whether you like the person or not.

When things go wrong or trials come your way, pray more and make more sacrifices.

Never eat more than necessary. Be always moderate in eating, sleeping, etc.

When you give anything to anyone, give always the best you can. Never give to others what is not good or what has no use for anybody.

Say some ejaculatory prayers as you walk along or while doing something, for example: *"Infant Jesus, teach me to love you"*; *"Holy Mother of the Infant Jesus, help me to love Jesus as you have loved Him"*; *"Mary, my mother, my trust!"* etc.

She used to tell us stories of many martyrs and saints, especially the tortures of saints like St. Sebastian, St. George and others; how they went through them and still preserved in their faith.

When we had some physical pain, cuts or hurts, or mental or moral trials of any sort she told us to say: *"Jesus, how much you have suffered, let me offer this pain in union with your sufferings."*

If anyone speaks ill of you, do not worry, Jesus the just judge sees all. Say simply: *"Forgive them for they do not know what they are saying."*

Never give up things easily because they are difficult, but persevere and do what you can. If you sow in tears, you will reap rejoicing.

Try to show your love more in deeds than in words.

She wanted us always to remain united to God, to acquire God's own qualities like pieces of iron stuck to a magnet, which eventually become part of the magnet. Prayer, sacrifice, patient endurance, fraternal love, and brotherly concern were the main means she taught us to achieve this goal.

My father and she were married on 9 February, 1931, and so had been married for over 67 years. My mother was over 82 when she went home to God. Now for her there are no more tears, nor pain, nor death, but an unending life of love and peace. It is to that world of love and peace we too have to prepare ourselves to go: *"I no longer desire anything except to love until I die of love."*

My father is 84 years old (he was born on May 2, 1914). It is very hard for him to live without my mother. He needs our spiritual and moral support, which I am sure will not be wanting. My father, together with all the members of our family, would like to express our heart-felt gratitude to all of you for what you were to us during those days and for what you have done to make *"our Yoke easy and our burden light."* Love and prayers. God bless you.

Fr. Sebastian M.C. and all Vazhakala family

October 2004

Born on 17 December 1945
TRIBUTE TO JOSEPH VAZHAKALA
Died on 03 October 2004

"The Lord gave, the Lord has taken away. Blessed be the name of the Lord.
Naked I came forth from my mother's womb and naked shall I go back again" (Job 1: 21)

It is almost impossible for me and the family of my brother Joseph to express our sincere thanks to so many of you, who have tried to share in our sorrow through telephone calls, email, fax, letters, cards...and for those who did it in person. Yes, you have learned to live the words of St. Paul who says: *"Rejoice with those who rejoice, and weep with those who weep."* (Rom 12: 15) Your words of comfort, your promise of assiduous prayers and generous sacrifices have made our sorrow lighter and the soul of my brother Joseph enter heaven faster. May the God of all consolation reward you for your great kindness and sublime generosity. You all made me reflect once again more deeply on the words: *"We are one in the Spirit, we are one in the Lord."* It is by the way we express our love for one another that the world will come to know that we indeed are Christians!

Joseph died, but his love and charity did not die. His soul was separated from his frail and broken body in order to be united to God, the source of all love. Love cannot be conquered but conquers everything and everyone. Is there anything that love cannot do? Love

225

has no boundaries; it never comes to an end; love never gives up. Love is more happy to give and share than to receive and enjoy (cf. 1Cor 13 1-13).

Every Sunday Joseph went to Holy Family Church to participate in the Mass. He used to go an hour before the Mass started for two reasons: to spend some time in prayer before Jesus in the Blessed Sacrament, and also to help the catechists who teach catechism to the children before the Mass began. His beloved wife Mary and their three children, Shiny Joseph (23 years), Shyju Joseph (20 years) and Shyrus Joseph (17 years) followed him.

On Sunday, 3 October in the morning (2004) they did the same. They all participated in the 8.30 a.m. Mass. Unlike other Sundays, that morning the priest for some reason, did not give the homily. So the Mass was short. As the Holy Mass was over, he came out that day earlier than usual and was crossing the road on foot when suddenly a loaded mini truck came in full speed and hit him from the back. He was lifted up in the air, fell on top of the truck and then his head hit on the road very strongly. With it he straight away went into coma and never woke up.

Needless to say it was a real shock for his daughter Shyny who saw the whole thing, and his wife who was a little behind. They rushed him to the hospital. As he had several fractures on his legs and hands and there were no real cuts or wounds visible, the doctors plastered his legs and hands, but before finishing he went home to God, about 11.00 a.m. on Sunday, 3 October, 2004; may he rest in peace.

As I received the unexpected and painful news of my brother's going home to God, it took time for me to respond as Job did (Job 1:21). I needed much reflection and contemplation to come to understand and accept the event as the will of God and thank God for it. The divine logic did not conform with my way of thinking and reasoning. The "kairos" of God must come to grips with the human "chronos". I questioned God, his will, his ways, his "kairos" for my brother.

Was I wrong to do so? I opened the Bible and I found my justification for questioning the divine logic, when at the age of twelve Jesus was found missing after a day's journey from the Jerusalem temple and only on the third day were Mary and Joseph able to find him. As they *"found him in the temple, sitting among the teachers, listening to them and asking them questions…* " (cf. Lk 2: 46), the sorrow-filled parents were astonished. And Mary said to Jesus: *"Son, why have you done this to us?"* (Lk 2: 48) With and like her I questioned: "Why have you done this to my brother Joseph, right in front of his daughter Shiny? How could your merciful heart permit such a tragedy to a family that was doing so much good to the poor victims of tuberculosis, without counting the cost, without seeking rest and reward, even in the teeth of terrible oppositions and objections, conflicts and ideological clashes? And who will carry on with the work Mr. Joseph and Mrs. Mary and their family have been doing for so long a time?"

Like Mary who treasured all these things, pondering them in her heart (Lk 2: 19), I too have to do in order to accept the divine logic, the will and the plan of God in our lives. It is only through *this pondering in our heart* that we come to understand and accept the mystery of life and death and the divine logic that goes with it.

By nature Joseph was a very generous, affectionate, friendly and joyful person. Even as a boy he thought more of others' needs and interests than his own. As years went by he grew with some of the more outstanding virtues of love and care in a heroic way, as he did not enjoy very good health since the age of eighteen, when he had the first attack of epilepsy. Far from making it into a stumbling block, he used it as a stepping stone to practice all the more the virtue of Charity.

To express his altruism and heroic Charity, Joseph as a young man of twenty-six went to Kolkata to join the Brothers of the Missionaries of Charity of Mother Teresa in April, 1972. There he showed his love and dedication to the poorest of the poor in an extraordinary manner. All those who came to know him not only admired his zeal, but were edified as well. The periodic attacks of epilepsy became an obstacle for him to make his vows in the Missionaries of Charity. So, in June, 1975, he said good-bye to the institute, but not to his intense desire to serve the poor.

He kept his contact with Mother Teresa, from whom he sought advice and guidance on a regular basis. Once he expressed to her his desire to join the Contemplative Branch. Blessed Teresa wrote to me about it in one of her letters : *"… your brother Joseph is very anxious to join the Br. of the W. So I have sent him to Fr. Bede in the South to make an experience of the contemplative life before we make another step."* That experience made him realize that his life was not meant to be purely contemplative.

It took a while for him to re-orientate his future, to decide who he was going to serve and the way of serving them. He consulted Blessed Teresa of Kolkata again, who offered time and advice to him whenever he sought her help, and Fr. Cukale S.J. who took a real interest in him and guided him spiritually and otherwise. Several local people too became interested in the program. After much prayer and reflection he founded in the outskirts of Kolkata "*Shanti Tuberculosis Control Society*". The then health minister of West Bengal inaugurated Shanti, and Blessed Mother Teresa graced it by her welcome presence and words of appreciation. He simply called it "*Shanti*", which means "Peace".

As years went by, "Shanti" grew into a considerably big institution... along with its growing problems. One of the things he always resisted was corruption. He fought against it with all his strength; he also had to watch from making it into a political entity. His sole intention was to give loving service to the poorest of the poor, especially the T.B. patients.

Joseph often neglected his health very much. So Blessed Mother Teresa asked him to find a suitable partner who could look after him and also help him in his mission. She gave him three months' time to find a girl; otherwise she said that she herself was going to choose his future partner. But God chose the right person, Mary Kanyarkuzhiyil, within a month or so. Blessed Teresa writes: "*Your brother Joseph came with his future wife-she seems a very good girl. They will marry on the 28th Dec. I feel bad I will not be in Calcutta as I have to be in Mangalore* (Karnataka, India). *He looks well and happy.*" (from Mother Teresa's letter to Fr. Sebastian, 10.12.1980)

His wedding was a big event for the family as well as for the parish. My parents travelled over 2,600 km to share their joy and to participate in the event. His Excellency Msgr. Linus Gomes, the Bishop of the place of Bariupur, with seven other priests concelebrated and blessed their marriage on 28 December, 1980. Ever since his wife Mary came into his life, not only was he well looked after, but she worked very closely with Joseph, remaining faithful and loyal to the very end.

Three children, one girl and two boys, were born to them: Shiny, who has taken her Master's degree in "Computer Application" (MCA) with distinction; Shyju in computer hardware and electronic repair and trying to take his Bachelor's Degree in "Computer application" (BCA); while Shyrus, is still in the final year (Plus Two-Final) in an English medium high school.

Joseph left Kolkata in 1987 and came with his family to live near to my parents' place for over a year. But he was not tranquil. His love for the poor and suffering victims of tuberculosis moved him again to travel over 600 km. Upon inquiry and search he came to know that there were many T.B. patients among the fishermen, who were much neglected. He spoke with some of the priests of the Roman Catholic Church of the area of his intentions; they encouraged him to go ahead with his plans. So he founded *"S.T.E.P.-Shanti Tuberculosis Elimination Programme"* in the Vizhynam-Poovar area in the district of Trivandrum, Kerala. He began in a rented building. It took much time, effort, and above all lots of prayer and reflection before he could find the present site for S.T.E.P. Neither the family nor their activity had a house of their own. He did not, however, concentrate in providing a home for himself and his family; that was not his first priority; he thought of building one for his own family only after building a house for the T.B. patients.

Joseph was a man of God and a man for God, before he was a man for others. He never tried to fly with one wing, which means only doing a lot of good work. He never ever started his work without first praying together with the staff for at least 15 minutes, beginning with a song, then a passage from the Bible, followed by the Lord's prayer and the offering of the work of the day. Every evening at home with his family he used to pray more than an hour, reading the Word of God, followed by the rosary, litanies, devotional prayers and songs. Prayer and work went hand in hand for him. Even with his broken legs and broken heart he used to go to attend to the needs of the T.B. patients. Such was his love and dedication. The day following his death many newspapers called him, "Joseph, the saviour of T.B. patients". The priest during his homily at Mass for the repose of his soul compared him with Blessed Damien of Molokai. He said that as the leprosy patients have Blessed Damien as their heavenly patron to pray for and bless, so now the T.B. patients also have Joseph as their heavenly patron to intercede for them.

Let us pray that from heaven, he may continue to "save" many TB patients, as he was a

soul of heroic charity and an angelic alleviator of human suffering on earth!

God bless you all.

Fr. Sebastian Vazhakala M.C.

A Visit to My Beloved Dying Father
2005

Dear beloved Brother and Sisters,

It was on Sunday 18 September 2005 that I left Rome to visit and assist my beloved dying father, who is over 91. To be exact he was born on 2 May 1914.

Since I left Rome my communications with you all have been very limited. It has been done through telephone with only a few of you on business matters, the various problems of the houses, traveling arrangements, visas and the like. Needless to say, I miss you all very much and I long to be with you all as soon as I can.

I reached the hospital on the evening of 19 September 2005. My sister and my brother-in-law were with my father. As a matter of fact, they never left him alone, not even for an hour, from the time he was admitted to the hospital. I saw my father's terrible suffering. He sat on his bed for twenty-four hours. I too spent that night with him in the hospital, even though I was very tired from the long journey, to keep vigil with him, to clean him, and to make him feel a little better. Of course, none of us slept that night, not even for an hour. I really admired the heroic dedication of my brother-in-law and my sister and their family.

On the following morning I spoke with the doctor, who was in agreement with me to take my father home, as there wasn't much to do for him in the hospital. What he did need was tender loving care. It was and is a grace for me to devote a couple of weeks to look after my old and dying father, to do everything necessary for him. Most times I just sat close to him, as I would sit near Jesus in the Blessed Sacrament exposed.

My adoration of Jesus these days took a different form. My father was my Jesus in agony, in excruciating pain and distress. In a sense I am like one of the three apostles Jesus took with him to watch and pray in the night of his terrible agony. As he never went to sleep, I tried several other ways to make him feel comfortable. At times I question Jesus in my mind: how can you, Jesus, allow a person suffer like this? Even Blessed Teresa said towards the end of her earthly life that Jesus was asking a bit too much form her. When will my father end his pilgrimage and enter into the presence of God? Who am I, who are we to question God, as we know that his ways are not our ways, and for the most part, they are incomprehensible. "For who has known the mind of the Lord, or who has been his counselor?" (cd.Rom 11:34).

Practically speaking, the night and the day for my father are the same – a prolonged agony. And my sister and my brother-in-law and I go on watching with "this Jesus" in agony. It is very demanding, and yet very rewarding. It is extremely painful to see him suffering so much. He suffers so much in body and we suffer so much in spirit. Our suffering is something like our Lady's suffering when she stood near the cross of Jesus on that first Good Friday watching her son die like a criminal, when her heart was pierced by a sword of sorrow, when her heart was drowned in pain, and she was not able to do anything for him. Her faith was strong enough to move mountains and save souls. "In his wounds we are healed". (Is 53:5) and our souls are saved. They both, i.e. Jesus and Mary gave their all to save souls.

I, too, must believe the redemptive value and the sense of this excruciating pain that is like a two edged sword which cuts all the way through to where soul and spirit meet, to where joints and marrow come together.

It is hard, very hard to see this unending agony of the one whom I love, who gave me life and existence. Yes, he is doing his purgatory here on earth. His soul is being purified through the crucible of pain.

How does my father react to all this?

Most time he make his groaning into a form of prayer, an expression of love, and acts of profound faith. He says: "It is better that I suffer than to make Jesus suffer." He continues to thank God and told me that it is better to try to accept the will of God in all things. He said that if we do not do the will of God, our suffering can become worse. "Let Jesus decide for me, let Jesus choose for me. Personally, I would like to die, but if he wants me to go on suffering like this, I want to suffer, provided he gives me the strength and the grace to endure."

But he is not always able to accept his terrible pain like this. At times the unbearable pain almost throws him into convulsions. His entire body begins to tremble. WE try to hold him tight. Sometimes we succeed, but not always. He is not able to pray. His prayer is simple outcry: "O, Jesus, my Jesus, please be near me, give me a good death, forgive all my sins; if I have done evil, forgive me." He then comes to a calm disposition, even though his suffering continues. Oh, I could write pages and pages every day on his battle with life and death, between agony and ecstasy. He tells me again and again to thank all of you who pray for him, who think of him, who inquire about his health. Hence, here and now, in his name, in the name of the members of my family and me, I thank you for all that you do. We feel your closeness, your nearness, your participation, your brotherly sharing. It is so consoling, so comforting, so much more uplifting. Here distances become closer; colour, culture and nationality become accidental. Here we become one in the spirit, one in the Lord in suffering…suffering that unites us to God, and to one another. May the good God bless you, reward you, and write your names n the book of life. This is my prayer; this is my deep desire; and this is my joy. Please continue to help us to understand the Christian meaning and the redemptive value of human suffering. May we accept it as our vocation, as we know that the cross is the proof of the greatest love. Love necessarily leads to suffering for the beloved. Yes, our "vocation is to love and suffer and save souls". This was Jesus' vocation, our Lady's vocation, and this was and is the vocation of all the saints and martyrs. It is our vocation as well. What we need is the faith and strength to endure, to baptize our suffering and to recycle our trials into channels of grace and ways and means to save souls!

After staying with and looking after my father for just about two weeks, I came to Deepashram community on Saturday 8th October night 2005 for a week. It is a great joy and comfort to see my beloved Brothers and children of Deepashram. We have altogether 43 brothers;

this includes Br. Damian MC, the house superior and Br. Jean Marie MC, the joint superior. These two brothers have so much work; their hands are extra full. They really need our prayers, support and words of encouragement for the faithful fulfillment of their respective responsibilities and duties. With them we have the four Tertians: Brs. Benedict, Tony, Jan Timo, and Barnabas, who have just started their tertianship (third year of novitiate before they make their final vows) on Saturday 1st October 2005. They have to share much with Br. Damian and Br. Jean Marie to do the work of Deepashram, as eh majority of the brothers are young and in formation. We have three second-year novices who, God willing, may make their first vows on Thursday 2nd February 2006, while the four first-year novices will continue their formation. The remaining ones are 15 postulants who are being prepared to begin their novitiate; the other 15 are aspirants who are at the very first stag e of their formation.

Our 66 mentally and physically challenged orphaned boys are growing very quickly. Because they need additional space, we have bought 12 acres of land about 16 km away from Deepashram to start a rehabilitation centre. It may take a while to develop the land, as we need many resources. Thanks to AISPO, the Italian Association, for all their help and support. They recently also donated one more vehicle, which is very helpful in doing our work. May God reward them all, especially Dr. Wanda, Dr. Laura, and Dr. Gloria, who are very closely associated with the hospital San Raffaele in Milan and the Indian Spinal Injury Centre in New Delhi. There is always so much more to be done. I also would like to thank God for all those who help our boys and Deepashram community through distant adoption and the coordinator, Gianna Tommasi LMC. Thanks to Luigi and Tilde of Rome. The children look better, cleaner and more tidy. The washing of the children's clothes is going to become much easier. A big, really a very big 'thank you' to all of Deepashrams' friends, benefactors, volunteers and all.

Our Society feast this year is on Thursday 27th October 2005. Hence we begin our novena of the holy Family on Tuesday 18th October 2005. The text can be found in our Spiritual Path: "Novena for our Society". We make every effort to make our novena a real experience of God, a personal encounter with Jesus, Mary, and Joseph. It can be a very good retreat with the Holy Family. It is a time of renewal…to renew individually and as a Society. It is a time to reaffirm our fidelity to our MC vocation….to love and suffer and save souls. It is a time to see whether we are really growing in holiness and helping our brothers to persevere in doing God's will against their likes and dislikes. We are in need of convinced brothers who fall in love with Jesus and with our Society. Let us pray much and prepare ourselves for this great feast. Happy and Holy Society feast to all. Thanks to all our general councilors and superiors: Br. Subash, Br. Damian, Br. Andre Marie, Br. Jean Marie, and Br. Leo, the superior of Kumasi, Ghana. Thanks to the dedicated service of all of you. Love and prayers.

God bless you.

Fr. Sebastian Vazhakala MC

December 2005

Born on 2 May 1914
Tribute to Mr. Devasia (Sebastian) **Vazhakala**
Died on 5 December 2005
"For the greater glory of God"

Dearly beloved brothers and sisters,

It was seven minutes past four in the morning on Monday 5 December 2005. I was in the chapel in adoration before the Blessed Sacrament exposed. The telephone started ringing. I ran to answer. It was my sister-in-law, Mary, from Trivandrum, Kerala, who was chocked-up and was unable to speak, as she was crying (sobbing). She somehow made me understand that just a few minutes ago my beloved father went home to God, leaving this valley of tears, pain and sorrow. He breathed his last in a nearby clinic as he was taken there the day before (Sunday 4 December 2005).

I closed the phone and returned to Jesus in the Chapel. I felt that Jesus was there alone waiting for me; and he wanted me to share with him my sorrow… the first person, the first and best friend I could share with. I do not think that it was accidental that I was before Jesus in the Blessed Sacrament exposed when I received such heart-renting news!

Although I wanted very much that our God called my father to himself as early as possible, freeing him from his excruciating pain, giving him comfort and eternal rest in his company, the news of his final and definitive departure still troubled my heart, and to my great surprise tears began to fall from my eyes. At one point I cried aloud, which only Jesus heard, as there was nobody else around me in the

Chapel. A few times to my great surprise there were such almost spontaneous outbursts.

I closed the tabernacle to make a few telephone calls to get more accurate news of the death of my father and to tell them not to wait for me for the funeral, as I had to travel to Kumasi, Ghana, Africa on the following day to give the 8-day retreat in preparation for the deaconate ordination of Br. Peter and priestly ordination of Br. Stephen, which was scheduled for the 17 December 2005 in Ghana.

My father and I had greatly desired that he would go home to God in my presence and that I would perform his last rites. More than once he expressed this desire during his last illness. I prayed to the Lord very ardently for it as well. But the Lord wanted this great sacrifice from both of us. There is nothing greater and nobler in life than accepting the will of God with interior joy and filial gratitude. Besides, for me it was a beautiful sacrificial gift to offer to our Lord, especially for the repose of the soul of my father. The more painful and demanding the sacrifice is the more beautiful and meritorious the gift of sacrifice is. Here the words of St. Thérèse of Lisieux come to mind: *"...I wish to suffer for love's sake, and for love's sake even to rejoice...and I will sing...I will sing always, even if my roses must be gathered from amidst thorns, and the longer and the sharper the thorns, the sweeter shall be my song."*

I called my sister's house, but she was still at the clinic with my father. I called my brother's house and he had gone out. Finally, through their mobile phone I was able to talk to my sister, who alone was beside my father's side, sitting next to him while he breathed his last. After a night's long vigil, my brother-in-law had gone to purchase some medicine for my father at the nearby town, while my sister continued to keep vigil with my father. My sister told me over the phone that he spent the entire night sitting, as usual, calling his children one by one by name; but in the morning, a few minutes before he breathed his last, he called just two of us by name and said that he was going home to God. He called my niece Biji, who had taken care of him for some years and me, his unworthy son, after which he spoke no more. It was 8.30 a.m. (Indian time, (4.00 a.m. Rome time) of Monday 5 December 2005. About the same time two of the nurses just walked into the room to take blood for all sorts of tests. But it was no more necessary. His immortal soul, purified in the crucible of suffering, had just departed his frail and worn out body for his eternal reward (R.I.P.).

Yes, the hour had now come for him to pass from this world of tears, suffering and death to that never ending world of peace and joy. The world of the past had gone for him (cf. Rev. 21: 1-4).

My father never wanted to make Jesus suffer, even if he suffered terribly. *"It is better that I suffer"*, he used to say, *"rather than make Jesus suffer."* He suffered enough for the past three months, making up for his long and healthy life. Except for one time in April-May 1959, he has never been hospitalized, as far as I can remember, for any serious sickness. He even had all his teeth till the day he died.

The last time I was with him was in the afternoon of Tuesday 22 November 2005. We said good-bye to each other. Every time I said good-bye, I used to ask his blessing and he too used to do the same. This time also we blessed each other, putting our hands on each other's head. As he put both his hands on my head, he said: *"May God take care of you wherever you go. May Jesus protect you from all dangers and deliver you from all evil."* He continued to whisper some more prayers. As we did this, tears fell from our eyes and they got mixed in the presence of my elder brother, his elder son, Jolly, my sister and her family, our pastor of the parish of St. Sebastian, in Charral, and the mother superior of the convent in our parish and several other visitors. My father asked me when I was going to come back to see him again. "Please come back, I want to see you soon." I was not able to answer, but walked out of the room without words, knowing too well that I was not going to see him again in this life. I entrusted him to the care and protection of the Holy Family and St. Thérèse of Lisieux, as I thought she would understand and help us, as she too had some similar experience with her father towards the end of his earthly life.

My father was born at Ettumanoor, Kerala, India on 2 May 1914 and was baptized in the Church of St. Sebastian Athirampuzha on 12 May 1914. His uncle (maternal), Dr. C.L. Varkey, was a renowned and leading lawyer of his time. My parents got married when they were still very young, on 9 February 1931. Of course after their marriage each one continued to stay with his/her respective family for a few more years, as was the custom of the time.

My father was a born leader. This leadership was shown in the various sectors of his life. He was a man of faith. He worked very hard to build up the parish church as well as the parish community. I remember when I was about 7 years old, he, together with Fr. Paul Rathappilly, one of the Carmelite priests, and several of his friends took the initiative to found the new parish church at Malippara, Kothamangalam, Kerala. Under his leadership they went around to collect the necessary funds to build the rectory. If ever he started anything, no matter how difficult the project might have turned out to be, he would never leave it half done or unfinished, but would do everything possible to bring it to completion. I have seen him sacrificing his rest, sleep and food for weeks to accomplish something he has taken in hand.

Towards the end of 1950 the whole family migrated to the northern part of Kerala, where for two hundred and fifty years nobody had lived. This meant that there was nothing but very thick forest. There were no roads, no schools, no churches, no houses or neighbourhoods… nothing but wild animals, monkeys and snakes. We were four families together to venture into such area. I still remember very vividly my father and his friends trying to build roads. He was one of the pioneers to take the lead in building roads, schools, churches, etc. Throughout those growing years I very closely watched and followed my father as well as I could. There was always something new to learn from him.

He worked in the religious, social and political field to build up a better society, sacrificing even his own personal needs and comforts and that of the family.

He made our home our first school and our parents and elders our first teachers, demanding rather strict order and discipline.

Our parents worked very closely to build up a real religious family. They taught us to love God in prayer and love God in our neighbour. People spontaneously came to visit us, and we too liked to visit our neighbours. We were a very happy family together.

My father had a special love for the old and the sick people. If any sick person needed to be accompanied to the hospital, he would go with him without counting the cost. I remember him taking a cancer patient to a very far away hospital and staying with him as long as it was necessary.

His love for the poor was something extraordinary. He told us all that we should never send a beggar or a poor person away empty handed. It was a custom in our family after meals to save some food for one person. Unlike today, during those early years we did not have electricity, refrigerator, telephones, etc. Life then was much more simple, poor and primitive. He also instructed us not to give to anybody the left over food or things that we did not like. If you give anything to anyone, then give the best and not the worst.

Every Wednesday was dedicated to the Holy Family. So it was our custom to invite periodically on Wednesdays a poor family – father, mother and their son to the house. They had to be welcomed as we would welcome Jesus, Mary and Joseph, serve them very respectfully with a well prepared meal after a short prayer.

My father used to organize monthly prayer meetings at our house to pray for the living and the dead, always followed by a meal.

The feast of St. Sebastian is the most solemnly and socially celebrated feast in the entire state of Kerala even today. There was a very solemn procession carrying the statue of St. Sebastian to the various parts of the spread out and mountainous parish, accompanied by music, band, fireworks, etc. My father always prepared a special place in our own land, near our house, beautifully decorated, where the entire group came in solemn procession and where they offered special prayers, songs and votive offerings. He made sure that we served a full meal to all. In all these he always went out of his way to prepare whatever was necessary, involving us all and making us all work very hard.

He always loved children, even to the very last day. When he saw them his face became spontaneously radiant. He would heed to their demands, so much so that we used his two years old grandniece, Angelina, to invite him to eat, to take medicine, etc. When he would say no to us, he would easily say yes to her with a smile.

Failures and tragedies did not become a stumbling block in his life, but he used them as stepping stones. He considered any failures as stepping stones to success.

Once he gave his word to anybody or agreed to do something, he made sure that he did it. He used to tell us that if you cannot do something, or if you don't want to do something for some reasons, do not say "I will do it" and then refrain from doing it.

Punctuality for him was very vital. He never liked to reach anywhere late on his own fault. Often he would be the first one to reach a place. "Never make a person wait on account of your fault". He used to instruct us.

He was very quick in everything… in getting ready, in doing things, etc.

He was a joyful person and liked to see others also joyful. He liked very much to create jokes and make people laugh.

He was very self-disciplined and moderate in eating and drinking. Nobody could force him to eat or drink; once he said no, that was it.

Well then, these are some of the positive qualities I have observed in my father. According to St. Thomas of Aquinas, the two pillars of humility are truth and justice. The truth is that whatever is good in a person comes from God, and justice is to give glory to God for all the gifts and blessings. So I have mentioned a few of these gifts of God in my father so that God may be praised and glorified. My father's life long desire was the same: *"Amen. Praise and glory and wisdom, thanksgiving and honour and power and strength to our God for ever and ever. Amen."* (Rev. 7: 12)

Thanks to you, brothers, thanks to you sisters, for all your prayers, letters, emails, faxes, telephone calls, through which you expressed your sympathy, shared our sorrow and pain, making our sorrow much lighter and the soul of my father enter heaven faster. This is what true charity is all about. God will never forget the good you have done, whether we deserve it or not, because anything we do for anyone, Christ counts as done for him. Besides, he will reward you a hundred times more blessings of every kind, spiritual and material, in this life, and eternal life in the world to come.

Let us hope and pray that my father is already in heaven and that he sends blessings in abundance for each one of you, especially in this holy season of Christmas and New Year. I too wish you a very happy and holy Christmas and a peace-filled New Year 2006.

With much love and prayers. God bless you.

Fr. Sebastian Vazhakala M.C. and family.

CHAPTER FIVE:
LENT AND EASTER

Lent 1995

Dearly beloved Brothers and Sisters,

Once again the Holy Season of Lent is near to prepare us all for the great event of the Death and Resurrection of Jesus our Lord and Saviour.

According to biblical tradition, Moses stayed on Mount Sinai 40 days in communion with **God** before he received the Law of the Covenant. Our Lord fasted and prayed 40 days in the desert before He started His public mission of loving service. We too need to join in this redemptive mission of Jesus through prayer, penance and works of mercy, especially in this Holy Season, which is meant to purify and sanctify us. We are called to be purer than we are. To reach this state of purity we need to pray **much,** which would make us more and more unselfish. Renunciation and immolation are a "must" and are therefore essential components for purity. This purity must be total, and one must also yearn and long for it. In simple terms the word **Purity** has six letters, each of which expresses an important element that demands self-denial and sacrifice:

P - Prayer
U - Unselfishness
R - Renunciation
I - Immolation
T - Total
Y - Yearning

All these elements are absolutely necessary to attain purity. The Season of Lent provides a better opportunity to practice them. Lent is the 40-day period of prayer, penance and spiritual endeavour in preparation for Easter. Lent is not an end in itself; it exists only to lead to the paschal feast and so can be rightly understood only in the light of Easter. Easter gives meaning to Lent and shows it for what it **is:** the great paschal retreat of the Church. "The season of Lent has a twofold character: primarily by recalling or preparing for Baptism and by penance, it disposes the faithful, who more diligently hear the word of God and devote themselves to prayer, to *celebrate the Paschal Mystery" (Constitution on the Sacred Liturgy 109).*

Fasting. The custom may have originated in the prescribed fast of candidates for Baptism; it is certain that the catechumenate had a great deal to do with the formation of Lent. The number 40 was suggested no doubt by Our Lord's 40-day fast in the desert. The manner of reckoning the 40 days, however, varied in the different Churches. The East as a rule spread Lent over seven weeks, with both Saturday and Sunday exempt from fasting; whereas the West had a six-week period, with only Sunday exempt. As a result there were only 36 actual fasting days, a situation that the Western Church remedied in the seventh century by adding four days, beginning with Ash Wednesday. In the 4th century, however, the concern was not so much about whether there were 40 actual fasting days or not; the approach was to the season as a whole. The emphasis was not so much on the fasting as on the spiritual renewal that the preparation for Easter demanded. It was simply a period marked by fasting, but not necessarily one in which the faithful fasted every day. However, as time went on, more and more emphasis was laid upon fasting, and consequently there is apparent a more precise calculation of the 40 days.

During the early centuries (from the 5th century on especially) the observance of the fast was very strict. Only one meal a day, toward evening, was allowed; flesh meat and fish, and in most places even eggs and diary products, were absolutely forbidden. Meat was not allowed even on Sundays. However, from the 9th century on the practice began to be considerably relaxed. The time for the one evening meal was anticipated so that by the 15th century it was the general custom even for religious to have this meal at noon. Once that was general the way was opened for a collation in the evening, which by the 13th century included some light food as well as drink. The prohibition against fish was removed during the Middle Ages, while dispensation permitting the use of diary products came to be more general.

In the course of the last few centuries the Holy See has granted other more substantial mitigations of the law of fasting. Meat was allowed at the principal meal on Sundays, then gradually on the weekdays, Fridays always excepted. The trend to greater emphasis on other form of penitential works than fasting and abstinence, particularly on exercises of piety and the works of charity, found legislative expression in the apostolic constitution *Poenitemini* of Pope Paul VI (Feb. 17,1966). According to this constitution, abstinence is to be observed on Ash Wednesday and on all Fridays of the year that do not fall on holy days of obligation, and fasting as well as abstinence is to be observed on Ash Wednesday and Good Friday.

Spirit. The popular idea of Lent, which prevailed until well into the 20th century, was that it was a time of prolonged meditation upon the Passion, with special emphasis upon the physical sufferings. This view finds little support in the texts of the Lenten liturgy, and in any case must be abandoned in the light of Vatican Council II's insistence that the season of Lent has the twofold character: by recalling or preparing for Baptism and Penance to dispose the faithful for a celebration of the paschal mystery. Furthermore, the *Constitution on the Sacred Liturgy* declares that it is important to impress upon the minds of the faithful not only the social consequences of sin, but also the true nature of the virtue of penance as leading to the detestation of sin as an offence against God.

Lent is unquestionably a time of penance, of asceticism, of spiritual discipline. However, making these things ends in themselves obscure the real purpose of Lent, as it is found in the sermons of the Fathers, especially St. Leo, and in the liturgy itself. The accumulated evidence of Christian tradition in this regard shows without any doubt that the real aim of Lent is, above all else, to prepare men for the celebration of the death and Resurrection of Christ. This celebration is not a matter only of commemorating the historical fact of man's Redemption, but even more of *reliving* the mystery of redemption in all its fullness, which means renewing in man the power of the Redemption and appropriating its effects for him. Consequently, the better the preparation the more effective the celebration will be. One can effectively relive the mystery only with purified mind and heart. The purpose of Lent is to provide that purification by weaning men from sin and selfishness through self-denial and prayer, by creating in them the desire to do God's will and to make His kingdom come by making it come first of all in their hearts.

Lent is then a collective retreat of 40 days, a time when one tries to live in the spirit of his Baptism, a time of penance in the ancient sense of repentance, *metanoia*, change of heart and mind, conversion.

Once Lent was established in the 4th century, it quickly became associated with Baptism, since Easter was the great baptismal feast. It was the time when those catechumens who would be baptized at the Easter feast were more immediately prepared for that Sacrament. Not only those who were to be baptized, but all Christians prepared themselves for Easter. The Lenten season consequently developed into a time of spiritual renewal for the whole Church, a more profound initiation into the mystery of Christ. The whole Church renews her spiritual youth, and the necessary prelude to this rejuvenation is the awakening of the consciousness of Baptism, of realizing what it means to be baptized. This explains the prominence of the themes of Baptism, new life, and Redemption in the Lenten liturgy.

Lent is especially consecrated to the purification of the heart. This purification is accomplished first of all by sorrow for sin, compunction of heart, and penance, but it involves also the positive element, which is growth in virtue. The Church often insists in these 40 days upon fasting from sin and from vice; in fact bodily fasting is the symbol of this true internal and spiritual fast, as well as the means to attain it. True conversion, which is the aim of Lent, means forsaking sin and sinful ways. The Lenten Office reminds us of this every day: "Return to me with your whole heart, with fasting and weeping and mourning; rend your hearts and not your garments says the Lord Almighty" (Joel 2.12-13). The bodily fasting and self-discipline in which the Christian engages during this time has for its main purpose to give him that control over himself that he needs to purify his heart and renew his life. We are not only to fast from sin, but by our very fasting pursue holiness. The Gospel periscopes of this season present the person of Christ as the model and source of all holiness. They focus attention upon Him and inspire the Christian to follow in His steps.

This conversion from sin and compunction of heart should take place at the very beginning of Lent and should not be deferred to the end of the season. Lent is not intended to be a kind of preparation for the Easter Confession. On the contrary, the original idea was that Confession was made before Lent began. The penance was imposed on Ash Wednesday, and penitents guilty of very serious sins were excluded from the Eucharist until they were absolved on Holy Thursday. The whole Lenten season is the time for penance, which means sorrow for sin and conversion to God. A further reason for confessing great sins before Lent begins is that the Holy Eucharist plays an important part in bringing about that purification of heart that is the goal of the Lenten observance. Over and over again the Church speaks of this special work that the Eucharist accomplishes in man during this season.

Lent emphasises both the unity of the Christian Community and as an important time of special prayer. It also shows that Lent is not an individualistic affair, but a corporate action that involves the whole community.

The texts of the older ferial Masses show strong influence of the themes of the Lenten season: penance, conversion, return to God, sorrow for sin, redemption, the Passion, and especially Baptism. The fact that Lent was the great baptismal retreat of the Church and the last stage of the catechumenate has greatly affected the liturgy of the season.

The last two weeks of Lent are known are Passiontide; the second of these weeks is called Holy Week; the theme of the Masses during this time is the Lord's Messianic mission achieved by means of His Passion. The prayers continue to refer to fasting, but most of the chants are drawn from those Psalms that allude to the voice of Christ in His Passion. The Gospels during this time present the Passion as a growing conflict between Christ and His enemies. The Office during Passiontide is remarkable, chiefly for the hymns that sing the triumph of the cross: the *Pange lingua* of Prudentius and the *Vexilla Regis* of Venantius Fortunatus. As Alleluia is so intimately associated with the joy of Easter, it is natural that it should be dropped out during so penitential a season as Lent. It also explains why we do not use flowers in the Chapel and limit the use of the organ only to sustain the music.

In accordance with our Constitutions and the Custom Book, each community decides concretely how best we can live this special season, which can be enlightened by the above given reflections and meditations. So please read them carefully before you meet together, and also read the 12th and 13th chapters of the constitutions and the part on penance in chapter 21 of the Custom Book.

I wish you a very joyful and holy Lent and the feasts of St. Joseph (Our Foundation Day) and the Annunciation of our Lord (Aspirants' and Postulants' Feast). Let us continue to pray for each other and for all. Thank you for all your prayers; please continue to pray for me.

God bless you.

Fr. Sebastian Vazhakala M.C.

Lent 1997

"God thirsts that we may thirst for Him" (St. Augustine)
"Prayer is the response of love to the thirst of the only Son of God."
(Catechism of the Catholic Church N. 2561)

Dearly beloved brothers and sisters in Christ,

One of the most holy seasons of the entire liturgical year is Lent, which originally meant Spring time. It begins with Ash Wednesday that opens the door to a more regulated human and Christian life. It touches the three areas of one's life: physical, psychological and moral. It invites us to re-examine the two essential dimensions of our life and existence: the vertical, i.e. our relationship with God, and the horizontal, i.e. our relationship with our neighbor. The ashes we receive on the forehead are symbolic as well as a reminder that our earthly lives are in constant need of reform and readjustments. The Gospel of Ash Wednesday and the successive readings bring home to us that the three basic aspects of human and Christian life are: *I. Almsgiving (Charity), 2. Prayer, and 3. Penance,* all of which are the very corner stones of the M.C. Charism. Can we ever imagine an M.C. without practicing Charity or devoid of any interest to pray nor any desire to practice asceticism and penance, all of which form and reform his character and tune his being, preparing him to be a citizen of the world to come? All the three points directly and immediately touch God, myself and my neighbor: *prayer* - my relationship with God; *penance* - my relationship with myself; and *almsgiving* - my relationship with my neighbor.

249

The earth is the arena of man to prepare himself for the life to come. No human being can become anything...good or bad, saints or sinners outside of this planet. It is here on earth and here alone he makes all his decision to be what he wants to be; it is here he determines his final goal; it is here he chooses heaven or hell!; it is here on earth he fights his battle with all his might and power against the evils and injustices of this world.

Lent, which prepares us for the great feast of the paschal mystery of Christ, reminds us of our many duties and obligations towards God, our neighbor and ourselves. All these aspects find home with the M.C.s and the M.C. family in various forms, degrees and levels. Your response to my Christmas letter was a clear sign of the Koinonia - Communion, this sharing in a very personal way with the sick and the weak, with the poor and the downtrodden. Some of us feel duty-bound to help those who have less or nothing. The project for the handicapped children in India has been executed. The work is in progress. Over 60 people are working daily almost seven days a week. They do most work manually. This enables many poor people to have a meal and some earning. About 30 families who otherwise will have no means of support stay at our place. Only God knows when we will be able to realize the entire project. But I am convinced that it is His work and in His own time and His own way it will be realized. Your thoughtful offerings are like bricks in a wall. With many bricks the house walls are built. It is the work of God accomplished through human hands and human minds. You all have a share in it through your prayer, penance and Charity. The question is not how much or how little, but how interested we are, how concerned we are, how eager we are to help our neediest brothers and sisters who are just like you and me, and yet they do not have the facilities and commodities that we have, and even perhaps the God-given spiritual and intellectual stamina that you have!

We are already in the month of March, which bridges the two seasons of Winter and Spring...that is like St. Joseph who is the bridge between the Old and the New Testament; Jesus' coming into the world was real Spring. And it was to St. Joseph the eternal Father entrusted the care of the "well Spring of life, Jesus" and of Mary the Virgin Mother of God. Let us pray much to St. Joseph that we may leave behind all our frozen attitudes and let new life appear in us. On March 19, which is also the foundation day of the M.C. Contemplative Brothers, we have the Diaconate ordination of Br. Mark Poulin M.C. It will be at 10 a.m. in the Cathedral Church in Shkodra, Albania. All of you are cordially invited to grace the occasion by your most welcome presence and ardent prayers.

The work in Albania is moving slowly. We have been there since September 8, 1991. Our Noviciate House is there, too. Both Houses need much repair. One of the churches we built five years ago needed repair of the entire roof, which thanks be to God is now completed. The Brothers' House needs new roofing, as does the Noviciate House. The good Lord continues to bless us with "our daily bread". Until **now Divine** Providence took care of us. It is always the amazing grace that brought us thus far and the same amazing grace will lead us on. The same is true of our little Society: its growth in holiness and in number, its expansion and consolidation.

The Sisters of the Missionaries of Charity have come from the four corners of the earth to Calcutta for their seventh General Chapter, which is still in session. The whole world is so eagerly waiting to know who can and who is going to replace someone like Mother Teresa. The answer is very simple: the same "Divine Providence" and the very same "amazing grace" that called Mother Teresa in the train on her way to Darjeeling will choose the one who can best serve the Society in humility and Charity and can lead on to its fulfillment. Let contemplation replace curiosity and unnecessary preoccupation as the future of the Society depends on contemplation. Unless we are contemplatives we will fail to proclaim Christ in a credible way (P.P. John Paul II).

Mother Teresa has been a contemplative in the heart of the world. Even in the midst of terrible discomfort and pain she keeps her prayer life intact. I saw this again while I was visiting her in the hospital in Calcutta last December, where I had the good fortune to celebrate or concelebrate many times the Holy Mass in her hospital bedroom and to pray with and for her. Her life continues to be a sacrificial offering of love in the name of and for the sake of the M.C. family, the Church and the world at large. And yet at times she too feels crushed by the weight of bitter suffering in body, mind and soul. Like Jesus and with Him she too prays: "Father, if possible let this chalice be taken away, but not my will but your will be done". Yes, she said to me: "Jesus is asking a lot from me". Like the psalmist we all feel at times that "we are at the end of our strength". Through struggle and contemplation we come to the shore of peace inviting us to experience the power of the Lord's death and resurrection which this holy Lent is preparing us to. It is in the contemplation of the crucified Christ in the silence of faith and adoration that all vocations find their inspiration and the strength to persevere unto death.

Before I conclude this letter I would once again like to express my heart-felt thanks in the name of my Brothers and of the poorest of the poor to all LMCs, to our spiritual and temporal benefactors, co-workers, volunteers and all those who help us in any way through their prayers, sacrifices and Charity, here in Rome, in Albania and India. May the good Lord reward you for your kindness and generosity.

May all of you have a blessed Easter that takes us through the Holy Week, especially through Good Friday. Please remember us in your prayers that we may not spoil God's work, but do it with ever greater enthusiasm and renewed fervor. I too pray for you every day. Love and prayers. God bless you.

Fr. Sebastian Vazhakala M.C.

Lent 2000

This is the great Jubilee Year 2000.

The Holy season of Lent and the Pascal event is very special this year. How fruitfully we try to live it is up to us. It is said that God loves a cheerful giver. The more generous we are, the more abundantly we receive...grace upon grace.

Lent is a unique period in the entire liturgical year. It is six weeks. It is not too long to prepare for the Easter event, the Pascal mystery that changed human history and life. The period that Jesus devoted to reflection, prayer and fasting is represented to us by the forty days of Lent. For Him it was decisive, a time of deliberate choice of the way He was going to walk. The path that He chose was one of suffering, rejection, humiliations, conflicts and contradictions, oppositions, false accusations, calumnies...all of which ended up in a most painful and shameful death on the Cross. Born among animals He was going to be hung on the Cross between two criminals.

For Jesus it was all deliberate and decisive. He was not going to be led into it by chance or by mistake. His long retreat was an immediate preparation for the *"road to Jerusalem"*. This rough road of suffering was also a gentle way of love. *"Greater love than this no man has..."*; *"God so loved the world that he gave His Son..."*; yes, *"He gave His Son"* to us sinners. *"Jesus died for us even when we were sinners"* (cf. Rom 5, 7).

Here we ask:

What have I done for Christ?

What am I doing for Christ?

What more must I do for Christ?

"Near the Cross of Jesus stood His mother…" (Jn 19, 25). Let us stand with Mary near the Cross of Jesus so that we can also share with Mary the joys of the resurrection of her beloved Son, Jesus.

"My people, what have I done to you? How have I offended you? Answer me!…"; *"What more could I have done for you…?"* (See Good Friday reproaches).

What more can I do for you, my adorable Jesus? Love for love; love with love…Love has to be shown in deeds. *"He does much who loves much"*. Hence:

Punctuality – to be on time for all community exercises…all without exception.

We begin the Divine Mercy Chaplet at 2.50 p.m. So the bell is rung at 2.45; and please, Brothers I would like you all to be present as we start the Chaplet. Tea can be taken before and also after if you wish, but not while praying the Chaplet.

Faithfulness to our duty: all sorts of duties, small and big, assigned to me: house cleaning, bell ringing, meal preparation…Casa Serena, etc.

Doing all things with great love, since we do everything to Jesus: *"You did it to Me."*

Praying all the prayers reflectively, with due attention and meditation, and not simply reading them as a formality or duty. This applies to all forms of prayers; and prayer leaders should pay special attention when starting and leading the prayers.

Days of silence: interior and exterior silence. Silence of the eyes, ears and tongue. Silence of the mind, memory and imagination.

Tuesday and Friday: total silence

Monday: singing practice in English during night recreation

Wednesday: singing practice in Italian.

"A r*eligious is a lay person turned into silence*".

Days of fasting and abstinence.

Tuesday: Church fast – simple breakfast, simple soup for supper, abstinence (lunch).

Friday: no lunch and simple supper.

Saturday: total abstinence.

Practicing the virtues:

a) The theological virtues of faith, hope and charity;

b) The moral virtues of prudence, justice, fortitude and temperance;

c) Virtue of humility and all the virtues opposed to the capital sins: pride, avarice, envy, wrath, lust, gluttony and sloth;

d) The virtue of love and forgiveness to a heroic degree; and help, love and serve "our enemies".

Reflective reading and study of the Scriptures...and the *Imitation of Christ*, and sharing with our Brothers and with all men of good will the fruit of our reading, study and reflection.

Other items of personal choice with permission.

Let us also pray for each other and try to be more kind, gentle, understanding and open, ready to dialogue rather than to argue or answer back.

"*Jesus meek and humble of heart make my heart like yours*".

Jesus, how much you have suffered for me. Let me offer this (whatever kind...physical, psychological or moral) suffering in union with your suffering.

"*Passion of Christ, strengthen me*".

"*Jesus, my Saviour, let me hide myself within your wounds*".

"*Water flowing from the side of Christ, wash me*".

Pray "The Litany of the Precious Blood"

Do bodily penances with peace, serenity and joy.

This is all for now. Please do pray for me as I do for you. You are most welcome to come for renewal of permissions. Wishing you a holy and fruitful Lent. "***He does much who loves much***".

Love and prayers.

God bless you.

Fr. Sebastian Vazhakala M.C.

Lent 2001

Smile more tenderly, offer more sacrifices, pray more fervently
Your vocation is to love, to suffer and to save souls (Jesus to Mother, 10 Sept., 1946)
Teach the people to pray the family Rosary (Our Lady to Mother)

Dearly beloved Brothers and Sisters,

We are in Lent. It is a time of many graces for all those who hunger and thirst for holiness through humility and charity.

Lent offers us many opportunities to express our love more fruitfully in service. Again and again we must assiduously beg God to make us worthy to serve our fellow men as Jesus served. The quality of our service is very important and it depends not on how much we do but on how much love we put into our doing. Service without love cannot be sincere. It can easily be felt and noticed. Like when we take our meals, we can easily notice whether there is enough salt in the food or not. The salt is very simple, but without it the food is tasteless. As the salt is necessary for the food to be tasty, love is necessary for our actions to be fruitful and effective.

Lent is a time for us to re-examine our actions...whether we do them with love, or without it. We may not need to do big things in this holy season, but to do ordinary things with extraordinary love and to be constant in doing them.

Just the other morning I was at the main train station in Rome (Termini). A man walked up to me and asked for some money. He didn't look that poor, sick or old. I asked why he did not look for a job, to which his answer was that nobody gave him a job. We talked for a while together, and then he asked me again for money to get some breakfast. So I told him to come with me to a bar and he was happy. He became so much more friendly. He had his coffee with joy. Very often it is easy for us to give a little money and walk by, but it can be more demanding to go the extra mile with our needy brother. Lent is the right time to do that.

One of the M.C. Brothers who was also a dear friend said one day to Mother Teresa: Mother, my vocation is to work for the lepers. Mother said: *No, brother, your vocation is to belong to Jesus and become holy like Him by doing God's will as Jesus did His Father's will.* If we are really holy, and if we try to do God's will, we also will be eager to love and serve our fellow men throughout the world who live and die in poverty and hunger. We will then want to pray: *Lord, give them through our hands this day their daily bread and by our understanding love, give them peace and joy.*

Hope to hear from you all soon. On 18 March at 5.00 p.m. we had the blessing of the continued renovated house by his Eminence Cardinal Mayer O.S.B. It was a profound experience of God. Thanks so much for your material and spiritual help.

On Wednesday 25 April, 2001, at 4.00 p.m., God willing we will have the priestly ordination of Br. Ivan Marie M.C. by Archbishop Piergiorgio Sivano Nesti, Secretary of the Congregation for Religious. All of you are cordially invited to participate in it by your welcome presence and fervent prayers.

Some suggestions for the holy season of Lent:

1) Some important virtues to practice especially during Lent:

- More silence: interior and exterior

- More humility, more charity, more joy

- More forgiveness, more mercy

- More gentleness and more tenderness, etc.

2) Greater fidelity to one's duties of state of life and also to the spiritual exercises:

- Examination of conscience

- Contemplation: contemplating the face of Jesus in the Eucharist, in each other and in the persons of the poor.

- Scripture reading

- All duties of the state of life; duties towards one's family, etc.

3) Meditative reading of the Passion: Mt. 26 and 27;

- Mk 14 and 15;

- Lk 22 and 23

- Jn 18 and 19

- Stations of the Cross

4) Fast and abstinence:

- From food (whatever little sacrifices one is able to make)

- From watching television (limited time, and only useful and beneficial programmes)

    However, it is a good and holy practice to humble ourselves by abstaining from other than mere food for the body. The eye should abstain from all vain and curious sights, the ears from listening to idle talks, the tongue from detraction and frivolous words. True sorrow for past sins can best be expressed through acts of love and charity towards our brothers.

5) Study of the Statutes for 15 minutes a day (recommended).

6) The evil one is going to be very active during the season of Lent. He knows our weaknesses and failures more than we ourselves know them. The devil has taken his degree in capital sins in Lucifer's university. Listen to our first Pope: *"Stay sober and alert. Your opponent, the devil, is prowling like a roaring lion looking for someone to devour. Resist him, remain solid in your faith."* (1Pt 5: 8-9a).

Let us pray for each other that we may have a very fruitful and joyful Lent that prepares us for the great and glorious feast of Easter.

God bless you

Fr. Sebastian Vazhakala M.C.

Holy Week 2002

Dearly beloved Brothers and Sisters in the Holy Family,

"Time has no pity for the human heart", wrote the mystic Indian Hindu poet R. N. Tagore. We continually experience this in our own lives. *"Time and tides wait for none"*. Our life on earth is a profound mystery. As the years pass by we slowly enter more deeply into this mystery through prayer and contemplation and through the various experiences of daily life.

My trip from 28 February to 17 March to Puerto Rico via Philadelphia and the East Coast area of the United States was very special. The main purpose of this long trip was to give an eight-day retreat to a group of 24 Senior Sisters coming from 17 houses of the Haiti region of the Missionaries of Charity. I'm very grateful to Sr. Ronald, the regional Superior, all the retreatants and all the others who took care of me so tenderly. It was such a great joy for me to meet and pray, to talk and share with so many of the M.C.s and LMCs in Puerto Rico, in Philadelphia, Washington DC, Connecticut, New Jersey and New York. Some of them could only be contacted by phone. All in all the meetings were very enriching and strengthening. Thanks be to God and thanks to each and every one of you for what you were and what you did for me. Many a time I thought of the Gospel of Mathew (10: 42): *"Whoever gives to one of these little ones, even a cup of cold water because he is a disciple, truly, I say to you, he shall not lose his reward"*. You gave me much more than cold water. What will your reward be in heaven? May the good Lord reward you in abundance for your kindness and generosity!

My flight to Rome was delayed for 36 hours. There was some trouble with the aircraft and twice they tried to detect and repair the fault. But in the end they gave up. During those hours, over 300 passengers remained on board. Then at about midnight we were told that our flight to Rome was postponed to 10 p.m. and that we had to claim our baggage and carry it to the hotels we were assigned to. You can imagine the restlessness, the confusion and the anxiety of the passengers, who seemed completely lost. There was a lot of running around, here and there, up and down, not knowing exactly what to do. By 2.30 a.m. I reached the hotel. In the morning I contacted our M.C. Sisters in Chester (PA) who so kindly came to pick me up. It turned out to be a very beautiful and fruitful day of prayer, meetings, sharing, confessions of the people in the shelter, etc. The day concluded with the Holy Mass. A very big 'Thank You' to the Superior, her Community in Chester, their co-workers and the poor.

I reached Rome in the afternoon of Sunday, 17 March instead of the early morning of Saturday, 16 March. It is better to arrive even a day or two late than to lose one's life in a plane crash. My hour had not yet come. But then I had my ransom, which I did not know then, but the Lord knew.

Before I left Rome for Puerto Rico we had scheduled a special Holy Mass for 18 March at 5.30 p.m., to be celebrated by one of the Archbishops from the Vatican who would bless the first stone for our home for homeless handicapped boys to be built in Bushat, Shkodra, Albania. It was a wonderful celebration. Thanks to Dr. Salvatore Sicignano, our beloved brother, friend, volunteer and benefactor who organized the entire evening celebration so well that all returned home glorifying and praising God. The participants were varied – from simple people to professionals, architects, engineers, chartered accountants, doctors and even the football player Abel Balbo and his wife, as well as the LMCs and volunteers. The Archbishop was extremely happy and enthusiastic about the new project in Albania.

There is no real joy and happiness in this world without some sadness and pain. This world is a mixture of sadness and joy, sorrow and happiness. This was again proved on 18 March, 2002 when my niece Mini and Dr. Gloria Lolli called me from my home in India. They were unable to speak except to cry aloud. For a couple of minutes

I only could hear their loud crying. The words were not coming out of them. My immediate thought was perhaps something bad might have happened to my 88-year-old beloved father. But no. My beloved brother Zacharia, 46 years of age, went home to God on the afternoon of 18 March, leaving behind his beloved ones including Mini, whom many of you have come to know as five years ago in July she fell from the terrace of her house and became paralyzed for life. I was dumbfounded, shocked and confused. If I had the *faith* and *patience* of *Job* I would also have said as he did when he lost everything and everyone dear to him except his wife:

"Naked I came from my mother's womb and naked shall I return;

The Lord gave and the Lord has taken away; blessed be the name of the Lord" (Job 1: 21)

He continued: *"Shall we receive good at the hand of God, and shall we not receive evil?"* (Job 2: 10).

Instead, from the depth of my heart I offered a prayer for the repose of his soul and then tried to calm Mini down, asking her how it all took place and how her beloved mother Mary was, her younger married sister Reni and Marvins, her 14 years old brother. It was difficult for her to tell or share, nor did she have all the news about the event as yet. The point became clearer to me that what matters is not any more the *"how and why"* it happened but the *"now"*. The fact is that he is no more there to support the family, to take care of them, to be their father, husband, friend and brother. He is gone to Him who is the Author of life and shall not return to us again, but we have to go to him as King David said of his child who died in spite of his fasting, prayer and supplications. God has His way, His Kairos – the appointed time - for each one of us. His clock doesn't always go with ours. His time is different from our time. Who am I to question God, but simply to surrender myself to His will with loving trust, like Jesus who said, even when everything seemed to be a complete failure: *"Father into your hands I commit my spirit"* (Lk 23: 46). *"Jesus' cry on the Cross, dear Brothers and Sisters, is not the cry of anguish of a man without hope, but the prayer of the Son who offers His life to the Father in love, for the salvation of all. At the very moment when he identifies with our sin, '**abandoned**' by the Father, He abandons Himself into the hands of the Father. His eyes remain fixed on the Father...More than an experience of physical pain, His passion is an agonising suffering of the* soul…"; "…On the Cross there is the paradoxical blending of bliss and pain" (Novo Millenio Ineunte, 26). "The soul is blissful and afflicted", says St. Catherine of Siena, "afflicted on account of the sins of its neighbour, blissful on account of the union and the affection of charity which it has inwardly received". To Mother Teresa Jesus said: "Your vocation is to love and to suffer and to save souls". He continued to say to her: "In your immolation, in your love for Me they (the poor) will see Me, know Me, want Me. Offer more sacrifices, smile more tenderly and pray more fervently". There is no Easter Sunday without Good Friday. Bliss and affliction are the two sides of the same coin. This is what we celebrate in the Holy Week year after year. Although the liturgical Good Friday and Easter Sunday may not coincide with our own personal Good Fridays and Easter Sundays in this life, the liturgical celebrations prepare us to go through life with the same attitude of Jesus.

The final and definitive separation of a beloved one from one's immediate family and friends, especially if the death is premature humanly speaking, creates a big gap in the family, imprinting an indelible pain and sorrow into hearts. This is what the loss of my brother Zacharia did to the family and to me, his brother and friend. Many of his friends did not give credence to the news of his death. Can I see in it a revelation of God's hand? I am in need of a much deeper faith, a faith like that of Abraham who was asked to sacrifice his only son whom he loved more than himself (cf. Gen. 22: 2). If God could give him a son at the age of hundred, Abraham believed that the same God could do the impossible. "Nothing is impossible with God". Elizabeth, the sterile woman, gave birth to John the Baptist in her old age; Mary, ever a virgin, became the Mother of the Messiah while remaining a virgin. These events always take place out of the normal course.

On the evening of 18 March, 2002, at the end of our night prayer, I almost had to force myself to sing: "Thank you Father…". I still wanted to express my gratitude to God for the beautiful celebration we had had with the Archbishop, for the prayers and supplications offered to God for the repose of my brother's soul, for the consoling words, for all who had showed me such closeness and shared our sorrow. For everything and for everyone we sang: "Thank you Father, thank you Jesus, thank you Spirit, thank you Mary, thank you Joseph". I felt that I was paying a big price for that "Thank you" song on that day. But I wanted very much to do it. "The sharper the thorns", says

St. Thérèse of Lisieux, *"the sweeter my song shall be"*. *"You will suffer much, and you suffer now"*, Jesus said to Mother Teresa. Yes, indeed, we are called to love until we die of love – ours is a suffering love, which alone can become salvific. Our sacrificial love is necessary to save souls.

Well, dearly beloved Brothers and Sisters, how can I thank you enough for sharing in our sorrow so generously, so lovingly, so loyally. I felt very humbled and unworthy to receive so many condolences through telephone calls, telegrams, e-mail, by post and in personal meetings and exchanges, and above all for all the prayers and sacrifices you have been offering for the repose of his soul and for the intentions of his family. They tell me that they see the power of your prayers and sacrifices working in them and in their midst and told me to extend their *"Thank You"* to all of you. I too offer part of my pain for your intentions and needs. Suffering, pain and sorrow accepted in and with love becomes a powerful means of expiation. Jesus told Mother Teresa: *"You did not die for souls; that is why you don't care what happens to them. Your heart was never drowned in sorrow, as was my Mother's. We both gave our all for souls, and you?"*. Elsewhere, Jesus said to Mother Teresa: *"You will suffer and suffer now; but if you are my own little Spouse, the Spouse of the Crucified Jesus, you will have to bear these torments in your heart. Trust me lovingly, trust me blindly. Little one, give Me souls…"*. In the apostolate, the money to buy souls, therefore, is suffering accepted with love. Suppress the Cross from our life, everything will crumble and fall. The Cross is the structure upon which our life on earth is built.

We are on the verge of celebrating the paschal Triduum in which we come to understand better the Christian meaning of human suffering; in other words we must *baptize* our daily human sufferings and pain and offer them for the salvation and sanctification of souls. In this way we become *"co-redeemers"* of souls, which Jesus wants from all of us. See again how Jesus complains to Mother Teresa: *"You did not die for souls, that is why you don't care what happens to them…"*.

In conclusion I would like to thank you once again for everything and wish you a very peaceful and holy Good Friday which may lead you to a very happy and holy Easter Sunday. Love and prayers.

God bless you.

Fr. Sebastian Vazhakala M.C.

Lent 2005

Dearly beloved Brothers and Sisters,

The liturgical year begins with the first Sunday of Advent and ends with the celebration of the feast of Christ the King. Its purpose is to recall and to relive again and again with enthusiasm the mysteries of our salvation accomplished in Jesus Christ the God-man. By doing so God is being glorified and we are being sanctified.

"…In the Liturgy the sanctification of man is signified by signs perceptible by the senses, and is affected in a way which corresponds to each of these signs. In the Liturgy the whole public worship is performed by the mystical Body of Jesus Christ, i.e. by the Head and His members."

"From this it follows that every liturgical celebration, because it is an action of Christ the priest and His Body, which is the Church, is a sacred action surpassing all others. No other action of the Church can equal its efficacy by the same title and to the same degree" (S.C. 7: 3, 4).

The liturgical year is divided into three main seasons.

> The season of Advent-Christmas-Epiphany. This holy season, the shortest of the three, ends with the celebration of the baptism of Jesus, during which all the faithful renew their baptismal consecration. We know that it is in the baptism of Jesus that our baptism has its foundation. Here each Christian is not only to renounce sin and Satan again, but also to renew and make every effort to understand and relive the gift of his Christian faith.

The season of Lent, Holy Week, Easter—Pentecost: the season of Lent begins with Ash Wednesday and ends with the celebration of the feast of Pentecost, the descent of the Holy Spirit upon our Lady and the Apostles in the upper room. Every Christian who seriously tries to live this all-important season is to receive the Holy Spirit this day, as our Lady and the Apostles in the upper room received Him then.

The season of Ordinary Time is divided into two parts – a short period between the Baptism of Jesus and Ash Wednesday, and a longer period from Pentecost Sunday to the feast of Christ the King.

The use of the various colours of vestments in the Latin Rite for liturgical celebrations are:

a) White vestments: used for Christmas, Easter and Sundays of Easter season, solemnities, feasts and memorials of our Lady and saints who are not martyrs. White vestments can be used also in case there is no other colour available for the proper feast, i.e. for the feast of a martyr, if the red vestment is not available, we are allowed to use the white one.

b) Green vestments: Sundays of Ordinary Time and the weekdays of Ordinary Time when there is no particular feast.

c) Purple Vestments: the seasons of Advent and Lent, including Sundays and as a rule also for funeral Masses.

d) Red Vestments: Palm Sunday, Good Friday, the feast of Pentecost, Solemnities, feasts and memorials of all the martyrs of the Church, including all the Apostles and evangelists, except St. John the evangelist.

The season of Lent: Lent is the 40-day period of fervent prayer, penance and generous spiritual and corporal works of mercy in preparation for Easter. St. Peter Chrysologus explains it so beautifully when he says: *"... There are three things by which faith stands firm, devotion remains constant and virtue endures. They are prayer, penance and works of mercy. Prayer knocks at the door, penance obtains, and works of mercy receive… These three are one, and they give life to each other.*

"Penance is the soul of prayer; works of mercy are the life-blood of penance. Let no one try to separate them. If you pray, fast; if you fast, show mercy; if you want your petition to be heard, hear the petition of others. If you do not close your ear to others, you open God's ear to yourself.

"When you fast, see the fasting of others. If you want God to know that you are hungry, know that another is hungry. If you hope for mercy, show mercy. If you look for kindness, show kindness. If you want to receive, give. If you ask for yourself what you deny to others, your asking is a mockery…

"Let prayer, penance and works of mercy be one single plea to God on our behalf, one speech in our defence, a threefold united prayers in our favour." (cf. S. Peter Chrysologus, Sermon 43)

How to give alms, how to do Charity, how to serve our fellow men? To do Charity is a must, to serve our fellow men who live and die in poverty and hunger is a necessity. But how?

Jesus wants us to pray unceasingly (see Lk 18: 1-8). "Prayer cannot be taken for granted," writes the Holy Father Pope John Paul II, "we have to learn to pray: as it were learning this art ever anew from the lips of the Divine master himself, like the first disciples: 'Lord, teach us to pray' (Lk 11: 1)."

Penance involves self-denial, mortification, sacrifices, and above all joyful acceptance of the trials and hardship of daily life. Life in community, in the family, etc. at times, can demand much suffering, pain and sorrow, as suffering can be physical, psychological and moral. Our very vocation can be a call to love and suffer and save souls, as Jesus told our Blessed Mother Teresa: *"Your vocation is to love and suffer and save souls."*

Jesus tells us that when we give alms, when we pray, when we fast (penance), what to do and how to do it (cf. Mt 6: 1-6, 16-18). Jesus spells out in clear terms the "how" and the "why" of our actions, whether it is charity, prayer or penance. In a way Jesus tells us to do the things the way He did, do them with love and for the glory of God and for the good of the people. Without love sacrifice and suffering cannot be redemptive.

It is also very important to know why we do what we do. We should not do things or practice Charity to receive the applause and the approval of people, nor for ostentation or self-satisfaction. "I, me and myself" should not be at the centre, but Jesus and our neighbour. "He must increase and I must decrease", should be our aim and our effort.

Jesus' list of priority is worth noting. He starts with almsgiving, and then prayer, which is at the centre. This too is vital. Prayer purifies, sustains and strengthens charity and penance. Only the experience of silence, prayer and contemplation can help us make the transition from the natural to the supernatural, from the human to the divine. That is why we say prayer is a school, where we learn each day more about his presence and actions in us, in others and in the world…and also about ourselves, our attitudes, our desires, our likes and dislikes. Prayer frees us from self-attachment in order to open ourselves to others. It teaches us to make the transition from an affective love to an effective love. For love is not merely a feeling; it is an act of will that consists of preferring in a constant manner the good of others to the good of oneself.

The season of Lent with the help of the Holy Spirit, prepares us to experience and relive the Paschal event and invites us to go deeper into the reality of the Cross, pain and suffering in our lives. We must come back to Jesus and learn of him. This Christological dimension of the Cross is the heart of Christian life. I must learn again and again that the crucified Jesus of Nazareth is my saviour and the saviour of all… and especially of our poor people. Jesus' own words to Blessed Teresa are worth noting: *"Your heart was never drowned in sorrow as it was my Mother's. We both gave our all for souls--and you?"* and again: *"Your vocation is to love and suffer and save souls."* He continued to tell her that she will suffer much: *"You will suffer and you suffer now--but if you are my own little Spouse, the Spouse of the crucified Jesus--you will have to bear these torments on your heart…"* (MGF p. 10-11). Suffering love then is a means to save souls, especially the souls of the poor. Blessed Teresa says: *"I long to be only His--to **burn** completely for Him and souls. I want Him to be loved tenderly by many"* (MFG p. 13).

Every Christian must know that he/she has to share in the Cross of Christ as he/she belongs to the Church, which is the spouse of Jesus crucified. Every Christian must know that the Cross is inseparable from his/her life. He/she is marked with the sign of the Cross. The Cross is the very structure of his/her life and so it is inevitable. Suppress the Cross from our lives and everything will crumble and fall. Every Christian must know that he/she must deny himself/herself, take up the Cross every day and follow Jesus. (Lk 9: 23) Every Christian must carry the Cross, but always with Jesus, never without him. No Christian can follow Jesus without taking the Cross, nor should he/she carry the Cross without Jesus. He/she must know that the merit of the Cross he carries does not depend on its weight but the way he/she carries it.

Above all every Christian must know that the Cross is not an end in itself, but the means to a greater and more joyful end. The Cross is just a ladder that takes him/her to the joys of Easter. He/she should neither see Good Friday without Easter Sunday nor Easter Sunday without Good Friday, as they are inseparable. They are two sides of the same coin. We should never allow ourselves to be crushed by our suffering, trials and pain, no matter how hard, demanding and heavy the trials of life can be at times. Here blessed Teresa can be our mother and our teacher who says: *"To accept whatever he gives and give whatever he takes with a big smile is holiness."* It is very hard at times to do that. And yet if we do it, we can be more happy and serene…unlike if we try to resist or rebel. God is the honour and the author of everything and everyone. He has full dominion over us, over our health of mind and body, over our possessions and positions, over our very lives. He can come at any time to call us, and we have to go in haste, whether we are ready or not.

The other day one of our family members was talking to the parish priest near his house. While talking he fell back and breathed his last. He was healthy, not very old, but could not tell God to wait at least a few days when he could be more prepared perhaps, and his family members could have accepted the tragic event with greater serenity and resignation. But it didn't happen.

Worse still is what happened on Sunday 26 December 2004 in the Indian Ocean. No one could stop it. The consequences can be seen positively or negatively. Negatively speaking so many lives have been lost, so many people have become poorer, so many more orphaned children, handicapped ones, homeless, penniless. There is no end to the list! On the other hand it has brought humanity closer. An incredible sense of fellowship, sharing in every way. It made people poorer on the one hand, but richer on the other. Those who participated and shared with the suffering victims in whatever manner or capacity have become richer than they were. There can be an apparent pain in the "breaking" but such richness in the sharing, together with great interior joy. *"There is greater joy in giving than in receiving"* (Acts 20:35)

Let this Lent be one of great breaking and greater sharing of our time, talents, health, our riches and whatever else we have. The more we give, the more we will receive.

I take this opportunity to thank each one of you for all that you are to us and all that you do for us and for our poor people. Our gratitude to you is our prayer for you and our effort to live our lives as faithfully as we can. Pray for us that we may not spoil God's work in any way.

I wish you a very holy and joy-filled season of Lent, which prepares us all to the solemn celebration of Easter. Love and prayer.

God bless you.

Fr. Sebastian Vazhakala M.C.

Lent 2007

Lent, a Spring Time for our Souls

The word **Lent** is an ancient word for spring. The season of Lent is a time in our personal lives for new life to appear, and for old, frozen attitudes to disappear. It is a time to clear the ground, to clear away any rubbish, to do the pruning. It is a time to prepare for the great Paschal event.

Lent is six weeks. It begins with Ash Wednesday proposing us to build around this holy time on Charity (works of mercy and almsgiving), prayer and penance. This is the order proposed by Jesus in the gospel of Ash Wednesday. The season of Lent, therefore, with its rich liturgy, is being built on and around these three fundamental themes. These are basic elements of Christian life, but they are emphasized especially in the season of Lent.

Jesus went through this time of reflection that these forty days of **Lent** present to us. In the vast Judean desert of silence, solitude and dryness, Jesus made his final, definitive and new choices. He thought about his direction in life, his awareness of the Father, doing faithfully his Father's will, his use of time, power and personal gifts. Mind you, it could have been a terrible temptation for Jesus throughout his earthly life to use his power according to convenience, to misuse his gifts and thus become a world hero in the eyes of men...which he never did, not even once. Jesus wanted to be neither a world hero, nor a politician; he wanted to be but a religious leader who was sent by the Father to show us the way to heaven. *"God loved the world so much that he gave his only Son, so that every one who believes in him may not die, but may* *have eternal life. God did not send his Son into the world to be its **judge**, but to be its Saviour."* (Jn 3: 16-17)

The place he chose was a dry desert, away from everything and everybody; and that too was not for a day or two, but for a long period of forty days.

The means he chose to arrive at real clarity of his convictions was intense prayer, along with frightening kinds of solitude and fasting... which during his public life made him break and give himself totally to others, to satisfy the hunger and thirst of the human heart, mind, soul and body. This he could do only because he totally belonged to his Father, unconditionally, unlimitedly, ungrudgingly. From this long retreat Jesus made, he became armed with the power of the Holy Spirit. At the same time he also became aware of the presence and the apparent power of the devil. Satan is really deceptive and false. His suggestions can never be a help in the long run. "He is the father of lies." There is neither goodness nor any truthfulness in him. He is totally evil. However, he is extremely clever to mislead people through his insidious machinations and tricks. He can come to us as an angel of light to deceive us at an opportune time, when perhaps we are tired, discouraged, hungry or weak in body, mind and soul. The devil has no shame. He continues to prey on weak souls, studying very carefully and attentively the weak points, times and places. He knows each one of us more than we know ourselves.

Imagine what he did to Jesus in the desert at the end of a forty day fast and prayer. The synoptic gospels give us the account of what satan tried to do with Jesus in the desert (Mt 4: 1-11; Mk 1: 12-13; Lk 4: 1-13) and on the Cross. (Mk 15:31-32)

Here he could not do with Jesus what he did with Eve in the garden, when she was looking at the forbidden fruit. Listen to what the book of Genesis says: *"The woman saw that the tree was good to eat, pleasing to the eye and desirable for gaining wisdom. So she took some of its fruit and ate it; she also gave some to her husband who was with her; and he ate it."* (Gen 3: 6)

On the other hand, we see Jesus, who was severely tempted, not once but three times in one stretch of time, but without any success. It is worth noting how St. Luke puts it at the end of the three temptations, when satan utterly lost his battle fought against Jesus: *"Having exhausted every way of putting him to the test, the devil left him for a while to return to him at an opportune moment."* (Lk 4: 13)

In this regard the document "Vita Consecrata" exhorts us, saying: *"It is also necessary to recognize and overcome certain temptations which sometimes, by diabolic deceit, present themselves under the appearance of good..."* (Vita Consecrata 38: 3)

Lent is a time of more

1 SOLITUDE: the solitude of the desert in order to contemplate the disfigured face of Jesus with Mary.

2 SILENCE: *"The call to holiness is accepted and can be cultivated only in the silence of adoration before the infinite transcendence of God..."* (Vita Consecrata 38)

3 SELF-DENIAL: infuse into our Community and in me the spirit of prayer, self-denial and charity.

4 PEACE: make me a channel of your peace.

5 JOY: where there is sadness, let me bring joy.

6 HOPE: where there is despair let me bring hope.

7 FAITH: where there is doubt let me bring faith.

8 LOVE: where there is hatred let me bring love.

9 FORGIVENESS: where there is wrong let me bring the spirit of forgiveness.

10 PRAYER: more fervent prayer.

11 SACRIFICE: to offer more sacrifices.

12 WORKS OF MERCY: spiritual and corporal works of mercy.

13 FIDELITY: to one's duties of state, duties assigned, etc.

14 PENANCE: to rediscover the value and importance of the traditional ascetical practices, such as fasting and abstinence. These practices should be carried out gently, assiduously and serenely in imitation of and solidarity with Jesus' suffering, and

in reparation for our sins and those of others and as a sign of one's desire to identify himself with the *"man of sorrows"*, as an expression of his love for the suffering members of the mystical body of Jesus Christ: *"I complete in my body what is lacking in the suffering of Christ."* (Col 1: 24)

15 *"Love one another as I have loved you... Greater love than this no man has that a man lay down his life for his friends...you are my friends if you do what I tell you."* (cf. Jn 15: 13)

16 Paying more attention to the liturgical readings, based on the three themes: prayer, penance and works of mercy.

17 Following very closely and very faithfully the liturgy of the Mass, the Liturgy of the Hours, including the Office of Readings.

18 To be more and more gentle, kind, caring and bearing the trials of life. *"It is better to make mistakes in kindness than to work miracles in unkindness."* (Blessed Teresa M.C.)

Let us read very meditatively the following passage several times during this holy season, together with "Vita Consecrata" n° 82:

"There are three things by which faith stands firm, devotion remains constant, and virtue endures. They are prayer, penance and works of mercy. Prayer knocks at the door, penance obtains and works of mercy receive... These three are one and they give light to each other.

Penance is the soul of prayer, works of mercy are the life-blood of penance. Let no one try to separate them... If you pray, fast; if you fast, show mercy; if you want your petition to be heard, hear the petition of others. If you do not close your ear to others, you open God's ear to yourself.

When you fast, see the fasting of others. If you want God to know that you are hungry, know that another is hungry. If you hope for mercy, show mercy. If you look for kindness, show kindness. If you want to receive, give. If you ask for yourself what you deny to others, your asking is a mockery...

Let prayer, penance and works of mercy be one single plea to God on our behalf, one speech in our defence, a threefold united prayer in our favour." (cf. St. Peter Chrysologus' Sermon 43. Office of Readings for Tuesday, Lent, week 3)

"The Gospel is made effective through charity, which is the Church's glory and the sign of her faithfulness to the Lord. This is demonstrated by the whole history of the consecrated life, which can be considered a living exegesis of Jesus' words: 'As you did it to the one of the least of these my brethren, you did it to me' (Mt. 25, 40). Many institutes, especially in modern times, were established precisely to address one or other of the needs of the poor. But even when such a purpose was not the determining factor, concern and care for the needy – expressed in prayer, assistance and hospitality – was always a normal part of every form of the consecrated life, even of the contemplative life. And how could it be otherwise, since the Christ encountered in contemplation is the same who lives and suffers in the poor? In this sense, the history of the consecrated life is rich with marvellous and sometimes ingenious examples. Saint Paulinus of Nola, after distributing his belongings to the poor in order to consecrate his life fully to God, built the cells of his monastery above a hospice for the poor. He rejoiced at the thought of this singular 'exchange of gifts': the poor, whom he helped, strengthened with their prayers the very 'foundations' of his house, wholly dedicated to the praise of God. Saint Vincent de Paul, for his part, loved to say that, when one is obliged to leave prayer to attend to a poor person in need, that prayer is not really interrupted, because 'one leaves God to serve God'." (Vita Consecrata 82)

Lent is a time of listening. The Word of God is given to us in abundance. Look at the texts of Lenten season, the rich parables, the choice of Gospels, the great themes of faith, conversion and turning back to a God who is already waiting and loving us. We are asked to do more than just listen in this Lenten season. We are asked to make the Word of God a judgement upon our lives.

Lent is a time for special penance and personal evaluation. We are reminded of the words of Christ that unless we do penance we shall all likewise perish: *"Deny yourself, take up your cross and follow me."* (Mk 8: 34) *"The ascetic practises typical of the Spiritual tradition of the Church and of the individual's own institute have been and continue to be a powerful aid to authentic progress in holiness. Asceticism, by helping to master and correct the inclination of human nature wounded by sin, is truly indispensable if consecrated persons are to remain faithful to their own vocation and follow Jesus on the way of the Cross."* (Vita Consecrata 38: 2)

Practical applications:

❖ Trying to smile more tenderly and maintaining the spirit of serenity and joy.

❖ Serious study of the Passion of Jesus and contemplating on it.

❖ Never waste time idly. Let us remember the famous saying: *"The idle man's heart is the workshop of the devil".* Let us not give any occasion to our adversary, the devil, who *"is prowling like a roaring lion looking for someone to devour; instead let us resist him, solid in our faith."* (cf. 1Pt 5: 8-9a)

❖ "The merit of the cross we bear does not depend on its weight but the way we bear it." (St. Francis of Sales)

❖ *You will catch more flies with one spoon full of honey than with a hundred barrels of vinegar."*

"This is done by those who from morning to night submit joyfully to a rule, who strive to be attentive to their prayers, and recollected all day long, who keep silence when they feel inclined to speak, who avoid the sight of such objects as excite curiosity, who suffer without complaint the unseasonableness of the weather, who show kindness to those towards whom they feel a natural antipathy, who accept humbly and patiently the reproaches made to them, who accommodate themselves to the tastes, desires and temperaments of others, who stand contradiction without irritation....to do all this, not once in passing, but habitually, to do so not merely patiently, but joyfully - this is already heroic virtue and when later on grave circumstances present themselves, heroic action will not prove too difficult: for we shall then have the strength of the Holy Spirit Himself " (A. Tanquerey).

Wish you a Joy-filled and Holy Lent.

God bless you.

Fr. Sebastian Vazhakala M.C.

Easter 1994

Dear Brothers and Sisters,

Once again this morning the M.C. Family is around the altar to celebrate the peace and joy of this wonderful feast that is Easter. It would really be sad and bad if we did not recognize its great significance in our lives and in the life of the rest of mankind. The more we understand the mystery of the resurrection of Jesus, the more happy and serene we become. It is a mystery not to be told, nor simply to be read, nor even can be reduced to just an annual celebration....but something to be lived and relived..."The resurrection of Jesus has to be seen not as something of a past event, but something that is taking place in the here and now of our daily existence. To grasp it better we are reminded to return to its very first days and see it the way the Apostles and the early Church saw it. How did the Apostles see the resurrection of Jesus? How did the early Church see it? How did the saints and martyrs down through the centuries see this wondrous mystery that brought radical changes to man's life and history.., and continues to do so?

Since the evening of Holy Thursday we have been asked to observe and do certain things. We have been asked to "reproduce in us the passion and death of Jesus"; we have been told by St. Paul that he completed in his body what has been lacking in the sufferings of Christ.

Coming back to the Apostles, what did Jesus' death do to them... how did they feel? I wish I could have been there with them to see what they were feeling...simply on the human level. The death of Jesus: that first Good Friday brought to them terrible disillusionment. "We had hoped...," but now... What happened to their hopes? That first Good

Friday made them feel terribly frightened... with the result that even the prince of the apostles was badly shaken, to the extent of denying his Master three times. "I do not know Whom you are talking about".

The death of Jesus brought complete confusion in the minds of the Apostles; they did not know what to do any more. It really shattered their feeble minds. It shook the foundation of their very existence. What were they going to do? All that they heard and saw made no more sense to them. Their own eyes and ears deceived them. What a terrible catastrophe that was! It was like the first day of Adam and Eve's sin. The Apostles were reliving at that moment what the first Adam and Eve experienced after disobeying Good's command by eating the forbidden fruit. Above all Peter felt even worse. He felt terribly humiliated, deceived and guilty. The spark of hope and trust that they had in Jesus was all shaken, if not totally disappeared.

They had two choices: either they all do as Judas did...'go and die in despair'...or follow Jesus to the Cross, for which they were not yet ready. "Their eyes were not yet opened", nor their minds ready to grasp the meaning of the cross and its necessity in their lives.

We could go on and on with the Apostles legitimate confusion and chaos. But since we have another and a better side of the coin, let us try to see it. The Good Friday experience, even though intensively painful, even excruciating, was a temporary one and was going to be overcome by the joy of Easter Sunday. And it was. If the Good Friday feeling was like the pain of a woman in labour, the Easter Sunday experience was like the joy of a mother after giving birth to her beloved child. That is what we should experience too. And that is what Jesus told the Apostles and also to us... not something to be read, but really to be lived.

What did Easter bring to the lives of the Apostles? And that is what we read and meditate upon these days. The same men, but totally transformed. The one who denied the Lord in the dark hours of the night of the Last Supper is now preaching loudly, publicly and boldly in the bright daylight. The men who saw the worst part of Jesus' earthly life now see the best.

The Apostles understood the meaning and importance of suffering as the only way to Heaven. Any other road, no matter how great and wonderful it may look like, will give us neither happiness nor peace; nor will it lead to eternal life. It is not the wide road of human pleasure, luxury and ease that takes us to Heaven, but the narrow road of suffering and pain accepted with love, as Jesus did and later on as the apostles, martyrs and saints did...and as the living saints continue to do.

Mind you, Jesus did not cancel suffering and pain from our everyday life, but He gave positive meaning to it and made it "the way to Heaven". "Father if possible"...the Father could have... but He did not do... "Father remove this rule from the Constitutions..., or remove this Sister, this Brother, this Superior, this in-charge, etc..." God the Father may not answer our prayers the way we want them to be answered. He did not hear His Son's prayer either. In the dark hours of our life, we too may cry and shout to our father like Jesus: "Father if possible, remove this cup from me", but never forget to pray the second part, namely; "but not my will, but your Will be done". Our prayer most always help us to accept the Divine Will for us...and say often: "Father, do with me what you will, but whatever you may do, I thank you." The Father could have removed the bitter cup of suffering and death from Jesus, but He did not; instead he sent an Angel to comfort and strengthen Him. Many a time He will do the same with us: He will give us the grace and the strength to face suffering with peace and joy, and make it meritorious for us, and a means for our salvation and sanctification, and the salvation and sanctification of others as well.

All the Apostles finally ended up in martyrdom, like Jesus... Do we expect something different? Should we ask an easier and more comfortable life; should we rebel...? Are we supposed to shout, or grumble, or murmur...or should our obedience be like that of Jesus?.... Obedience is easier when we are asked to do something we like to do; or when I am asked to go to a place of my own liking...

God bless you

Fr. Sebastian Vazhakala M.C.

Easter 2001

"All I want is to know Christ and the power flowing from His resurrection; likewise to know how to share in His sufferings by being moulded to the pattern of His death, striving toward the goal of resurrection from the dead" (Phil.3, 10-11)

Holy Week is the week of all weeks for those who believe and practice their faith. It can be said that Holy Week is the foundational week of our faith, especially from the eve of Good Friday to Easter Sunday. Good Friday and Easter Sunday are like two sides of the same coin, or two pages of the same sheet of paper. Our life on earth is a mixture of sorrow and joy, pain and bliss. Through often painful experiences we are being prepared and brought into blissful endings, reminding us of an unending life of joy and eternal peace. Every human being is meant to pass through many "*Good Fridays*" before he/she arrives at the shore of unending bliss and eternal life of peace and joy. "*Not infrequently,*" says our supreme pontiff John Paul II in his apostolic letter "Novo Millenio Ineunte," "*the saints have undergone something akin to Jesus' experience on the Cross in the paradoxical blending of bliss and pain. In the 'Dialogue of Divine Providence', God, the Father shows Catherine of Siena how joy and suffering can be present together in holy souls. 'Thus the soul is blissful and afflicted: afflicted on account of the sins of its neighbour, blissful on account of the union and the affection of charity, which it has inwardly received. These souls imitate the spotless Lamb, my only begotten Son, who on the Cross was both blissful and afflicted. In the same way, St. Thérèse of Lisieux lived her agony in communion with the agony of Jesus, 'experiencing' in her the very paradox of Jesus' on bliss and anguish. 'In the Garden of Olives our Lord was blessed with all the joys of the Trinity, yet His dying was no less harsh. It is a mystery, but I assure you that, on the basis of what I myself am feeling, I can understand something of it'* (St. Thérèse of Lisieux – Last conversations, yellow booklet...6 July 1897)...Jesus in the depths of His pain, died imploring forgiveness for his executioners (cf. Lk. 23: 34) and expressing to the Father His ultimate filial abandonment: *'Father, into your hands I commend my Spirit'* (Lk 23: 46)" (M.M.I., 27).

Our contemplation must not stop with the tragic event of Good Friday, but must go further and deeper. Otherwise we will all end up in the same unfortunate fate of Judas the betrayer. Novo Millenio Ineunte continues: *"As on Good Friday and Holy Saturday the Church pauses in contemplation of the bleeding face, which conceals the life of God and offers salvation to the world. But her contemplation of Christ's face cannot stop at the image of the Crucified one. He is the Risen One. Were this not so, our preaching would be in vain and our faith empty (cf. 1Core 15: 14). The Resurrection was the Father's response to Christ's obedience, as we learn from the letter to the Hebrews: 'In the days of His flesh, Jesus offered up prayers and supplications, with loud cries and tears, to Him who was able to save Him from death, and he was heard for His godly fear. Son though He was, He learned obedience through what He suffered; and being made perfect, He became the source of eternal salvation to all who obey Him' (Heb 5: 7-9). It is the Risen Christ to whom the Church now looks. And she does so in the footsteps of Peter, who wept for his denial, and started out again by confessing, with understandable trepidation, his love for Christ: 'You know that I love you' (Jn 21: 15-17). She does so in the company of Paul, who encountered the Lord on the road to Damascus and was overwhelmed: 'For me to live is Christ, and to die is gain' (*Phil 1: 21) (N.M.I., 28).

Our religious and particularly our M.C. vocation makes sense only in the light of the Easter event. It not only makes sense to it but also becomes the reason to live the way we live. Our vows of chastity, poverty, obedience and charity are essentially based on the paschal mystery of the suffering, death and resurrection of Jesus. Our absolute faith in the risen Lord stirs us to live our vows even more faithfully and most perfectly.

The Easter event gives meaning not only to all that we are and all we do, but also gives strength to endure humbly, patiently and joyfully all our daily trials, dark nights, desolations, misunderstandings, false accusations, humiliations; in a word all sorts of physical, psychological and moral trials we have to endure during our earthly pilgrimage. How could we give wholehearted free service to the most repugnant ones of our society without taking into consideration their colour, creed or nationality, without counting the cost, without asking for reward or seeking rest, even when it hurts us, even when we are being humiliated for whatever reasons. Holy Mass and Communion would have made no sense without the resurrection of Christ. Does it make any sense to the penances we do: our first Thursday night vigils, our Friday fasts, our Saturday whole night adorations, or our rising so early in the morning or going very late to bed, spending so much time in prayer in the silence of faith often without seeing any spectacular results, and even more, to submit joyfully to rules from morning to night, to strive to be attentive to all our prayers and to be recollected all day long, to keep silence when we feel inclined to speak, to avoid the sight of objects that excite curiosity, to suffer without complaint the unseasonableness of the weather, to show kindness to those towards whom we feel a natural antipathy, to accept humbly and patiently the reproaches made to us, to accommodate ourselves to the tastes, desires and temperaments of others, to stand contradiction without irritation… to do all these not once in passing, but habitually, to do so not merely patiently, but joyfully – these and similar practices would have no sense if we did not believe firmly with all the powers and fibres of our being in the resurrection of the Lord.

"Tell us, Mary what did you see on the way?" "I saw the tomb of the now living Christ. I saw the glory of Christ, now risen. I saw angels who gave witness. Christ, my hope has risen." "We know and we are convinced that **Christ has indeed risen from the dead**. *Life's captain died; now He reigns, never more to die. Amen. Alleluia."* Like the apostles we not only believe in the resurrection of the Lord Jesus but also proclaim it in words and in deeds in season and out of season. *"This is the Jesus God raised up, and we are His witnesses"* (Acts 2: 32) and our joy goes to fever pitch.

It is true: Jesus suffered and died for our sins, but it is equally true that He rose again for our justification and salvation. With the risen Lord I greet you. His peace I wish to impart to each and every one of you, especially in this glorious and joyful season of Easter, while we eagerly wait to receive the gift of the Holy Spirit at Pentecost. Come, Holy Spirit, come! Fill our hearts with the peace and joy of the Risen Lord and the fire of your Divine Love. Love and prayers.

God bless you.

Fr. Sebastian Vazhakala M.C.

Preparation for the Feast of Pentecost
2001

Dearly beloved Brothers, and Sisters,

The feast of Pentecost is close at hand. Once again we are going to celebrate the solemn descent of the Holy Spirit upon Our Lady and the Apostles, who were united in prayer for nine full days in the upper room, as the Acts of the Apostles account it: "*After Jesus had ascended into heaven, the apostles returned to Jerusalem from the mount called Olivet near Jerusalem. Entering the city, they went to the upstairs room where they were staying... Together they devoted themselves to constant prayer. There were some women in their company, and Mary the mother of Jesus, and his brothers*" (Acts 1, 12-14).

The nine-day retreat the apostles made in the upper room with Our Lady and other disciples disposed them to receive the promised Holy Spirit, the "Paraclete", the advocate, the consoler, the helper. And they were no more the same. There came a radical transformation in their lives. Fear was replaced by courage. St. Peter, for example, who was so afraid to confess before a servant girl on that first Holy Thursday night was now preaching, teaching and even challenging the authorities publicly. "*It was you who accused the Holy and upright One, you who demanded that a murderer should be released to you while you killed the Author of life...*" (Acts 3, 14-15).

The rulers and elders were "*astonished at the fearlessness shown by Peter and John, considering that they were uneducated laymen; and they recognized them as associates of Jesus*" (Acts 4, 13). Peter and John continued: "*Judge for yourselves whether it is right in God's sight for us to obey you rather than God. Surely we cannot help speaking of what we have heard and seen*" (Acts 4, 19).

The apostles went beyond any human limits in their apostolic and missionary zeal since the Pentecost experience: "*The apostles for their part left the Sanhedrin full of joy that they had been judged worthy of ill-treatment for the sake of the name*" (Acts 5, 41). Nothing and nobody could separate them from the love of Christ: "*Who will separate us from the love of Christ? Trial, or distress, or persecution, or hunger, or nakedness, or danger, or the sword?...For I am certain that neither death nor life, neither angels nor principalities, neither the present nor the future, nor powers, neither height nor depth nor any other creature, will be able to separate us from the love of God that comes to us in Christ Jesus, our Lord*" (Rom 5, 31-39).

St. Paul also tells us that we are the temple of the Holy Spirit. If we take the Bible seriously and go over it page by page we see that the "Ruha Yahweh" i.e. the Breath of God, the Holy Spirit, was always at work in all of God's activities and interventions. The same Holy Spirit that descended upon Our Lady and the apostles descended upon each one of us at our baptism and then again at our confirmation. As Christians, and as religious in particular, all our words, actions and activities are to be subjected according to the promptings of the Holy Spirit and to be led by Him. So much so that the apostles could say at the first Jerusalem Council: "*It is the decision of the Holy Spirit and ours*" (Acts 15, 28). St. Augustine prayed: "*Breathe into me, Holy Spirit, that my thoughts may all be holy; Move in me, Holy Spirit, that my work too may be holy; Attract my heart, Holy Spirit, that I may love only what is holy; Strengthen me, Holy Spirit, that I may defend all that is holy; Protect me, Holy Spirit, that I always may be holy*".

There were three things the apostles did before they made any important decisions regarding the New Way: they prayed, they fasted and they discussed together and then discerned God's will. The apostles and the disciples no longer lived for themselves or for their own interests but for Christ and for others. Even when they had to go through severe trials, terrible sufferings and hardships, they experienced profound peace and abiding joy.

The apostles prayed constantly. Before their eyes and in their transfigured memories they had the example of Jesus praying from the first day they met Him till He was taken away from the visible horizons of their lives. Jesus not only prayed, but he also taught the apostles the art of prayer. Prayer became their life-breath. *"Now it happened that He (Jesus) was in a certain place praying, and when He had finished one of His disciples said: 'Lord, teach us to pray, as John taught his disciples…"* (cf. Lk 11, 1-13).

No longer were they able to lead their lives for the Master, no longer could they remain faithful to their Master if they did not pray. Praying meant asking, consulting, clarifying, forgiving, and even being merciful. It was not one more among many things they did; prayer became the heart and the soul of their life and work. Prayer for them was like breathing. The moment one stops breathing, one starts dying. *"Pray at all times and in all places…."*, the apostles instructed the Christians.

The second means was fasting and bearing all hardships for the spread of the Gospel: *"I have done more work, I have been in prison more, I have been flogged more severely, many times exposed to death. Five times I have been given the thirty-nine lashes by the Jews; three times I have been beaten with sticks; once I was stoned; three times I have been shipwrecked, and once I have been in the open sea for a night and a day; continually travelling, I have been in danger from rivers, in danger from brigands, in danger from my own people and in danger from the Gentiles, in danger in the towns and in danger in the open country, in danger at sea and in danger from people masquerading as brothers; I have worked with unsparing energy for many nights without sleep; I have been hungry and thirsty, and often altogether without food or drink; I have been cold and lack clothing. And, besides all the external things, there is, day in day out, the pressure on me of my anxiety for all the churches. If anyone weakens, I am weakened as well; and when anyone is made to fall, I burn in agony myself"* (2Cor 11, 23-29).

And the third effective means the apostles used to solve their given problems, whether small or big, was by way of discussion and dialogue. After having fasted and prayed they came together to speak, not to fight and to argue, but to discuss, discover and discern the will of God in humility and charity. They no longer lived for anything except to do the will of God in love until they died for the same.

Our Novena week in preparation for the feast of Pentecost must have at least these three elements: prayer, fasting and dialogue. It begins on Ascension Thursday and ends on Pentecost Sunday. Concretely it means two Fridays of fast: Friday after Ascension and Friday before Pentecost.

Regarding prayer, we try to keep a silent, prayerful atmosphere during these nine days of Novena, staying with Our Lady and the apostles in the upper room.

As it is also a time for intense prayer; praying especially for our enemies, for growth in holiness and for good and holy vocations, for one's own intentions, etc. Also when praying, trying to pray with greater attention and devotion.

Our dialogue can be done in two ways through:

Family prayer: *"Family that prays together stays together"*

Family dialogue: *"Dialogue is another name for Charity"* (Pope Paul VI)

Let us use the following prayer for our Novena week:

"Come, Holy Spirit, and from heaven direct on men the rays of your light. Come, Father of the poor; come, giver of God's gifts; come, light of men's hearts.

Kindly Paraclete, in your gracious visits to men's soul you bring relief and consolation. If it is weary with toil, you bring it ease; in the heat of temptations, your grace cools it; if sorrowful your words console it.

Light most blessed, shine on the hearts of your faithful – even into their darkest corners; for without your aid man can do nothing good, and everything is sinful.

Wash clean the sinful soul, rain down your grace on the parched soul and heal the injured soul. Soften the hard heart, cherish and warm the ice-cold heart, and give direction to the wayward.

Give your seven holy gifts to your faithful, for their trust is in you. Give them reward for their virtuous acts; give them a death that ensures salvation; give them unending bliss. Amen. Alleluia".

For the coming eleven days, that is from Ascension Thursday to Pentecost Sunday, we will use the Litany to the Holy Spirit. Let us pray for each other and for all. Happy and holy feast of Pentecost to all.

Love and prayers.

God bless you.

Fr. Sebastian Vazhakala M.C.

After the Resurrection

"You are witnesses of all this"

Every year the Church all over the world celebrates the Passover of the Lord Jesus. It consists of his Last Supper with his Twelve Apostles, his agony in the Garden of Gethsemane, the trial, the way of the Cross and the Crucifixion on Good Friday, and the glorious Resurrection on Easter Sunday. This is called the Pasch: and for a practicing Catholic these events make a tremendous impact on his life, making his faith, hope and charity deeper and stronger. His everyday life becomes an expression and an extension of these great events in the life of Jesus.

Since the evening of Holy Thursday, when Jesus got up from the table and began to wash the feet of his disciples, the Apostles were puzzled; they were even more puzzled when he told them that one of them was going to betray him. That paschal meal was not a very peaceful and comfortable one. It threw the Apostles into confusion, making them feel very sad and uneasy.

What was still to come was even worse, namely, the Gethsemane experience. From a distance they could hear Jesus' cry of helplessness. And then he came to three of the Apostles, Peter, James and John, asking for their prayers and their help. *"He began to feel terror and anguish"* (Mt 26: 37). Shortly after they heard the shouts and noise of a strange and exited crowd with lanterns, torches and weapons entering the garden, led not by a stranger but by one of their own company, Judas Iscariot (cf. Jn 18: 1ff).

"It is fulfilled". It would have been better if those hours of the night did not exist. But unfortunately, they did, and Jesus and the Apostles had to face the consequences, one hour after another. The cup the Father was offering them to drink was a bitter one. The Apostles were totally unprepared, not yet ready for such an adventurous enterprise.

Unexpected and, for that matter, unrepeatable days still awaited them. Their eyes were still closed and their minds unable to grasp the profound and positive meaning and significance of those events. For them, those minutes were like hours, and hours like days.

The worst was the Crucifixion, which was the climax. It was the culmination, completion and fulfilment of the entire Scriptures, as Jesus himself testified just before he breathed his last: *"It is fulfilled"* (Jn 19: 30). This appointed hour waged the hardest battle the world had ever seen or heard. The victory over sin and death became doubtful and precarious. Jesus fought the battle alone, all alone; his disciples and Apostles had already abandoned him.

Where was Peter, the rock, who once so boldly answered Jesus' question *"Will you also go away?"* with these words: *"Lord, to whom shall we go? You have the words of eternal life"* (Jn 6: 68)? Where have they all gone? The same Peter, to whom Jesus said: *"You are Peter, and on this rock I will built my Church",* to whom he entrusted the keys of the Kingdom, giving him the authority to bind and loose whatever on earth (cf. Mt 16: 18-19), had already denied him three times.

The one who held the common purse for Jesus' band of men sold his Master for 30 silver pieces and betrayed him. Worse still was that the betrayer ended his earthly life by committing suicide in utter despair.

What an incredible and tragic drama was played out on the stage on that first Good Friday when we see the Teacher and Lord (cf. Jn 13: 13) hanging on the Cross between two criminals, totally helpless and utterly powerless. We see Judas Iscariot, the betrayer, hanging himself on another tree. We see a few hours earlier Peter denying the Master three times and all the other Apostles deserting him. *"And they all deserted him and ran away"* (Mk 14: 50). This was the tragedy of all tragedies, the failure of all failures, and the humiliation of humiliations that the world could ever have faced. This was the Son of God and the Saviour of the world. But whom did he come to save?

Hope: the force for life. There was no doubt or ambiguity in the mind of Jesus; in the minds of the Apostles and disciples, however, nothing was clear.

The apostles became disillusioned, totally discouraged, sad, upset and angry. They felt stupid, humiliated, deceived. They became the object of ridicule; they could no longer walk around or look at the people's faces. Their own eyes and ears had deceived them. For they had seen incredible things with their own eyes, and heard words of wisdom that no one had ever spoken. They had many hopes and expectations: *"We were hoping that he was the one who would set Israel free"* (cf. Lk 24: 21).

To live without hope is a terrible thing, because hope is meant to be the driving force of our life. The Apostles came to the stage of utter despair. They had no more desire to go on living. Not only had their own eyes and ears deceived them, but also their mind and reason. All life's roads were blocked for them, and the light that illumined their path was now extinguished. What was there to hope for? To whom could they turn to for guidance, for clarity, for direction?

The Apostles needed extraordinary grace and strength to go through that Good Friday, Holy Saturday and Easter Sunday. With patient endurance, we too can win many battles and can go through many struggles to reach our goal. Have we ever endured the experiences that Our Lady and the Apostles have gone through? Drowned in sorrow, sadness, darkness and despair!

Many questions crossed the minds of the Apostles of Jesus: O God, why did we listen to the call of that carpenter's son, that Galilean? We knew that nothing good could ever come from Nazareth, and yet we left everything and followed him for three years. We were really blind, stupid and foolish to waste our time, our energy and our future!

Jesus: the light of life. Easter Sunday morning was even worse. Not even the body of Jesus could be found, for the tomb was empty. The women saw the empty tomb; as did Peter and John on the morning of that first Sunday. More confusion, more pain, more sorrow, more bewilderment. It was too much. They could not take any more.

They were too overwhelmed and came to the end of their strength. They decided to return to their old job of fishing. *"Simon Peter said to them, 'I'm going fishing'. They said to him, 'We will go with you'...but that night they caught nothing"* (Jn 21: 1ff), because they were not doing the will of God and Jesus was not with them. For without Jesus we can do nothing (cf. Jn 15: 5).

It is against this background that we have to approach the unprecedented and unique event of Easter, which can and does illumine even the darkest and innermost corners of our earthly existence.

The resurrection of Jesus became the most powerful light that was capable of removing all the darkness, all the sadness and despair from the lives of the Apostles and all the people concerned. Not only had the Risen Lord removed their doubts and questionings; he replaced sadness with joy, despair with hope, and humiliation with exaltation.

The Risen Lord made every effort to make the disciples and Apostles understand that the same Jesus who died on the Cross like a criminal on that first Good Friday was now alive and speaking to them. He made Mary Magdalene recognize him by calling her by name: *"Mary!"*. She turned and said to him in Hebrew *'Rabboni!'*, which means Teacher" (Jn 20: 16).

Two of his disciples were totally discouraged and were leaving Jerusalem. Jesus met them on the road and walked with them all the way, engaging in lively conversation. He explained to them the passages throughout Scriptures that were about himself. And then, in the breaking of bread, *"Their eyes were opened and they recognized him"* (cf. Lk 24: 25ff). Not only did he make their hearts burn within them as he talked to them on the road and explained the Scriptures to them, but he opened their minds to understand the Scriptures.

The Apostles were still terribly shocked and did not expect Jesus to rise from the dead at all. So when Jesus came to them where they were and said to them *"Peace be with you"*, they thought they were seeing a ghost. Jesus said *"Why are you troubled, and why are these doubts rising in your hearts?…And as he said this he showed them his hands and feet…"* Their joy was so great that they still could not believe it, as they were dumbfounded (cf. Lk 24: 36-43). Jesus even ate with them to reassure them that it was the same person (Lk 24:43).

Embracing the Cross. To the doubting Thomas Jesus said: *"'Put your finger here and see my hands; and put out your hand and place it in my side; do not be faithless, but believing'. Thomas replied, 'My Lord and my God' "* (Jn 20 27-28).

Jesus opened their minds to understand the Scriptures, showing how necessary it was for him to suffer before entering into his glory: *"Was it not necessary that the Christ should suffer and enter into glory?"* (Lk 24: 26). And he said to them, *"Thus it is written that the Christ should suffer these things and on the third day rise from the dead and that repentance and forgiveness of sins should be preached in his name to all nations, beginning from Jerusalem"* (Lk 24: 26).

In this light the Apostles understood the Christian meaning and significance of human suffering and death. They came to believe that suffering accepted with love becomes a means of salvation and sanctification, both for themselves and others as well.

Through contemplation of the Easter event the Apostles came to understand the power and wisdom of the Cross, the force and strength of accepting and welcoming calumnies, humiliations, insults, false accusations. Yes, *"It is in the contemplation of the crucified Christ together with the primordial gift of the Holy Spirit that all vocations, especially the gift of the consecrated life, takes its inspiration and origin."* (Vita Consecrata, n. 23).

The Easter experience of the Apostles sanctified, perfected and illumined the Good Friday experience, which became a necessary means to true and lasting joy and perennial happiness. Now they realized that their three years of life with Jesus were no mere waste of time but rich with meaning and fruit. They were years of sowing in tears so that in time both they and others could have rich harvests. They understood the profound meaning of Jesus' words:

"Unless a grain of wheat falls into the earth and dies, it remains alone; but if it dies, it bears much fruit" (Jn 12: 24).

Recognizing the Lord. The grain of wheat fell into the ground on that first Good Friday, after which many more grains of wheat have been added and continue to be added all the time. *"O foolish men, and slow of heart to believe all that the prophets have spoken! Was it not necessary that the Christ should suffer these things and enter his glory."* (Lk 24: 25-26) The Risen Lord opened their eyes and they recognized Jesus in the breaking of Bread; he opened their minds to the understanding of Scriptures. Even more, Mary Magdalene recognized the Risen Lord while her name was being called by the Master (Jn 20).

Happy is the hour when our eyes are opened to recognize him in the breaking of the Bread and in the broken bodies of the poorest of the poor. Happy is the hour when our minds are open to the understanding of Scriptures and our ears to hear the cry of the needy. Human life on earth has rediscovered its original meaning and dimension with the Easter event.

Let the Spirit of Easter pervade our whole being and guide our paths of life, illumining our faith, hope and charity in order to work ever more for the glory of God and for the salvation of souls. *"As they were saying this, Jesus himself stood among them and said to them, '**Peace to you.**'...He said to them, '**Why are you troubled, and why do questionings rise in your hearts**'...he showed them his hands and his feet...they still disbelieved for joy, and wonder"* (Lk 24: 36 ff.).

After the Resurrection Jesus suddenly appears when the doors were closed (cf. Jn 20: 19), which explains their surprised reactions. *Subtility,* which is one of the qualities of the glorified body, means that "the body is totally subject to the soul and ever ready to obey its wishes" (St. Pius V), with the result that it can pass through material obstacles without any difficulty.

Jesus wanted now for the Apostles to be witnesses, not only of his painful death on Good Friday but more so of his glorious Resurrection on Easter Sunday. They have been asked to be *"witnesses of all this"* (Lk 24: 48). And now it is our turn to be witnesses of all this in the heart of the world.

When our mood changes from sadness to joy, and we begin to hope again, we feel the need to share our joy with others, thus becoming heralds and witnesses of the Risen Christ. Let us go in peace and joy to love and serve the Lord and one another.

God bless you.

Fr. Sebastian Vazhakala M.C.

Pentecost 2004

Dearly beloved Brothers and Sisters,

May the grace and peace of the Lord Jesus Christ and the love of God the Father and the fellowship of the Holy Spirit be with each and everyone of you. We have celebrated the great feast of Pentecost. This event made radical changes in the lives of the apostles, who were simple, weak and ordinary men before, as we read in the various accounts given in the Acts of the Apostles. For example Acts 4: 13, which says: *"Now when they saw the boldness of Peter and John, and perceived that they were uneducated, common men, they wondered; and they recognized that they had been with Jesus…"* There was no proportion between what they were before and what they had become after receiving the Holy Spirit. The Holy Spirit opened not only their eyes to recognize Jesus, but also their minds to the understanding of the Scriptures, and above all the courage to live the Gospel and bear witness to it.

Jesus said: *"From the fruit you shall know the tree."* (cf. Mt 7: 16-20) It is impossible for a good tree not to produce good fruit. In the same way it is impossible for a good and practicing Catholic Christian not to love God and love one's neighbour.

Who among us would not want to hear the consoling words of Jesus in the evening of our life when we appear before God: *"Come, blessed of my Father, inherit the kingdom prepared for you since the foundation of the world, for I was hungry and you gave me to eat, I was thirsty and you gave me to drink, I was naked and you clothed Me, I was homeless and you welcomed Me, I was sick and you took care of Me, and in prison you visited Me."* *"When did we see you hungry, thirsty, naked, homeless…?* The king will answer: *"As long as you did to one of the least of my brothers, you did it to Me,"* or the opposite: *"As long as you did not do to one of the least of my brothers you failed to do to Me."* (cf. Mt 25: 31-46)

We then have to help one another while on earth to get rich in heaven. Each sigh, each look, each act of ours must become an act of love divine.

Everything we do must be done for love of Jesus. We must have two bank accounts: one in heaven and one on earth. Even if our bank on earth is empty because we transferred everything to our bank in heaven, it is much better. Let us do ordinary things of everyday life with extraordinary love, simple things with great love. Even a cup of cold water given in Jesus' name (cf. Mt 10: 42) will not lose its reward. That is why we must be formed in our spiritual life so that our life on earth may not become a waste and we may not feel sorry in the evening of life when we appear before God. St. Thérèse of Lisieux said: *"In the evening of life when I appear before God, I must be empty handed, having distributed everything for the salvation of souls."* We must all be consumed with the one desire: *"to love and suffer and save souls."* In the end, the value of all our actions is based not on its quantity but on the quality, not how much we did, but how we did it. In other words, how much love we put in our actions. The merit of our actions does not depend on their size or amount, but on the love with which we do what we do. This applies to our sacrifices too. *"The merit of the cross we carry,"* says St. Francis de Sales, *"does not depend on its weight but the way we bear it."* Our spiritual, psychological and moral formation must be based then on how we form our attitudes, why we do what we do, how we see things and the desire to become better than what we are.

The thought of the "evil one" came to my mind. I took the word "devil" and saw that if we add the letter "d" before the word "evil", it becomes "devil=d+evil." This means the devils cannot be formed, as there is no good in them at all. They have no postulancy or noviciate. They do not have even a grain of desire to be good, to improve the quality of their life. So they cannot be formed. Formation is possible and necessary only for those who can and want to become better than what they are. In any case, we have the capacity to change from what is good in us to what is better. This can be in all three levels: physical, psychological and spiritual. This transformation is not meant to be static but dynamic. There is so much good in the worst of us and so much bad in the best of us. There are many things in us that cannot be changed, while some other things need to be discarded, reformed, reshaped--sometimes to be chiselled out; at other times smoothened. Jesus told our Blessed Mother Teresa: *"to offer more sacrifices, to smile more tenderly and pray more fervently."* These are part of an on-going formation. Unlike the devil, there is in us a strong desire to be better than what we are. The devils are terribly jealous when they see their clients pray fervently when they try to become holy. They may even do some physical harm to them. They sin continually but never go to confession because they cannot be sorry for their sins. They become more and more bad, evil and proud. Human beings are meant to be just the opposite; they desire to change and want to become better and better each day. Here we are not speaking of this and that individual, but we are considering the nature of man and woman in whom there is the immortal soul, created in the image and likeness of God (cf. Gen 1: 26). This immortal soul must be redeemed. So let us try to overcome not evil with evil, hatred with hatred, but evil with good, hatred with love, pride with humility, etc.

Perhaps the following points may help us to form ourselves and others:

1) The desire to improve the quality of one's life in accordance with God's will and for His glory.

2) The effort to know and the humility to accept the things we cannot change and the courage to change things we can and wisdom to know the difference. In any change of life effort, is a must.

3) Courage, constancy and perseverance.

4) To be firm and to be convinced of what one is up to. Avoid negatively speaking, not easily giving up or simply being discouraged.

5) Motivation--why I do what I do and to whom and for whom? The more I know that whenever I do, even the most insignificant actions done with love and for Jesus, the more easy and meritorious my actions become. Love for Jesus makes even the most difficult work easier and sweeter.

6) Be patient with oneself and others while praying for the gift of understanding..

7) Charity in word and action. *"Charity covers a multitude of sins"* (St. Peter, St. James).

> *"Breathe into me Holy Spirit that my thoughts* (desires) *may all be holy"* (St. Augustine).

> *" Move in me Holy Spirit that my work may all be holy".*

10) Apostolic zeal and fervour, ardently desiring to save all souls, embracing all the different vocations (see St. Thérèse of Lisieux): martyr, apostle, saint, priest.

11) To become a true Missionary in heart, mind and soul, and not simply travelling around. This means that to learn that to go out of oneself as a true missionary is not one who leaves his home and native land, but one who goes out of oneself, sees the needs of others, wherever one is placed. In other words, try to become what Jesus wants you to become and bloom where you are. Not all can go around and preach to the people and not all are meant to go around. Some are called to be contemplative missionaries like St. Thérèse of Lisieux, while others like St. Francis Xavier or Blessed Mother Teresa became missionary contemplatives, going around and preaching the Gospel.

12) Faithfulness in everything. Many a time one may not be successful, but one can try to be faithful in the little things of everyday life, such as:

- One's duties, one's state of life.

- The vows one has taken.

- The appointments and engagements.

- One's spiritual life and especially to one's life of prayer.

- Family or community duties and functions.

- The Spirit and charism of our Society.

- The apostolate among the poorest of the poor, that is to carry Jesus to them and bring them to Jesus.

13) One must be trained to do things not according to one's feelings and moods but knowingly and willingly do things to Jesus and for his glory. *"So never hesitate to do good to others whether they deserve it or not. God will never forget"* (6th Station of the Cross).

14) One must have the conviction that whatever we do to the least of our brethren we do it to Jesus and for Jesus. The more repugnant the work and the more difficult the person or situation is, the more faith is required. For example, at times our superior/the link can be hard and harsh, not understanding nor forgiving. But in the superior we

must see the will and plan of God. St. Thérèse says: *"If my prioress was not hard and harsh I would not have become a saint. Jesus made her act toward me without much kindness and tenderness."* See Jesus before Pilate. In Pilate, Jesus saw the will and plan of his Father. In obeying Pilate, Jesus was obeying his beloved Father. *"Never look upon your Superior otherwise than if you were looking upon God. Keep a careful watch over yourself in this matter, and do not reflect upon the character, ways, conversation and habits of your Superior. If you do, you will injure yourself and you will change your obedience from divine into human, and you will be influenced by what you see in your Superior, and not by the invisible God whom you should obey in him"* [St. John of the Cross]. (R. 94).

15) It should be possible for us to have "unity in essential things, freedom in doubtful matters and Charity in all things". It must be possible for us to differ and disagree and yet remain friends and work together. We may disagree with a person in his way of thinking, but we can still love the person and work with him or her.

16) We must be determined to become not only saints but martyrs. Then we will be longing for suffering, will be able to accept humiliations, mistreatments, false accusations, calumnies and the like. St. Thérèse said: *"The sharper the thorns, the sweeter my song shall be."* Blessed Mother Teresa said: *"I love you not for what you give, but for what you take, Jesus"..."Even if I suffer more than now, still I want to do your Holy Will."* As a woman in labour pain gives birth to her beloved child, Mother Teresa was giving birth to the Society of the Missionaries of Charity in darkness and in pain. For she writes on 16 February 1949: *"Even if I suffer more than now, still I want to do your Holy Will. This is the dark night of the birth of the Society. My God, give me courage now, this moment to persevere in following Your call."*

17) This martyrdom can lead us to the experience of rejection, feeling of loneliness, complete spiritual darkness, feeling of withdrawal of any grace and spiritual consolation. One can experience real hell on earth, which means to experience the absence of the presence and action of God in and around us. Mother Teresa

writes on 28 February 1949: *Today, my God, what tortures of loneliness, I wonder how long will my heart suffer this. Tears rolled and rolled, Everyone sees my weakness. My God, give me courage now to fight self and the tempter. Let me not draw back from the sacrifice I have made of my free choice and conviction. Immaculate Heart of my Mother, have pity on Thy poor child. For love of Thee I want to live and die an M.C."*

18) Our experience of martyrdom can be very long, tedious and continuous. Here it is necessary for us to distinguish between a true saint and an average person. The saint is able to discern and distinguish and knows how to use hardships, sufferings, trials, temptations and the like as channels of grace. St. Thérèse of Lisieux writes: *"Even the wildest fancies that cross my mind, I use them as means to save souls."* The saints and mystics are real artists. Blessed Teresa of Calcutta wrote to one of her spiritual Fathers back in 1965: *"As for me what will I tell you I have nothing--since I have not got Him whom my heart and soul long to possess. Aloneness is so great from within and from without. I find no one to turn to. He has taken not only spiritual, but even the human help...If there is hell, this must be one. How terrible it is to be without God--no prayer, no faith, no love. The only thing that still remains is the conviction that the work is His, that the Brothers and Sisters are His, and I cling to this as a person, having nothing, clings to the straw before drowning--and yet Father in spite of all this I want to be faithful to Him, to spend myself for Him, to love Him not for what He gives but for what He takes, to be at His disposal. I do not ask Him to change His attitude towards me or His plans for me. I only ask Him to use me."* (from Mother Teresa's letter to her Spiritual Father)

19) Whatever adversities, trials, oppositions may come, we must be trained to use them not as stumbling blocks but as stepping stones. These trials may come from within oneself or from outside. We must learn to baptize our sufferings and recycle our trials. When Jesus spoke to the apostles of His impending passion and death, he said, *"I have a baptism to be baptized with..."* Jesus did not remove suffering from our lives, but he

made them channels and means. He made suffering our royal road to heaven. *"We adore you, O Christ and we praise you, because by your holy Cross you have redeemed the world."* There is now only one way of redemption, Jesus' way, and it is the royal road of the Holy Cross (cf. Imitation of Christ, book II, Ch. 12).

20) We must be trained to know, love and live the Liturgy. Our life must be centred around the Liturgy, especially the Eucharist. The Liturgy of the Hours is meant either to prepare us or to help us to continue to live the Mass and the Eucharist; as we read in S.C., that the "Eucharistic celebration is the source and summit of our Christian life and vocation". The celebration of the Liturgy re-enacts the work of our redemption, glorifying God and sanctifying us. It not only prepares us for heaven, but in a certain sense it anticipates the heavenly life on earth singing songs of praise and thanksgiving, although in an imperfect manner.

21) "Let your communities/your family be another Nazareth." The families are the domestic sanctuaries of the Church. In this, the Holy Family of Nazareth stands out as an edifying example not only for families, but also for religious communities. Here we can come to know the basic virtues of faith, hope and above all Charity, coupled with the virtue of humility. The Holy Family is the foreshadowing on earth of the Holy Trinity in heaven. It was a unique family where Jesus was the centre, where all three persons had only one desire, namely to do the will of God in the most perfect way possible. There was no room for any sins or selfishness. The Holy Family underwent severe trials, but they became means of salvation and redemption. Far from being drowned and sunk, they used them as channels of grace. They used hardships and trials as stepping stones for them and ladders for all those who try to follow their example. They sanctified the family life and gave a new and noble dimension. It became a means to fulfil their call to holiness. When love and Charity reign in a religious community or in a family, the members not only experience for themselves heavenly peace,

but radiate and share it with all around. That is the reason why we have the board with the following words in our refectories: *"Christ is the head of this family, the unseen guest at every meal, the silent listener at every conversation."* We must have a childlike devotion to Jesus, Mary and Joseph.

22) Formation enables us to see the preciousness of silence and enables us to live it in our everyday life, the silence which becomes meekness, mercy, patience, humility, faith, adoration.
The Silence is Meekness.
When you do not defend yourself against offences;
When you do not claim your rights;
When you let God defend you.
The Silence is Mercy.
When you do not reveal the faults of your brothers to others;
When you readily forgive without enquiring into the past,
When you do not judge, but pray in your heart.
The Silence is Patience.
When you accept suffering not with grumbling but joyfully,
When you do not look for human consolations,
When you do not become too anxious, but
Wait in patience for the seed to germinate.
The Silence is Humility.
When there is no competition;
When you consider the other person to be better than yourself;
When you let your brothers emerge, grow and mature;
When you joyfully abandon all to the lord;
When your actions may be misinterpreted;
When you leave to others the glory of the enterprise.
The Silence is Faith.
When you keep quiet because you know that the Lord will act;
When you renounce the voice of the world to remain in the presence of the Lord;
When you do not labour yourself to be understood,
Because it is enough for you to know that the Lord understands you.
The Silence is Adoration
When you embrace the cross without asking "Why?"
"But Jesus was silent."

23) Formation in ascetical life, in other words, to teach the members to practise self-denial and abnegation. Blessed Mother Teresa writes: *"For if they are not in love with God, they will not be able to lead this life of continual immolation for souls. Each must understand that, if he/she wants to become a Missionary of Charity, he/she must be in love with the Crucified and be His victim for the souls of the poor...We are called to lead a life of continual self-forgetfulness and immolation for others. To do so we need interior souls, burning with love for God and for souls...Free souls who would be able to sacrifice everything for this one thing only: to bring souls to God. The work will need much deep, fervent prayers and much penance to bring souls to God and God to souls."* (cf. Founding Grace: 22, 23, 24) It is clear that not only self-denial and abnegation are inevitable to save souls, but the purpose of leading an ascetical life is primarily meant to save souls. Blessed Teresa's main preoccupation was how to save the souls of the poor.

All the saints and mystics who fall in love with God are also passionately in love with souls, especially of sinners. St. Francis Xavier, the patron saint of the Missions, cried out: *"Give me souls and take everything else from me."* Blessed Teresa of Calcutta writes: *"These desires to satiate the longing of our Lord for the souls of the poor--for pure victims of His love, goes on increasing with every Mass and Holy Communion."*

It is through self-sacrifice and immolation that the world of the poor will come to see, know and want Jesus. Jesus said to Blessed Teresa of Calcutta: *"Come, be their victim. In your immolation, in your love for Me, they will see Me, know Me, want Me. Offer more sacrifices. Smile more tenderly, pray more fervently and all the difficulties will disappear."* Jesus continued: *"You will suffer, suffer very much but remember I am with you."* Never follow Jesus without the Cross and never carry the Cross alone, i.e. without Jesus. It is so easy to be crushed by the weight of the Cross if Jesus is not with us and if we carry it alone. But Jesus' presence helps our Cross to become light and sweet. For Jesus says: *"...my yoke is easy, and my burden light."* (Mt 11: 30)

24) From the beginning of our formation we must have clear knowledge and understanding of our relationship with God. This knowledge

and understanding of God must grow deeper and deeper, which would enable us to know also ourselves better and deeper. It is in the unfathomable mystery of God that we discover the mystery and miracle of our own existence and life. We realize that whatever is good in us comes from God and so we should not feel proud, better or superior. If we come to understand this truth of our existence, we may not have inferiority or superiority complexes, nor will we be carried away by the praises, applauses or flatteries of men. Whatever experiences we go through, we learn to thank God and praise Him; this we do even when we suffer from hurts and injuries. If we follow Jesus' admonition to *"love your enemies and pray for those who persecute you,"* (Mc 5: 44) we will experience profound peace and unspeakable joy. There is a great strength and power in praising God and thanking Him for good times and for bad, for good people and the less good people, for those who may do harm, hurt or injure us, or those who are kind and friendly to us.

We must never cease to thank God and praise Him: "Jesus, I praise you and I thank you for such and such a person, or such and such situation". Do this as many times as possible. In place of grumbling and murmuring or getting angry or upset, we must learn to praise and thank God for everything. The Holy Spirit will help us to understand that everything is God's gift. With Job we can say then: *"if we have received good things from God, must we not take bad..."* (Job 2: 10). As Blessed Teresa of Calcutta said: *"Accept whatever God gives and give whatever He takes with a big smile."* If we do this we will experience untold joy and profound peace.

25) Coming to know what the capital sins are and what they do to us.

There are seven capital sins, which work against us. They are our spiritual enemies. They are like weeds which choke in us the good seed of grace and peace. We are taught to practise the virtues that work like antidotes to the capital sins. In other words, if there are seven capital sins, we are taught to practise seven virtues against these vices.

Our spiritual enemies are three: concupiscence of the flesh, the world and the devil. Concupiscence is the foe we carry within us. The world and the devil are the foes from without that feed the fire of concupiscence and fan its flames.

The capital sins are tendencies rather than sins; however, they are called sins because they lead us to sins; they are termed capital because they are the fountainhead or source of other sins.

These tendencies can be referred to the threefold concupiscence in the following way: from pride are born vain glory, envy and anger; from the concupiscence of the flesh, issue gluttony, lust and sloth; lastly, the concupiscence of the eyes is one with avarice.

26) Come to know, love and live the Constitutions/Statutes as we make our vows according to them. Therefore, we are duty-bound to know them well; here again, it is not something that we read once or twice and pass by, but we read and study regularly so that they become part of our daily routine like the food we eat. We come to love them in order to live them in all their entirety with God's help.

Besides our Constitutions/Statutes, we must also come to know, love and live our Mother Teresa's Founding Grace document, the Spiritual path and other materials, which are of great help for us to live our M.C. vocation and become holy. Fidelity to our call and not spoiling God's work is vitally important. To do so we have to pray more fervently, offer more sacrifices and do the works of mercy more perseveringly, in humility, charity and joy.

God bless you.

Fr. Sebastian Vazhakala M.C.

CHAPTER SIX
ADVENT AND CHRISTMAS

Christmas, 1984

"Pause a while and know that I am God"

Dearest Mother and all the Sisters,

"Pause a while and know that I am God". This verse from Psalm 46 struck me as I opened my Bible at random; and I came to realize that the Lord is telling me (us) to cease from all hectic activities, to take a moment to myself to pause, especially during this season of Advent and Christmas. Only when one enters into the inner sanctuary of his own being will his eyes begin to open up and will he see the Lord of his own being, secretly seated in his innermost recess. There he falls on his knees in profound adoration before the inscrutable God, who in the fullness of time came down from his own world of glory to a world doomed to destruction (Wis 18 15) in the form of a weak and tiny baby. Can any human mind grasp this unspeakable condescension of the Almighty! Human words are inadequate to translate the meaning and significance of this divine act. And yet day after day this condescension, this kenosis (self-emptying), this Christmas takes place throughout the world in a thousand and one ways.

Pause a while, take your time and see the sacrament of the Eucharist, for example; it is a real Christmas...the coming down of a God on the altar to become food and drink for us. Man, and he alone, is God's preoccupation. Restlessly and untiringly God works out His plan of salvation for fallen man. Misusing the most precious gift of his freedom, man is constantly tempted to walk away from the Father's house. A merciful and generous God with infinite patience and tender love waits for the return of His 'prodigals'.

303

We live in a complex world of many contradictions. There is the constant battle cry for peace and justice, in a world of hatred and war. Violence has become man's prerogative, his way of living and surviving. Most of man's life is controlled by fear! People hardly trust each other any more. Compelled by tyranny and fear, a mother kills her own child when no resistance or defence is possible...a defenceless victim so brutally attacked. Mankind is moving toward atrocious insanity. In a world like ours, when materialism has the highest power and the last word, all spiritual and supernatural values crumble. For the materialists, supernatural values are an obstacle to progress and prosperity. The world is being more and more moved away from its true centre, with the result that there is so much insecurity, fear and mistrust. In search of a better and more comfortable life, man replaces God for material things and finally ends up in utter despair. Even the feast of Christmas has become a commercial event, a time to make more money, a time for competitive enterprises. It has so sadly lost its original spirit, beauty and simplicity, meaning and significance. Who will have the courage to take up the challenge to try to revive the original spirit of Christmas?

Pause a while, take your time and see the self emptying of a God who makes himself visible and lives among us in the form of our grandparents or elderly persons, in the form of our children or parents, in the form of husband or wife, in the form of the poorest of the poor, or in the form of the rich and the affluent… Often we are like the disciples of Emmaus (Lk 24): we do not recognize Him, because we live in our own world of preconceived ideas, prejudices and feelings. And so, even when we live with Him, walk with Him, work or converse with Him, we fail to recognize Him, unless and until He opens our eyes "at the breaking of the bread". It is very interesting to note that only when the disciples pressed him to stay with them and were willing to break bread together, their eyes were opened and they were able to recognize Him. Every time we see the coming of Christ in some form we have our Christmas.

Here I recall one of my recent experiences. I went into a Church as I was passing by to pay a visit to the Blessed Sacrament. The Holy Mass was in progress and the church was rather full. I knelt at the back of the church and prayed in silence. All of a sudden a strange sort of a feeling and desire "to see the face of Jesus" dawned on me. Cherishing it in my heart, I prayed with greater earnestness. As I opened my eyes

I saw the people leaving the church as the Holy Mass was over. In a way I was happy, thinking that once the people had gone, Jesus might grant me "a private audience". I waited and prayed even harder, but to my great disappointment I had to leave the church without my prayer being answered. Leaving the church I headed toward home. As I walked along the side walk, a man came to me asking for a few coins for a cup of coffee. His eyes were heavy; his clothes filthy; he looked exhausted and worried. I felt that his need was more than a cup of coffee. So I asked him to come with me to our house where he could wash himself, change his clothes, eat, rest and relax. Above all it was very evident that he needed someone to talk to. As I pressed him to come with me, he came and together we did all that was necessary to be done. He was helped to take off his clothes; he was also helped to peal off the dirt. During all this ordeal he would look at me with eyes filled and ask: who are you? And why are you doing this to me? Don't you know that I have no money to give you...He had his bath, change of clothes and meal, during which he shared his long and tragic story. He was on the verge of despair to the point of committing suicide. His constant experience of rejection and the consequent feeling of unwantedness left an indelible mark on him. For years he had not received the warmth of love of affection. We went to the chapel. He knelt down, prayed, cried, and made his confession after many years. He thanked God and the brothers and then left saying that he would like to return to us later.

In the evening as usual I was making my examination of conscience when suddenly my eyes were opened and I remembered my 'crazy' desire to see the face of Jesus. Jesus did hear my prayer, but not the way I wanted. He made Himself visible in that person who came to our house, hungry, filthy and friendless. That was a Real Christmas Day for me. Meeting this sort of person has become almost a daily experience for us in Rome. In our competitive society where 'survival of the fittest and the strongest' is the law, we often find people who are utterly broken and deeply wounded, people not knowing where to go or whom to turn to. Passing from hunger to starvation they have lost the sense of brotherly love and true friendship, in a world of scaring indifference and shocking apathy. More and more the world is becoming a "Huge Home for the Dying"; so much spiritual poverty, so much want of love, even in families, among husband and wife, between parents and children, among and between brothers and sisters. Television takes the place of family prayer, family life and sharing. The same can be said of religious families and communities. If television replaces our tabernacle, then there is no true religious life either.

Pause a while and know that I am God. It is only when I took a little time to pause that my eyes were opened and I was able to recognize Jesus in the person who came my way. It was then that I heard Him say, "As long as you did this to one of the least of these brothers of mine, you did it to Me" (Mt 25: 40). These least ones of his are everywhere. Here in Rome we find them in the hospitals, prisons, apartment houses, in public parks, on street corners and also in our house. Often the really poor people do not come to us; we must go to them. The brothers spend several hours a day visiting the poor. These visits renew their spirit, bringing them 'Christmas' joy and peace. Many of them want to pray together; some like to sing hymns or songs; while others like to tell their long and painful stories. What we are and what we do are not that important; we are the weakest and the least, and our actions are quite insignificant. It is the promise and assurance of Jesus: *"Whatever you do... you do it to Me"* that makes the whole difference. This always gives us the incentive to do small things with great love, to make every kind of service into prayer, as we do it with Jesus, for Him and to Him. "Lord, give us the strength to make our love more fruitful in service".

At the end of a long and full year, when we look back, there is so much to thank God, for so many of you my dear brothers and sisters in the faith for your uninterrupted assistance at all the major events of our life and activities, especially in building our new prefabricated house. Thanks to each one of you for offering so much material help and man power, for devoting so much of your precious time to give us timely advice and practical suggestion. Even from long distances people support us through their unceasing prayers, words of encouragement, timely donations, etc. All these are little sparks of love that always sustain our fire. While thanking God for each one of you, we pray that you may continue to be the reflection of His love in action.

We would like to express our sincere thanks to his Eminence Ugo Cardinal Poletti for kindly coming to bless our new house, for the beautiful words he spoke at the homily, for his keen interest and paternal care and concern. Thanks to the Mayor of Rome for so kindly sending his personal representatives, all other civil and religious representatives and all the participants, for your active co-operation to make November the 7th a great success. Just before leaving, his Eminence said that Missionaries of the Word is a real gift to the diocese of Rome. Please pray that we may be a real gift not only to the diocese of Rome but to the whole world.

Born out of our weekly meeting, sharing and prayer (every Wednesday of the week a group of people meet regularly from 7 p.m. to 9 p.m. in the chapel of the Brothers, to pray, to hear and reflect together on the Word of God...) is the 'Holy Family Movement'. It is a response to the call of God to live more authentically and generously their Christian and baptismal consecration. On April 16th four married persons made the profession of Conjugal Chastity, poverty, i.e. adherence to a simpler life style, obedience to the Church and to Her teachings, sincere and free service to the poorest of the poor, in the chapel of the Brothers, in their presence, in the presence of Mother Teresa of Calcutta, in the presence of their family members and friends. This new movement, though only a tiny seed, has already become an incentive for many to follow their example. Let us support them by our prayer and words of encouragement. Our Wednesday meeting also has become a real source of strength and grace for us to live a better Christian life, to appreciate each other's ideas and views. It is also helping ±o understand and to participate more actively in the liturgy of the Mass, prayers and Sacraments. "Where two or three meet in my name, I shall be there with them" (Mt.18: 20).

Writing this letter I realize that one year is too long and the events are too many to describe in one letter like this. Already this has become quite long. At the end of everything it is gratitude to God that fills our minds for His 'amazing grace'. We can never thank Him enough neither by words nor by deeds. Often God speaks to us not through the 'big and spectacular events' but through the simple and ordinary activities of the day. The words and works of Jesus clearly teach us (Lk.21: 1-4) that the merit of our actions does not consist in its size or weight ,i.e. in quantity, but rather the way we are and the way we do things. Saints like St. Therese of Lisieux and Blessed Elizabeth of Trinity tell us to do ordinary things with great love; to find holiness in our everyday life.

Christmas is the feast of the poor and little ones. Jesus was one with them and one of them. Moreover he was sent to announce the good news to the poor. He was poor at birth, poorer in life and poorest on the cross. Working among and with the poor make us realize that we too are poor like them.

307

Only when we are filled with the power of the Holy Spirit do we become His strong hands to serve, His sweet lips to speak His Word and His warm heart to love. We are like a bulb. In itself it has no power unless connected to the source through a wire. To be His light, we have to have continuous connection with God, the Source of all light; prayer unites us to God. Each one of us is God's bulb through whom He shines. Happy and holy Christmas and a prosperous New Year.

God bless you.

Fr. Sebastian Vazhakala M.C.

CHRISTMAS 1987

Dear Brothers and Sisters,

The preface to the 2nd Eucharistic prayer begins with: "Father, it is our duty and our salvation, always and everywhere, to give You thanks through your beloved Son Jesus Christ." This is how I feel and I do on the eve of the solemnity of Christmas when our hearts are filled with joy as we recognize in Christ the revelation of our Father's love. This is how I feel and I do at the end of a long and eventful year of His many blessings and graces. This is how I feel and I do when I think of you, my dear brothers and sisters in the Lord, Lay Missionaries of Charity, benefactors, co-workers and friends and all men of good will. You have become so much a part and parcel of our life. We thank you and thank God for you and pray that the spiritual journey we have started together in the spirit of love, prayer and fellowship may continue to grow and mature, bearing fruit in abundance.

One of the major events for us of this year was our chapel repairs. Thanks to God's unfailing assistance! He has made His dwelling place more beautiful than ever before. It was God's work and was very evident for us the way things happened. There were times when we did not have the sufficient amount to pay the bills, but by evening somehow help was offered without being asked. I am so convinced that Jesus, who sees all our needs both spiritual and material more than us, inspires people to help us. That is exactly what happened. Even a group of scouts from Cassino, 120 Km. from Rome, came twice to work with us. God's Providence is so evident in all our undertakings!

The work went on for months. One family took care of the floor tiles, while another of the doors, and a third one of the windows. Even some kids made their offering, saying this is for your church repairs; this summer we will not eat ice-cream. A burden shared is no more a burden too heavy to carry. Besides, so many people, including some of the grown-up children, worked for days. Here I remember a little poem I studied while I was in high school:

> "Little drops of water
> Little grains of sand
> Make a mighty ocean".

Throughout the work I thought of the repairs of my interior self, refashioning after the example of Jesus who is meek and humble of heart. It takes not only months and years but the whole life time. Again and again I said to Jesus: repair me, my Brothers and all those who are in need of putting things in order in their lives, in their families and communities. When we allow Jesus to do that we will experience profound peace in our hearts.

I spoke so much about the chapel repairs, because it was one of the main events for our community this year and so many of you have been over generous in helping us. May the good Lord reward you for your kindness and generosity!

We also had other great moments. In the first place we joyfully recall and cherish the memory of the many visits with us of our beloved Mother and founders, Mother Teresa of Calcutta, especially the one in May(16th) together with his Grace Henry D'Souza, the Archbishop of Calcutta .

August was a month of spiritual repairs and renewal. We had a very beautiful and fruitful eight-day Ignatian retreat. Thanks to Fr. Francis Furlong S.J. who directed the work of God in us.

Br. Luke made his first profession and Br. Piet his final. Both were very moving experiences and God's blessing for our community. It is our duty, Lord, to give you thanks and praise always and everywhere!

Throughout the year we have been very fervently praying for vocations and to have another community of ours beside S. Agapito. Well, Jesus heard our prayer, not perhaps the way in which we all expected, but the way He wanted it to happen. And it literally happened on October 4th, when we happily welcomed a new community in Sao Paulo, Brazil, and the Brother In-charge, Br. James, making his final vows. The joy was immense. The homeless boys who stay with the Brothers sang songs of praise and thanksgiving. Thanks to all the co-workers who help the

Brothers to run the place so well, making it into a house of God and a home of love.

To one of the older boys I asked: Where is your father? "There", he said pointing, "my father is Bro. James". It is true, I thought: when one is homeless, friendless and penniless, whoever shows kindness and provides his needs is his father, brother, or sister, and at the same time he does it to Jesus. "I tell you solemnly, in so far as you did this to one of the least of these brothers of mine, you did it to Me".

Beyond doubt Christmas is essentially a time of sharing and joyful celebration. Everything around us speaks of a forthcoming great event. The shops are well set, attractively arranged and beautifully decorated. Many seek to renew their friendships and intimacy through telephone calls, greeting cards and personal meetings; and rightly so. For such things are very necessary and precious to renew, rebuild and restore human and personal relationships.

But then, behind such sharing and celebrity there is another group of weaklings, who hardly receive any telephone calls, greeting cards or personal visits. Their existence is even often forgotten or ignored. They are the sick, the aged and the poor, the misfit to our highly competitive, product-oriented and consumer society. Today more than ever the sick and the aged suffer from such terrible loneliness and feelings of rejection. On top of all, our society makes them feel useless nay even a burden to others. How often and how many old people with tears in their eyes tell me of their state of affairs. "It is so terrible to be an old person; my own never come to see me and nobody really wants me…why should I live? Why should I live? Christmas only makes me feel sad". Inconsolable loneliness and feeling of rejection are written on all over their faces. "I looked for someone to console me, and there was none"!

Just the other day one of my friends came to see me. His face was bruised all over, his eyes red, and his eyebrows swollen. "What happened to you, my friend?" I enquired. "Some accident of some sort?" He sighed deeply. His eyes were full. "Well, you know, Father, I scolded my son for something and this was the result. My own son! Yes my own son did this to me". He could not continue any longer; he was choked up. I thought of the Good Friday reproaches: "My people, what have I done to you, how have I offended you? Answer me". How often we do worse than this to Jesus in our neighbours…!

I can go on giving examples which then will never end. Against this background Jesus comes again with the message of peace and joy. "Listen, I bring you news of great joy, a joy to be shared by the whole people. Today in the town of David a Saviour has been born to you."

Jesus will not be born any more in the crib of Bethlehem, but he seeks an entry to our crowded hearts, and often they are poorer than the Bethlehem crib. But his birth in our lives makes a world of difference. We can no longer be the same. Dying to ourselves and to our own interests, we live in Him and for others. When that happens we would be able to say with St. Paul: "The life I live is no longer mine, but Christ who lives in me".

Before I close this letter I would like to say a word about our movement known as the Lay Missionaries of Charity. We know very well that God doesn't call all to become religious or priests, but he wants all to become holy and perfect like him. So many of us want to be so but do not know how. The Lay Missionaries of Charity (LMC) was founded to help lay people who are not yet fully holy and saints but want to be so. This they do by trying to live the Missionaries of Charity spirit and spirituality in their homes and surroundings. The members make private vows. We already have groups in various parts of Italy, France and the United States. Our Statutes and Way of Life are approved by the Church and are already translated into several languages. Those who want to know more about it can always write to our address.

As I conclude this letter let me wish each one of you very personally for a really happy and holy Christmas and a blessed New Year 1988 and say:

A world without Jesus is a world worse than a dark dungeon;

A world without Jesus is the actual "third world";

A world without Jesus is a world of utter despair;

A world without Jesus is a world of hatred and war;

A world without Jesus is a world without peace and joy

Where people live more and more like strangers and enemies.

The same can be said of each individual person without Jesus living in him or her.

A family where there is no more room for Jesus is no family anymore. As the days pass by the couples slowly begin to live like strangers, and then like enemies, and finally end up in divorce.

Without Jesus we can do nothing. Let us then pray:
"Stay with us, Lord, for it is nearly evening".
God bless you.

Fr. Sebastian Vazhakala M.C.

Christmas 1994

**Jesus was born in the House of Bread (Beth-lehem)
in order to become the Bread of life for us.**

Dear Friends,

Greetings of peace and joy to all of you in this holy season of Advent that prepares us with eager longing for the coming of the Messiah, our Saviour and Lord. Our cribs are getting ready, I suppose, both within and outside. Our straw, which means our sacrifices to prepare a crib in our heart for Jesus, is getting finished. We have seven candidates, four of whom are sent for their home visit and also to bring more vocations, as they are all very enthusiastic. They will be back on December 29, God willing.

Gianna, after her Culcutta experience, went to make a charismatic retreat in Kerala, and will be back in Delhi to return to Rome on the 10 December. She will have a little tour in the Southern part of the country.

My mission in the U.S.A. went quite well, thanks to all your prayers and sacrifices, which I could feel through and through. People were very kind, loving and caring. Since I had a bronchitic fever, my voice wasn't that good; still they listened to every word I spoke. There were about 6,000 people in all. I had many surprise meetings. Also I met some of the U.S. LMCs, including Br. Mark's parents, and talked to some others by telephone.

Now, our Society is completing one year on December 8 and it is going to be our first Thanksgiving Day of this sort. Our Lady has been so kind and considerate to bless our tiny little Society from the first moment of her sinless existence. She couldn't be tinier than the first moment of her being conceived in the womb of her beloved and holy mother St. Ann. And Our Lady knew very well that like Her our Society too is really tiny.

Looking back at the past year we can see that it has been eventful, and we cannot thank God enough for His countless blessings. We had the first thanksgiving Holy Mass together with Mother Teresa, some of our Brothers, and many Sisters, at Via Casilina on December 13, for the ecclesial recognition of our Society. As some of you may remember, on December 31 we had the official Canonical Erection and for the first time the solemn profession of six of our Senior Brothers and simple vows of Br. Luke. Many of the participants said that it was a very moving experience of God. Then on February 2, we had an event in the renovated Shkodra Cathedral for the first time after several years of severe communist regime: the first profession of the three lucky Brothers: Br. Thaddeus, Br. Thomas and Br. Martin. It was another moving experience of God, as many remarked. March 24 marked the solemn perpetual profession of Br. Matthew, who missed December 31, as he was at home with his dying mother to help her to go home to God in peace and to console the rest of the family members by his presence and prayers. To complete the stream of experiences, on September 15, we celebrated the moving spiritual experience of Br. Simon's first profession. Now let us pray for our continued growth in holiness and for our final perseverance.

Another great blessing is and always will be the new and fervent vocations. Let us thank Our Lady for the four new zealous novices and the three enthusiastic postulants. May our Blessed Mother help them to grow in holiness, covering them with Her mantle of purity and humility.

In Albania Br. Paul and Br. Joseph have begun their intensive preparation under the wise direction of Br. Piet. Usually it starts with a day of prayer, special Holy Mass, etc., at the end of which they write the application for admission to profession. Who knows, we may even have their profession ceremony in India, as we know that nothing is impossible with God.

There is still another reason to thank God and Our Lady, namely for the new foundation in India and the several aspirants who are very eager to learn our way of life in order to become holy. Of course we, like Mary, have to go through many trials before we get this new house properly established in the Indian soil. At this time last year we were offering prayers and supplications with loud cries and tears for the canonical erection of our Society, which we finally obtained with God's grace and Our Lady's intercession. This year we ask Our Lady instead to help us to establish us here in India, especially giving us a proper house with the minimum requirements. I am sure that what we ask in deep faith and trust will be granted us in love, but in God's own time, way and place. We need to be patient. Please pray for us.

December 8 then is a great day of thanksgiving; at the same time it is a day of examination, evaluation and renewal for everybody, and especially for our Society. We thank God and Our Lady with all the powers and fibers of our being. The real thanksgiving does not finish in one day...it is a continuous one. Our daily life lived according to our Constitutions in fidelity and love itself is a great thanksgiving.

There are many ways we can and we should express our gratitude. One simple way is to pray our family - group - community Rosary with greater love and devotion. It unites us with the thousands of devout and simple Catholics around and across the globe who pray the same prayer. The Rosary is prayed in all the five Continents. In order to be more united with the people everywhere in our daily meditative praying of the Rosary, we make the following intentions before each decade:

1. For new, holy and fervent vocations. For Asia and Australia.

2. For our Aspirants and Postulants and their in-charges. For Europe, for the conversion of sinners, "and for our own Community here".

3. For the Novices and their Master(s). For Africa, for all our other communities, for the poorest of the poor, especially those whom we know.

4. For our Junior Professed Brothers, for their growth in holiness and perseverance. For South and Central America, for our beloved parents, brothers and sisters and their families, for the LMCs, Co-workers and our Benefactors.

5. For our Finally Professed Brothers, especially for our Superiors, for North America and all the islands around the world. For our tiny little Society, for our Holy Father, and for our entire MC Family.

N.B. Besides these intentions, there are those listed in our Prayer Book, and others may be added at will.

I also would like to thank Mr. Carlo and Mrs. Piera Mercuri, and thank God for them, for all that they were and are and for what they have done for the LMCs in Italy as national Links. Carlo has retired from his work; he would like now somebody else to take his place as LMC national Link. Thanks be to God Mr. Adolfo Costa from Parma has kindly consented to be the national LMC Link for Italy and Magì Scanziani as national Secretary while Sr. Gianna Tommasi continues as General Secretary. Let us pray that our LMCs may continue to grow in holiness and in number through their wise direction. They are the editors and publishers of the Newsletter "L'avete fatto a me".

I also take this opportunity to wish each one of you a very happy and holy Christmas and a peace-filled New Year. Let us try to make the coming year a year of peace and joy for all, especially for the poorest of the poor. Let there be peace and joy and let it begin with me.

Well, my dearest friends, thank you for all your love and care. God loves you immensely; more than you and I love Him. He loves you more than I love you. He also loves you through me. Please pray that I may be totally free so that He can love you and others through me as He wants and as much as He wants, that I may never be an obstacle to Him. In other words, that I may be totally transparent to Him. I pray much for you every day and thank God for each one of you.

Love and prayers.

God bless you

Fr. Sebastian Vazhakala M.C.

Christmas 1995

Dearly beloved brothers and sisters in Jesus Christ,

Christmas is a feast of freedom! Jesus came to set men free. Only one who is truly free can set others free. There are three kinds of freedom: physical, psychological and moral.

When a person is imprisoned he loses his physical freedom. Sickness or accidents can also curtail one's physical freedom. Lack of physical freedom does not automatically cripple one's psychological or moral freedom. St. Maximillian Maria Kolbe, for example, was put in the starvation bunker, and yet he retained his psychological and moral freedom to his last breath. So many people down through the ages who lost their physical freedom one way or another have retained their spiritual freedom intact and have become great saints and martyrs. We have the examples of all the martyrs of the Church in the various parts of the world. "Freedom is what we have; Christ has set us free," says the Apostle of the Gentiles (St. Paul).

The majority of the people are physically free, but only a minority are free psychologically and morally. How often we become victims of our own fears, anxieties, worries and cares! How often people become so nervous that they make a mess of the situation, like the Roman Governor Pontius Pilate. In the judgment scene, all except Jesus were upset and disturbed. Jesus alone remained calm, even on the Cross; so much so that He was able to pronounce forgiveness over the repentant thief and promise him paradise. Jesus was truly free and wants all to be free like Him. It is worse to be physically free and then to be slaves psychologically and morally. So many get addicted to drugs, alcohol and other bad habits to the extent that they have lost all control over themselves and are controlled by these bad habits. A drug addict is psychologically not free as long as he has to have his daily dose, just like an alcoholic's drinking habit controls his life. Jesus came to set men free. "The spirit of the Lord is upon me...He sent me to give freedom to the captives..."(Lc 4).

The birth of Jesus is the birth of peace on earth. He came that all men of good will may enjoy peace in its fullness. Only one who is free can experience peace and become a prophet of peace..."Lord, help me to have profound peace and make me a channel of this peace"!

We live in a world of rapid changes. Mankind has never been so much in move. People have never traveled as they do today; and yet never before were people so unhappy and discontent as today. The result is often disastrous. Husbands are not happy with their wives, so they change, and vice versa. Pregnant women are unhappy because they do not have the freedom they want, so they destroy the fruit of their love, the innocent and defenseless child which God formed in their womb in His own image. Employees are not happy with their jobs, nor with the salary they receive, so they change jobs or go on striking. Consecrated persons, men and women religious, after a while get tired of their state of life or their Order and they want to change. The religious who bear the habit at times think that their ministry could be more effective without the habit.

One lady wanted me to bless her house because she was afraid that her fourth husband was going to leave her as the other three had done. Obviously, it is not the house that needs the blessing, but she herself, so that her heart can be changed.

Another lady comes to me asking for a general absolution, since she did not have any serious sin to confess. "Well, when did you make your last confession and what are the main sins that you think you should confess?" I asked. "I do not remember any serious sins". "Have you done any abortion?" "Abortion? What? Is it a sin? Nobody so far has ever told me, and every time I went to the clinic I saw 15 to 20 persons like me..." "So have you had some abortions?" "Yes, Father". "How many times?" "Well, I do not remember the exact number. I think somewhere between 25 and 30".

Someone thinks that others must be kind to us, must love us, appreciate us...that we have these rights, while we may treat them like slaves. But Jesus says: "Treat others as you like them to treat you". Let us not try to change places, jobs, persons, but first of all let us change our own hearts. That is the most important change to do, *metanoia - conversion of heart and change of attitudes.*

One married woman told me: "Father, I made a big mistake in getting married. If I were a religious, I could have been holier, more gentle and kind". I said to her: "You need to practice all these virtues and more in your married state, to live a happy family life. Do you obey your husband, respect him and listen? Do you see Jesus in him, even in distressing disguise? You have to find real holiness in the place where you are and what God wants you to be. Your married state is not an obstacle to holiness for you but a means. Now that you are married you can become holy only through your family. Holiness is not a luxury of the few but a simple duty of all. Everyone is called to holiness, but no one automatically becomes holy...not even the Pope because he is Pope, or cardinal because he is a cardinal. It is only by doing God's will and being what God wants us to be that we become holy. There are no shortcuts to holiness, and if I do not fulfill the duties of my state of life, no matter what I am...cardinal or pope...**I** am not going to be holy.

One priest told me if he were a bishop, he would have enacted many reforms in the diocese; but "I am only a pastor in a parish," he said. "Well," I said, "St. John Maria Vianney was sent to a remote and unknown parish. He was not a bishop. He changed not only his parish and the people around him, but also the whole world. He spent hours in the confessional, became a great saint, and a shining example for all pastors. His way of life changed the lives of many people and reformed many parishes!"

A little girl of fourteen, Bernadette of Lourdes, did not do much to change others, but she listened to our Blessed Mother, endured all the trials patiently, and died a peaceful and holy death at the age of 35. How many hundred thousands of people have been and are being touched by her life and example?

St Thérèse, a girl of fifteen, entered the convent, never to come out, dying there at the age of 24. Her life became a legend in no time, and millions of people follow her way of spiritual childhood that is total abandonment to God's holy will. She taught the world the value of small things...to do ordinary things with extraordinary love. She writes: "I will let no little sacrifice escape me, not a word, not a look (each sigh, each look, each act of mine shall be an act of love divine), I will make use of the smallest action and I will do them all for love".

On my recent trip to India I visited my aging parents for a couple of days. My father is 85 and my mother 83. We organized a Mass together. As the Church is on the top of a hill and my mother has some serious difficulty walking up the hill, I took her by hand by a round about way. While we were walking a car was just about there, and I told her that we could ask the driver to drop us in two minutes. "No," she said, "I must offer this with Jesus' way of the Cross to Calvary..." I still remember some of the ejaculatory prayers she taught me when I was small, especially when I am hurt: "Jesus, how much you have suffered for me, let me offer this pain in union with your suffering and death for the departed faithful, for the conversion of **sinners.**" Fifty years later she renewed that prayer through her unforgettable example. My eyes were full and I was choked. I tried not to show my reaction. We together slowly climbed up the hill. I could feel God's love all the more by being with my parents for few days. O my dearly beloved parents, I thank you and thank God for you. May the good Lord reward you for your loving kindness. Who can ever substitute our worthy parents' sacrificial love?

I still have to give you some news about our Brothers and our various communities. We are still a very tiny little Society. Pray that we may have more holy and fervent vocations and for our perseverance. In Albania we have two houses, including the Novitiate. Six novices from different countries spend the major part of their time in prayer and study, while twice a week they are involved with apostolic work among the prisoners, teach children catechism, and visit the families, especially the sick and the aged. The priest Brothers also involve themselves in pastoral works in several parishes, as there are no other priests working there. The other house in Bushat, besides prayers, teaches catechism, and prepares the young people and children for the various sacraments. From the beginning in Albania the Brothers were doing both corporal and spiritual works of mercy. Unlike the beginning now with money things can be bought. But the poor are always with you...much remains to be done. We really need help. We also need more priest

Brothers to take care of their spiritual needs. Several villages are still without priestly assistance. Any priest volunteers to work in Albania or elsewhere? We also need many good and holy vocations. Please help us by your prayers, words of encouragement and good example.

On July 3, 1994, we began a little community in India, about 14 Km. away from the International airport in Delhi. We finally bought a piece of land and constructed a small house for the Brothers. The main one is still to be constructed, and we need everybody's help. On Nov. 18th we had its blessing and inauguration. Mother Teresa was present. She, like a young girl, climbed up the stairs and visited the whole house. The auxiliary bishop Vincent blessed our humble house and Mother Teresa inaugurated it in the presence of many priests, religious nuns and over 1,500 Hindu people. Br. Damien (house superior), Br. Matthew, who was the first brother to begin the community there, and Br. Joseph from Peoria (Illinois) really worked hard to make it beautiful and colorful. The presence of Br. Piet (Vicar), Br. André Marie (house superior and Novice Master - Kukel, Albania) and Br. Subash (house superior - Bushat, Albania) was also a great help and encouragement for the brothers and the people there. Thanks to all who made the day a moving and enriching experience of peace and joy. Mother Teresa's presence made all the more aware of our duty toward the poorest of the poor. Much remains to be done, but the beginning has been made. Our tiny little Society is slowly growing, under the shadow of the Cross... making its steps little by little. After the blessing, Gianna LMC from Rome, proceeded to Calcutta to work with the poorest of the poor for three weeks in one of the houses of the Brothers.

Our night shelter in Rome houses about 50 people who otherwise would have been homeless and friendless, left to fight against the cold, drink and die. God is good.

I also take this opportunity to thank all our spiritual and temporal benefactors, co-workers, volunteers and LMCs, with their national and group links and spiritual directors, for your untiring and constant help, without which our work would not have been possible. May the good Lord reward you for your kindness and generosity. May this holy season be a time of special graces and blessings for you. Please pray that we together continue to build the kingdom of love and peace.

The LMCs are looking forward to our gathering in Sept., 1996 (22 to 29 Sept., 1996) in Lourdes. Much is to be done by way of preparation, etc. Plus, we need to pray much for its success and fruitfulness.

Christmas, then, calls for reform and renewal - that means I have to do it. The priests and religious often think the lay people need to be reformed; the husbands want their wives and children to be different; the wives want their husbands and children to be kind, loving and caring...But this holy season wants each one of us to examine his/her conscience and see what the good God is asking of me for my own benefit and for the benefit of all. Let there be peace and joy, and let it begin with me; let there be charity and love until I die of it. Happy and holy Christmas and a peace-filled New Year 1996 to all.

God bless you.

Fr. Sebastian Vazhakala M. C.

Christmas 1996

Dear brothers and sisters in Christ,

As I think of you, as I think of the year 1996, as I reflect again on the forthcoming Feast of Christmas, my heart gets filled with a profound sense of gratitude to God for you, for the year's many events and the incomprehensible divine condescension of God at Christmas. Never before have I felt God's merciful and undefeatable love so much in my life as was shown through you throughout this year...all the more to realise the words of St. Paul when he says: "Love never gives up", which is a phrase for all of us to ponder over and over and then translate into our everyday life. If it were not true of God, I wonder what would have happened to so many of us...yes it is true: "Love never gives up", which is the same as saying: "God never gives us up". The same truth is said in another way when God said: "Can a woman forget her sucking child, even if she forgets, I will not forget you".

It is very true, then, that there is Someone to love us all the time, that Someone can be loved by us all the time, and that Someone's love is unconditional, enduring and all encompassing. There is Someone to forgive us all the time, provided we humbly ask His forgiveness and forgive each other's faults. Love and forgiveness go hand in hand. God can forgive us because He loves us beyond measure. For us, too, the measure with which to love God is to love Him without measure. More than ever I came to realise God's tender love and care for me through you, which you showed in so many different ways through the different events of this year:

1) The Profession of the Brothers. With God's grace seven novices made their first vows this year: Br. Ivan Marie on January 24th in

Rome; Br. Jean Marie in the Sacred Heart cathedral in Delhi on May 10; and Br. Michael Joseph, Br. Lawrence, Br. Francis, Br. Leo and Br. Stephen in the Mother House Chapel in Calcutta on September 8, in the presence of our dearest Mother and the M.C. Family, all of which were profound experiences of God for all. Still more moving was the perpetual profession of Br. Luke on Sunday, February 4 in our Chapel in Rome, presided over by His Eminence Cardinal Arinze.

2) This year some of us were fortunate to participate in the Jubilee celebrations of:

a) Our Beloved Holy Father John Paul II: the 50th Anniversary of his priestly ordination celebrated in St. Peter's Basilica on November 1st. With him we thanked God and for him we offered up our prayers.

b) The 50th anniversary of the Inspiration day celebrated in the Mother' House Chapel in Calcutta by Mother Teresa and all the five Branches of the Missionaries of Charity Family, plus the Lay Missionaries of Charity and the co-workers. As we just had our Brothers' Professions in Calcutta on September 8, we were still around to thank God together with Mother for the wonders of God accomplished through her over the past 50 years. Words are inadequate to express our gratitude to God for her!

c) We also had the 25 years of my priestly service celebrated in various places, but more specially celebrated in our Chapel in Rome in the afternoon of November 1. Thanks to his Grace, Archbishop Giuseppe Mani, and all of you, who so happily came to thank God together with me and pray with me and for me. I also thank God very specially for the presence of my beloved parents (86 and 84), my brother and my sister, and for all those who have helped to realise it. May the good Lord reward them for their kindness and generosity.

3) Another major event of this year for us was the Lay Missionaries of Charity's 2nd International Meeting in Lourdes from 22 September to 29th. 145 Persons from 20 countries or so participated in the Convention. Thanks to Fr. Mc Guire who enriched us so much with his beautiful and inspiring talks which have taken deep roots in our hearts. Thanks also to Msg. Maloney for his enlightening talks; thanks to Msg. Flusk, and all our LMC Spiritual Directors who continue to work so hard in the various parts of the world. Thanks to the Lay links, both international and national, especially to Mr. and Mrs. Jean Claude & Fabienne Bastide, who have led the LMC for the past four years despite many difficulties, and also to Gianna Tommasi for her untiring work as secretary General of the LMCs, and for so many of you who have worked so hard or are working so hard or are going to do so in the future. To all I say thank **you,** while offering my humble and unceasing prayer and sacrifices.

My special thanks to Mr. Roger D'Haen from Belgium, who so willingly agreed to be the International LMC link, about which I am very happy. Let us pray that he may be able to help the Movement to accomplish God's will. Welcome to all the new Links in whatever capacity you are links: group, regional, national or international. Let us pray much, especially when we all know that Mother Teresa is suffering much and is making reparation for our sins and of all humanity. Even if her physical heart stops beating, her spirit will continue to beat in our hearts and in the hearts of all...her sublime virtue of Charity will be for us a constant source of strength and inspiration. As she diminishes and becomes weaker and weaker in body, we hope and pray that the entire M.C. Family becomes stronger, humbler and holier. To this end we pray and ask the prayers of all.

Advent is a time of preparation and Christmas is a time of sharing. God made so big a sacrifice in giving Jesus, His Son, to us through Mary. He gave, in Jesus, the best and everything. "God loved the world (us) so much that he gave His only begotten Son". The other day we met a girl of 17-18 in the North of Italy who was found in a trash can. She took shelter in it to protect herself from the cold. **Luckily,** now she is in a Franciscan Convent of Sisters. We met another man from Albania at Bologna railway station at night, poorly clad and suffering from cold. As we saw him we thought that he was in need of help. So we approached him to see what he really needed. Among many other things, he said that he had come two weeks before from Albania and now only wanted to go back. He had tried several times to buy the train ticket to go to Bari, but did not succeed, as he did not know the language, plus the counter did not accept the money in coins. Luckily, Br. Lawrence from Albania was with us, so we were able to help him and to send him to Bari, from where he was going to take the boat to Albania. You cannot imagine how happy he was and how grateful he felt! These two experiences of the past week (Nov. 30) made me think much...if I were she, if I were he...and I could easily be...What poverty and misery can do, how easily we can be reduced to a helpless and hopeless situation, and how important it is for us to share what we have with those who have less or nothing. It made me appreciate all the more the beauty and the importance of our vocation as M.C., who are called to give whole-hearted free service to the poorest of the poor; and how important for us to live our vocation of loving service in all its fullness.

I would also like to say a word about the project we have in India for the handicapped boys. They are really the poorest of the poor who have no home of their own except the street; no one to belong to except God, our Heavenly Father. Left to their own, they will die and vanish from the earth; and yet they are the beloved of God, and at the same time our brothers. They too have a life to live. I also spoke of distant adoption: i.e. an individual or a couple adopt one of the handicapped boys from a distance, remembering him in their prayers, helping them also materially if they can and if they so wish. Any donation made is better to send to Via S. Agapito, 8 - 00177 Rome. Since we scarcely have room enough for 10 boys, we started building a home for about 50 to 60 handicapped boys. We are also building a Chapel for the people of the area and a house of formation for the Brothers. Let us pray much so that these boys can have a home where they can experience love and peace. When we die and go home to God, we are going to be judged on our deeds of love. Hence let us make every effort to help one another to love God and love God in one another, and especially in the poor, abandoned and unloved. "Love never gives up".

Wishing you a very happy and holy Christmas and a bright New Year. Love and prayers, God bless you.

Fr. Sebastian Vazhakala M.C.

Christmas 1997

Dearly beloved Brothers and Sisters,

So many of you have remembered us and our poor people during the Holy season of Christmas and New Year 1998 by sending prayerful greetings through letters, cards and gifts. It made us feel one family again. More and more we come to discover the depth of our oneness in the mystery of God. No matter whether we are rich or poor, black or white, we are all children of the same Father. These celebrations remind us that colour and culture are accidental and we are called to go beyond the external appearances. We discover all the time that we have more essential things in common and our differences are merely accidental. Let us praise the Lord and tank him for the gift of one another. It's our heavenly Father who enables his children to meet and share. It is he who inspires us with sublime thoughts and heart-felt affection. It is he who offers us the opportunity to make our love more fruitful in service. It is his Spirit working in us that make us experience deep joy and profound peace when we get out of ourselves to meet "the other" in need. There is so much to thank God for in the past year, for the persons who have been instrumental for us to grow and mature in the Spirit, to express and experience the fire of Divine Love in action.

We all felt deep gratitude to God for our beloved Mother Teresa, who even though not with us physically is more present among us in Spirit. Her death on September 5th is to be seen in the light of the Gospel of John: *"Unless the grain of wheat falls to the earth and dies, it remains a grain of wheat. But if it dies, it produces much fruit"* (12: 24). Mother Teresa's death is going to bring rich and abundant fruits.

In Rome there is always much movement: the night shelter, "Casa Serena", where 60 men are housed and fed each night and the on-gong pressure from all sides to receive the homeless who may not qualify as candidates for "Casa Serena"; the continual coming and going of people with problems and possibilities; the many generous and dedicated volunteers who are always ready and available to serve our guests and the community of Brothers; the many people who come to our gate with used clothes, surplus food and other items; the in and out-of-time telephone calls, all of which make our day alive and active. Isn't it true that the more contemplative we are the more active we become in charity! In spite of all these things our Brothers are able to pray, study and serve one another and the poor in "Casa Serena", in the prison, in the homes and streets, hospital visiting, especially AIDS patients. Thanks be to God for the strength he gives us each day to do his work, for all that he is to us. He is always just there to help us. The words of the psalm really become alive: *"It is he who gives us the strength…"*

May 16th to July 19th, 1997 were very special days of grace upon grace for us. Mother Teresa arrived on May16th from Calcutta, together with Sr. Nirmala M.C., Sr. Gertrude M.C. and some other Sisters from the first group. We had the Eucharistic celebration in V. Casilina 222. During the homily I mentioned what Mother Teresa used to tell me in the hospital in Calcutta in December, 1996, where she was critically ill. To my surprise, after Holy Mass in her room, Mother taking my hand said: "Fr. Sebastian, when I come to Rome, we will go to see the Holy Father". It hurt me much, as her condition then did not give me hope that she would come to Rome or travel long distances again. Still, I said to her: "Yes, Mother, we will do it, God willing". Now her prophecy came true. Lo and behold, we did go to see the Holy Father on Tuesday 20th. It was an unforgettable visit with the Holy Father. Her wish was thus granted by the Lord. *"If you have enough faith like a mustard seed, say to the mountain…* Over the years her faith moved many a mountain and I was fortunate to be an eye-witness of so many of them for over 30 years. *"How can I thank God for all his goodness to me".*

Knowing that this was going to be her last and final visit to Rome, all our Brothers were asked to come to Rome to be with her to celebrate the Eucharist, to listen to her talks. First of all, all the senior Brothers came for a mini-Chapter, in which the General Councillors were elected: Br. Piet M.C., Br. Damien M.C. and Br. André Marie M.C. It was a time of real grace for our Society. Mother Teresa was extra generous with her time, with profound reflections on humility, charity and joy. The novices from Albania were also brought to Rome to meet her, to pray with her, to listen to her words. On the day of her departure from Rome for Calcutta, her last testament was a long conference on how to be humble and how easy our life can be as Jesus makes himself present in the persons of the poor and in each other: *"Whatever you did to the least of my brothers, you did it to me"*.

Mother Teresa left Rome on Saturday 19th July, 1997 for the last time, never to return to the terrestrial eternal city, which she always loved and respected, to go and to prepare for the everlasting city of heaven. We all accompanied her to the airport and saw her off, remaining close to her till the last minute. There wasn't any more time for clarification. It was time to leave. Air India carried her away into the blue sky of the eternal city. Who knows what was going on in her mind concerning her final and definitive departure, about which she was more than certain. I felt like Elisha who watched his master and guide Elijah being carried away in a fiery chariot (2Kgs 2: 11-12). Here that fiery chariot was Air India. I did not hear from her again until her 87th birthday, on August 26, when I called Calcutta to wish her a happy birthday. She was exuberant and gay as usual. She made enquiries how the Brothers were in Albania, as we were all there for our annual retreat for eight days. So it was that I spoke to her for the last time from Albania, where the remains of her mother and sister are laid. Our conversation wasn't too long, but always the same feeling as ever: a son speaking to his mother and a mother to her son, which began on 30th November, 1966 and ended for me on this day, 26th August,1997. And yet did it all end?

Since September 8, 1991 our brothers are in Albania, about 100 Km north of Tirana, the capital city. It is where the Brothers transformed a theatre into a place of prayer and worship. It meant time, money and tireless work. The Lord again worked miracles through weak humans. Blessed be his name. Thanks to many of our Italian benefactors and volunteers we were able to construct two churches, both of which are full on Sundays and feast days. The Brothers have gone through fire and flood there, especially in this past year, with total lawlessness in the country.

Thanks to God's help and grace, neither did the flood swallow us nor the fire burn us so far. More than once we were attacked with guns and other arms. Still vivid in our minds is the event of August 26th 1997, when 24 of us retreatants, with our retreat preacher Fr. Konrad SJ from Malta, and our guest priest, Fr. Darius from Poland, were attacked by a young man with an automatic rifle and two grenades. We remained motionless, not knowing what to expect or do except to pray, which Br. Piet and some of the Brothers started doing. The "hour" had not come yet for us to depart from this world to the home of the Father. More than half an hour of strenuous battle! Looking back now it all looks like a drama; it wasn't then; then it was a matter of life and death and the minutes were counted. There wasn't much time for reflection before acting. We had to be prudent and quick. The Spirit's assistance arrived. The young man agreed to surrender to the Brothers and walked quickly into the police van. In the evening Br. Subash and I went to the police inspector who was waiting for us. All that we wanted was peace and security, and we did not want him to be in jail as he had a family to take care of, and as long as he was willing to amend his life. We prayed hard for him. Three days later he came in person and asked for forgiveness. But his story did not finish there. This twenty-five years old Fatmir, father of two children, two weeks later tried to force entry into a nearby house where he was shot to death by a sixty years old woman. R.I.P.

Life in Albania goes on in the midst of all the turmoil and confusion. Our Brothers, both professed and novices, go on proclaiming the good news in spite of the many insurmountable dangers and difficulties. It is not success we must look for but fidelity and perseverance.

The journey that we began in Rome through Albania, now takes us to "Deepashram", Gurgaon, in the state of Haryana, 14 Km south of Delhi International Airport, India. There Br. Damien M.C. and the Community of twelve more dedicated Brothers, together with about twenty handicapped boys, welcome us warmly to their still unfinished house. Even a quick and short visit to the place can immediately tell us of the enormous amount of work to be done there. We very quickly see that taking care of the handicapped children demands time, divine patience, great dedication and generosity. Whoever goes there cannot stand aloof and watch. The children need to be washed and dressed, fed and cared; one sees the amount of energy each child demands. More than anything we notice that they are hungry for love and affection, warmth and protection of a loving father, and the love and affection of a caring mother.

When finished, the house is meant to accommodate over sixty handicapped boys, a community of a good number of Brothers, a group of paid workers and many volunteers from India and abroad. The building work still goes on. We cannot thank the Lord enough for the numerous benefactors, especially "Missio" in Aachen, Germany, and the many generous and dedicated Italian volunteers and others whose timely help and support have brought us so far, and we believe that the same Lord will continue to bless his beloved children from heaven through the M.C. family.

Deepashram has had three beginnings: the first was on July 3rd, 1994, thanks to Br. Berchmanns and the patrician Brothers who offered one of their buildings in Gurgaon, where we stayed for about a year. The second was on November 18, 1995, when Mother Teresa came in person to the present site, together with His Excellency Msgr. Vincent Concessao, the auxiliary bishop of Delhi, to bless and inaugurate the new place. It was an unforgettable experience for many in and around the area who had never met Mother Teresa before except through the media. We hope and pray that the prophecy which she uttered on her way back from Deepahram becomes more and more true: "It is going to be a real centre". Amidst the numberless stars of God let Deepashram be a little lamp burning all the time, giving light to all who come in contact with "her".

The third "beginning" was the blessing of the new church and the handicapped boys' home on November 22, 1997. It was another Pentecostal experience, mixed with pain due to the final and definitive departure of Mother Pia on the same evening. God bless that great soul who from the very beginning was the one who stood by us in all our joys and sorrows, which we hope she continues to do from heaven in another form.

In conclusion, what more can I say except to thank you and thank God for you from the bottom of my heart for all that you are and all that you do to share in whatever manner and form. Let us desire nothing except to love God and love one another until we die of love.

God bless you.

Fr. Sebastian Vazhakala M.C.

DECEMBER 2000

Dearly beloved Brothers and Sisters,

Once again we are preparing ourselves for Christmas - that wondrous "mysterium fidei" - and we want our Christmas to be happy and holy for us, for our friends, for "*all men of good will*," and in a very special way for our poor people. When we love people we want them to be happy and at peace. We want them to experience joy. This is what many of you have expressed through your prayerful greetings, wishes and sharing of material goods.

Thank you for all that *you are*: our beloved LMCs, volunteers, co-workers, benefactors and the parents of distant adoption, "Thank you" for all that *you do* for us and for our poor people in so many different ways. It is important to remember that it is not how *much* we do, but with *how much* love we do. **Your** little deeds of love, your little words of joy, your gentle looks and tender smiles make our world like a mighty ocean of love. May our Lord Jesus Christ bless you and reward you. May our blessed Mother intercede for you, keeping you healthy in mind and body. May St. Joseph, our beloved heavenly patron and protector and intercessor, take care of you, and help you to grow in holiness through profound humility and heroic charity. May your patron saints and holy guardian angels continue to inspire and guide you all the days of your life on the path of greater perfection.

Love we all must, cost what it may, count not its cost. Love must hurt. To love is to give, to break and share. Love necessarily leads to sacrifice. God loved the world so much: He loved us so much that He gave, He offered His only beloved and begotten Son. It must have cost God very much to do that. But He did. Love is like that. Love is love only when it knows how to give, how to share, how to make the other person feel better and happier. "*Nothing is sweeter, nothing stronger, nothing higher, nothing more sublime, nothing more expansive, nothing more joyful, nothing more abundant, nothing more pleasing in Heaven or on earth; because love is born of God, nor can it rest upon created things, but only in God*" (Imitation of Christ, Book III, Ch. 5, 3). "*Love often knows no measure, but burns beyond all measure*".

Jesus loved us by dying on the Cross for us. "*Greater love than this no man has that a man lays down his life for his friends*" (Jn 15, 13). He loved us to the very end. In His wounds we were healed. He gave all to us. Because he loved us God became man. Because He loves us Jesus becomes the Bread of Life to feed us so that we will have the strength to feed His poor: both physically and spiritually. He feeds them through us; He loves and cares for them through us; He saves them through us because He suffers in the hungry and thirsty, in the homeless, in the sick, the aged, the lonely, and in the shut-ins. He calls us to feed Him in the hungry, to satiate His thirst in the thirsty, to shelter Him in the homeless, visit Him in the sick, and comfort and console Him in the aged, sick and the lonely. For "*as long as you did to one of the least of my brothers you did it to me*" (Mt 25, 40).

Therefore, every time we feed the hungry, clothe the naked, welcome the homeless, comfort the sick and visit the prisoners, it is Christmas for us and a happy and holy Christmas for the ones we feed, clothe, shelter, comfort or visit. Christmas is a feast, having joy as its very essence. The angels said to the shepherds: "*I give you good news of great joy*". It is a feast of great joy because it is essentially a feast of sharing. God shared in our humanity so that we could share in His divinity.

Rome has had a happy and holy *Christmas* throughout this great jubilee year. Jesus came into so many people's lives. The 22nd of October this year was a great jubilee day of and for the Missionaries. Missionaries from all five continents represented us all in St. Peter's Square for the jubilee Mass. It was a cold morning. I decided to spent half a day in prayer and went to the Basilica of St. John Lateran. Since the Basilica was overcrowded, I went to the Franciscan church on Via Merulana, went to confession, holy Mass and Communion, then I was going to visit a patient in the hospital, when I came across a man sitting on the floor on the sidewalk. I went over to him and made enquiries about his situation. I realized that he needed help. I told him to stay there until I returned from the hospital. On my return I found him still sitting there as if he had no other choice. When I told him to get up, he tried but could not. He had been sitting there the whole night until late morning, and he could no longer get up on his own. Several people passed by. My several attempts to make him stand were in vain, as if he had been nailed to the floor of the cross. His legs had gone numb; blood circulation stopped. He was no longer able to get up and stand on his feet without help.

God is the lover of the poor. His only beloved and begotten Son suffered and died for each poor person. We can be indifferent to people, but God cannot. He is like a mother. A mother cannot be indifferent to the cry of her helpless baby. Others can hear the baby crying and pass by. Jesus cannot be indifferent to the poor, because for them He suffered, died, shed every drop of His blood. "*Can a woman forget her sucking child…even if she forgets, I will not forget you…*". No, He cannot. Love cannot forget. Love can only give and forgive. You cannot love a person and continue to be indifferent to him or her. God is never indifferent to any one of us. His love is real, invincible, unconditional. He never gives us up, even when we are sinners. "*It is proof of God's own love for us, that Christ died for us while we were still sinners*" (Rom 5, 8).

Out of a clear blue sky a friend came along who saw me trying but unable to lift the man up. The man finally stood but needed support. He leaned on my shoulder…half-carried, half- limping…to the tram, dirty and smelling. I had received Jesus in the Bread of Life an hour before, and now I was receiving Him in the distressing disguise of this poor man. This was much more difficult and demanding. It was the same Jesus but in two different forms. We both had a happy and holy Christmas already, even though it was only the month of October. Many moved away from us in the tram because of the terrible smell. Reaching home, the Brothers had to spend a couple of hours cleaning him up and dressing him with fresh clothes. He had no other possession except the dirty, smelling clothes on him: a really 'poorest of the poor'. Weeks have passed, and after much care, treatment and rest, his health has improved, although it has not yet been fully regained.

Every visit to a lonely person, even if it is not Christmas time is somehow wishing the person a happy *Christmas* without words. Every time one makes a sacramental confession there is a very happy and holy *Christmas*...Every time the volunteers and benefactors come to the homes of the poor to cook, clean, help or serve there is *Christmas*. Christmas continues...

There is *Christmas* each day in Casa Serena, our night shelter in Rome, where so many volunteers come to serve and share their joy with our people. This summer Casa Serena went through some serious cleaning and repairs. Thanks to our Australian volunteer, Mr Gerry, who did such wonderful plumbing work. May the good Lord reward him for his untiring work and sincere dedication.

Rome is a beautiful city, organized and orderly. It is also called the 'ETERNAL CITY', filled with monumental churches and ancient holy places. There is also a growing open Church of the poor in this magnificent city. It is very Catholic in nature, as people come from all five continents...living under the bridges, parks and around the railway stations. Our Brothers, with the help of many generous and dedicated volunteers, go every morning to serve breakfast to some of them. Their number is always on the increase.

In the month of July our Brothers in Rome made their eight-day annual retreat. It was a real Pentecostal experience for all the retreatants. On July 30 Br. Mathew and Br. Ivan Marie were ordained deacons, a very moving ceremony indeed! On the Dedication of Our Lady of Mary Major, the 5th of August, three Brothers - Alphonse, Benedict and Tony Mary Jose - made their first vows, while on the day after, the feast of the Transfiguration, Br. Charbel solemnly pronounced his vows of Chastity, Poverty, Obedience and Whole-Hearted Free Service to the poorest of the poor for life. All three celebrations made the participants completely forget about earthly happiness and comforts to be united to God alone, like the three apostles on the mount of the Transfiguration.

Besides our 60 usual guests, we were happy to house over 60 young people from Poland during the jubilee for the youth in August. Our priest Brothers helped the youth with confessions.

It was a joy for me to preach a retreat to 77 priests of the diocese of Lucena, in the Philippines. The points were mainly four:

> By virtue of his priestly ordination every priest is entrusted with the key to open the door of eternity for sinful souls through

the sacrament of confession. This key is only to open the door for penitent sinners and never to lock the door under any circumstances.

Every priest is a sinner whom Jesus turns into a saviour. "*Do not be afraid, I will make you fishers of men*" (Lk 5, 10). Every priest is a wounded healer; priests are vessels of clay. Let us sustain them with assiduous prayers and generous sacrifices instead of criticizing and finding faults with them in their worst.

Every priest is called to experience his own unworthiness and sinfulness before he is made a co-redeemer of the world with Christ, the high priest (Is 6, 1ff).

Every priest is meant to be a good shepherd like Jesus, and with Him must be willing to lay down his life for the sheep (Ez 34; Ps 23; Jn 10).

Thanks for the prayers of so many of you for the success of the priests' retreat.

In Rome the Lay Missionaries of Charity held their International Planning Committee meeting in October. Representatives from 16 countries came. We had a week of real Pentecostal experience in this jubilee year. Included in the week's activities was a pilgrimage to St. Paul Outside the Walls and the Holy Mass celebrated there. On the morning of October 8 in St. Peter's Square, many were able to participate in the Bishops' jubilee Mass and entrustment of the whole world to the Immaculate Heart of Mary. A noticeable sense of joy and peace pervaded everyone.

We finally obtained the necessary permission to complete the repairing works of our Brothers' house. It may take three or four months to complete it. If everything goes well, by March 19 we may be able to do the blessing and inauguration. All of you are most welcome. Thank you so much for your prayers, and let us continue to pray for each other.

Wishing you a very happy and holy Christmas and a peace-filled New Year 2001. Love and prayers.

God bless you.

Father Sebastian Vazhakala, M.C.

Christmas 2002

Dearly beloved Brothers and Sisters,
"It is better that you suffer than you make Jesus suffer"
These are the words of my father who is confined to bed since the month of October last. Since so many of you have been praying for my father's health and well being and wanted to know how he was doing, I thought of sharing with you some news of him.

First of all I would like to express my sincere thanks in the name of my father and all the members of my family for all your prayers offered and sacrifices made and are still doing so for my father's speedy recovery. My father told me to tell you that he is extremely grateful to you and to God for you. He told me that all that he wants is to do God's will. He will willingly accept all the suffering as God wants and as long as He wants it. He continues to beg prayers for courage to accept suffering, strength to endure it, and wisdom to christianize it and make it all the more redemptive. I do know that he is what he is by the grace of God and because of all the prayers and sacrifices of so many of you. May the good Lord bless and reward you abundantly

My father was born on 2 May, 1914 in the State of Kerala, which is in the Southwest of India. Until two months ago his health was quite well and his mind extremely lucid and his memory active. But then he had a fall, which made him confined to bed. He slowly began to lose his memory and his mind became confused. My sister and her family, who take such wonderful care of him, decided to admit him in a good hospital and told me that he was getting worse. They also felt that he was critical. Not only that, but he was really going from bad to worse. Those who were with him did not know what to do with him in the situation he was in. They began to feel frightened and insisted that my sister and I should go to visit him, as he was continually asking for us. He became one of the poorest of the poor…reduced so unexpectedly and so suddenly from his life-long independence to complete dependence.

Many days went by. It was hard for me to decide. I prayed hard and prayed much; and I drew lots twice, as St. Peter did when he wanted to choose another apostle in the place of Judas (cf. Acts 1, 23-26). Both times the answer was positive, that I should go. My doubts disappeared with regard to whether it was God's will or not that I should go to visit him, but my pain and suffering continued. I prayed even more ardently. The experience was rich and profound.

And finally I left Rome in the morning of Sunday 24th November, 2002 and reached on the 25th late morning in Mangalore, in the State of Karnataka. From the airport I went directly to the hospital, which is about 27-Km's distance. Before I went to see my father, I decided to go to the nearby parish and beg the priest for hospitality. This I did. The pastor came running to welcome me as if he knew me for all his life and as if he was waiting for me. He did not want to listen to my explanations. I felt humbled for such warm welcome and generous hospitality. Leaving my luggage, I went to see my father straight away.

I was shocked to see **him:** both hands tied, all kinds of tubes and needles on his body. He was being fed with a tube through the nose. For me it was like Jesus hanging on the cross. If it were not for the prayers and sacrifices of my Brothers and so many of you, it would have been very hard for me to accept. My brother, brother-in-law and my nephew were with him. It was difficult for him to speak. I waited for the doctor to talk with and see what was the best thing to do for him. The doctor was so kind and gentle. He told me that he too was Catholic. I could sense it from his words and behavior. From the scanning it became clear to him that there was not much more to do or any real hospital treatment that would make my father feel better. He told me that it was up to us to keep him in the hospital or take him home.

We decided to do the latter on Wednesday 29th November evening. My sister Leelamma from California arrived in the morning and then in the evening as planned we traveled home, over three hours' drive in an ambulance. Since then he receives home care and home nursing, surrounded by many family members, immediate and distant, and the neighbors. He had an average of thirty to forty visitors a day, at least when we were there.

When Leelamma arrived I asked my father whether he knew her at all. His answer was "I do not remember to have seen her before". It took sometime to recognize her. And then he cried, saying that he had given up hope of ever seeing her again except in heaven. We took off all the tubes and started giving him liquids through the mouth, even though it was rather demanding for him. His hands too are now free. His face is very radiant. Although he is becoming weaker and weaker in body, he looks very graceful. Each day I prayed with him at least five decades of the rosary and some other prayers. He is very happy to be able to pray, he and prays alone a lot. Then he gives pieces of advice and beautiful messages. He told one of my nephews that it is better that he suffers rather than he makes Jesus suffer. One time I asked him whether he would like to come with me to see one of my brothers. His answer to that was, "I must go where Jesus calls me". I told him that we should go together to Jesus. Straight away he said, "It is not for us to decide but Jesus". He told another nephew: "Remember that God created us to love. We must love as Jesus loved. Never offend God. If we do not love Him and each other, then we offend Him. We make Him suffer".

He asked for a priest. The parish priest came to anoint him and to give him Holy Communion. Of course, in his presence he made me to administer the sacraments of the sick and Holy Communion.

It was a grace for me to be with him, to take some little care of him, and above all to listen to him and pray with him. I came to understand the depth of his faith and his profound conviction of accepting and doing God's will. But then the time came for me and Leelamma to part from him and from the rest of the family.

It was hard and heart renting, but I entrusted him and all those who look after him so well to the care and protection of the Holy Family. My sister and I left on Friday, 6 December in two different directions. She returned home in S. Francisco, while I to our home for our homeless handicapped boys in Delhi, about 2,600 km from my home. On the way I stopped to see my brother; he had met with a motorcycle accident and was in bed with a broken leg. My brother-in-law, who is doing such wonderful job with my father, has also been sick in bed with a swollen foot.

At times it is hard for us to understand the will and plan of God, and what he really wants to communicate. My everyday life teaches me to love God all the more, to trust Him more lovingly and more blindly. *"Surrender to God and he will do everything for you"*. And yet my long experience of religious life tells me that our life on earth is a struggle, a battle and *a dark night experience*. This is especially true if we have to do something worthwhile. Gold is to be melted and purified in the fire, and the more the gold is tested the brighter it becomes. Our growth in holiness demands much pain, which has to be baptized. The Christian's suffering in love then becomes a vocation…as Jesus told Mother Teresa: *"Your vocation is to love and to suffer and to save souls"*. Only through contemplation do we come to understand the Christian meaning and the redemptive value of human suffering.

Christmas is not a time to speak much about suffering, because the joy is so great that it makes us forget all the pain. It is not that the Holy Family, Mary and Joseph, did not suffer. No, they suffered many inconveniences, much pain and sorrow. But the birth of Jesus made them forget all their poverty, misery and destitution. The center of their life was the newborn child, and their concern was to make him feel happy and his life comfortable.

Since 20th December, Mother Teresa has been proclaimed Venerable. What a great privilege for us all to see that someone whom we knew so well and so long is going to be beatified on Mission Sunday 19th October, 2003. Let us praise and thank God for this great gift and try to become humble like Mary and holy like Jesus. Those who intend to participate in the beatification ceremony may contact the M.C. Sisters in your area, where you will get all the necessary information required to obtain the tickets and also any other information connected with it. There is only one kind of ticket for all the participants. The number of tickets is unlimited and free of charge. You also need to tell how many will attend the Thanksgiving Mass at St. Peter's i.e.20 October, 2003. Please do not wait to ask for tickets until the last minute. This applies as well with regard to your travel arrangements and lodgings. You may have to do all these without delay.

I conclude this letter by wishing you all a very happy and holy Christmas and a peace-filled New Year 2003. Because he loved us God became man; because he loves us Jesus becomes the Bread of Life; and because he wants us to become holy Jesus comes to us through the hungry one, the thirsty one, the naked one, the homeless one, etc. (cf. Jn 3, 16; Jn 6, 54; Mt 25, 31-46).

Thank you for everything. I'm praying much for all of you, especially at this holy season of Christmas and New Year.

God blesses you.
Fr. Sebastian Vazhakala M.C.

Christmas 2003

"A Joy to be shared by the whole people"

Dearly beloved Brothers and Sisters,

On Christmas eve some of us went to visit an elderly woman of 82 whom we have not visited for quite some time. She lives close to the center part of the city of Rome. Even though she did not look too happy and did not welcome us very enthusiastically as she used to do at other times, we tried to remain calm, joyful and open to listen to her. We sat around the table and listened to her many sad and painful stories and experiences. At the end of our visit with her, she became more exuberant and joyous and said: *"Now I can say that it is Christmas"*.

This experience made me reflect on the real meaning and significance of the Christmas event, which is both spiritual and social at the same time. The feast of Christmas then has two essential and inseparable dimensions: the vertical and horizontal. God and neighbor. God and I and my neighbor.

Christmas is essentially a feast of sharing. In other words, there is no real Christmas if we do not share with those who have less or nothing. Where charity and love prevail, there is Emmanuel-God with us. Any authentic Christian life of sharing is an on-going Christmas.

Christmas is a feast of joy, a joy to be shared. On Christmas day I called one of my friends after a very long time. He lives many miles away. He and his family went through some serious trials. He was full to the brim. There was a downpour. At the end of a long conversation he said that it was the best Christmas gift I could ever give him. Just a telephone call can make someone's yoke easy and the burdens of life lighter. There are so many in the world that are being crushed by loneliness, indifference, apathy and hatred. And then comes the voice of the angel from heaven: *"Do not be afraid. Look, I bring you news of great joy,* **a joy to be shared by the whole people***"* (Lk 2, 10). The evangelist then gives us the content of the good news of this great joy: *"Today in the town of David a Savior has been born for you; he is Christ the Lord"* (Lk 2, 11).

The world we live in is becoming more and more materialistic and atheistic and so joyless, sad and gloomy. Material things are ephemeral and transitory. Nothing except God can give us true joy and authentic happiness. There is no substitute for God. God cannot be exchanged or bought with money. Wealth and riches count but little and can even become an obstacle to true happiness. People are forgetting to smile. Many know how to laugh and often laugh at someone, instead of smiling. It is better to smile from the heart while you smile.

God is aware of all the anomalies of man taking place in every nook and corner of the world. His effort to substitute God with himself, wealth or power is a complete failure. God is the only one absolute. He cannot be replaced with anyone or anything. He is our rock, our stronghold, our shield, our protector and redeemer. He is our refuge and our strength (cf. Ps 62). He is omnipotent, omniscient and omnipresent, i.e. he is all-powerful, all knowing and present everywhere.

Christmas is a feast of hope and joy. Even here mere superficial celebrations and social gatherings are not enough and will not give us the real and profound spirit of Christmas. The celebration of Christmas must call us to contemplation. It is our birthright to go deeper and deeper into the mystery and reality of the *In-carnation* of the eternal Word who was in the bosom of the Father. The Word eternally contemplates the Father and loves him infinitely and immeasurably. His contemplation of the Father is at the same time his love for the Father. Jesus' contemplation of the Father is identical with his love of the Father.

The Father on the other hand equally contemplates his beloved Son in absolute and unfathomable love. This contemplation of the Son by the Father is identical with the Father's unfathomable and infinite love. From this intense love we have the Holy Spirit. In other words, the Holy Spirit is the subsisting love between the Father and the Son and vice versa. There is eternal contemplation in the heart of the Blessed Trinity. Our life of contemplation is rooted in the heart of the Holy Trinity. It is from the heart of the Trinity that we draw the waters of contemplation.

Love is contemplated and shared. The more we contemplate the mysteries of God, who is love, the more we want to share. Contemplation is our thirst for God and our thirst for souls who are created in the image and likeness of God. A real contemplative is also a real lover of creatures in profound freedom. Yearning for God increases in us to the extent that we contemplate him in love. *"My heart cannot truly rest nor be entirely contented till it rests in God"* (cf. St. Augustine)

St. John in his letters gives us the simplest definition of God when he says, *"God is love"*. We can also say that God is contemplation in absolute. God's love is irresistible. A very simple example can make it clear. Take a piece of a magnet and a little piece of iron. In one sense we can say that the magnet is thirsty for iron. God's thirst for us is his love for us. Christmas, which celebrates the mystery of the Incarnation, is a celebration of the thirst of God. God's thirst for man is so irresistible that he sends his only Son. Jesus is the incarnation of the thirst of the Father for mankind. Jesus, the God-man, is the extended magnetic power of the Father. We are free to name this power as thirst, as love, as yearning. Because Jesus is God, his thirst is infinite.

Every time we celebrate the feast of Christmas we must not only realize but experience God's thirst for us and for souls. I must know that Jesus, the second person of the Blessed Trinity, whom the Father contemplates eternally, is the concrete and human expression of his thirst.

The magnet has the power to attract the iron, and the iron has the disposition to be attracted by the magnet and has the capacity to receive the magnetic power as long as the iron is stuck to the magnet. To some extent we can say that the iron is thirsty for the magnet. This is true much more of God and human beings. God has the tremendous power to attract souls to him, because he is love and he is in love, and the human soul has the disposition to be irresistibly attracted by God. God is in thirst with man and man is in thirst with God. In other words God is in love with man and man is in love with God. *"The wonder of prayer is revealed beside the well where we come seeking water:*

there, Christ comes to meet every human being. It is he who first seeks us and asks us for a drink. Jesus thirsts; his asking arises from the depths of God's desire for us. Whether we realize it or not, prayer is the encounter of God's thirst with ours. **'God thirsts that we may thirst for him'** *(St. Augustine)"* (C.C.C. N°. 2560).

The year two thousand and two has been a historical one. Many things have taken place around and across the globe, leaving behind many an unforgettable memory. These historical events have far reaching consequences both in our personal lives and in the life of the society as a whole. The more the world around us advances in science and technology, which are meant to make our lives easier, happier and more comfortable, the more insecure, fearful and unhappy we apparently become. Unless and until Christ is born in us again, recognized, loved, adored and served, mankind will continue to grope in darkness and the fundamental values of life will go into oblivion.

Here too, the recognition of the Emmanuel-God with us is the answer to all our vexing problems. Most of us are so easily ready to cast stones at others rather than seeing our own blunders, weaknesses, inadequacies and sins. Jesus' words to those who came to stone the woman caught in adultery continue to resound in our day: *"Let the one among you who is guiltless be the first to throw a stone at her"* (Jn 8, 7). Our antenna has to be attuned more to the voice of God than to the voice of the world. In all of us there is a divine antenna capable of absorbing the voice of God, assimilate, transform and transmit it to the world around and across us.

We were fortunate to come to know and live with some of the great saints of our time, such as St. Pio of Pietrelcina, Venerable Teresa of Calcutta etc., whose divine antennas worked twenty-four hours a day, for three hundred and sixty-five days a year. Mother Teresa, for example continually confessed the secret to her force and strength, her inspiring words, her magnetic power to draw people to God and God to people. The story of her vocation, the life of heroic virtues of faith, hope and charity and all other connected virtues were all due to her unbroken union with her Crucified Spouse in the Eucharist. Her antenna received the words of the Master in the silence of faith to give whole-hearted free service to the poorest of the poor, which she transmitted through her life of sacrifice, immolation and heroic

Charity *"until it hurt"* her. She saw Jesus not only in the Bread of Life but also in the disguise of the broken bodies of the poorest of the poor. She loved and adored Jesus in the Bread of Life and loved and served him in the distressed disguise of the poorest of the poor. *"And how could it be otherwise, since the Christ encountered in contemplation is the same who lives and suffers in the poor?"* (V.C. 82 §3).

The General Chapters: The year 2002 for me was a year of many travels, meetings and giving spiritual exercises. The Brothers and the LMCs had their General Chapters held in Rome in the month of June and July respectively. Both were profound experiences of God, not only for the participants but also for our Society and for the Movement as well. All went home praising God in a loud voice. Once again thanks to all those who have worked very hard to make these events a great success. The reports of both Chapters, the Brothers' and the LMCs', are being prepared. Please have a little more patience with us. We will try our best to have them ready at the earliest possible moment.

Our house in Rome moves ahead with the new Administrative Body. As you know in the General Chapter of the Brothers held in Rome from 11 to 29th June there were elections of the Father General in the presence of the Vicar for Religious in the diocese of Rome, Msgr. Natalino Zagotto, on the morning of Wednesday 26th June. On the same day our Vicar General, Br. Subash M.C., and our General Secretary, Br. Ivan Marie M.C., were elected and appointed as such. The other two General Councilors, Br. Damien M.C. and Br. André Marie M.C., also were elected. Br. Subash is also our house Superior, assisted by Br. Jean Marie M.C. and the community.

From 6th to 14th July 2002 the Lay Missionaries of Charity held their third International Meeting and their first General Chapter in Rome. The theme was *"The doctrinal, juridical and the M.C. Charism that are the basis of the Movement of the Lay Missionaries of Charity and its Role in the Church and in the contemporary world"*. During the week of the Chapter there were various interesting and enriching events taking place. We also had the Holy Masses celebrated by three Cardinals on different days of the Chapter week: H. E. Cardinal Francis Stafford, President of the Pontifical Council for the Laity; Cardinal Francis Arinze, President of the Pontifical Council for Inter-religious Dialogue, Cardinal José Saraiva Martins, President of the Congregation for the

Cause of Saints. Msgr. Natalino Zagotto was sent by Cardinal Camillo Ruini, the cardinal Vicar of Rome, to represent him. While in Loreto we had Holy Mass with H.E. Msgr. Angelo Comastri, Archbishop of Loreto, where the original Holy Family house rests.

On Friday 12th July evening the LMCs had their elections. Accordingly Mr. Antonio Serangeli Lmc from Rome, one of the first LMCs, was elected to be the third International LMC Link and Gianna Tommasi Lmc was reconfirmed as International General Secretary. They are to be assisted by three Vicars, representing three major language groups: English, Spanish and Italian. They are Mrs. Ann Burridge Lmc, Vancouver (Canada), Mrs. Tai Pearn Lmc, S.Diego (U.S.A.) helped by Yolanda Rodriguez Lmc, (Puerto Rico), Anita De Orezzoli Lmc, (Perù), and Prof. Giuseppe Gandolfo Lmc, Rome. Let us pray that the Holy Spirit may descent upon them, melt them, mould them, fill them and use them for the greater glory of God and for the salvation of souls.

Casa Serena, Rome, home for the homeless men: The majority of our Brothers in the Roman community are students either of philosophy or theology. Our life of prayer, study and works of mercy become heavy and even strained at times. *Casa Serena*, our night shelter for homeless men, keeps Br. Stephen M.C. and Br. Benedict M.C. quite busy, while Br. Jan Timo M.C. is involved in ordering things in the kitchen and feeding us all. Thanks to all our Brothers, to so many of our volunteers, LMCs and benefactors, without whom I wonder if we would ever be able to run *Casa Serena*.

Your heavenly bank: Dearly beloved Brothers, volunteers, LMCs and benefactors, when you come at the gate of Paradise, you will hear the consoling words of the Master: "*Come, blessed of my Father, inherit the kingdom prepared for you since the foundation of the world, for I was hungry, thirsty, naked, homeless, sick and in prison…As long as you did to one of the least of my brothers, you did it to Me*" (cf. Mt 25, 31-46). *Casa Serena* has become your heavenly bank on earth. You will be repaid with interest on the judgement day whatever you put in it now. It can be a sigh, a look, or a little act of kindness, as long as they become acts of love divine. It is important that everything you do may always be done for the love of God. In other words, you may do ordinary things with extraordinary love, simple things with great love, even as simple as a cup of cold water (cf. Mt 10, 42). *"It is not how much we do, but how much love we put in our doing that matters"* (Mother Teresa).

Right now we have about fifty homeless men in *Casa Serena*, some of whom are disabled and handicapped. Paolo Santelia, our faithful gate keeper and hard worker, had a stroke, followed by an operation for a brain tumor in C.T.O. hospital in Rome. Since it did not go too well, he is now admitted in San Raffaele hospital in Milan. Let us pray that Paolo may get better and regain his senses of sight and hearing. The Brothers in Rome also have other regular ministries, such as family visits, sick calls and communion services to elderly people, holy Mass and confessions in the prison, visiting the sick people in the hospitals, especially the AIDS patients, street ministry and periodic night apostolate on the streets.

The Brothers also have an intense prayer life. Praying for the living and the dead is one of the seven spiritual works of mercy. And we have almost six hours of community prayer a day.

In Albania: Our community is mainly busy with spiritual works of mercy. It is one of the seven spiritual works of mercy to help a person to turn away from his/her evil ways of life, to make his/her sacramental confession and thus amend his/her way of life. To teach children and adults the Catechism of the Catholic Church and the mysteries of our faith by word and example is another spiritual work of mercy. We also come across many that no longer even know what is sin and what is not. Some young couples think there is nothing wrong in the use of contraceptives and other forms of preventing conception. Some even are ignorant of the seriousness of procuring an abortion, especially in the very early stages of pregnancy. One of the main reasons they give is that because many are doing it, why can't we also do it? There is also the unbelievable propaganda about all these things, which does brain wash and black mail their minds. There is so much to do everywhere.

For many, to miss Holy Mass on Sunday without a serious reason is no longer a sin to be confessed before one goes to Communion. People must be told the importance of making every effort to participate regularly and actively in the Sunday liturgy of the Mass. Sin of omission is a very serious one. There are so many daily neglects which not only we have to be sorry for, but we have to make up for the good we ought to have done. The priests, religious, LMCs and all practicing Catholics not only have the duty to live their authentic Christian lives, but they are duty-bound to teach and preach the faithful of their obligations.

In the story of Lazarus and the rich man we see very clearly that the rich man was condemned to hell, **not** for any wrong he did, but for the good that he ought to have done, but neglected to do (cf. Lk.6, 19-31). Here we see very clearly the terrible sin of indifference, negligence and omission. God wants us all to be our brothers' keepers. All of us may hear in the silence of our hearts *"Where is your brother, sister, father, mother, husband or wife or children or parents"*. Where are they? How are they? Are they OK? Do they need your help, some of your time, your comforting presence, your sweet smile and consoling words or even your gentle and fraternal corrections and admonitions? Your love of God will open your eyes not only to see the necessities of your neighbour but also to respond to them with generosity and enthusiasm. It is not enough to praise Mother Teresa's heroic virtues and great works of Charity, and longing to participate in her beatification ceremony. It is absolutely necessary to understand and absorb her spirit of love for the poor in action, her heroic Charity, her blind and loving trust in the providence of God and his unfailing guidance, her love and devotion to Jesus in the Eucharist, her filial love and reverence to Our Lady, her spirit of prayer, her sacrifices, and her unwavering faith. She not only saw Jesus in the distressing disguise of the poorest of the poor, but instead of leaving them there alone to face many unborn tomorrows, she did whatever she could to help them as she would have done to Jesus: *"You did it to Me"* (Mt 24, 40).

Those who have much must give much and those who have less, give less. *"Better practice almsgiving than hoard up gold. Almsgiving saves from death and purges every kind of sin"* (Tobit 12, 9).

All of us go through various kinds of experiences in life, good and bad ones. All of us are in need of periodic physical help, psychological and moral assistance. There are so many sorrowful people who live among and around us. Consoling and comforting the sorrowful is another spiritual work of mercy, especially in Albania where the Old Testament law of retaliation is still so prevalent: Tooth for tooth, eye for eye, life for life. How many young people were shot dead for some serious wrong their ancestors did in the past? At times human life is taken so cheaply. In our day people no longer have the good will and the humility to forgive from the heart the past injuries, hurts and wounds. Instead, homicide and fratricide have become so spontaneous a response to any hurt or injury. Hardly anybody is willing to bear wrongs patiently. Only one who has understood the meaning of Christian forgiveness can also bear all the wrongs patiently as Jesus and Mary did. *"Forgive them, Father, for they do not know what they are doing"* (Lk 23, 34).

It strikes me so much whenever I reflect on the attitude of Our Lady who stood beneath the Cross of her Son hanging between heaven and earth in agony and in excruciating pain. It is hard for us to understand how she could really accept such inhuman cruelty done to her innocent Son. And yet there was no anger or retaliation in her. Instead she let her heart be pierced with the sword of sorrow (cf. Lk 2, 35; Jn 19, 25).

Back in 1946 Jesus told Mother Teresa that his mother's heart was drowned in sorrow, that Jesus and his Mother gave their all for souls. Here is the text: *"Your heart was never drowned in sorrow as it was My Mother's. We both gave our all for souls, and you?"* (M.F.G. p. 10). Instead of getting upset and angry our Lady understands and forgives and joins so closely with her Son's redemptive suffering, thus making it a more effective and powerful means of salvation and sanctification for souls. It was not that the redemptive suffering of Jesus was insufficient to save mankind, but that his Mother's understanding and acceptance of the meaning of his suffering, strengthened and consoled the human heart of Jesus.

In her second vision of the crowd in sorrow, our Lady told Mother Teresa: *"Take care of them. They are mine – bring them to Jesus – carry Jesus to them. Fear not. Teach them to pray the Rosary, the family Rosary and all will be well. Fear not. Jesus and I will be with you and your children"* (M.F.G. p. 19).

The seventh spiritual works of mercy is praying for the living and the dead. This too is very important and it is a big mission. *"When you and your daughter in law, Sarah prayed, I brought a reminder of your prayer before the Holy One; and when you buried the dead, I was likewise present with you. When you did not hesitate to rise and leave your dinner in order to go and lay out the dead, your good deed was not hidden from me, I was with you. So now God sent me to heal you and your daughter-in-law, Sarah. I am Raphael, one of the seven holy angels who present the prayers of the saints and enter into the presence of the glory of the Holy One* (Tobit 12, 11-15). *"Prayer is good when accompanied by fasting, almsgiving and righteousness"* (Tobit 12, 8).

In the Albanian context there is much spiritual works of mercy to be done. As the country is becoming economically better off, there is the perennial danger of forgetting God, his blessings and benefits. However, we have our project ready to build the home for the homeless handicapped boys. The ground is ready to do the foundational work. **Then, as** the continuous rain and cold set in, the work was stopped until such time when the weather will be more favorable to begin the work again. Till then we keep praying and gathering material for the construction. Please do keep the project in your prayers that it may be realized in God's own time.

Deepashram, India: Home for the homeless handicapped boys. It was 3 July 1994, on the feast of St. Thomas, one of the twelve apostles of our Lord and the first apostle of India, that the Brothers began a tiny little community in Gurgaon, in the state of Haryana. It is about 15 km South of the International Airport in New Delhi. With the grace of God and with the help of so many, we have purchased some land, built a Church, a home for the homeless, orphaned handicapped boys and the house for the Brothers. Right now we have about seventy (70) boys, aging from five (5) to thirty-five (35). Not only are the boys homeless and orphans, but they are also handicapped in one form or another, i.e. either physically or psychologically or both. So many of our boys have gone through various kinds of treatments. Quite a few of them have undergone several surgeries, either to make them stand or to make them walk, even if some of them may never walk again properly. Thanks to the doctors and nurses of St. Stephen's Hospital in Delhi who help us so much and do practically all the surgeries free of charge. Like our *Casa Serena* Bank in Rome, in India we have *Deepashram* bank. In this spiritual bank people are free to put any little things; but you must do it with humility and Charity. It will all be repaid in full with interest, if not in this life, in the life to come. What we may put in now can be extremely little, but what we may receive can be beyond any measure or calculations. Working for the Lord does not pay you much, but the retirement program is out of this world!

Some of our boys were unable to speak a word when they came to *Deepashram*. But through specialized and qualified speech therapists many of them started talking, which makes the boys' lives happier and the future brighter.

Even though the boys are handicapped, they do grow in every sense of the word with growing problems. *Deepashram* looks very big and imposing. But with the present number of boys the space is becoming smaller. The boys are desperately in need of a bigger place and a rehabilitation center. The land nearby is almost impossible to purchase as its price has gone so high.

The children of *Deepashram* need tender love and care. Periodically we do have some volunteers, mainly from Italy. But we need more, especially trained nurses. *Deepashram* has a place for volunteers in the same compound. They do not have to look for accommodation outside. In the past up to twenty (20) volunteers have stayed and have helped the boys. There was a retired nurse from Sweden who was able to obtain a visa to India for ten (10) years. She wanted to live and help our boys and then die in India. But the Lord had other plans for her. He could not wait too long. He called her to himself quite unexpectedly. Our children lost a real mother. She loved them and the children loved her. We think of her with gratitude.

I also would like to say a word of thanks to all our generous people who have enrolled themselves in our distant adoption programme. Thanks to your generosity and constancy. The children send you their love and regards, and wish you a very happy Christmas and a peace filled New Year 2003.

Some of the artistically minded children make Christmas cards, or Deepali cards (Hindu festival of lights, which is celebrated at the end of the month of October or in the beginning of November). Some others make candles and sell them. A few do mechanical works. Although handicapped we try to encourage them to do various activities, which in themselves are a real therapy for the handicapped boys. If you have any further suggestions, please feel free to do so.

Our children, though handicapped, pray much. They pray and sing before each meal; pray the daily Rosary together with the Brothers; and participate in the Sunday liturgy. Some of them also join in the Charismatic night vigil every second Saturday of the month conducted by Br. Mathew M.C. In all their prayers our children think of you, pray for you and thank God for you.

As I wish you all a very happy New Year 2003, I also impart upon you all the Lord's blessing of peace and joy:

"May he grant you unwavering faith, constant hope and love that endures to the end.

May his face shine upon you and be gracious to you.

May he look upon you with kindness

And give you his peace".

May almighty God bless you.

Fr. Sebastian Vazhakala M.C

"A friendship to be renewed"

Dearly beloved Brothers and Sisters,

True joy and abiding peace are the most precious gifts of this holy season of Christmas. So many of you have shared *this Christmas Spirit* with us and with our poor people through telephone calls, fax messages, emails, cards, letters and gifts; while some others through the welcomed visits in person, and others still through the assurance of prayers and sacrifices. In whatever way or manner you have been sharing *the Spirit*, our friendship with God and with one another has been renewed, deepened, purified and strengthened. You made us and our poor people feel that it is all true, that God did really become man and lived with, like, among and for us, as we pray in our profession of faith: *"For us men and for our salvation He came down from heaven"*.

This friendship results in service, in humility and charity. No merely and purely horizontal friendship can last; i.e. the friendship based on likes and dislikes, based on selfishness and pride. True friendship demands due respect, trust, sacrifice, forgiveness, constancy, humility, understanding, appreciation. True friendship is based on the two-fold love of God and love of one's neighbour. Friendship without sacrificial and enduring love and loving service in humility and joy is an intolerable mockery.

More and more I come to realize that Christmas is a time of renewal. It is a time to renew our friendship with God and our friendship with one another. They are not parallel ones, but two inseparable realities blended into one. Christmas is a time also to reestablish broken friendships, and to build new ones. It is a time to repair and renew, or to build new bridges. This is why we send Christmas cards and letters with promises and assurances of prayers. It is also a time to clear the ground and to throw the rubbish away.

On Friday, 19th December 2003, two very important personalities visited us: His Eminence Cardinal José Saraiva Martins, the Prefect of the

Congregation for the Cause of the Saints, who so kindly celebrated the Holy Mass with us and for us, and Senator for life, his Excellency Giulio Andreotti, who has been the number one politician, patriot and a very fervent Catholic in Italy. The presence of these two among us during this holy season has made a great impact on many people, especially the Missionaries of Charity, the Lay Missionaries of Charity, and our volunteers and benefactors, all of whom are here to take care of the poor, to bring them to Jesus and carry Jesus to them.

For some of our friends *Senator Andreotti's coming to the Missionaries of Charity Contemplative* meant coming down many steps below his status, and this made me reflect on the great event of Christmas. There are several passages in the Bible that came to my mind. Two of them from the letters of St. Paul are of great importance to understand not only the joy of Christmas but also its richness. *"Christ Jesus became poor for our sake so that in his poverty we may become rich"* (2 Cor 8: 9). For Jesus, becoming man meant becoming the poorest of the poor. The book of Wisdom is more explicit as we read: *"When peaceful silence lay over...Your all-powerful Word leaped from the royal throne into a land doomed to destruction"* (Wis 18: 14). By becoming man, in human terms it was a big loss for Jesus. But for people of good will it was the greatest gift and blessing. When celebrating the holy Mass the priest mixes a few drops of water with the wine, saying: *"By the mystery of this water and wine we may share in the divinity of Christ who humbled himself to share in our humanity"*.

The Creator of the universe has deigned to become a creature so that human beings could regain the dignity that was lost by the disobedience of our first parents. Ever since that day of their radical refusal, mankind was distanced from its Creator, God and Father. The distance was infinite and could not be bridged anymore by any man. It might have been easier to try to build a bridge between the five continents through the ocean than for man to come out of his terrible fall by his own power and strength. The fall was so terrible that man became the poorest of the poor, the weakest of the weak and the most miserable of the miserable creatures. This refusal of Adam and Eve not only affected mankind, but the entire universe. What was good and was in perfect harmony is no longer the same. Chaos, disorder, confusion and division within man and in the outside world resulted. The world became man's enemy and was doomed to destruction (cf. Gen 3: 1-19).

It is to this world of sin, hatred, vengeance, retaliation and evil, *"down from the heavens, from the royal throne, leapt Your all-powerful Word...carrying Your unambiguous command like a sharp sword..."* (cf. Wis 18: 15) to be the *Way, the Life and the Truth*. He became one of us in every way except sin to teach us to walk the way he walked, the way of the royal road of the holy

Cross: *"If you want to be a follower of mine, deny yourself, take up your cross and follow Me"* (Lk 9: 23). This was Jesus' way, Our Lady's way, St. Joseph's way. It was and it still is the way of all saints and martyrs, and it was the way of our Blessed Mother Teresa. Whoever takes this way with Jesus and follows Him will never lose the way to eternal life. No one should walk this way alone; no one is meant to carry his Cross alone. If he does, he is bound to lose his way and be crushed by the Cross! With Jesus, he must carry his cross.

Jesus' way is the way of humility and charity. Here is the second scriptural passage that says: *"Though he was in form of God, Jesus did not deem equality with God something to be grasped at. Rather he emptied himself and took the form of a slave being born in the likeness of men. He was known to be of human estate and it was thus that he humbled himself, obediently accepting even death, death on a cross"* (cf. Phil 2: 6-11). His way is narrow and his path is difficult, but always a sure one.

Whoever understands this passage of the Scriptures can be raised or lowered to any position, transferred to any place; he can even be accused, blamed and condemned----even to a shameful and painful death. Whoever contemplates this passage can accept misunderstandings, false accusations, calumnies, humiliations, and mistreatments with a certain equanimity and serenity; and not only that, he can go beyond human likes and dislikes and can accept any evil with a certain serenity and tranquility. Shame or blame for Jesus' sake one does not even count, but it is desired and looked for. One is never satisfied enough or content with some superficial way of pleasing God, but wants to identify self with Jesus out of love, and tries to please God rather than trying to please himself or others. This attempt to identify self with Jesus is the process of *Kenosis – self-emptying* – seen as a necessity for one's progress in spiritual life.

Humility does not make us poor and miserable as pride and jealousy do. The humbler we are, the nobler we become. It is only when we are ready to share in the humility of God, who became man like us in all things except sin, that we share in the divinity of God and become great and divinized. Satan is furiously in war with the friends and lovers of God. His main effort is to make us enemies of God by making us enemies to our neighbour, making us feel jealous and over-ambitious. Satan works very hard to create disunity by breaking our friendship with God and one another. The devil attacks on our prayer life; he tries to break our friendship with God, which is built on faith, hope and charity and is sustained, nourished and strengthened by prayer, contemplation and works of mercy. He knows that if we relax and become careless with our life of prayer, he can easily break our friendship with one another. It is impossible to sustain and befriend our neighbour if we do not sustain and befriend God in the first place.

God is not only our Father, but he is also our life-long faithful friend. This friendship is reciprocal and two dimensional. Friendship with God immediately and spontaneously seeks to establish friendship with one another. This is something normal, as we are children of the same heavenly Father. Just or unjust, good or bad, normal or abnormal, saint or sinner, black, brown, yellow or white, we are still children of the same heavenly Father, like the cows and the milk. The cows can be of different colours, but milk is always white. The colour of the skin is something superficial and is not the criterion to judge people, but our love for God and our neighbour is ontological. This twofold love is not something injected into us, but something that is part of our very being.

If we do not know how to love God and love God in one another, we become spiritually handicapped. There are more spiritually handicapped and crippled people in the world than there are physically handicapped and crippled ones. If our love is based on colour, nationality, culture, or religion, or on political ideologies, then we are spiritually handicapped people. We need help. Blessed Mother Teresa of Calcutta, through whom Jesus opened the eyes of many to this all important reality of the great Brotherhood of man and woman in the one and only Fatherhood of God, is an inspiring and edifying example for us.

Christmas is also essentially a time to share. So many of you have done that. *"God loves a cheerful giver"*. Thanks to so many of you who share so much of your time, energy, money and material things for and with our poor people. We are edified by your untiring generosity and good will. So many of you go out of your way to help us and our poor people of *Casa Serena*. In our night shelter in Rome we have over 70 men, who otherwise would have slept in the open and perhaps succumbed to decease and death. Our *Casa Serena* volunteers are very special. At times I am dumb-founded by the heroic charity, constancy and loyalty of so many of them. In the name of our *Casa Serena* men and the Brothers of our Community, I thank each one of you who is blessed by our heavenly Father. The same can be said of all who help our orphaned-handicapped boys of *Deepashram*, Gurgaon, India whom so many of you continually help in many ways. May the good Lord reward those who love God without measure and love and serve Him in the poor without limits. You are the ones who will be hearing when you go home to God: *"Come blessed of my Father, inherit the kingdom prepared for you since the foundation of the world. For I was hungry, thirsty, naked, homeless…As long as you did it to one of the least of my brothers you did it to me"* (cf. Mt 25: 31-46). God bless each one of you, Lay Missionaries of Charity, volunteers, benefactors and co-workers. With you we thank God, and for you we pray. May the very same spirit of loving service pervade your homes and families as well. This my prayer. Our home in *Albania* for the handicapped boys is being built very slowly with many complications. It may take many more months, a lot more money, and above all much prayer and sacrifices in order to complete the project.

Mother Teresa's beatification has touched so many people. From heaven she continues her mission of bringing souls to Jesus and carrying Jesus to the poor. She intercedes for all those who ask her intercession and blesses all those who sincerely try to do ordinary things with extraordinary love, whether this is done in one's community, at one's home, or to the poor people. In connection with her beatification a tiny little community was opened in the Archdiocese of Kumasi, in the land of Ghana. The official opening was on 1st October 2003, on the feast of St. Thérèse of Lisieux, the patroness of the missions. Br. Stephen M.C. is the superior and Tertian In-charge and Brs. Gaspar M.C. and Peter M.C. are the Tertians. Please remember this little community in your prayers and sacrifices so that it can grow under the shadow of the Cross led by the Holy Spirit.

You might have heard of the book that came out in Italian entitled *"Vita con Madre Teresa"* ("Life with Mother Teresa"). I did not really and truly write any book, nor did I ever think that what I wrote was going to be translated, and worse still, to be published and read by the public, as it is not a work of art, nor is it a biography of Blessed Teresa, nor is it a theological treatise or a historical and a chronological account. It is not one more book on Mother Teresa either. It is simply some reflections on the personal experience of one who lived and worked very close to her over thirty years. For me, she has been my second mother. I hope and pray that whoever reads this "book" may be touched by the unction of the Spirit and may have her hunger and thirst for souls, especially the souls of the poor...and that Jesus may be recognized, welcomed, respected and served more and more. She is near to all those who try to light a candle rather than curse the darkness. In other words, she works with those who try to be a light of hope for those who live in despair, a light of joy for those who are sad, a sign of love for those who try to forgive and reconcile. She is a channel of peace for all those who have lost their peace of mind and joy of heart. She is a strength to all those who try to help those who are sick and weak, irrespective of caste, colour, religion or nationality. Blessed Teresa, Virgin and Foundress and our Mother, intercede for us, for our families and all those who are poor both materially and spiritually.

Let us pray then that God may be glorified in our becoming a little more kind and a little less harsh, a little more humble and a little less proud, a little more generous and a little less selfish, a little more docile and obedient and a little less arrogant and rebellious, a little more thoughtful and understanding and a little less critical and judgmental. The holier we are, the humbler we become and the more God is being glorified.

Three of our deacons and Br. Ricardo, our novice, had a three week experience in Fatima in preparation for their priestly ordination and Br. Ricardo for his first vows, which takes place on Wednesday, 31st December 2003. God's providence also took care of all our needs, including free lodging and stay. Thanks to Fr. Gary M.C. who preached the eight-day retreat and gave the seminar for the deacons. Thanks to Mr. Philip, who gave his brand new villa free of charge. May the good Lord reward him, and Mr. Jerry Coniker, the M.C. Sisters in Lisbon, Portugal and others who helped to make our stay enriching and strengthening.

Saturday, 27th December 2003 has been another important date in the history of the M.C. Contemplatives. On that day three of our Brothers: Br. Subash M.C. (India), Br. Charbel M.C. (Lebanon), Br. Leo M.C. (Ghana) were ordained priests by His Eminence Cardinal Giovanni Battista Re, President of the Congregation for the Bishops in the parish Church of Santa Maria Consolatrice of Casalbertone, Rome. While congratulating them and thanking God for this great gift of three new priests, we also must constantly sustain them by our prayers, sacrifices and edifying examples. They are His priests today and forever. They are called to sanctify themselves and the people, especially the members of the Society and the poorest of the poor.

To the newly ordained priests the ordaining Bishop said:

"Accept from the holy people of God the gifts to be offered to Him.
Know what you are doing and imitate the mysteries you celebrate:
Model your life on the mystery of the Lord's Cross"
(from the Rite for the Ordination of Priests).

Holy Christmas and a peace-filled New Year 2004.
God bless you.
Fr. Sebastian Vazhakala M.C.

2004

"Serve with love, serve in humility"

Dearly beloved Brothers and Sisters,

Though I wanted to greet each one of you personally, and waited for the day and the time to do that, it only prolongs, and that "tomorrow" never comes. So I have decided to write a few lines to:

Thank you for all your letters, cards, email, telephone calls, personal exchanges of this holy season of Christmas and the New year 2005.

I also would like to express my sincere thanks in the name of our poor people and for the community of the Missionaries of Charity Contemplative for all your generous gifts in cash, cheque and kind. May the new born Babe of Bethlehem who, though rich, became poor for our sake, reward you for your kindness and generosity. He shared his richest divinity with our sinful, broken, miserable humanity. It is impossible for us to comprehend this unfathomable divine condescension! "It is easier to understand the greatness of God, but difficult to understand the humility of God" (Blessed Mother Teresa).

He did this so that we may share in his divine nature through humbling himself to share in our wounded, sinful, broken humanity. Yes, because he loved us so much God sent his only Son so that whoever believes in him may have eternal life. (cf. Jn 3: 16)

Today Jesus is not born among animals, but among sinners, for sinners. He is not only born in Bethlehem of Judea, but on every consecrated altar where the Holy Mass is being celebrated. The word *"Bethlehem"* means *"house of bread"*. He is no more born in "the house of bread"; instead he becomes the *"Bread of Life"* at every Mass. We are invited not only to love and adore this wondrous mystery, but to *"take and eat"* with love and reverence, with profound faith and deep humility. Before every Holy Communion we say: *"**Lord, I am not worthy** to receive you, but only say the word and I shall be healed."* After Communion we usually pray: *"**Make us worthy**, Lord, to serve our fellowmen throughout the world, who, live and die in poverty and hunger…"* We are neither worthy to receive him in the Bread of life, nor worthy to serve him in the hungry, thirsty, naked, homeless, sick or imprisoned ones" (cf. Mt 25: 31-46). We pray more and more humbly and fervently to the Lord to make us worthy to receive and make us worthy to serve. Each time we approach the altar to receive Jesus, we feel unworthy. Each time we stoop down to serve our fellowmen –father, mother, brothers, sisters, husband, wife, parents, children, countryman or foreigner, black or white, rich or poor, we must pray: *"Lord, make us worthy to serve this person, who represents you"*, to serve with love, to serve in humility.

Because Jesus loves us now, he becomes the Bread of Life; because he wants us to be with him where he is now, he makes himself the hungry one, the suffering one, the sick one, the lonely one…so that by serving these. our fellowmen, we prepare our dwelling place in the world to come. It can be very demanding now, but then we will be rewarded. Now we may be sowing in tears; then we will have the harvest in joy. In the evening of life, when we appear before God, we will be judged on love. *"Come blessed of my Father, inherit the kingdom prepared for you from the foundation of the world; for I was hungry, you gave me to eat, I was thirsty, you gave me to drink, I was naked, you clothed me, I was a stranger, you welcomed me…etc"* (cf. Mt 25: 31-46).

This year Jesus gave us added opportunities to **share** with our suffering fellowmen who were hit by the earthquake in South East Asia. It is hard to understand "the how and why" of such tragic events. But one thing is clear, namely that while the wars create more hatred, anger, division and disunity, natural calamities unite us in love and open up the door to loving service and generous sharing. Thousands have died and gone within twenty-four hours, while many more thousands have become more poor and miserable, if not utterly destitute. There was a great world bewailing because thousands were no more, and many are still inconsolable. God alone knows the "how and why" of such a terrible catastrophe; he alone is capable of bringing good out of evil. He is the divine pedagogue who can teach us great value even from such horrible situations. Let us then try to light a candle rather than to curse the darkness.

On Saturday, 22 January at 5:00 p.m., God willing, Br. Stephen M.C. will be ordained deacon in the parish church of St. Bernadette Subirous, in Rome. All are cordially invited to participate in the celebration. On the other hand, Br. Jean Marie M.C.'s priestly ordination is on Saturday, 2nd April 2005 in the Holy Family Chapel, Deepashram, Gurgaon at 10:00 a.m. by His Excellency Mgr. Vincent Concessao, the Archbishop of Delhi. Br. George, our second year novice, will make his religious profession on Wednesday, 2 February 2005 at 4:30 p.m. in Deepashram. Let us pray for our beloved Brothers that they continue to grow in holiness and persevere in their vocation. All are cordially invited to participate.

I just wanted to thank you all for your kindness, concern and generosity, but as usual my letter has become rather long. Another reason to write these few lines quickly was to request your prayers for our various intentions, especially from Monday-Thursday, January 3-6 in the evening. I am engaged in giving a retreat to a group of approximately 42 priests. Please, I would like you all to remember them and me in a very special way in your prayers.

I hope to come back to you as soon as I can. In the meantime we pray for each other.

Happy and holy feast of the Epiphany and a peace-filled New Year 2005.

Love and prayers.

God bless you.

Fr. Sebastian Vazhakala M.C.

EPIPHANY 2006

"…I have absolutely no one for my very poor…I cannot go alone…Carry Me with you into them." (MFG 18)

Dearly beloved brothers and sisters,

Once again I would like to wish you a very happy and holy New Year 2006. Let us pray very fervently that the New Year 2006 may be a year of many graces and blessings for all, especially for our Movement so that our Movement can continue to grow in holiness and increase in number in order to bring many souls to Jesus and carry Jesus to them.

In Rome we had a day of prayer on Thursday 29.12.05, in preparation for the New Year. It was also a day of thanksgiving for all the graces and blessings of God for each one of us, for our Society, for our families, for our LMC groups and for the whole MC Family in the past year.

Our main theme was:

RENEWAL (cf. Daniel 9: 4b-10). Renewal is necessary because we are weak, sinful and unworthy.

Renewal demands reorganization of our lives as individuals, as families, as groups in accordance with our LMC Statutes and way of life and other documents of the Church, especially 'Christi Fideles Laici' and 'Familiaris Consortio':

1) Our life of prayer.

2) Our life of sacrifice and penance.

3) Our life in the family and in the group.

4) Our contemplative-missionary apostolate.

Our life of prayer demands we establish proper relationships with:

- God

- Oneself in God.

- God in one another, especially with one's family members and our poor people (cf. Mt 5: 23-26).

Our life of sacrifice and penance demands us:

- To be victims of Jesus' love so as to pour out his love on souls.

- To be totally free to be covered with the poverty of the Cross.

- Obedience of the Cross: Jesus learned obedience through suffering, through loud cries and tears (cf. Heb 5: 8).

- Charity of the Cross: *"Your vocation is to love and suffer and to save souls"* Yes this is our vocation: no love without suffering, no Jesus without the Cross. "If you want to be a follower of me, deny yourself, take up your Cross and follow me..." (cf. Lk 9: 23-26)

- A fish is created to live and grow in the water. The human soul, created in God's image, is meant to live and grow in God's light, as God is light and there is no darkness in him at all (cf. 1Jn 1: 5). A fish, when taken out of the water feels uneasy, becomes restless, jumps up and down and finally dies if it stays out of water for a considerable amount of time. In the same way the human soul, when it lives in the darkness of sin, feels uneasy, becomes restless and nervous and eventually dies.

- *"The body dies when the soul departs, but the soul dies when God departs."* (St. Augustine)

Our life in the family demands:

- To reestablish our relationship with one another in the family.

- To have genuine brotherly love for each other.

Our apostolate demands:

- To have deep love and concern for the poor.

- To be contemplative missionaries and missionary contemplatives.

RECONCILIATION (Mt 6: 12-13):

- With God.

- With oneself.

- With one another.

REPARATION means:

- To make reparation for all the damages caused by our many infidelities, our lack of the observance of our vows, our pride, tepidity, sloth, jealousy, anger, vain glory, lack of self-control, etc.

RESTORATION:

- Of all things in Christ-Instaurare omnia in Christo. (St. Paul) This was the motto of St. Pius X.

RESOLUTION: to resolve to live our LMC vocation more faithfully and more perseveringly: to be faithful in doing ordinary things with extraordinary love.

These five **"R"** you may take and reflect: What is meant by **RENEWAL**?

People sometimes ask us: "What is your specialization?" I do not know what you say to people, when they ask you what our specialization consists in.' Does it not consist in the CHARITY of Christ? When we make our vows we get the degree in Charity, plus in Chastity, Poverty and Obedience. So you are studying in the M.C., LMC University to get this degree. I sent Br. Nicholas to our Deepashram university of Charity. People who join us must get this degree so that you and I can teach others by words and example. Otherwise we waste our precious time for nothing.

This Charity must be in thought, in words, in actions as well as in omission. One must become more and more sensitive.

Brothers and sisters, Jesus said to our Blessed Mother Teresa: *"In your immolation, in your love for me, they will see Me, know Me, want Me. Offer more sacrifices, smile more tenderly and pray more fervently…"* (MFG)

Come and see,
Come and know,
Come and want,
Come and love and come and serve.

Come to see, come to know, come to love, come and serve. Come to see Jesus, come to know Jesus, come to love Jesus and come and serve Jesus in you, in each other, in the poor. See, know, love and come and serve Jesus…It is a lifelong process.

Connected with the virtue of Charity is HUMILITY, to be specialized also in it. Humility is built on the twofold pillars of (cf. St. Thomas of Aquinas):

- TRUTH: whatever is good in us comes from God and

- JUSTICE: demands therefore to give to God what belongs to God and give to Caesar what belongs to Caesar; namely all praise, honour and glory should be given to God. Here, too, Our Lady is our example: "The Almighty has done great things for me, holy is his name." (Lk 1: 49)

I still want to go to the school of the Holy Family of Nazareth and learn from Jesus, Mary and Joseph all the virtues they have practised. Praying the litany of the Holy Family can help us to practice those virtues.

Let us Live with Mary,
Walk with Mary,
Work with Mary,
Pray with Mary,
Suffer with Mary

Serve one another and the poor with Mary all the days of our life,
To be a cause of joy with Mary.

Every day I think of each one of you in the presence of Jesus; I thank God for you and pray that you may continue to resemble Jesus, who is our mirror and our model.

Br. Stephen's ordination went very well, also Br. Peter's deaconate ordination (shortly you may receive the letter), as they were planned on 17 December 2005 in the parish church of Kumavu, in the diocese of Konongo-Mampong, Ghana (Africa).

On the feast of the Epiphany (06.01.06) Br. Stephen celebrated his first Holy Mass in our Holy Family Chapel in Rome, with and for the people to reveal Jesus' glory.

I leave for Deepashram, Gurgaon, India on 20 January 2006. We begin our 8-day retreat on 23rd January (06) for our Tertians, Novices and 14 Postulants who are going to begin their novitiate on Thursday2, Feb. 2006. At 12.00 p.m. of the same day, God willing, we will have the first profession of Br. Jees, Br. Panithason, Br. Vimal Chand and Br. Nicholas at Deepashram. His Excellency, Archbishop Vincent Concessao is going to preside over the celebration. I count much on your prayers.

In this trip I have two more retreats for the M.C. Sisters of Kolkata and Mumbai regions. I am in need of your fervent prayers.

We have fixed Thursday 20 April 2006 for the blessing and inauguration of our new home for the handicapped boys in Bushat, Albania, known as "Bethel-Banesa e Zotit", House of God. We cannot express enough our gratitude to Dr. Salvatore Sicignano, without whose untiring effort, hard work and persistence this work of God might not have been realized. Please thank the Lord for him and pray much for all his intentions and all those who have worked with him, especially our community of Brothers in Bushat past and present. May the good Lord reward them all. Before any of our major events, please make a novena to the Holy Spirit or to the Holy Family. Let us continue to remember the past with gratitude, to live the present with enthusiasm, and to look forward to the future with confidence, remembering that it is better to light a candle than to curse the darkness. Love and prayers. God bless you.

Fr. Sebastian Vazhakala M.C.

369